"Kiernan . . . extends his [...] ith this spellbinding fable of sanctuary, art, and recovery. . . . A dramatic and transfixing tale that responds to life's horrors by celebrating beauty, resiliency, and soulfulness."

—*Booklist* (starred review) on *The Glass Château*

"The fragility of the glass cradled in the hands of the artists, sensitive to the slightest tremor from outside, is a beautiful metaphor for the fragility of emotion in men and women who are grieving and healing. A marvelous and moving book."

—Historical Novel Society on *The Glass Château*

"A bittersweet story of beauty . . . Kiernan has written a lovely, moving elegy for those who were lost and resilient survivors who long for redemption."

—*Star Tribune* (Minneapolis) on *The Glass Château*

"The most tender, terrifying, relevant book you'll read this year."

—JENNA BLUM, *New York Times* bestselling author, on *Universe of Two*

"This thought-provoking novel is both heart-wrenching and inspiring. . . . Kiernan has created characters who are well-developed, beautifully flawed, and unforgettable."

—Washington Independent Review of Books on *The Baker's Secret*

"A tale beautifully, wisely, and masterfully told."

—PAULA McLAIN, author of *The Paris Wife,* on *The Baker's Secret*

The Glass Château

The
Glass Château

A NOVEL

Stephen P. Kiernan

WILLIAM MORROW
An Imprint of HarperCollinsPublishers

THE GLASS CHÂTEAU. Copyright © 2023 by Stephen P. Kiernan. All rights reserved. Printed in the United States of America. No part of this book may be used or reproduced in any manner whatsoever without written permission except in the case of brief quotations embodied in critical articles and reviews. For information in the US, address HarperCollins Publishers, 195 Broadway, New York, NY 10007. In Canada, address HarperCollins Publishers Ltd, Bay Adelaide Centre, East Tower, 22 Adelaide Street West, 41st Floor, Toronto, Ontario, M5H 4E3, Canada.

HarperCollins books may be purchased for educational, business, or sales promotional use. For information, please email the Special Markets Department at SPsales@harpercollins.com or in Canada at HCOrder@harpercollins.com.

A hardcover edition of this book was published in 2023 by William Morrow, an imprint of HarperCollins Publishers.

FIRST WILLIAM MORROW PAPERBACK EDITION PUBLISHED 2024.

Designed by Nancy Singer

Title page/chapter opener painting by Jose M. Izquierdo/stock.adobe.com
Glass flower illustration by Fred Whitson

Library of Congress Cataloging-in-Publication Data has been applied for. Library and Archives Canada Cataloguing-in-Publication information is available upon request.

ISBN 978-0-06-322730-9
ISBN 978-1-4434-7094-0 (Canada)

24 25 26 27 28 LBC 5 4 3 2 1

For Ziggy and Beulah, and all that they imagine

A stained glass window represents the transparent partition between my heart and the world's heart. The stained glass window is thrilling, it needs to be serious and fascinating. It has to live by the light which passes through it.

—Marc Chagall

What is art for, if not precisely this moment?

—Lacy Johnson

CHAPTER I

After the end of a slaughter that nearly devoured a continent, the last thing anyone expected to hear was laughter.

Yet that was what reached Asher's ears, echoing up the narrow street as he navigated toward what remained of the town square: the sinister snickering of Levi, a conniving thief allergic to guilt, and the lusty guffaw of Eli, a cow of a man even in days of want. Something had made them laugh together.

It was a reassuring sound. Both men had been Asher's schoolmates and, for the past four years, members of the same Resistance cell. Sabotage and espionage, communication and assassination, they'd fought a covert war. As locals, they were experts in rivers and roads, hedgerow shortcuts and abandoned buildings. They'd shivered together in haylofts and forests, hidden in cellars and cisterns, slept in belfries and basements and under the thinnest blankets of leaves. And on this unseasonably hot day in June, Germany's surrender only one month past, Asher rounded the corner to where the town fountain had gushed for a century until a bomb destroyed it, to see his friends allowing themselves to be seen in full public view.

"Hello, hello," Eli hailed from the entryway of St. Anne's Church, its façade concussed, its heavy wooden doors splayed wide. The iron hinges were bent much as a torturer might ruin the fingers of a spy. Eli patted the stone step beside him. "You're just in time for the show."

He pointed at Levi, who stood to one side shifting his weight from foot to foot, pretending not to know them. He'd pilfered a yardstick from somewhere, but it was several times thicker than the kind a schoolmaster might use to discipline wayward boys. Perhaps it had belonged to a draftsman or architect. Now it rested on his shoulder like a rifle, while Levi scanned the square, eager to find a use for it.

"His eyes are deeper set now," Eli observed. "Don't you think? His cheekbones are more prominent too. Starvation has made our friend beautiful."

Asher did not answer. Friends before, during, and now after the war, these men were his only remaining links to the past. Asher surveyed the remains of the fountain—in which they had frolicked as children, and eventually in whose waters his toddler daughter had played. Now, where the carved statue of a seal had spouted water from its mouth, a bare tin pipe pointed skyward. Where a low wall of marble had contained the water, a circle of broken stone memorialized the basin's shape. Everywhere Asher looked, everything was gone.

As if scheduled for their entertainment, an Allied guard unit arrived, armed men shepherding a flock of weary enemy soldiers in brown uniforms into that marble circle, to await the trucks for the next leg of their journey home. The guards were smiling, jawboning while they shared cigarettes and clustered around the one with a lighter. Well fed, equipped thoroughly from the bandoliers draped over their shoulders to the grenades clipped on their chests, they moved with an ease that was nearly athletic.

The prisoners of war displayed no such swagger. Stripped of rank, insignia, and swastikas, they found seats on the ground beneath a blazing sun, having marched under armed escort all the way from Dieppe, an exertion of three days. Part of Asher's job was to know information of that kind. The guards corralled them inside the marble circle—beside a stack of tires that had been smoldering for a week, defying all efforts at extinguishment, and producing an oily stink that had persuaded Eli, hardly the churchgoing kind, to make his seat upwind at the feet of Saint Anne. Again he patted the stone steps, again Asher hesitated.

After fifty months of concealment, it was terrifying to appear in broad day. Also, Asher was unarmed, an uncomfortable situation for a man who still considered himself a soldier. Yet he knew that his circumstances—despite the rags he wore, despite uncertainty about where or when he might next eat a meal—remained stratospherically superior to those of the men sitting before him.

In a stupor of thirst, they awaited a convoy to remove them from the place of capitulation, survivors of combat but bearing the wounds of disgrace. Iron-fisted warriors only weeks ago, now they were being trucked home like so much cargo. Mothers would seek to console them, as would the sweethearts they'd left in tears. Could anything be more humiliating than pity?

They were young too, none older than twenty-one, the blank page of their futures already inked with mortification. No wonder they did not care that they were thirsty. Compared with the depths of their shame, a dry throat was beneath notice.

Cautious as a cat, Asher wove through the stones to sit. Eli was already talking.

"Of all the fabrications propagated during this masterpiece of savagery," he said, "none is worse than the lie that victory is the same thing as peace."

This was classic Eli. The man was his own sort of fountain. "Tell me more," Asher said.

"We know victory when we see it." He gestured at the prisoners, who, to keep the square clear for traffic, were squeezed into the former fountain's shape. Cars and trucks could maneuver easily in the available space, but the region hadn't possessed petrol for household use in years. Villagers relied on wagons pulled by horses, which required wider lanes of travel.

As a hayrick entered the square, Levi saw his opportunity. Instead of rushing over, though, he savored it like an amuse bouche: approaching the guards, smiling, tapping fingers to his lips. They gave him a cigarette. He stood smoking with them, yardstick on his shoulder, assessing the situation.

"Victory was a distant notion in the minds of French men and women," Eli continued. He fancied himself a future mayor of Bonheur, their seaside hometown halfway between Bayeux and Le Havre, and considered oratory his greatest asset. This was a man who savored rolling his r's. "Recently we dared to imagine it, and now the impossible has arrived."

Levi idled over to the prisoners, most of whom hung their heads in silence, their misery sharpened by the intensity of the sun. One soldier's legs stuck out into the roadway. Levi lowered the yardstick to tap the bottom of his boots.

"Yet there is no evidence of what you or I would recognize as peace," Eli said. As if to prove his point, a noxious gust of tire smoke passed over, causing them both to hold their breath a moment. "Every bridge in this nation," he continued eventually, "every major road, rail line, gas line, and power line, every church, school, factory, or hospital, lies flattened. In a nation so thoroughly shattered, peace is a cruel fantasy."

The prisoner raised his eyes, and although Levi wore no uniform and carried no weapon, the boy curled his boots in close, out of the way. Levi gave his friends on the church steps a wink. Then, proceeding around the perimeter, he tapped the yardstick against any boot that strayed out of the circle.

"He wants to start something," Asher observed to Eli. "Isn't the war over?"

"Why end a good thing before its time?"

"A good thing? What kind of idiot—"

"Don't you miss your mission and purpose?" Eli replied, unruffled. "Your former reason for being?"

Asher was caught by the questions. No doubt the intensity of wartime, the responsibilities and dangers, made ordinary life seem pale. He could not imagine sitting in a quiet shop, sewing a shank to a sole, and considering it meaningful. Oh look, here's a customer. "I'm not thrilled about making boots again, if that's what you mean."

"The people of France," Eli continued, shifting his rump on the stones, "are as damaged as their bridges. On the right are the appeasers, who signed an armistice with the Nazis, and now congratulate themselves on having prevented millions of deaths. They forget the tens of thousands they sent to the enemy, to their deaths. On the left are the rabble-rousers and the Resistance, who praise themselves for weakening enemy forces, making them easier for the Allies to defeat. They forget how their deeds often brought far greater retaliation." He laughed. "Anyone not of these extremes is a Communist, and they forget everything."

Levi reversed direction, and one prisoner whose boot he'd tapped inward had stuck it out again. Like an affronted schoolmaster, Levi paused, resting the yardstick on the offender's shoulder. As the soldier squinted up, Levi brought the stick to hover over the boy's knuckles. His eyes narrowed. The boy still had some fight in him.

"This," Asher predicted, "will not end well."

The boy glanced toward his captors, but they'd left for a meal. One guard alone remained on duty, and he was fully occupied with cooling off: guzzling from a canteen, splashing water on his back, rubbing it around his neck much as a dog might position itself under a caress. The guard's rifle leaned unattended against a wall, a temptation no combat veteran, regardless of age, would miss. The prisoner calculated how many steps it would take to reach that gun, until Levi circled the yardstick before his eyes. It was clear: if this were a race, he would lose. Lowering his gaze, he drew his boots inside the circle. Levi recommenced his patrol, crowding the soldiers in the heat.

"Each side," Eli continued, "has erred. Each believes the other side is not only wrong, but also immoral. And these are the people who are supposed to rebuild our nation?" He slapped his leg and laughed. "They cannot agree about the time of day."

Levi, having reached the point in his circuit where the guard stood, spun on his heel as though he were an actual soldier, not a carpenter who had never worn a uniform, and who'd avoided conscription into the enemy's factory labor system by hiding in the woods. Already he could see that the bold youth had straightened his legs again. Levi all but skipped in his direction.

"He's spoiling for a fight," Asher said.

"Yes," Eli replied. "And that fool might just oblige him."

Levi did not use his yardstick this time. He kicked the prisoner's boot—hard. "Move back," he barked, unconcerned about whether the soldier understood French.

The boy did not budge, if anything stiffening his legs. Prisoners around him were showing agitation too, shifting positions, freeing their hands as if they might need them. Levi's game was becoming a test of authority.

"I said move back." He kicked the boy's boot again.

At that the soldier burst into motion, raising an arm, trying to stand. But he held the lowest of low ground, and in a flash he was on his back, the yardstick hard against his throat. Levi was pressing down, not strangling the boy but definitely compromising his airway. The prisoner flailed his arms, his eyes a mix of determination and fear.

"Should we intervene?" Asher said.

"When he's like this?" Eli shook his head. "He would kill us both."

Yet to Asher, the situation was darkly familiar: the heightened tension, the ritual of antagonism, the sudden turbulence of uneven power. Each time he had stepped out of the shadows before one of his nineteen victims, they instantly knew why he had come, and waited only to learn how much it would hurt.

"What's your opinion of what I said?" Eli asked. "About two sides incapable of rebuilding?"

"Let me mull it a minute," Asher replied, looking away from Levi, focusing on the ground between his knees. Sometimes the sturdy earth was the only effective solace.

But he could not ignore the moment in the balance, a tension, as if a violinist stood on a nearby roof, playing a long high note. He raised his head again.

"You choose." Levi snarled at the boy. "Boots back, or die."

AT FIRST ASHER HAD THOUGHT the rumors of surrender were an enemy trick, to draw the Resistance out of hiding and into the crosshairs. He was not alone in his skepticism. The people of the woods continued to hide as they had for years, waiting for assignments, except that the orders did not come. No commands from the leadership of Asher's cell, no word from the regional team in Colmar, total silence from Lyon, the hub of Resistance organization for half of the country.

Days accumulated, then weeks, during which the war had reportedly been over. Yet having a chest constantly clenched with anxiety remained as familiar as breathing, jerking upright was the usual way of waking, and Asher remained familiar with the acidic cough caused by an empty stomach. He mistrusted the word victory because he did not believe it was possible. This war could never end.

Yet somehow it had. They heard reports of enemy soldiers rounded up like herds, their supplies distributed among the starving, their artifacts seized and shared. One by one, resisters emerged, the human mice of Bonheur's attics, abandoning their platforms in the trees, crawling out of caves to wash dirt from their faces. Last of all came Asher, shy as a fox, poking his nose out of the woods for a long slow sniff.

The stench was worse than smoldering tires. Bodies unburied, crops abandoned, fields that a passing battalion had used as an impromptu latrine. So he sought the places where he'd felt safest before the war.

First, the synagogue his family had attended. He came up the lane and found it burned to the ground. Only one corner remained upright, a few boards waist-high. Perhaps during the blaze the wind had come from that direction. Asher touched the charred wood and it crumbled inward, blackening his fingers. Was this victory? Everything fragile and torched?

He peered at the wreckage. In this building he had whiled away his childhood boredom by watching the colors of stained glass make their way across the floor, dust motes in the beams. Here he studied and recited for his bar mitzvah. Here, on the night of the puppet show, he did not want to go.

Asher's mother had insisted, so he could help with nieces and nephews. For him, age seventeen, an evening performance on the grass outside the synagogue would be unspeakably dull, but for the little ones? A treat. Sullen, foot-dragging, he obeyed.

The show turned out to be not puppets, but marionettes, and they were larger than he'd expected—as tall as his leg, which made them oddly realistic. Not wood and wire, but people, with motives and emotions. Asher forgot the manipulators existed, despite their hands visibly working above the miniature stage.

It was the story of Noah and the ark, told with imagination and ingenuity. God's voice through a long echoing tube. Keen imitations of animals: bleating goat, grunting pig, whinnying horse. The children were entranced, while Asher discovered the pleasure of invention. Dried peas rolled in a pan to make the sound of rain. For God's promise never to bring another flood, they aimed a flashlight through a prism, casting a rainbow on the backdrop.

Asher's older brothers and their wives carried sleepy toddlers home, but he stayed to watch the puppeteers collapse their little stage. Each marionette went into a box, lifeless like it was a coffin. Only when the company started up their grumbling trucks did he notice that someone else had been similarly captivated. A young woman, Asher remembered her vaguely from school, stood on the opposite side of the lawn.

"Wasn't that magical?" she asked. Her eyes were bright despite the hour, her jaw set as though she had just won an argument.

"Pardon me," Asher answered, approaching. "What is your name?"

So long ago, and it happened here. It was fitting that the synagogue had burned. With all he had witnessed, all he had done, all he had lost, what case could there be for the existence of God? He kicked over the remaining bit of wall—it did not resist—and rushed away across the grass. The scent of charcoal trailed him.

Next he set out for home, where he and Aube had lived. Rubble and destruction made the roads confusing. He reached what he thought was his street, but all of the buildings had been bulldozed, all the houses flattened. When Asher found a pile of red bricks, he remembered the Schwartz family, friendly, talkative day and night, who'd lived in a red-brick house. That meant his former home was just across the way.

Asher crept closer. The walls were gone, the roof caved in. A sink stood free on its pedestal, pipes connecting to nothing. He stood at the lintel, over which he had carried Aube on the day they were married. At the back there had been stairs to a loft, where that night they gave one another their virginities. There too, some years later, she parted her knees and seemingly tore herself in half, delivering into the world a perfect girl with her father's wide-set eyes and her mother's determined jaw. Rachel.

There was no way around the rubble, no path to the back, where Aube's garden had grown until he made it the resting place for her and Rachel—buried together as they were killed together, a Nazi soldier firing a single bullet, passing through mother into daughter, while Asher stood exactly where he stood now, calling them to hurry in, then watching his world vanish.

Someone had bulldozed the house over their graves. How could there be a God?

Wind rattled something down the way, a curtain rod tapping against stone, and he changed direction. There was one more place to which he might yet return.

His shop. In an era of machine-made footwear, the farmer wanted better gear that could withstand fieldwork in all weathers. The hunter sought to keep his feet dry. The horseman desired boots that held a polish and made stirrups comfortable. The gentleman ordered boots of taste and class, with a hard oak heel to give his stride an authoritative sound. Given a decent oiling each spring, Asher's boots would outlive their wearer. People drove from as far as Brittany to do business with the cobbler of Bonheur.

He could live in his shop till demand returned. It had smelled heavenly, rich leathers stored in the workroom. After the way Asher had lived for the past four years, sleeping on an even floor, with a roof overhead, would be a huge improvement.

As soon as he reached that block, though, he knew his hope was foolish. A bomb had struck halfway down, exploding buildings outward, collapsing the ones alongside. His shop was filled with debris like sand in a child's beach bucket. Leaning in his workshop's window, he saw the empty tool rack, the forms and nails gone. Even the door was swollen and warped, and with its glass shattered, his name was therefore erased.

He tried the door anyway. It barely moved, yet his tug was enough to ring a bell, which he had forgotten, the tin bell on the door that called him out from the workroom because a customer had entered. The chime of that bell took Asher back: how ordinary it was, how exquisite the ordinary had been.

Asher hoped that whoever stole his tools had melted them down into bullets, his hammers and tongs and awls now lodged in enemy bodies. When those corpses decayed into dust, the lumps of metal would float in the soil, perpetual evidence of the evil that had been conquered, and the evil required to accomplish the conquering.

He grabbed the doorknob with both hands, pulling and lifting and shaking with all his strength. The bell rang like insanity, and nothing else moved.

In a moment his passion had passed, and he marched dully away. Nothing remained there for him to open. No place from his past existed anymore.

FINALLY, ONE OF THE OTHER prisoners of war barked something in German. Those near him murmured agreement. The young soldier tucked his feet back inside the circle.

"Good decision," Levi said, standing straight again, lifting the yard-stick, while the boy gasped and gagged and clutched his throat. "I re-spect you as a warrior."

Asher exhaled, the whole square deflating. He had no interest in witnessing one more death. He'd seen enough of them.

"That was an interesting little drama," Eli said.

With a hubbub like a team returning from the halftime break, the Allied troops reappeared, bearing tins of rations for the guard who'd stayed to keep watch.

Levi swaggered over, swinging the yardstick like a conductor's ba-ton. "*Mes amis,*" he said, grinning. "*Vive l'Amerique. Vive l'Angleterre. Vive Canada.*"

"*Oui, oui,*" one soldier said. "*Merci beaucoup.*"

"*Vive la France aussi,*" Levi added.

"Hell, yes, bub, *vive la France,*" the group's commander answered. "That's what the hell we're here for."

"Maybe I could try again," Asher told Eli. "Nothing extravagant. Ordinary life. Let me make and sell good boots. It would be a start."

Eli burst out laughing, so loudly that everyone looked, guards and prisoners alike, though there was nothing to see but two ragged men on the church steps, one quite still while the other jiggled with mirth.

"Not in this lifetime, friend." Eli shook his head. "Those political factions I described are every bit as entrenched as the enemies' armies were. Attaining ordinary life will take a generation, maybe two. Care to hear my prediction?"

Asher squinted at him. "Probably not."

He waved three fingers aloft. "Levi, first, will go the cynical route. Scorn everyone, take what he can get, a bit more if he can get away with it. I love him, but the man will be a conniving loner all of his days."

"Not a very sunny forecast," Asher observed.

"Secondly, you, my sensitive friend? You will grieve. You've lost ev-erything. Even the war, an ideal mechanism for your revenge."

"That's not what motivated me," Asher said.

"But it is what made you deadly. Now you'll stay in Bonheur forever, lamenting the town it once was. You, poor fellow, will grieve for all of France."

"I sincerely hope not."

"Otherwise, you'll wander the country 'round, looking for a reason to live."

"That's no better." Asher noticed Levi slinking out of the square, apparently tired of his game, hiding something under his coat. The yardstick lay abandoned in the road, as feckless as a pebble. "What about you?"

"The realist?" He wiggled the third finger. "I shall ride."

"Excuse me?"

Eli heaved himself to his feet. "Like you, I have lost everything . . . except my pluck." He ambled toward one of the broken chapel doors. "I intend to live by it, and honestly, but with all the hedonism a man can attain."

"What in the world does that mean?"

From behind the door Eli produced a bicycle, its frame as upright as a pious spinster, with a wicker basket on the front. Asher stood. "Where did you find that?"

"Someone didn't need it anymore." Eli wheeled it forward. "Now it's mine."

"For all of us without a car or horse, it's a treasure. You know that?"

"I do." Eli's grin seemed as wide as the handlebars. "I intend to travel, dooryard to churchyard to barnyard, from here to Marseille if need be, on a mission to convince the widows of France—there must be hundreds of thousands of them, the poor sorrowing dears—that virtue is a luxury beyond our means, and that there is no comfort better than contact with another human being."

Asher chuckled, as soft as a shoe shuffle. Already he had seen evidence that Eli was right: In the afternoons, couples kissed in the streets, against walls, under bridges. At dusk in the doorways, they groped themselves disheveled. At night in the alleys, they strove like horses, all buckles and flanks, as if reclaiming territory from the vast dominion over which death had for a time been sovereign. But an opposite image surfaced too: an enemy soldier dead at the roadside, his skin pale and body stiff like a statue, as Eli—strolling past, lecturing about how to forecast weather by the clouds, and without pausing his speech—spat on the corpse.

Eli remained his friend, but the spitting, and the plan to play predator on the widows, called the man's character into question. "Which are you, Eli? A pig or a dog?"

"Neither one, my friend. I am solace personified." Eli threw a ham-thighed leg over the bicycle's frame. "Sincere as sugar, and twice as sweet."

He pushed on the pedals, bounced down the three church steps with surprising grace given his girth, and pedaled away.

From childhood friend to fellow warrior, and one of the few remaining people who could connect Asher's prewar life to the future, yet this was how he last saw Eli, without so much as a farewell, riding out of the square and around the corner, into the unknown. The last few threads to Asher's past were unraveling. Soon he might become completely untethered.

At least there was one link left. He still had Levi. Allied soldiers shouted at the prisoners—get up, move out. They rose wearily and proceeded toward where the highway used to be. Their backsides were all white, from polishing dust off the marble circle. As they shuffled out of sight, one laggard was wincing and rubbing his throat.

Asher stood alone in a flattened world. No mission, no assignments, no occupation, no money, no food, no family, no home. He searched his soul for a sliver of faith, any remnant, and found none.

A cold thought occurred to him, there on the steps of a church of a different religion: Maybe he wasn't meant to survive the war. Maybe it was time for him to die.

CHAPTER 2

Levi was sitting in the harbor, leaning against a pier. Beside him lay two empty tins of rations, and he was digging his fingers into a third. Here was one person who knew Asher past and present. Gruff, yes, but Levi was a living link.

Out of habit Asher checked left and right—spying no suspicious people, seeing no potential weapons, identifying two potential escape routes—before drawing closer. "I don't suppose you have any extra."

"Nope." Levi continued eating, licking into the tin's corners, grease on his stubbled chin. Gulls hung back a cagey distance, eyes on the food.

Asher felt like those birds, hoping for a morsel however low the odds. He inhaled the waterfront's salty air, the stink of fish rot, the oily smell of diesel boats. "You are a skillful thief." He sat, checking the discarded tins. They too were licked clean. "I didn't even see you snatch them."

"Hunger makes opportunists of us all."

A modest fishing boat was motoring up to its slip, and Levi bobbed his head in its direction. "Wonder where he found the fuel."

"Another opportunist."

Levi settled against the post. "Do you ever think about your . . . what, sixteen?"

"Nineteen. And yes, many times a day."

"You enjoyed them that much?"

"Enjoyed?" Asher's eyes bulged. "I was a murderer."

"Who volunteered for that role, as I recall." Levi licked his fingers. "I only had nine, but I'm proud of them. Each one persuades me that I will do what is necessary to secure my survival. Everyone else can take a horse's hind leg."

"I witnessed one of yours, and I'll never forget it."

"The major." Levi sniggered. "That knife went in dirty and came out clean."

"I still don't understand why you didn't finish him."

"A day, a week, a month of suffering, who cares? An infected kidney will always kill you eventually. Besides, the women he raped did their share of suffering too."

"I know." Asher hugged a knee to his chest. "I can still hear him gurgling."

"Maybe that sound will appear in one of your stories." Levi dug a dirty fingernail between his front teeth. "Your endless supply. How about telling one now? I have eaten too much, and your tales keep me from getting sick."

Asher tossed a splinter of decking wood into the water, where it floated. "You want something medicinal?"

"The opposite. Something dire and dark."

"That makes it easier." Asher shoved the empty tins away. "This isn't mine, but one I heard. You remember how the surrenders came one by one, starting in April?"

"An encouraging trickle that became a wonderful cascade."

"Yes. Finland, Denmark, Italy, and finally Berlin. For Allied troops, May eighth was the official day. War over, V-E, all the front pages. That afternoon, one infantry unit in Caen found alcohol of some kind. A drunk soldier celebrated the victory by firing his rifle into the air. But the bullet struck a member of his troop, and killed him."

Levi laughed. "That will teach me to ask for dire and dark."

"Terrible story." Asher blinked several times. "I don't know why I told you."

"Because." Levi wiped his chin on a sleeve. "You don't believe it."

"Do you think the war is not capable of this degree of irony?"

"Are you kidding? This war's ironies have been positively spiteful."

"Because it's too easy to picture, then, so it must be contrived?"

"No." Levi examined the last tin, making sure it was empty. "I could easily see myself in that situation. Either the idiot shooting or the idiot who gets shot."

"Then what's the problem?"

He tossed the tin on the others, a little metallic clank. "The soldier wasn't drunk. You and I have hidden in enough cellars, and have had enough occasions of wanting a good stupor, to be experts on this topic. We know that the enemy found, confiscated, and guzzled every drop of alcohol anywhere around here a long time ago. History may enshrine it as their most thorough accomplishment."

"Now that you say it, I know you're right. The man was careless and stupid. Drink was just his excuse."

"We all must find a way to live with ourselves." Levi chuckled. "I would surely enjoy a decent intoxication right now. For two years."

"You've already identified the main obstacle. No booze." Asher shifted in his seat, hugging his knee. "What will you do now? Back to carpentry? There's plenty of rebuilding to be done."

Levi took out a pack of cigarettes, shaking one loose. In another time, it would have been the equivalent of flashing a wad of hundred-franc notes.

"Where did you find those?" Asher said.

"Same place as lunch. Carpentry? No, no." He lit the cigarette, using a lighter Asher hadn't seen before. "I'll steal. Squat. Whatever's necessary."

"Doesn't sound like you have much regard for your fellow man."

"My fellow man has been trying to kill me for several years now. And kill you."

"Sometimes I wish he had succeeded." Asher muttered it while looking away, but Levi snickered again.

"Everyone does, Asher. Who wants the job of cleaning up this mess? Basic things, like an honest day's work, a dry place to sleep, reliable meals." He scowled at the tins. "They're all years away. Ages. Till then we fight and scrape."

"Eli was saying the same thing. Victory does not equal peace."

"Victory?" Levi stood, brushing off his pants. He drew on his cigarette and stared across the harbor. "Victory is a lie."

Asher rested his chin on his knee. "I hope not."

Levi shrugged and strolled away. Childhood friend and Resistance comrade, connection between Asher's past and present, this was the last he saw of him: bumping into an older man, snarling, "Watch where you're going," and continuing on his course as straight as a tank.

Another thread, gone. Maybe Asher's last.

He had visited these piers countless times, when he was ten and had an endless supply of questions for the fishermen, early teen years when he wondered what it might be like to work on a boat, the summer he was seventeen and did so, and while he was proud of his biceps growing from hauling the nets and his legs becoming steady on a heaving deck, all he did besides work was eat and sleep to recover so he could work again. There was no income to be had from his favorite pastime of drawing, despite his grandmother's fervent encouragement, and one morning Asher's grandfather took him to meet a cobbler. The shop smelled splendidly of leather, each tool had an artfully specific purpose, and the cobbler himself seemed comfortable living somewhere between peasant and artisan. He had a small but well-kept home and was ready to retire. As if the economy were a century in the past, he was also willing to take an apprentice.

That put an end to Asher's days on the docks. Marriage and fatherhood and a mortgage followed, a modest domestic comfort until the war disrupted everything, ruining life's pleasures with a cruelty so thorough you sometimes had to admire it.

At that moment, however, Asher remembered one of his favorite childhood things to do in the harbor. Lying on his belly, he tilted his body over the side of the pier and looked under, his head upside down, so that the dock was the ground, and the waves were the sky. The confusion had a unique pleasure, defying gravity and sense.

The sea was dark blue, as always in spring. Under the dock it had peaks and valleys of a thousand different shades, a different color for every shape the water made.

He jerked upright, scampering back on hands and knees.

"Are you all right?" a passing woman bent to ask.

"Beauty," Asher told her, shielding his eyes. "I'm not ready to see it yet."

The woman gave him a wide berth, hurrying down the dock with a basket she brought to a fisherman on his boat. She must have said something, because the man climbed onto the pier with a long wrench in his hand and gave Asher a severe look.

He waved in reply, feeble as grass in the wind, before staggering away.

ASHER WAS EXHAUSTED, A CANYON of fatigue that would take years of sleep to refill. He had performed his duty, and now that duty was done. It had shaped his days, formed his attitudes, and vanished with the swiftness of lightning. Nothing remained except—with a determination to persist that baffled him—his breath.

He followed it down a path, inhale and exhale, in with sorrow over what he'd lost, out with guilt over what he'd done. He knew where escape might be found, not a thousand steps away. Weaving through shore grass, the path left harbor and village behind, descending, opening, delivering Asher to the beach.

White, wind-whipped, and the tide gone out, the beach was deserted. Warm but not as oppressively as by the fountain. Ideal for his purposes.

What mattered, now that the war was done? His wife, Aube, named for the rising of the sun. Gardener, lover, stern spur to better himself. And she was gone. His daughter, Rachel, named after Asher's grandmother, a determined girl who, if she was awake, was running. Chasing her had been the joy of his days. She was gone too. His home, his work, his friends, his role in the Resistance. Meanwhile, before him, sunlight glinted off the sea in invitation.

Oddly, the idea that his time had come did not feel at all dramatic. For a man disconnected from everything he had been before the war, and now from the war as well, to end his life was to dispense of an empty rations tin. Afterward there would be no one to notify. He crossed the wet sand with a purposeful stride.

Yet as the first wave spilled over the toes of his boots, Asher backpedaled. He'd called them his babies, these wonders in calfskin he made by hand eight years ago, preserving them through the war while friends wore all sorts of disasters on their feet, and suffered for it. These boots were still sound, and he was not going to waste them.

He reversed direction, planning to leave the boots above the high tide mark. But someone was there. He was no longer alone.

A woman with a dog. That was exceptional, because the enemy had confiscated and killed all dogs years before. This one was gray-muzzled, white-chested as though he wore a tuxedo shirt, which meant he was born before the war and had survived it.

Walking in soft sand was tiring, so he saved his breath till the distance was shorter. As a result, the woman greeted him first.

"Are you thirsty, man about to swim fully clothed?" She held up a large canteen.

"Pardon me?"

"I'm not accustomed to this heat," the woman said, arranging layers of clothes around herself. She had brought a folding stool of some sort, on which she seemed entirely comfortable. Beside her, the dog sat at perfect attention, pink tongue hanging. "Here." She reached the canteen toward Asher. "Be kind to yourself."

He gave her a sidelong assessment. Her hair was a white bird's nest, her clothes as ragged as his. She was not smiling, but there was humor in her expression.

"Actually, I'm dying of thirst," he said. He accepted the canteen, but hesitated. What if it was poison? Wouldn't that be ironic? He poured water into his mouth.

"Take all you like," she said. "Thirst is not a thing worth dying of."

Asher felt his mouth soften, his whole throat relax. It felt as if water had just been invented, the sensations were so strong, his relief so profound. When he lowered the canteen, he saw she had produced a loaf of bread from somewhere, round and high.

"You have yeast?" he marveled.

"Shhh." She broke an end off the loaf. "My secret."

He took the piece she offered, dark brown, and the crust required hard chewing.

"Excuse my forwardness," the woman said. "But you appear to be in distress."

Asher stopped to consider her straight-on. "I don't want to spend the rest of my life grieving for France."

"But we will," she answered without hesitation.

"I don't want to grieve at all."

"Why would you feel that way?" The woman tossed a bit of bread toward her dog, who snatched it from the air expertly. "Grief is the most involuntary form of love."

He looked down the beach, jaw working, and did not answer.

"Where are you headed?"

Asher took another bite of bread. "I thought I knew a minute ago."

"I have heard that good things are happening in Clovide."

"Clovide? Where is that?"

She pointed a thumb over her shoulder. "South of here. Southeast. Good things."

Asher paused his chewing to gulp from the canteen again. His stomach growled at its sudden satisfaction. "What is your definition of good things?"

"It doesn't feel right to say, since I haven't seen for myself." Now she was smiling. "Too far for these old knees."

Asher looked out at the waves, as if he'd forgotten they were there. They curled and collapsed, brilliant in the sun, indifferent to their beauty. "It has been a long time since I heard of good things happening anywhere."

"As rare as fish in the sky." She grunted, leaning forward, rising to her feet. The dog stood too, tail wagging, as the woman slipped her arm through a strap, folding the stool to rest it on her back. "I've delayed you long enough. Have a nice swim."

Slow as a turtle, she began to make her way up the beach, woman and dog casting a single shadow.

"Thank you," he called. She waved a hand and kept walking.

He still had bread in his hand, and he wolfed it down. Then, remembering why he had come, Asher slipped out of his boots, gave them a long look of gratitude, and started back toward the sea. Where was Clovide? What was happening there? Were good things possible anymore?

He had many more questions he wanted to ask the woman. After a few steps he glanced back—she was gone. Asher shook his head as if to clear it, but there was no doubt. A distance that had taken him several minutes to walk, she and her dog had covered in seconds.

"What the hell?" he asked the air.

The moisture in his throat was real, the fullness in his belly. He hadn't imagined her. There must be another trail from the beach, he thought, made during the war, that he did not know yet. How had she arrived so quickly, and vanished even faster, and where were her tracks in the sand?

Asher found himself back at his boots again. Clovide? Curiosity was not enough to live for, but good things might be. And he hadn't even asked the name of her dog.

Right and left, he pulled his boots back on. With slow steps and uncertain direction, he began to hike away, and when he'd left the beach he kept at it, and when he reached the fountain he picked up his pace, and after he'd left the town he lengthened his stride.

No food, no money, no weapon, Asher did not look back once, because there was nothing left for him to see. All of the threads were gone. So began the period in his life he would later call the time of wandering.

CHAPTER 3

Everyone had heard of Clovide. No one knew where it was.

"Good people are there."

"It is supposed to be a place of healing."

"I've heard there is a sanctuary."

"Their food, I'm told, is excellent."

Then people would point right or left, south or east, and Asher would stagger on, town by village by hamlet, untethered, rudderless, so hungry he sometimes hallucinated. Was the world actually assembled from pieces, like cuts of leather for making boots? Was everything as fragile as glass? Could there be a fish in the sky?

Most often, what brought Asher back to reality was the arguing. France had become a nation of houses with closed shutters, as if a storm were forecast. But he'd linger outside a café hoping for a scrap, hover near a street market, or sip from a fountain in the square, and people would be shouting at each other.

Either the armistice with the Nazis had prevented battles and saved countless lives, or it was a fatal sacrifice of national pride. Either the Resistance showed courage, taking spectacular risks to disrupt enemy plans, or it cost more lives than it saved.

One or both arguers would look Asher's way, seeking to enlist his agreement. If you weren't a Communist, you were a Nazi, or so each of them accused the other. When Asher declined to speak, both sides viewed him with suspicion. But he never knew whose passions might turn violent, and he was traveling unarmed. He'd found a knife, its blade dull but hard. One morning, inexplicably, he'd wandered off without it. It was just as well; hunger had weakened him beyond defending himself anyway.

One time the arguers did catch his attention, on a blistering day when heat rose from the road like a neglected pan on the stove. The men were disputing about Pétain, former head of the Vichy government, who was now on trial in Paris.

"I tell you," the bearded man said, grinding a fist into his palm, "he was right to support the Germans. It was the only way to save Europe from communism."

"But the Jews," the other man exclaimed. "Pétain handed tens of thousands of them over to their executioners."

Asher stopped in his tracks. His brothers, his cousins, all those children of Israel had appeared at the rail station as ordered, crowded obediently aboard the cattle cars, and never returned. Of his family, he alone defied the orders, took to the woods, and struck up with Levi and Eli. Yes, there were Communists in the Resistance. Socialists made up the majority of his cell. But politics were trivial compared with the brutal reality of his family taken away, and his wartime determination to make the takers pay.

"What are you looking at, mule?"

Asher came to his senses. The men had stopped arguing to glare at him. With slow care, he bent and picked up a brick, hiding it with his body.

"Which are you, deaf or stupid?" asked the bearded man.

"Or all three?" quipped the other man, and they laughed.

Asher shuffled away, suffering the heat. Out of their sight, he tossed the brick in a gutter. Why should he have survived, and not his beautiful brothers? Why him, and not his daughter and wife?

He could hear the arguers rejoining their debate, ardent as ever. He heard them everywhere he went. Meanwhile, the rails stayed bent, the bridges reached halfway, the roads remained potholed or bomb-cratered. Meanwhile, the rivers proved their disinterest by continuing to find a path through what had once been greatness. In his time of wandering Asher found himself on riverbank after riverbank, his direction pulled this way and that like a kite by the wind.

There were women whose heads had been forcibly shaved. One was paraded naked in the streets, her breasts bruised, her arms jerked this way and that by a rope around her wrists. At night there was gunfire in the distance. Nothing connected Asher with any place or time or purpose. He became a leaf on the river.

One day he arrived at a town whose sign had unusual spelling: SAARBRÜCKEN. The accent was puzzling, the umlaut, until the truth stunned him. In his search for a sanctuary in France, he had wandered all the way to its eastern border. Germany.

Asher did an about-face, and from that moment on, he began to starve in earnest. To complete what he had begun at the seaside, before the woman and her dog had beguiled him into changing his mind.

Starvation was not always terrible, aside from taking too long. He felt the acid in his belly, a body gnawing on itself. The scent of food cooking, when he encountered it, made him angry. His thirst was unquenchable. People eyed him with suspicion; rough men kicked him in his sleep. Some nights he lay at the roadside scowling at the stars, attempting to organize the constellations in the shape of his daughter's face, and failing.

Yet the world was not content to let him go. Someone would insist that he accept a piece of fruit. Or they'd leave a plate outside for him. Sometimes at dusk there would be a wagon, a bonfire, strangers willing to feed a stranger.

"We have food," a man said, guiding Asher along. "It's not far."

The fire burned high, people circling it. The man helped him sit against a fence post. Asher found a rock that fit his palm, and tucked it under his leg in case of trouble. The man brought him a metal plate. "It's only a little, so you don't make yourself sick."

A charred potato, baked in the coals. As the man backed away, Asher squeezed it with his hand, splitting it open, scooping the scalding-hot insides into his mouth. It burned his tongue, at the same time he felt flooded with flavor. Salt, and then rosemary. Where could these people possibly have found salt and rosemary?

Asher's stomach clenched to have food in it, a pain he bore without complaint. He watched the man minister to the group—a piece of bread here, a pat on the back there. He returned with a cup of water, which Asher instantly gulped dry.

"Which is greater," the man asked, "the appetite of your body, or the hunger of your soul?"

Asher laughed, the question was so immense. The man did not flinch, though, waiting easily. Asher handed back the cup. "Is it that obvious?" he said at last.

The man peered momentarily into the empty cup. "You look like someone with a thousand stories to tell, almost all of them sad."

"Are you a clergyman?" Asher asked.

It was the man's turn to laugh. "Sheep farmer. And I used to keep bees."

Someone by the fire took up a tune, a spirited ditty, but everyone shushed him.

"Not yet," the farmer called to his people. "Too soon for song."

Watching him amble back to the fire, Asher recalled when he had last heard music. He knew down to the minute. Aube had a habit of humming to herself while she was gardening. He would bring a stool outside and pretend to work, just to hear her song. Along came Rachel one day, toting her beloved Dolly, whom she instructed in toddler gibberish on how gardening was done. Eventually tiring of that play, Rachel crawled up beside her mother, humming bits of a tune as well. He sat there thrilled, as they unconsciously harmonized. An hour later, they left to bring beet greens to a neighbor, and on the way home the enemy soldier fired and ended everything. But that moment with their two voices humming at once? He heard it in his mind as clearly as if he were still seated on that stool, sewing tools in hand, and the memory was so sweet, he felt as though it might split him in half there against the fence post. It might as well have been the last music on earth. All Asher could do was close his eyes and hurt.

After a time, he dozed off, but the nightmare was waiting as usual: the man on fire, his face distorted by agony, his skin making a smell Asher would never forget.

"Sorry to bother you," the farmer said, at which Asher jumped awake. "I thought you might want another." He dropped a second potato on the metal plate. And backed away before Asher could collect himself enough to express thanks.

Later, when the coals burned low, the farmer returned. Asher put a hand on his rock for security, but the man only sat beside him. He wore patched clothes and a collapsed hat, but Asher noticed that his boots were well maintained. In his lap he tossed a pebble hand to hand, like an idea about which he was of two minds. "As I said, you look like a man with some stories. How about earning your supper by telling one?"

Asher released the rock. "What kind do you want?"

"One from your travels, that reflects the time we're in. I have heard, for example, about hangings. Not only collaborators, but sympathizers, or people who got rich doing business with the enemy, rounded up without a trial and executed."

"I hope not," Asher replied. "The people of France are better than that."

The farmer fingered the pebble in his palm, as if he were stirring something. "I don't mean to dispute with you. But one hundred and fifty years ago, our country guillotined fifteen thousand people, cut their heads off, for the crime of being royal or rich. I imagine that same nation, these days, would not have much difficulty deciding that a few hundred Nazi friends deserved a rope around their necks."

"I suppose you're right. But compared with the fate of millions in the death camps, our old revolution looks practically *gentille*."

"Fair point. So, tell me a story," the man persisted, "that teaches me something."

Asher hesitated. Could he tell this farmer how grief uproots a man? How guilt makes each footstep heavier? And how, combined, these forces could make him wander the earth, casting about for a reason to live?

He looked away into the dark. The dwindling fire revealed a sty, a fence, a tree. From the low dance of the flames, shadows lurched and heaved.

"Whenever I enter a village," he began, "I find the well first, because I am thirsty. Also, people gather there. I ask for work, sometimes food, if the pangs are too strong, then shelter, in that order. Each time I think, Is this where I belong? Could this be home for the person I have become?"

"Are people generous to you?" the farmer asked.

"As they are able. No one has abundance. One day, at a town's well, I found two men who were fistfighting. It was the middle of the day, they both appeared sober, and it seemed almost businesslike. No one attended, no voyeurs gathered to goad them on or pull them apart."

"That's strange."

"Yes, and they fought half-heartedly. As if they didn't hate one another, but were doing someone's bidding. Yet on they battled, pummeling in the stomach, jabbing in the jaw, until I couldn't bear it. I called out, I moved between them."

Asher watched the man's hands. He had stopped fiddling with the pebble.

"They seemed relieved," Asher continued. "Dropping their fists, chests heaving like oxen at plow. Make peace, I said, and left them to that task."

"This is an uplifting story."

Asher shook his head. "I was less than a block away when I heard the thud of blows. They'd started again. No one stopped them. No one cared."

The man pondered what he had heard, before tossing the pebble aside. "I cannot leave because of my children. But I hear that Clovide is the place."

"What place?"

The farmer checked right and left, as if to confirm that no one was eavesdropping. A battered farmstead, the shapes of sleeping bodies. "Where fighting has stopped."

"I've heard that rumor and many others. But where is Clovide?"

The man pointed across Asher's chest. "South. Not forty kilometers."

"I have heard that before too."

"Before the war I sold wool and honey there. This is the right road."

"Where in the city should I go?"

"The cathedral, I imagine," the farmer said. "A holy place. When France had kings, that was where coronations took place."

"Is that right? A holy place?" Asher decided to keep his faith to himself. If another religion offered a meal and a place to sleep, he would not object.

All at once there was a pull in the air, a restlessness. Still susceptible to the seduction of hope, he stood and clasped the farmer's hand. "Thank you for your kindness. I'm leaving now, while I have strength from the meal you gave me."

"The gratitude is mine."

"I've done nothing but eat your food. Why would you be grateful?"

"I will be chewing on your story long after these potatoes are digested."

TWO DAYS LATER, WHEN THE afternoon offered slanting light, celestial beams through the clouds, Asher dragged himself to the crest of a hill. In the distance, like an island in the sea, there lay a city: roads and buildings and a river flowing through. Vultures circled in the between lands, floating without moving a wing tip. Here was a species that subsisted entirely on the dead, yet appeared to hunt with a kind of ease, a laziness, so steady was the supply. If he died in the open, they would feast on him.

Papers blew past like tumbling leaves. Asher's attention followed their somersaults till one sheet flattened on a post—the top of which held a broken sign: CLOV. The farmer had told the truth. Asher had arrived.

Once he'd crossed the vulture road, the city was larger than he'd expected, and more confusing. He'd intended to use the river as a reference point, but lost track of it in the buildings and lanes. Eventually he sought high ground. There he found a square, less littered than most. Two toddlers sat with a dog, their legs wide, rolling a brown ball back and forth between them. The wire-haired terrier eyed the ball, a bored babysitter, but did not play.

"Excuse me, boys," Asher said, at which the older one snatched the ball up to his chest. These children were clean, he noticed. They were loved, someone had survived to take care of them. "I'm looking for the cathedral. Can you direct me?"

The younger one had a glint in his eye, the spark of mischief. He murmured something to the older one, whose eyes lit up identically. Lowering the ball, he tossed it past Asher, into the gutter and down the hill. Asher scurried after, rushing to catch it before the gutter emptied into a sewer pipe. Swooping low at the last second, he grabbed the ball and felt an odd thrill.

Straightening, he saw the spires. The cathedral was in as plain sight as if the boys had drawn him a map. His mood lifted, he climbed back to return the ball.

The brothers weren't there. Nor the terrier. Nor any sign of where they'd gone. All the house doors in the square remained closed. It was a puzzle. He went to the nearest stoop and placed the ball there, taking care that it would not roll away.

Nearly a year into his time of wandering, Asher set out toward the spires.

THE CATHEDRAL SAT AT THE back of a large parvis, its stone edifice presiding over the broad courtyard. Thick wooden doors bore charred evidence of attempts at destruction. Statues of saints lined the entry, most damaged but some intact, this one holding a handful of wheat, that one a book. Despite the thrumming in his chest, he marched forward slowly, formally, as if in a procession.

As soon as he entered, though, the march came to a halt. The holy place was as damaged as everywhere else. Collapsed walls on the near side. Stones the size of coffins lying haphazardly, like blocks that playing children had abandoned.

He heard the raucous call of a crow. The bird swooped overhead, sailing toward the cathedral's rear wall—which remained intact except for openings where the windows had been, the stained glass. Again, the bird cawed, whether in encouragement or warning Asher could not say, as it soared through the gap and away.

He clambered over the mess for a closer look. The altar lay on its front. Though side chapels remained intact, many of the pews had been splintered by falling stones.

There was no denying reality. Clovide was no sanctuary.

There was movement to one side, a scraping sound like a chair moving. As Asher snatched up a rock just in case, a hand drew back a curtain, and an old woman emerged. Bent, wrinkled, she wore a black kerchief on her head. She wrung her hands like a concerned mouse. "Are you a priest?"

"No," Asher said.

"You cannot hear my confession?" Her voice was a warble, high as a wren's.

He shook his head. "I don't know what that is."

"A sacrament." The woman tiptoed closer, eking a path through the disorder. "I wish to reconcile with God before I die."

"So do I." He brushed pebbles away, and sat. "I was told this was a place for people to accomplish that goal."

"Oh, years ago, that might have been the truth." As she approached the broken altar rail, Asher could see that the woman was not old, only hollowed by famine.

"Until they discovered the priests were hiding Jewish families," she continued. "They gathered us all to witness, then shot them in the square. That was not enough, we had to see the holy men profaned. They prohibited any burial, and left the bodies to rot. By day, vultures feasted. By night, we heard dogs fighting over what remained." She picked at her apron. "Later someone bombed our city. As you can see."

Asher tilted his head toward the damaged ceiling, beyond that a crimson sky. He shut his eyes, unwilling to experience beauty, but quickly blinked them open. That color meant the sun was setting, and soon he would need a safe place to sleep.

"Everyone lost something." The woman knelt at the rail. "No one was spared. My mother? Ancient, frail, prayed herself to sleep at night. A soldier shot her, for what reason I cannot imagine. She was as harmless as a cricket." She lowered her head. "How can anyone have faith, after God abandoned us?"

"I wonder the same thing." Again, Asher assessed the open archways at the rear, the spaces for windows that did not survive the war.

"The left panel was the Visitation." The woman was up again, approaching with arms raised. "On the right, the Annunciation. In the center, the wedding at Cana. It was lovely. You would have thought the lilies were real."

"The wedding where?"

"Someone took the rest, though." She waved at the sides of the building, where dozens of window openings looked like missing teeth. "They actually robbed a cathedral."

"Why would anyone commit such a crime?" Asher asked.

"That was the goal of the war." The woman had reached his side, and spoke as if offering condolences. "To take everything, and never give it back."

CHAPTER 4

In his memory the colors touched everywhere: the sun's yellow in the aisle, green from leaves on the book of Torah, red from Eve's apple on the believers' hands. And that was from the Garden of Eden window alone. There were others, all the way down the synagogue's southern wall. Slowly, almost painfully as the sun progressed through the hours, the colors moved. Only a boy, bored as a turtle, he waited for the day to advance enough that a bit of colored light would fall on him. Around him the congregation droned and sang and prayed, while the earth dawdled in its spin.

Near the end of services, the tints reached his lap at last. He waved his hands in the beams, moving back and forth from one color to another, until his mother yanked them down, squeezing his wrist hard enough to be a corrective, and whisper-growled that he'd better pay attention to the rabbi, or by heaven, when we get home . . .

Asher's eyes jerked open, his arms tensed, finding himself still inside the damaged cathedral. The warbling woman was gone. She had mistaken him for a priest. In a way, he was: A minister of wandering. The patron saint of nowhere left to go.

At the scent of cooking meat, he sat up, his senses sharpened. It came from behind the cathedral, and he set off at once.

Outside, the stars were an insanity, not one streetlamp to dim their brilliance. But there was a campfire under the bridge, revealed by its reflection off the river, a warm orange glow. A grumbled comment, a gargled laugh. Asher drew closer. Once again he was without a weapon. He would have been content with a simple carving knife, a tire iron, any form of self-protection before approaching strangers. But the scent was irresistible. Something was roasting on that fire.

He approached without sound, not scuffing or kicking the least pebble. Two men, large as tree trunks and looking nearly as solid, sat under the bridge. One of them rotated something over the fire, causing drops of fat to fall hissing into the flame.

"Euclid," said the seated one. "Would you truly have drowned yourself?"

"Without this dinner?" the nearer one replied. "Pascal, you know I would have."

"And left me alone?"

"You'd be having twice the feast."

Pascal scratched his massive chest. "But you are the chef. If I tried to roast a chicken, I would have one half burnt and the other half raw. We need one another."

Euclid poked the fire. "Have you never once considered drowning yourself?"

Asher hesitated. Was his impulse, that day on the beach, a common idea?

Firelight tossed shadows on Pascal's brow. "Not while she lives and breathes."

"To fall in love with a married woman." Euclid sighed. "You have my pity."

The aroma pulled at a part of Asher that refused to die. It had taken two full days after Aube and Rachel died before he would accept a plate of food, yet within minutes he was sponging up the last of the sauce with his bread. That same stubborn animal hovered at the edge of the firelight, goading him forward. "Hello?"

Both men jumped. Pascal drew a knife as long as his forearm. Euclid seized a truncheon. In the firelight Asher could see him better, and the man had the thighs of a horse, a barrel chest, a head larger than a bucket. He was too large to stand upright under the bridge. "Who's there?"

"Whoever it is," Pascal said, jabbing the knife, "kill him for interrupting."

Asher stepped fully into the light, hands open. "Go ahead. I have no fight left."

"What do you want?" Euclid circled the head of the club, flexing his stovepipe wrist. "And what makes you think we have it?"

He was barefoot, Asher noticed, and his nose was bent to one side as if it had been pressed by a great weight. Pascal also lacked shoes, his feet dirty and scarred.

"Boots," Asher said. "I heard that there were friendly men under the bridge wearing fine boots. Apparently I was misinformed."

"Are you making a joke?" Pascal asked. "Because we are not laughing."

For some odd reason, Asher felt no fear. These men were huge, and belligerent, and yet he had no sense that they would harm him.

"If you kill me," he replied, "please throw my body into the river, so the fish at least will not starve."

"You are peculiar," Euclid said, pointing his weapon. "What is your name?"

"Asher is what my mother called me," he replied. "But I bear so little resemblance to that boy, I might be called anything."

"What changed you so much, Anything?"

He did not hesitate. "Killing."

"It is no great thing." Euclid shrugged. "The times required it."

"For me it remains a gigantic thing."

Euclid studied him with one eye, while Pascal interjected. "I had a cousin named Asher. I admired him when I was young, because he knew how to juggle."

"I would gladly juggle for you," Asher said with a bow, "if you are entertained by seeing various objects artfully dropped to the ground."

"Stand here, Anything." Euclid pointed with the truncheon. "Supper's cooking but we're starved for conversation. Let's chat before I kill you."

"Such politesse." Asher ducked under the bridge. "We must be countrymen."

"Tell us a story," Pascal said. He sat like a gargoyle, surveying his domain—if the gargoyle held a long, gleaming knife.

In that moment the behemoth could have been Levi or Eli, who demanded stories as if Asher had an unlimited supply. "What makes you think I am a storyteller?"

"I can hear your brain machine grinding all the way over here. A story to lift our spirits."

"That's no easy task in these times."

"Do it anyway," Euclid growled. "Or die."

Stalling for time, Asher pointed. "What kind of meat is that?"

"Have you forgotten what a chicken looks like?"

"And tastes like too, I'm afraid." It was as bold a hint as he dared to make.

"I said tell us a story," Pascal whispered, knife blade glinting in the firelight. The quietness of his voice made it all the more threatening.

"Yes, you did." Asher lowered into a squat, rubbing his hands at the flames. "And here it is. During the labor for her fifth son, my mother hemorrhaged. Blood on the sheets, her body, everywhere."

"We said uplifting." Pascal stabbed the air.

"Patience, please," Asher replied. "After one particularly strong and bloody contraction, the midwife checked my mother and could not find a pulse. Her heart had stopped. The woman went for a knife, with a plan to deliver me before I smothered. Of course, with the blade over my mother's womb, she hesitated. For the rest of her days my mother described that moment as entering a place of mild light and sweet tones, kindness without limit, and all of it coming from the other side of a gate. Her own mother, long buried, stood inside with arms wide. My mother moved to open the gate, intending to enter this divine place, when a loud sound from behind caused her to stop. She turned back, to learn what had caused the noise. The midwife said at that moment, her heart began to beat again."

Euclid and Pascal exchanged a look so identical, Asher wondered if they were twins. Pascal rubbed his thumb on the jut of his chin. It was a giant thumb, a sausage. "All right, what was the sound?"

"My birth cry."

For a moment no one spoke, while Asher observed the men more clearly. They were the largest humans he had ever seen. Bearded, long-haired, wearing many layers of clothing, all ragged with holes. Pascal's nose was damaged identically to Euclid's, folded over like the page of a book.

"Good story," Pascal said, tucking the knife away. "Good enough."

"Sit." Euclid gestured at the dirt beside the fire. "Tell us what you have seen."

"It would be quicker to list what I have not seen." Asher eased himself down. "Food, humor, rebuilding." Closer now, he could see that the chicken was nearly done. It was impaled on a wooden spit. His mouth watered so, he had to swallow before speaking again. "I heard there is a place near here where the war is genuinely over."

"It's true," said Euclid.

"How do you know?"

"We make deliveries there," Pascal answered. "The vegetable girl brings her cart, a cooper sells them wood, and we provide sand by the wagonload."

Asher forced himself to look away from the chicken. "Why do they need sand?"

"To give them the opportunity to pay us francs," Pascal said. "I fill my wagon with all it can bear. I strain the load uphill to the sacred old château—"

"Sacred?"

"It was once an abbey. Five hundred years ago, that is. I wheel the wagon around to where I delivered my last pile, which is all gone by that time, for what use I do not care one twig. I tip the wagon to relieve it, the husband gives me coins—though I wish it were his beautiful wife, alas—then I pull the empty wagon down and home."

"Unless I come too," Euclid added, "bringing ash or lime, which they also sometimes need. Which earns me a coin, and prevents the rattling of an empty wagon on the return trip from making my friend here melancholy."

"Some days the lady pays." Pascal brightened. "And I am not melancholy."

"Her breasts," Euclid explained, wagging his head. "A national treasure."

"You make jokes," Pascal lamented, "about the love of my life."

"I'm sorry." Euclid put a hand on his chest and lowered his gaze.

"If you are earning coins," Asher interjected, "why are you under a bridge?"

They were silent awhile. "There is nothing to buy," Pascal said at last. "Food, shelter, none to be had for good money nor bad. This chicken? We did not buy it."

"Nor did we steal it," Euclid hurried to add. "We are workingmen, creatures of honor. Not thieves."

"I am no one's judge," Asher said, hands raised with open palms.

"It crossed our path too slowly," Pascal explained. "Meaning it was lost. A lost bird belongs to whoever should find it."

"Can you tell me where this château is?"

"We can," Euclid answered, "but we have a better idea."

"We do?" Pascal shifted in his seat. "What idea do we have?"

"Suppose we possess an inkling of whose chicken this used to be, before it crossed our path too slowly. Suppose we committed a fraction of a wrong by making it our dinner. The tiniest of misdeeds on our conscience. But." He frowned, a serious solicitor making closing arguments. "If we did a good deed now, and gave a portion to an obviously starving person, might we regain that lost grace in the eyes of the Lord?"

"You certainly would," Asher blurted.

Pascal considered. "You're not a priest, are you?"

"Not a fraction."

"I was hoping you were, so you might adjudicate my friend's idea."

"Well, perhaps a speck of a fraction . . ."

"I'm decided on the matter," Euclid announced, reaching nearly into the flames. He tore a leg off the bird and flung it in Asher's direction. "Here's to virtue."

Asher tossed the leg from palm to palm to avoid burning himself, before dropping it to cool on the flank of his coat.

"See?" Pascal winked at his brother. "He can juggle after all."

Euclid used his truncheon to lift the bird, setting it on a flat stone. He and Pascal blessed themselves, then dove into the chicken like wild dogs on a fresh kill.

With his portion, Asher peeled away the skin and put it in his mouth. The sensation was overwhelming—fat, crunchiness, juice. It took all of his self-control not to devour the rest, like the behemoths now gnashing and gulping. Sinking his teeth into the warm meat, Asher felt his body rejoice in a hundred ways—the sustenance, the flavor, the liquid down his chin, the pleasure, when had he last felt pleasure?

"Here," Pascal said. "To improve your juggling." And he tossed a chicken wing.

"Now," Asher responded, gnawing away. "Now I am a wealthy man."

THE FIRE DWINDLED, THE MOON spilled milk on the river, the men sat in satisfied silence. Euclid used a sliver of bone to pick his teeth. "Why do you wish to visit the château?"

"I am untethered." Asher held his stomach with one hand. "What the war took from me, what it required me to do, and what I'd hoped to return to—"

"You are telling the story of everyone we know," Pascal interrupted.

"I am looking for a place where the war is truly ended, where there is no killing and perhaps rebuilding has begun. Because if it exists in one place, it is possible in every place."

"You want peace, reconciliation, and reconstruction, in that order," Euclid said.

"It sounds sensible when you say it. To me, it feels more like wanting a terrible storm to pass."

"What you seek is unattainable." With fingers deft despite their size, Euclid rolled his truncheon back and forth. "Why should we rebuild the world anyway?"

"To eat decently. To sleep in a dry place. Perhaps to mend our broken hearts."

Pascal responded with a sorrowful sigh, a lone dog with no bone, so Asher knew he had suffered his share.

"Before we give directions to this sanctuary across the river," Pascal said, "do you have questions for us?"

"Will they accept me there?"

"No," Euclid replied. "You would be another mouth to feed."

"No." Pascal shook his head. "They have no use for you."

"No," said Euclid. "They have everyone they need."

"No," said Pascal. "They seek people with skills that you lack."

Asher sat speechless. Were they joking behind their beards? Why did they seem safe, though they appeared dangerous? More importantly, why did he feel a small—perhaps tiny, perhaps the most minuscule—sense of progress? The man who shared his potatoes had directed him accurately to Clovide. Hunger had led him to these men, who knew the château and why it was worth seeking. The marvel was not that people were helping. It was that, despite being completely untethered from the world, Asher had drifted nearer to a place where he might wish to remain alive. Also, he'd eaten twice in three days. His body wrestled to digest the meat, a problem he welcomed.

"No more questions?" Pascal bellowed. "Did we discourage you too well?"

"What happened to you?" Asher asked.

"What do you mean?" Euclid said.

"Both of you. I'm curious what it was."

Pascal elbowed his companion. "Do you know what he is talking about?"

Euclid shrugged. "I have no idea."

"Here, I mean." Asher waved at his own face. "What happened to your noses?"

At that the men snickered like chimps. "Few dare to ask," Pascal said. "We make them say it. Most back down."

Asher realized he was being played with. "You would not feed me if you planned to kill me. A waste of food."

"It's never too late to kill a nosy-bones," Euclid said, nudging his truncheon. "Wham and bam and story over."

"What did happen?" Pascal asked his companion. "Remind me. We used to be so handsome. What happened to our beautiful faces?"

"Boots," Euclid said, mock-woeful, wiggling his toes. "Enemy boots."

They both burst out laughing. Asher did not get the joke. But under the dome of the bridge, their peals echoed wildly. Instead of two voices, it sounded like twenty.

CHAPTER 5

The man on fire had staggered like a drunkard, flames racing up his back. Intoxicated with pain. The wind blew smoke from his body to where Asher hid, the scent straight into his nose, memory, dreams.

Asher shuddered awake. It was morning, he was alone. A mound of charred coals was the only evidence that Euclid and Pascal existed. How had such large and coarse men escaped without causing him to stir? And why had he not insisted they give him directions to the château before they all fell asleep? All he knew was that it was across the river.

The morning was chilly for late summer. At his feet, sticks sped past on the smooth water, and he wondered why rivers were always in a hurry. Perhaps they were restless. Feeling likewise, Asher emerged from under the bridge.

A gunmetal sky greeted him. Set back from the banks there stood a row of houses, each one caved in or collapsed. It was as bad as Bonheur, not one remained intact. But these homes were finer, their windows looked like eyes and the front doors like mouths. They reminded him of the people in his Resistance cell—whose response to the enemy's surrender was to heave a sigh and march off in the direction of home, hoping something remained. Some limped, others used crutches, still others walked well but flinched at the least sound.

Artifacts of damage as much as any row of houses. And as unlikely to be repaired.

When he turned away, what he saw surprised him. The bridge was intact. In all his time of wandering he had not seen one other span that was complete, riverbank to riverbank. He jogged across at once, as if combat might recommence at any moment.

On the opposite bank Asher saw another thing that cheered him: grapevines. In rows they rose, flourishing in spite of everything. Yes, their trellises were tilted and broken, the vines neglected and unkempt. Yet the plants were fat with fruit. Green clusters, huddled like refugees, intent upon ripening.

The vines did not care that there had been a war. They insisted on being alive. Asher imagined it would be years before anyone wanted champagne. The vines did not care about that either. Sun shone, rain fell, grapes grew—the seasons doing their business. He shuffled forward, encouraged.

Half an hour along he saw a fork ahead, and paused at the roadside to consider: south to follow the river, or east into the highlands. In the distance there stood a medieval village, walls and spires and red-tiled roofs. They lifted a person's eyes to the sky, where God had lived before mankind destroyed the possibility of his existence. What deity would engineer beings in his own image, then observe impartially while they killed one another with the efficiency of a plague?

A sound from behind interrupted his thoughts. A cart approached, pulled by a stiff-haired donkey. The rear of the wagon was heaped with vegetables, pale lettuce and forest-green cucumbers. But what arrested Asher's attention was the driver.

She wore a wide-brimmed hat, contrary to the fashion of the time, and red canvas overalls that sun and labor had worn to peach-pink, which accented her tanned skin. The young woman held the reins lightly, but her forearms were strong. Inclining her head as she approached, she used the hat brim for concealment as much as shade.

The woman rumbled up the road, as determined as a grapevine.

The wagon raised enough dust above the grasses that he could follow where she steered left, uphill, and disappeared in the trees. He needed no better compass.

With every step the road's condition improved, while his stamina did the opposite. As the morning sun gathered strength, Asher felt weary. Noticing a grove of poplars ahead, he drew under their shade. They were noisy, thanks to a north wind sweeping the sky clear.

The air revived him too. Eventually he reached the road's last fork. One route rose to the village, while the other, a leafy lane, rounded the hill out of sight. With no way of knowing which way the woman with the cart had chosen, he stood as if mute.

Seconds later a donkey brayed, directing him to follow the lane. Plodding forward, Asher smelled an unusual scent. A wood fire, yes, but something else was burning too, something peculiar. He reached a sign on an iron gate: LE CHÂTEAU GUERIN, 1588. Here was the place. How had it withstood all the wars of those centuries?

The answer lay around the next corner, where the view opened. A great house stood in handsome dominion over the land: splendid, three stories tall, with four chimneys rising higher still. The approaching field was grass, with pens to one side for pigs and goats. A sacred place it may once have been, as the men under the bridge said, but its setting indicated a martial history too. Anyone storming this place would spend two hundred yards in steep climbing with no protection—not a stone to hide behind, not a tree. Beyond lay broad fields dotted with sheep and cows, and farther, cropland sloped toward the valley. From the nearby brush, he heard the hum of bees.

Asher paused, perspiring, taking it in, while again the donkey complained. A melodic female voice urged the animal along. Before Asher could hide, the young woman rode up briskly. All Asher could muster was to touch the brim of an imaginary hat, by which time she had brushed past, trailing a breath of wind.

He watched her go. Sitting smartly erect, she did not look back.

Her cart dipped into a pothole, however, and something bounced free. Asher hastened to pick it up. A tomato, so enriched by sun its skin bore a yellowed split, as if it were about to burst.

"Madamoiselle?" he called, holding the fruit aloft. "Hello?"

But she continued on her way, taking the lane that led up to the village. He found himself alone in the road.

A tomato. It had been ages, and this one was a specimen. Asher gave it a good long sniff, and it seemed as though he were smelling the sun itself, and the rain that had fallen in spring. Sitting on a roadside stump, he nibbled into the flesh. Flavor flooded him, nectar so bright and strong he had to close his eyes. Could a life be saved by so little a thing? Certainly a day could, so his second bite was a big one. The tomato burst, spraying, he had to jerk forward to keep seeds and juice from spilling on him. By reflex he cupped his free hand below, to catch whatever might fall.

His wife, Aube, had tended their garden, and defended her territory. Each spring it grew, tidy and orderly on the house's south side. By August it became wild abandon: overburdened beanpoles, makeshift pea ladders, wide leaves where melons snaked the ground, a fence to protect cucumbers and peppers from garden animals. To one side, lattices for the tomatoes to lean upon as they fattened and plummed. Asher's job was to bring carts of manure at planting time, then stay out of the way while Aube worked and weeded and hummed to herself. When the goods of the earth were ripe, she would bring them to the table, or make a surprise dish for dinner—or, on one memorable day, when she was proud, present him in his workshop with a perfect red orb made of no ingredients so much as her effort and patience.

That tomato had been eaten as if by another man: a husband and father, who kept his shop organized and clean. A person who had never killed another human being, who had not yet learned the finality of death and the bottomlessness of grief.

Aube lingered that afternoon, Rachel away playing at a friend's house, sitting in the shop with him as he ate, asking about his work, chatting about what time the sun had come up. The memory was its own piece of perfect fruit.

And so, there at the roadside, he wept. No matter how depleted his body might be, somehow his reservoir never ran dry. Because grief had grown familiar, however, companion of all his travels, he continued eating despite the tears that streaked his grimy cheeks, spilling from his chin. When Asher finished the tomato, he licked the hand below for every drop. His sorrow had salted the juice, improving the flavor.

Ahead lay the château, and he noticed one more chimney, to the rear, twice the height of the others. Made of brown brick, newer by centuries, it issued a smoke that must have been the strange scent he'd noticed. Metallic, as though the monks he imagined to be laboring within were operating not a place of prayer, but rather some sort of foundry.

As he neared the entry, Asher moved on tiptoe. A memory surfaced, another time he had been quiet. He was carrying a pistol, one bullet in its chamber, one in its magazine, as he crept behind an enemy major taking his breakfast *en pleine air*. He was eating sausage and eggs while concentrating on the map he was reading, which gave him the hearing of a deaf man. This major, a burly fellow with the mustache of a walrus, supervised a unit called the "housekeepers." They saw homes they liked, waited till the men of the house stepped outside, demanded their papers, and, having confirmed them as the owners, shot them where they stood, impounding the homes for military billeting. The "housekeepers" had entertainments too. They seized a Bonheur man known for boxing prowess, matching him against one enemy soldier after another until he could no longer lift his arms, and rewarded his victories by hanging him. Perhaps at home this breakfasting major was a loving father and devoted husband who attended church often. But the "housekeepers" were his invention, and he had nearly finished his meal.

Asher raised the pistol, steadied his hand, and fired—from the side so that the food would remain unmarred. He swabbed the man's plate with his fingers, stuffing his mouth with sausage before darting back into the trees. Later Levi praised him for the economy of using one bullet, preserving the other for future use.

Stealth, therefore, had a moral dimension. What was the meaning of his quiet approach to the château? Perhaps he had reached the end of his homelessness, the destination of his wandering. With each step his hopes soared higher.

Asher was startled to see someone dart out from the bushes just ahead. He paused at the entry, a short man who glared at him with the beady eyes of a mole. Was he some sort of guard? Had he gone for reinforcements?

Asher scanned his surroundings for a weapon, but there was nothing. Not a tree branch on the ground. No matter; he had no interest in fighting his way into this place—or any place. And he needed all of his nerve to keep walking.

The courtyard stood open, the house entrance straight ahead. He paused, aware of himself, wishing he had bathed in the river that morning. Shabby clothes and hunger did not repel people nearly as much as having a stink. Too late to do anything about that now. He strode into the courtyard. Immediately a committee of chickens charged out at him, angry hens squawking and jabbing their beaks at him, while a grouchy rooster, full of opinions, crowed at them from behind.

Startled so much he jumped at the sound of them, Asher gave a swift kick. "Get away, you pests." The birds, quick-footed, dodged him effortlessly. He started after them, booting left and right. "Go on, get away with you."

"Who taught you that?"

Asher spun to see where the voice had originated. A man dressed entirely in black sat curled up in a recess in the courtyard wall. "Excuse me?"

"A child is not born with the inclination to injure creatures weaker than himself. Someone taught you that this behavior was acceptable." Unfolding from his perch, the man proved to be gangly and slender, with long hair and long fingers. He was holding a crystal prism, which he now tucked away. "Who was it? Your mother or your father?"

"Neither." Asher held his hands out and open, displaying that he was unarmed. "Everything I know about causing injury I learned as an adult, by experiencing injuries from which I will never heal."

The tall man folded his hands on his stomach like a plump lord, though he was as slim as a fasting monk. "I once knew a fellow whose wife was often unfaithful, up to her death. When he remarried, he told his new bride that she could depend on his lifelong loyalty, because he knew how deeply infidelity hurt a person."

"What are you saying? I'm not following you."

The man smirked. "If experience taught you what it is like to receive an injury, I imagine it would deter you from causing injury. Like kicking at chickens."

"You speak in riddles." He held out his hand. "I am Asher. I was told that this place was a sanctuary where a stranger might find peace."

"I am Etienne." The tall man shook hands with light pressure, his manner suggesting not weakness but indifference. "You have been misinformed. This is not a sanctuary, peace is not what we make here, and strangers are not welcome."

"Another riddle." Asher glanced left and right, wondering when that short man who had run away would reappear. Seeing no feed on the ground, the chickens wandered off too. "Could you—in plain terms, please—tell me how I might find the lady of the house?"

"At the moment you would find her impatient. A project is behind schedule."

"There, you see?" The conversation felt like a game, and he was enjoying the play. "Helping hands are needed. I've come just in time."

The tall man crossed his arms. "Do you know how to operate an annealing kiln?"

Asher crossed his arms as well. "Soon I'll be an expert at it."

"Expertise of that sort takes years to attain."

"Every expert begins with a first day."

The tall man leaned closer. "Many first days conclude with an injured novice."

"Etienne," a voice called from inside, high yet full of gusto. "Where are you hiding yourself now?"

Consternation crossed the man's face. "In the courtyard, lady."

The front door burst open, and out waddled a woman with hair as unruly as a hayloft. She was carrying a plate of food, which caught Asher's attention as keenly as it would a dog's. "What are you doing with yourself? You know the hurry we're in."

Asher took in the sight of her: ruddy cheeks shining with perspiration, her bodice unbuttoned low enough that he had to look away.

"Are you on vacation?" she continued, whacking Etienne's chemise with the back of her hand. "Imagining a restful weekend at the sea?"

"Merely contemplating how to excel in your service."

"You should have been a salesman." She handed him the plate. Greens, bread, slices of cold meat.

He held the plate by his hip, not eating, not even looking at it. Asher marveled. "I am the opposite of a salesman. But I've cooled off now, and it's back to work."

Etienne gave him a nod, set the plate on a café table to one side, then bowed to the lady. Leaning as if to fall forward, his body followed his head past her, across the threshold—making the sign of the cross on himself, Asher noticed—and into the house.

"Go, go, go," she growled after him, though once he'd gone she turned to Asher and winked. He stood with eyes averted. "Yes? Is there something you want?"

"Several things," he answered. "I have come a great dist—"

"Make a list," she interrupted, "write it down, and come again on a quieter day." With a cloth, she patted the exposed portion of her bosom. "If we ever have one."

"Yes, ma'am." Like a weather vane rusted to perpetual east, he remained sideways. She was spilling out of her shirt.

His interest was not lust. No woman had interested Asher since

Aube. Neither the scented ones selling themselves, nor the solemn ones, seeking a night of comfort. He was impenetrable to their allure, and that included this plum of a woman with her blouse undone.

"Well, aren't we the proper gentleman?" she said with a snicker. "Modesty has no value beside the heat of a working kiln," she explained, though he did not understand. With one hand she patted her wild hair, half attempting to tame it. "Particularly while serving those blessed with skills such as Etienne's."

He felt confused; who was serving whom? "What skills are those?"

"The man was born with the gift of perfect breath."

"He is a tenor, I assume?"

The woman laughed, fanning herself. "A gaffer. But of such impeccable consistency, he outperforms the finest bellows. The man's exhale is an art form."

What was a gaffer? She had bound her bodice up somewhat. "Does everyone here speak in riddles?"

"I hope so, to keep our minds supple. But—" She raised a finger. "Not my husband. He's sensible. Deep in his faith, feet on the ground. Thank heaven there's one such among us." With a wave, she began toward the house. "Farewell, sir."

She was leaving without the plate. This was a moment when he should have tried to convince her to hire him, or take him in, but all he could think about was the food on that little table.

"Farewell," he said.

As she waddled into the château, Asher all but pounced on the plate. He gulped and gobbled, nearly choking. Eating three times in four days was better than he'd done in months, and his body was ravenous.

"Look at you," the woman said, returning. She'd remembered the plate.

"I'm sorry," he said, unable to stop till he'd wolfed the last morsel— though she did not try to take the plate away, only stood by the door watching him.

"I have seen many kinds of hunger since the war, but none as honest as yours."

As Asher gulped the last of it, his original intent returned. "I heard that you are behind schedule today."

"It's often the case."

"I'm willing to work to earn the meal."

She reached out for the plate. "What do you know how to do?"

How to assassinate. How to mourn. How to wander with nothing and yet survive. "A great many things," he answered, handing it over.

"For example? And be specific."

"I can make boots that outlive the man who wears them." Asher angled one foot sideways to prove his point.

"Perfect," she said with a guffaw. "We lack leather, yet have no shortage of feet. A fitting metaphor for these famished times. Good day."

He held his arms out. "I would work to my utmost. I have come a long way."

The woman wiped her brow with her cloth. "Let me see your hands."

As Asher held them out, she turned them palms-up for inspection: miniature battlefields, blistered and furrowed and gouged. From calluses to a spot of pitch to the sheen of last night's chicken fat, they told the story of his life since the day an impatient enemy corporal had ordered the people of Bonheur to clear the streets.

"You're not a rich man, that's certain." She put one fist on her hip. "Do you know how to lift heavy things, and carry them, and put them safely down?"

"At tasks such as those, I have a lifetime of experience."

"You amuse me. And I am not in a mood to be easily amused." The woman buttoned her smock. "Break your back for me, I'll pay a wage that's more than fair."

"How would it be if I bend my back, but not quite break it?"

"Fine. But I can't feed you or take you in. There's no room here."

"You've already fed me. And I'm grateful."

"We have a contract." She seized his hand, pumping it up and down once. "I am Brigitte. Now come see the atelier."

"And I am—" But she had already scurried into the house, also crossing herself on the threshold.

Not knowing the actual gesture, Asher pretended by raising his right hand, jerking it right and left, as if conducting an imaginary orchestra. With one last look around the courtyard—vines and stones and dappled light—and with the undeniable sensation that he was taking leave of one thing and embracing another, carrying no bags yet plenty of burdens, he trotted along after her.

CHAPTER 6

The smell hit him first, the same metallic scent he'd noticed back on the road, but more acrid and eye-watering now that he neared the source. They'd hurried through the house—handsome wooden floors with worn rugs that slid underfoot, plaster walls covered with giant paintings and faded tapestries—until they reached a door propped open with a milk bucket. It opened into a rear courtyard, where a great chestnut tree arched overhead like some muscular overseer.

He hustled after Brigitte into another building, with broad doors like a stable, though he hadn't seen any sign of horses. Inside, while his eyes adjusted, she gave him gloves of hard leather, stiff against his skin.

"Don't touch anything," she said. "Nothing is more painful than a burn."

Immediately he understood why her blouse was open. He had never experienced a place so hot, the air so breathless. Like a blacksmith's forge, but the size of a building. The killer in him knew: a foretaste of Hades.

Asher followed, gloves against his chest, as she stepped past bins of various powders. A scowling man was shoveling them into a stone structure that looked like a giant oven. Inside, Asher saw molten coals below a ceramic bowl that was wider than the length of his arm, filled with a boiling orange soup. Even five steps away he could feel his hair singe. The scowling man grunted, scooping another shovelful into the maw.

Beyond the oven, two men were dipping long metal poles into the boiling soup. One of them lifted his pole, a shiny glob stuck to its tip, which he rotated with nimble fingers. Asher recognized the black clothes of Etienne, and he paused, hoping to learn what a gaffer did, and how breathing could be an art form. Stepping back to a workbench, Etienne put his mouth to the pole's cool tip. The orange glob on the other end bulged, then grew into a sphere of glass. Asher stood stunned.

The other man working in that area broke the reverie, however, when the globe on his pipe snapped off, crashing to the floor. Everyone in the atelier stopped at the sound, everyone looked, while the man cursed and banged his pipe on the floor, then kicked the surviving half of the orb so that it shattered against the furnace. Noticing Asher, he snarled, jabbing the pipe in his direction as though he had caused the mishap.

Brigitte sidled over, calm as a pond, and spoke to the man in a voice low enough that he had to bend closer to hear. His forehead was inches from her breasts. He scowled, but stayed inclined toward her, eventually nodding. As she left him, he put his pipe aside and returned with a push broom and dustpan.

"Don't dawdle," she told Asher, sashaying past. "Come on with me."

But this place is terrifying, he wanted to say. He'd just seen a madman. Also, each workbench had a rack of tools—tongs, knives, shears—all excellent weapons. He scanned the floors, expecting bloodstains, wondering why he couldn't find any.

Brigitte led him past a row of empty horse stalls, through a set of doors large enough to accommodate a wagon, to a dirt workyard. Pieces of wood the size of his legs lay all akimbo, hundreds of them in a chaotic stack, like a giant version of the children's pick-up-sticks game.

The woman was pointing here and there at the stack. "Birch and poplar, with the lighter-colored bark, are good for getting the kiln started. But they burn fast. After that we need a higher temperature that lasts longer. Oak, ash, and elm. You carry it in, and put it where Bondurant can reach it handily."

"Which one is Bondurant?"

"The grouch with the shovel. He hates work, so don't take his anger personally."

"I'm carrying wood. What could I do that would make him angry?"

She laughed. "You'll see. But if you do this job, I can attend to the kitchen. Good luck." With a wave, she was gone.

Removing his coat, Asher studied the woodpile—the chaos of it, and how much extra effort its disorganization made necessary. He was reminded of an evening Aube announced that she was about to throw away a skein of yarn the size of her head. Somehow in her basket it had become a continuous knot, and she had reached her limit of untying frustration. Asher attempted to untangle it, standing in the kitchen, till she shooed him away. Even watching him was annoying. But he sat in the corner, and spent the better part of an hour unwinding and unknotting. Which pleasure was greater—bringing the yarn into order, or eventually presenting a tangle-free skein to his wife—he could not say. She placed a slender hand on each side of his head and kissed all over his face.

They were newlyweds then. Love gestures came easily. Some, like that moment, were indelible—for which Asher was unspeakably grateful. They were all he had left.

Pulling on the heavy gloves, he reached for the nearest logs. Of course, they were all birch or poplar. He wrestled several out of the mess to set aside. Now he could reach the harder woods. Three logs at a time he toted through the large doors and up beside the kiln, adding them to the existing stack.

Bondurant gave him no notice. Asher made trips out and back until the pile was knee-high. On one circuit he saw Bondurant use his shovel's blade to lift the handle on the furnace's fuel door, swinging it open. Asher watched with disbelief as the man, bare-handed, fed wood to the fire. How was he not covered in burns?

Back outside, Asher shed his vest, continuing to bring logs until the stack inside was chest-high. Therefore, he was ahead. Asher used that time to pull more of the light woods from the pile, collecting them by the wall. His desire for organization was taking over, he recognized it, the assurance that came from reducing chaos. As a cobbler he'd finish every day by wiping down his workbench, arranging cuts of leather in the order he would need them in the morning, storing his tools each in its proper spot. Even as a saboteur, this had been his way. Securing the dynamite in a knot of bailing rope before tucking it under the bridge. Leaving impeccable directions to safe meeting places. Shooting a man but saving the extra bullet.

His reverie broke as one side of the pile collapsed, logs tumbling. Asher hopped back, saving his feet from a mashing, but after that the dividing became easier. He grabbed more wood to carry inside.

The supply was down to one log. Bondurant gave him a frown made of lightning bolts, and brandished the shovel in his direction. Asher hurried to replenish the pile, and when there were ten extra logs, he went back to sorting outside.

Each time he made a delivery, Bondurant answered with more of a scowl. There was plenty of wood, though. What was the problem? Outside, the air was clear and cool, which made sorting more pleasant. Every armload he carried inside meant entering a stifling heat, avoiding the dangerous kiln, and experiencing Bondurant's discontent, until he began to connect the furnace's heat with the man's rage. As Asher set the next load of logs down, he felt a hard poke in his side—the shovel's handle.

Asher grabbed the handle and they had a brief tug-of-war. Bondurant yanked back, prevailing, and raised the shovel's blade as if to strike him.

Asher pointed at the stack ready for burning. "You have plenty."

"I don't like men who rest while I work." Bondurant shone with perspiration, the yoke of his shirt darkened by sweat.

"I'm not resting," Asher said, sweating himself. "I'm organizing."

"I don't like it." He jabbed the shovel in the air. "And I don't like you."

Asher strode away, but his blood was up. Who dared to threaten him? He knew what powers he possessed, if need be. He knew his brutality. He paused at the doors to watch Bondurant shoveling, his back turned and head exposed. Etienne and the other gaffer were working around the corner. There were others, he'd noticed them in back. No one would see if he lifted a log and clubbed the man. And if Asher shoved the body in the fuel door, in half a minute there would be no evidence.

Nineteen deaths or twenty, what was the difference? Either way meant eternity in the same hell. Asher grabbed a log, weighing it, relishing its aptness for the task.

Etienne happened to step around the kiln at that moment, eyes darting from Bondurant to Asher. Dropping his metal pole with a clang, he trotted over carrying a bucket, approached Bondurant, dunked a ladle in the bucket, and held it out.

Bondurant's shoulders dropped, as if the fight had gone out of him. Leaning his shovel against a workbench, he raised the ladle and tipped it. Water poured into his mouth as he gulped, with plenty spilling down his neck and chest. He offered the ladle back, but Etienne shook his head. The man took another dip, savoring that one slowly.

Asher slinked back outside, overheated and ashamed. This was what the years had done to him. The war was still in his blood. He would have ruined his whole opportunity at the château, over nothing. He was not a cobbler, but a killer.

He accelerated his work, with less time sorting. During one delivery, a man came from the gloomy back area—the mole-eyed fellow he'd seen outside. He scurried past, grabbing a log from the pile himself, gesturing for Asher to do the same. When they both had armloads, he tilted his head to direct Asher back inside, dancing a caprice as he skittered ahead. But he veered left, pretending to stumble away from the kiln, heading toward the dimly lit back area.

"Aren't you a playful one?" Asher said.

The short man continued to smile, as he led the way up a few steps to another kiln, a smaller one. Inside, there was not a cauldron but a series of racks. The fire within was low, only starting. The man set his log down, then held both hands toward the spot in a formal way, a footman showing a duchess where she was invited to sit.

Asher placed his wood on top. "What's this fire for?"

The man shook his head vehemently, pointing at his throat.

"Don't get angry with me," Asher said. "I don't understand you."

"Henri doesn't speak," called yet another man, a bearded fellow who sat farther back by a small window. He was holding a hand tool over a sheet of green glass.

"Why doesn't he speak?"

"You could ask him, but you won't get an answer." The man smiled. "Life is a mystery, new fellow. Be a good Christian and tote us a stack of starter wood, all right?"

Good Christian? Asher only backed away and down the steps.

Bondurant had been watching. "Don't cross that one." He leaned on his shovel. "He's the boss-man here."

"Which one?"

"Marc. Keeps this place ticking. Supplies, money, the works." Bondurant gave a conspiratorial wink. "If you or I trip up? Replaced in a heartbeat. If Marc stumbles, everything falls."

Asher bustled back outside, ashamed that he had felt a murderous impulse toward this person. He began lifting four logs at a time: two for the main kiln, two for the little one. Greater effort required greater concentration, and his mind released.

It is possible for a human to become all animal, if the exertion is demanding enough. As the sun traveled its path in the sky, the entirety of Asher's thoughts came to settle on desire. Not for sex or wealth or material things, though—those lusts of comfortable men—but for food and drink and rest. Yet his craving was every bit as keen.

He had no opportunity to observe Etienne, aside from that first globe. Nor the angry one, nor the others in the atelier. The fires must be fed continuously, he realized.

Bondurant sneered at each delivery, though Asher could not imagine why. The angry gaffer stomped his feet and banged his pole on the floor. Yet Marc appeared to be unperturbed. He supervised without leaving his work: craning his neck to confirm, nodding approval, or tilting his head side to side in an unimpressed way, *comme ci, comme ça*. Once he spun his forefinger in a circle, like a mouse on a wheel: Hurry up. Though there were plenty of logs on hand, Asher promptly did.

By late in the day, he completed the division of wood: orderly piles on opposite walls, softwoods apart from hard, with clear working space between them. To the west, the undersides of clouds glowed gold. To the east, the first star glimmered. At one time such sights would have given him comfort. Now? Night was coming and he did not know where he would sleep.

Asher's shoulders ached, his back. The gloves' rough interior had blistered his hands anyway. He ruminated on that ladle of water. Was he permitted to drink? Between Bondurant's madness and Henri's silence, he had not dared to ask. Instead, again he bent for another load, and hobbled inside.

Everyone had gone. All of the men, all at once. Both furnaces' doors were shut tight. The shovel was stabbed blade-first into a bin of sand.

Asher crept over to see where Marc the boss had worked. The table was covered with pieces of glass, carved in odd shapes, with a green hue as pale as April leaves.

Everything Etienne had said in the courtyard had proved to be true. This place was no sanctuary. It was a forge. They did not make peace, they made glass.

Etienne was also right about inexperience. Expertise in glass would take a lifetime to develop. The boot maker in Asher respected this reality; he'd spent decades honing his skills. Becoming an assassin, that too required years. Learning to carry immense losses, plus the weight of his crimes, would likely take the rest of his life.

Le Château Guerin could not repair such a creature. It was too busy and strange, and what they made was too fragile. Despite all his time of wandering, Asher had to accept the truth: He'd come to the wrong place. And now he was hungry again.

He ambled outside to collect his vest and coat. The woodpiles were tidy, at least he'd accomplished that. But his throat was tight. What if his punishment for the nineteen did not come in the afterlife, but in the present day? Asher had found the place of sanctuary, only to confirm his unworthiness. He started to pull on his vest.

"There you are."

It was Brigitte, attired now in an apron, a fresh blouse properly buttoned. She wore an apple of a smile. "I was wondering what had become of you." She jingled a few francs. "Etienne gave you a fine report."

"He did?" Asher, still half in his reverie, held out his good hand. "Thank you."

The woman dropped the coins into his palm. "Was this your idea?" She pointed at the stacks of wood. "Did you separate them?"

He tucked the money in a vest pocket, fingers counting without looking: three francs. "Softwoods here, hardwoods there. I hope that's all right."

"All right?" She laughed, a bright, two-note chuckle. "What is your name, ragamuffin man who works so hard in my atelier?"

"I am Asher."

She lowered her chin an inch. "Asher, who told you to do this?"

"Did I do something wrong?"

"Wrong?" She laughed again, easy as a breeze. "We have no beds to spare." She waddled back toward the house. "But you are welcome to stay for dinner."

CHAPTER 7

When Asher entered the main house, the scent of cooking made his stomach clench. In the past two days he'd eaten chicken scraps, a tomato, and a stolen lunch—a feast compared with his starving times. And now he was to eat again? He followed Brigitte, who bustled down the hall, pointing him straight ahead as she ducked aside into the kitchen. He paused outside the door, hesitant, hearing conversation within.

Yes he smelled flavors in that moment, but also something greater. He was inhaling the past, his country, what a meal had meant before the war: hours to prepare, hours to eat. Many mornings Aube had something simmering—a broth, a reduction—for dinner ten hours later. Those days he'd come home from his workshop and the whole house would smell glorious. What had become of time?

"Come, my new expert," Etienne called from the dining room. "Snails eat last."

Asher walked into the room. Men sat the length of the table on both sides, Etienne with his aristocratic air, dressed all in black and his hair pulled back. The angry man who worked beside him, glowering. Silent Henri, who followed the conversation with keen eyes. Across from them Bondurant fumed like a kettle about to boil. Marc presided from the head of the table, while the empty seat at the foot could only be for the lady of the house. Aside from Marc, who was washed and decently dressed, the men looked like misfits, stringy hair and skeptical eyes. Desperate cases all. Asher would fit right in.

A basket of bread progressed down one side of the table and no one was grabbing, no one gobbling it down. The men took one piece at a time, setting it on their plate without a nibble, passing the basket along. Asher blinked in disbelief.

Henri raised a finger, then pointed. The chair beside him was empty.

Asher moved to the seat slowly. The moment he sat, though, the bread basket arrived—still holding plenty. Reaching, he saw how filthy his hand was, and took a piece without touching any others. As he passed the bread along, Brigitte arrived in oven gloves, toting a cauldron of wrought iron.

"Gentlemen," Marc called, and to a one they stood. Asher hurried to follow suit.

"Eat now, please, or my work will be wasted," she replied. "Stew's best when it's steaming."

As they sat she removed the pot's lid, and a cloud did indeed rise. She circled the table. One by one the men filled their bowls. Asher saw turnips, carrots, and meat, chunks of it, in dark sauce. Again, the men were restrained in their portions. They were gruff in the atelier, but at table they behaved as politely as dukes. There was only one possible explanation: they were not starving.

"Come, now, Asher," Brigitte said, lowering the pot. "You earned your share."

After glancing at Henri's portion for a guide, he ladled into his bowl a complete impossibility: lamb. He recognized the smell, with a hint of mint leaves, and vegetables in the rich stock. He took his share, or perhaps less out of caution against overstepping, and she proceeded around the table. Raising his spoon, Asher noticed that the others had not yet begun eating, nor did they when Brigitte took her seat.

Instead that was a cue for Marc, who folded his hands together and bowed his head. "Heavenly Father, make us instruments of your peace.

Where there is hatred, let us sow love. Where there is injury, forgiveness. Where there is doubt, faith. Where there is despair, hope. And above all, in this humble atelier of glass, where there is darkness, let us bring light. May our work serve in some small way to illuminate your unwavering love for a recovering world."

"Amen," the men said as one.

"Amen," Asher whispered.

They were making the sign of the cross again, which he imitated—but starting with his left hand before switching. No one noticed, or so he hoped.

At last Marc picked up his spoon, and the table exploded with activity: plates clanking, men sopping the broth with bread, four conversations at once. Asher chomped on the piece of baguette, and it was sublime: the hard crust requiring teeth, the interior soft like a secret. He closed his eyes, savoring. An actual meal, with noisy people. It was almost too much.

He opened his eyes to take up the spoon. Henri on his left remained as silent as a stone. Brigitte consulted with Etienne about why Marie delivered extra lettuce that day.

"Perhaps to lighten her cart, for the climb to the village," Etienne answered. "Though lettuce weighs almost nothing."

So her name was Marie. Asher tucked it away like a fourth franc.

With the first spoonful of stew in his mouth, he nearly wept. Food, since the victory, had been a means of appeasing a stomach angry at its emptiness, nothing more. This lamb was soft in the succulent way that can only happen if it has stewed at a low temperature for many hours, perhaps all day. The onions dissolved in his mouth, slippery and sweet. The carrots were still firm, and the turnips hot enough he had to breathe with his mouth open to cool them.

"What do you think?" Marc was looking down the table. "You, I mean." He gestured his piece of bread at Asher.

He gulped down what was in his mouth. "Think, sir?"

All conversation had stopped.

"About this meal," Marc continued. "About what is in your bowl and in your body. Have you an opinion?"

"It's delicious, sir." He looked around the table; everyone was watching him. "It's the most delicious thing I've tasted in years."

"That's not an opinion. That is the gratification of the senses. What does your mind tell you about this meal?"

"That he's a lucky pigeon?" Etienne asked, and the men laughed.

"That I am eating for the fourth time in four days. I feel like a sultan."

"Again with sensations." Marc shook his head. "I want your mind. And if not that"—he blew on his spoonful of stew—"then your soul."

Asher felt seized by a fear that this place was too prayerful, too well-fed for a starving man. "I think . . ."

"I doubt that," Bondurant growled, and while some of the men chuckled, Marc gave him a look like a rap on the knuckles.

"Patience, gents," Brigitte said. "There's a new soul at the table."

Their attention returned to Asher. "Well," he said, "I believe . . ."

"That's better," Marc responded. "Tell us about your belief."

And now speechless Henri, at his side, his small eyes bright, elbowed him. Taking it as encouragement, Asher sat up straight.

"I remember when food tasted this good at every dinner, on every day."

"I'm not bored quite yet," said the man who worked with Etienne. "But almost."

Annoyed, Asher took his first real look at him. The man was as bald as a boulder, with a large hooked nose. His chin jutted, and he'd added a goatee, brushed from beneath to aim it forward. In all, the appearance of a living gargoyle.

"A meal this delicious," Asher continued, "requires a hundred favorable opportunities. Weather, soil, delivery, refrigeration, an intact kitchen, many things."

Hearing no wisecracks, he pressed on. "I have walked this beautiful, broken country from the weeks immediately after victory till I arrived here this morning. Everything I have seen is about the war: the cost, the damage, the need for repair. I have not witnessed five favorable opportunities, much less hundreds. I believe . . ."

They were all listening now. Asher began to address the whole table. "If a meal this good can exist here, as a start, a cornerstone, even if it's just in this one place, then, for the first time since the war, I believe that our country may actually have a future."

"Well said," Marc cried, rapping the table with his knuckles. "Faith is nourishment. And vice versa."

"Boo-hoo-hoo," mocked Bondurant. "Bring on the violins and weeping virgins."

"Be civil, please," Brigitte said. "He's new."

"He's also correct," Marc said.

"He speaks in platitudes." Bondurant frowned as if he'd tasted something sour. "All broth and no meat. Heartfelt maybe, but as shallow as a puddle."

"In point of fact," Marc declared, "the farms that produced this meal, ours and Marie's, are the reason France will recover before more industrial nations do. While Britain rebuilds its mills, and Germany piles its rubble to one side to erect new factories for what we hope are peaceable purposes, all that time our farms will be feeding us, enriching us, while we regain our culture, converse with one another, and remember who we are in the sight of God."

"I can't speak for you empty eggs," Bondurant said, "but I know exactly who I am. Also you left out the Soviets, whose only God is their desire to rule all of Europe."

"What about the Yanks?" Etienne asked Marc. "What's their fate?"

"Not one bomb fell on their soil," he answered. "Their farms and factories remain intact. For the foreseeable future, America will rule the world."

"Precisely what I mean about empty declarations," Bondurant said. "You laud a nation that very conveniently kept the war an entire ocean away."

"I am grateful for what the Americans did," Asher replied, bringing everyone to look in his direction again. "I lived in Bonheur, where they came ashore, and died by the thousands for our liberation. With my own eyes I saw great valor, and courage, and beaches stained with their blood. In your heart, I believe you are grateful too."

"Do not dare to presume about my heart, about which you know nothing."

"Easy, now," Etienne said.

"Does that mean you are ungrateful?" Asher asked.

"I said do not *dare*." Jerking up from his seat, Bondurant snatched his knife and slashed it in Asher's direction. "Tonight, I vow, you pedantic twit, I will slit your throat while you sleep."

The table erupted immediately.

"You pulled a knife over that?" Etienne asked.

"Imbecile," snapped the man who worked with him. "Complete imbecile."

Henri pounded the table, rattling silverware and making the candle flames flail.

Asher had already armed himself. Clasping his own knife by his thigh, he assessed the odds. If Bondurant attacked, the width of the table would require him to stretch forward, so the easiest target would be his chest.

"As if this fool knows anything about my heart," he bellowed, knife high.

Marc shouted over the din, "Pull yourselves together. Everyone."

They quieted slightly, while Brigitte pointed at Bondurant's knife. "Put it down," she commanded.

Bondurant snarled, swinging the knife in the air.

"Planning to stab all of us?" the man without a name scoffed. "What a fool."

Henri banged the table twice more.

"Listen to me." Brigitte raised her voice. "All of you." And the men murmured into silence. Folding her napkin, she placed it on the table. "Listen."

Bondurant's hand stilled.

"No more knives," Brigitte crooned. "No weapons of any kind. Those times are over. The enemy is gone. We can all put down what is no longer necessary."

She rose, eased down the table to Bondurant's side, and held out her hand. Brigitte showed no fear, approaching empty-handed, but Asher could see her immense maternal strength. Bondurant quaked for a moment, as if to weep, though he shed no tears. Shoulders lowering, he placed the knife in her hands.

"All of us, please," she said. "Put it down."

Asher observed the others: Etienne moved his hands into his lap, away from his knife. The man whose name he did not know was lowering the ladle back into the stewpot. Asher had not even seen him grab it.

"Thank you, gentlemen. Well done." Brigitte took her seat again, but paused to address Asher. "Where's your knife?"

"I don't have one," he answered, feeling it snug under his leg.

"You're new, so you don't understand," Brigitte said. Her tone was warm, but as firm as a boulder. "The enemy is gone. Weapons are no longer needed."

Asher lowered his head. Once again everyone was looking at him.

"Come, now." She curled her hand in, as if calling a dog. "Give it up."

He felt doubly foolish, for hiding the knife and for the obvious lie. If this place was a genuine sanctuary, he had just blown his chance. But there was no alternative. He had been threatened by an armed man.

She sat, tucking the napkin back in her lap. "Do you think I set the table," Brigitte said lightly, "and do not know who I gave a knife?"

Asher slid the knife out, set it down, and flattened both hands on the table.

"Well." Marc stroked his beard. "Mr. Bondurant, you're finished here."

His hands fell to his sides. "You can't mean it."

"We know what you have endured." Brigitte's throat tightened. "All of us hoped you were capable of recovering."

"We prayed for it," said the man who worked beside Etienne.

"We prayed," Marc said. "All of us."

Nodding, Henri pressed his hands palm to palm.

"It was rhetorical," Bondurant said. "I didn't mean an actual threat."

Marc shook his head. "The last incident was only three days ago. I warned you then that you were down to your last chance."

Asher followed their exchange, not saying a word, not missing a thing.

"Can't we discuss it, though?"

"You raised a knife at a new arrival." Marc shrugged. "What is there to discuss?"

"This is much too abrupt. Who will stand with me?" Bondurant opened his arms. "Who will plead my case?"

Trying not to move his head, Asher watched the others' reactions. No one spoke. It occurred to him, given his murderous impulse earlier at the furnace, and his readiness to kill in self-defense half a minute ago, that he and Bondurant might not be that different. And this moment might be instructive.

"No one?" Bondurant stood, eyes flashing. "You have blown glass, cut glass, colored glass, all your pretty little tasks, thanks to my sweat and strain. Every log in the fire, every shovel of sand, without it you would have made nothing. Nothing. And this is the gratitude you show?"

"I am grateful," Etienne said, eyes on the stoneware goblet he rotated with his long fingers. To Asher, it resembled how he'd rotated the metal pole that afternoon. "Your labors have indeed kept our crucibles busy. Thank you."

"Etienne, it is I who owe you thanks, for the wonders of art that you made from my dull work. You believe I should stay, right? Should have another chance?"

"I don't understand why you threatened to kill him." Etienne pointed his chin at Asher. "In rage or jest, it doesn't matter. There is no room here for murderous declarations. This atelier is a place where war has ended."

"So, you are a coward, like the rest?"

Etienne stopped turning the goblet. "Clearly the river of my gratitude runs deeper than yours. But I also know better than to wade in over my head."

Bondurant snorted. "What does that mean, you prickly thistle?"

"It means do not test your friends' tempers," said the man who worked beside Etienne. "Particularly when the misconduct is not theirs, but your own."

"Take your plate to the kitchen," Marc said. Though his voice was calm, a vein had risen in the center of his forehead. "Do not break it, or make any display of anger, because that will accomplish nothing. Accept that this is what you deserve, for behavior that we have repeatedly tried to help you overcome."

"And," Brigitte added, "we have repeatedly failed."

Bondurant's hands fell to his sides. "I am more ashamed than angry."

"That is your conscience speaking." Her tone was soft, as if to soothe a teething child. "If you listen, it will be your unfailing guide."

"All right. I'll go." He picked up his plate. "The passion that made me grab the knife comes from a great river of bitterness. Some of you know what flows there, and why the waters are so high. But if I cannot tame my rage here, where on earth could I?"

"That is no longer our concern." Marc cleared his throat. "We've done our best. Now gather your belongings and depart."

"Tonight?"

"Now." Marc took up his spoon and began eating again.

Bondurant addressed the table's other end. "Brigitte? Lady? Have mercy?"

"In the days ahead, we will think hard how we might have done better. *Bonne chance*."

"So be it, then." Bondurant collected his utensils. "So be it." Head hanging, he started for the kitchen. But in the doorway he spun on his heel. "Damn you," he spat. "Every one of you. Self-righteous hypocrites, smug with your worthless windows, this isn't the last you'll see of me. Damn you all to the fires of hell."

He flung the plate down, shattering it on the stone floor. With a cry, he fled.

They were silent, until Brigitte waved a hand in the air in annoyance at Marc. "A perfectly good plate, and you had to suggest the idea of breaking it."

"Which is why I shall be the one to sweep it up," he replied.

Everyone laughed, and commenced to eating again. As he savored his stew, Asher had much to ponder: Misbehavior would lead to ejection. Rage had no lodging here. This château might be a sanctuary after all.

"We appear to have an empty billet." Marc addressed his bowl. "And need of another pair of hands."

"Consider the idea, at least." Brigitte took up her spoon. "We can discuss it in the morning."

Asher looked up and down the table. Had they already forgotten his lie? "Are you speaking to me?"

Another round of laughter. Etienne leaned over his plate. "It appears, boot maker, that you have found a place to sleep tonight."

CHAPTER 8

The man whose name Asher did not know held the lamp ahead, lighting his own way. Asher had to navigate in shadows. The man who sat beside Etienne, who worked with him at the kiln, had no regard for Asher's unfamiliarity with the darkened hall. At the back of the house, they reached a set of stairs that curved tightly upward, and climbed without conversation. On the wall, the lamplight cast moving shadows, while Asher held the railing for balance. The man's boot-heels, he observed, were worn nearly flat. Two stories up they reached a narrow hall with doors on either side.

"It's how I've always imagined a dormitory," Asher said.

"Nothing so posh," the man replied. "Picture a monk in each cell, hundreds of years ago, roasting in summer, shivering in winter, and thanking God for all of it."

"To each his own definition of comfort. I am Asher, by the way."

"I heard," he said without reciprocating. Down the left-hand side, the man paused by an open door. "Here."

Asher hesitated. In all his time of wandering, he had only a handful of nights under a roof, and then always in a barn or church, with high ceilings and a feeling of openness. This room's ceiling was low, and sloped steeply like the roof.

"There." Brigitte emerged from the far corner. "Better." She bundled her rags into a ball, dropped them on a crumpled blanket on the floor. "Always does the soul good to wipe dust away. Bondurant, the poor man, is not ready to stop suffering."

Asher did not enter, for fear of breaking the spell. A clean room. His room.

The nameless man brushed past, throwing the window open as if it were his own room. He stuck his head out and took a good sniff. "He'll be fine. It's summer."

"Do you remember your first night?" Brigitte unfolded the fresh blanket she'd been carrying under one arm.

He spoke out the window. "Sick in my belly and worse in my lungs. Etienne all but carried me to my room."

With a snap of her wrists, the blanket opened like a parachute over the bed, floating down to the mattress. "And?"

"It wasn't tuberculosis after all. Only famine. A dozen of your meals, and I was able to work." He stood before Asher in the doorway, sizing him up. "You've arrived in better condition than most." He strode off, the hollow sound of his bootheels receding down the stairs.

"I have?" He could not imagine being hungrier, or more uncertain.

"Sleep well." Brigitte tucked the blanket in at the foot of the bed. "I'll send someone to wake you. If I may boast, breakfast includes excellent cheese."

Ducking his head, he entered the room. "This is all a bit incredible."

"Dream of making great glass." She gathered the laundry from the floor.

"I may dream of cheese instead. But why won't that fellow tell me his name?"

Brigitte paused in the doorway, the bundle in her arms. "He's not yet healed enough to be himself." She smiled, bright as a bobbin. "Anyway, the question is not how sick you are when you arrive here. It's how well you become."

As soon as he was alone, he went to the window. Moonlight spilled on the fields and valley, a million contrasts in blue. Sheep bleated in the meadow, ewes calling their kids, while overhead bats darted and swooped.

Then a cow lowed, long and loud, somewhere down the hill in the dark. When it moaned again, another cow mooed from the middle of the fields. But the sounds confused Asher: Was the second one a reply, or only an echo off of the château's stone façade—which ran three stories from his window to the grass below?

Now both cows were singing, with the echoes goading them on. Four bassoons, though he could not tell which were real and which were reverberation. The combined sound seemed to rise into the moonlit clouds. It was as if they were cows too, calling to their kindred below, hearing the response and repeating it, heaven and earth in bovine chorus, musical and strange, and Asher had to brace his arms against the window frame to bear it.

The song passed quickly, as beauty mercifully does, but left him marveling at the expanse of his day. Waking by the river, his stomach appeased by the brothers' chicken, would have been enough. Noticing the grapevines would have been enough. Seeing the lovely woman pass in her cart would have been enough. The tomato falling for him to eat and mourn would have been enough. A few francs in his pocket would have been enough. A bed, cheese for breakfast, peace in the valley? Enough enough enough.

It had happened so suddenly, after the long ache of seeking, he worried that the situation might be like poplar wood, quick to catch but fast to burn. How long could it last? Until he lost his temper like Bondurant. Or revealed that he did not share their religion. Or burned himself terribly. Pitfalls lurked in every direction.

Asher sat on the bed and wrestled off one boot, massaging his foot before stretching out, planning to remove the other boot in a moment, but drawing the blanket up. Scratchy wool. He should pray now, and give thanks. And cry too, because his life might be starting a new chapter—without his wife and daughter.

Weeping and prayer, what was the difference? Three deep breaths, and he slept.

FOR ONCE, THE NIGHTMARE DID not wake him. The man on fire remained distant, small, impeded by a tangle of grapevines. In the morning it was true about the cheese—thick, creamy chevre. Brigitte had stirred in basil and honey, and he slathered it on a hunk of baguette. A bowl of pears sat on the table, ripe as newlyweds, but he couldn't get to them for filling himself with cheese.

"Eat all you can," Etienne said, rising from his seat, tying a string to hold his hair back. "It's a long day ahead."

"I've had enough," Asher declared, which was untrue, but he stood as well. Better not to claim his share before he knew it was secure.

Henri remained at the table's far end, spooning something onto a split pear. The nameless man arrived with nose high, a prince arriving at his stables. "*Ancipiti plus ferit ense gula.*"

"Translation, please," Etienne said.

With his fingertips, he selected one pear. "Gluttony kills more than the sword."

"So does hunger," Etienne replied, pocketing a pear in his black pants for later.

Asher started as he'd been told, with poplar. The day before had left his arms sore, his palms testy where the rough gloves had abraded them. When he brought his first piece of oak, the nameless man snarled in Etienne's ear. He ambled over to Asher.

"Not yet," he said. "We're gaining on it, but a bit longer before hardwoods."

Asher nodded, bent at the waist, sweat dripping from his chin. "Fine."

Etienne started back toward his spot. "Remember," he said, waving at the bucket and ladle. "Water equals stamina."

"I didn't know whether I was allowed."

"Of course you are. Drink all you can."

The nameless man had come up beside him. "Also anticipate," he instructed. "Predict what the kiln requires. The thermometer must remain above that red line"—with his pole he tapped a circular dial on the kiln—"fifteen hundred degrees Celsius, or the batch will fail. Stay ahead on wood, so you'll have time to shovel."

Straightening, Asher wiped his eyes on a sleeve. "I appreciate the advice."

"It's not advice. It's what's necessary if you wish to stay here. Don't screw up."

"Listen," Asher began, "you can't—"

Clapping hands interrupted. Marc had appeared by the wood entry door, and now he held up both fists. "To work, people. To work. Let's begin the day."

Asher wanted to inform him that he had been laboring for an hour already, thank you. But he knew better. Sincere or not, silence implied respect.

With Henri at his heels, Marc carried large curling sheets of paper into the back, where he flattened them on a worktable, a slug of gray metal on each corner. The two men leaned over, scrutinizing the papers, their heads nearly touching.

Etienne stirred the cauldron, studying the flames below. The nameless man departed, as stiff as a stilt. Asher glowered at his back, before returning to toting logs.

When he made a midmorning delivery to the second furnace, Marc and Henri looked up from their papers. "Not needed yet, thanks. Not till afternoon."

"Good news," Asher said, pausing to rest while he examined the back area, where they worked: tools on tables instead of in racks, shelves of glass in a motley of colors, buckets and loose papers, and stacks of metal ingots. It would take longer to find a tool than to use it. The cobbler in him wanted to organize the whole area.

Worse, the room was dim: lanterns hung willy-nilly, tallow candles encircled where the men worked. Being up a few steps meant the ceiling was too low to stand upright. The primary window was half-blocked by a pipe for the furnace's exhaust.

"If it's not a bother, may I ask why you cook the glass twice?"

Marc held up two fingers. "First: It's not a bother. If you want to be of value here, this atelier offers neither classes nor books. So ask. The only way to advance is to learn."

Henri stood at his elbow, his nodding as exaggerated as a puppet's.

"Second: It's called annealing, to purify the glass into finished form."

Asher's expression must have shown incomprehension, because Marc put his pencil down. "Our windows must last centuries. The slower and more uniformly glass cools, the more strongly its crystals will remain fixed. We fire the annealer after noon, and allow it to cool all night."

Asher nodded, pretending to understand, then trotted down the steps to fetch more wood. Making glass was complex, and his rank was one step above mule.

"Asher," Marc called, which halted him. "Once you get far enough ahead on the wood, Henri and I can show you a bit of what we're doing." He tapped the papers with a pencil. "Designs, for example."

"Thank you." Asher tried to absorb what that offer implied— allowing for curiosity, making room in a day to learn something. After a long dark tunnel of grief, here was a glimmer. He reached the wood stacks, and bent to lift the next load.

Within the hour, the thermometer reached the red line. Under Etienne's direction, he began shoveling material from the bins: dumplings of potash, the fine powder of ground limestone, and above all sand—not the blond of the beaches at Bonheur, but a coarse, dull brown. From time to time the nameless man would shout something Asher could not hear clearly. Etienne would come over, and direct him to add more of one or the other ingredient.

Henri arrived from the back, and with hand motions indicated that it was time to begin feeding the annealer. For the first hour Asher stayed ahead, but gradually his lead shortened. If he concentrated on the wood, the crucible needed feeding. The nameless man would stand with the scowl of a disappointed duke. If Asher put shoveling first, the furnace temperature fell, twice coming perilously close to the red mark. Meanwhile the atelier warmed, till he was working bare-chested and his body gleamed. Again, he became an animal, brute exertion with limited powers of reason.

Etienne appeared with the water bucket. Asher dipped the ladle and drank. No wonder Bondurant had been grouchy. This job was a circle of hell.

He heard the sound of cracking wood, and Brigitte was waddling out the large shed doors, having deposited two logs by the furnace. While he recovered, she brought a load for the annealing furnace, taking a moment to pump its bellows as well. The next trip she'd unbuttoned her smock, her bosom as exposed as it had been the day before.

Now he knew why she was not embarrassed. They had seen her displayed countless times. To Asher her open bodice seemed scandalous, but she did not disdain their attention. The men would take a full gander, then focus again on the cauldron. The dragon must be fed.

Leaving the water bucket to retrieve more wood, Asher tried to remember the last time he had noticed a woman's figure. When Aube died, he lost all appetites. But the next day his stomach began to growl. After two nights, fitfully, he slept. The want for a female, however? Not yet. The soldier's bullet had killed desire simultaneously with his wife and daughter. Nor did Brigitte's open smock cause it to revive.

The afternoon passed in a long blur of exertion. His arms grew weak, his legs wobbly. Gradually, in the later hours, the burden eased. When the crucible was fully fed, Etienne told him to set aside his shovel for the day. Once the annealer reached proper temperature, Brigitte left for the kitchen, fanning herself with both hands. Asher maintained his trips to the main furnace, and to the annealer, like a machine, until with loaded arms he found the nameless man blocking the doorway.

"Surprise," he sneered. "You made it through a day."

Too tired to feel relieved, Asher dropped the wood where he stood. "Why won't you tell me your name?"

"Because you won't last here long enough to bother."

Asher had no reply. As he relaxed his hands, the rough gloves fell to the dirt.

He shuffled out to the side yard. The gardens were weedless, impeccable. Herbs flourished by the kitchen door, fragrant and pale. Brigitte was singing to herself, which recalled his wife's humming in the garden. He had not thought to ask if she'd had any particular song in mind. Now he would never know.

In that moment, fatigue and defeat felt like cousins, relatives who knew one another well. At a bench beside the cobbled path, Asher sat with a sigh. Bent forward, for a mindless while he was content to watch sweat drip from his face onto the stones.

"Excuse me, are you weeping?"

A woman's voice. He lifted his head and she was leaning toward him, her brow creased with concern. She wore a dress the color of daisies, yellow and white.

"Marie," he declared. "Just perspiring, thank you."

"I'm relieved," she replied, straightening. "Have we met?"

"I'm Asher." He stood, hand out, but his head went blank and he nearly toppled.

"Steady, now." She clasped his arm until the blood reached his brain. "Hold on here a moment." Marie ducked behind her cart, reappearing with metal canteen in a green canvas sling. "Water."

"Thank you," he said, unscrewing the top, taking a generous gulp.

"Drink all you like," she said, "as long as you're not a Nazi or a Communist."

Asher lowered the canteen. He remembered cell meetings, his friend Levi ranting about the promise of communism, while others called out in agreement. Asher did not want to create a new nation, though, only to defeat the enemy. It felt so long ago, Marie might as well have asked about his childhood. "No. I'm not partisan now."

"But you were at one time?"

Asher blinked at her. The woman had a kind of acuity, a keenness. "I was on the side of France."

"Exactly." Marie clapped once. "That's why I'm boiling about the upcoming elections. The Communists keep shouting about three hundred and forty thousand tons of grain that Russia claims are on their way here. But they won't even whisper about the seven *million* tons the Americans have already delivered."

"Since the war ended, I've paid almost no attention to the news."

"How comfortable that must be for you," she said with a bit of bite.

"Marie," Asher said, not hiding his exhaustion, "I don't want to argue."

"What if I do want to?" Marie asked. "What if I think the recovery of France is everyone's responsibility? What if I think that victory is not the same thing as peace?"

"That's exactly what my childhood friend Eli said, right after the war ended."

"Well, childhood friend Eli was right."

"So are you," Asher conceded. "But I need to find peace for myself first. Otherwise, I'll be inflicting my hard times on everyone else."

He expected another sharp comeback, but instead her expression became wistful. Marie withdrew, contemplating, then brightened and made a shoveling gesture with her hands. "Drink, drink."

Needing no further instruction, Asher tilted the canteen and guzzled.

"De Gaulle gave a brilliant speech last week," she continued, "in Bayeux."

He paused for breath. "That's not far from my hometown."

"In the pouring rain, in fact, though he wore no hat." She moved back behind her wagon. "He predicted the Communists would lose."

Another long drink, and the canteen was empty. Marie was certainly comfortable with discussing politics. Eighteen months earlier, that would have been perilous. He screwed the top back in place. "How did you come to possess military gear?"

"Armies leave all sorts of things behind," she called over the donkey's back, then brought him two apricots, small and pink. "I can't give you all I have. Two are reserved for the doctor, up in the village."

"Fruit," Asher marveled. "Are you an angel of some kind?"

Marie laughed, eyes glinting like sunlight off the ocean. "Just a gardener."

"So was Eve, and look what mischief she made." Asher bit into one of the apricots. It was wet and tart, awakening some gland at the back of his jaw. "Sweet."

She stepped back to pat the donkey's neck, moving into the late sun's glare, which shadowed her face while giving her head a halo. "We had a late frost during blossom time this year, so the bees only pollenated some of the buds. But the yield is tasty, don't you think?"

Asher squinted into the light. "So sweet."

AFTER SHE'D GONE, HE FOLLOWED the path around the château to the front courtyard. "*So was Eve,*" he mocked himself. "What an idiotic thing to say."

Rounding the wall, Asher took in the view again: the valley, the distant fields. He heard sheep bleating, one cow's nasal complaint. A bee veered close to him before buzzing away on his business. Evening summer sun spilled through the trees.

Inside the courtyard he sat in that dappled light—back against the house, legs out straight. Although he wanted only a moment's rest, that was where Etienne found him later, when supper was ready, shaking his shoulder till Asher jumped, eyes wide.

"Good." Etienne chuckled. "You're still breathing."

"I'm fine," Asher replied, fists clenched, peering left and right to locate himself.

Etienne hoisted him to his feet. "You don't weigh much more than your clothes."

"I'll be awake momentarily," Asher replied, but Etienne led him into the house. They passed everyone gathering for dinner, up the winding stairs, Etienne's arm supporting Asher as though he were drunk.

"Really," Asher protested. "Give me a quarter of a minute."

"Shush." Steering Asher down the hall, Etienne deposited him on the bed. "Whew. You're as ripe as old fish," he said, pulling up the blanket. And he was gone.

Late in the night Asher awoke, his throat parched. The château contained a depth of quiet: not a leaf stirring, no farm animals awake. Moonlight poured in the window, casting milky rectangles on the floor—enough for him to see two mugs of water, and beside them a plate of food. Another consecutive night of dinner. The generosity had not worn off, and neither had his amazement.

He set the plate in his lap. Slices of ham, fatty and thick. Buttery mashed potatoes, which a fingerful told him were flavored with tarragon. Celery, crisp and barely dressed in vinegar. He drank, and ate, and drank again. His body seemed to absorb everything before it had reached his belly, so ravenous was his appetite. Had celery always possessed such a strong flavor?

He knew who brought this meal. Who noticed his absence at the table. She was caretaker to them all. With each bite his gratitude deepened.

Another day of that workload would crush him like a walnut. The promise of this château was great, but not if it killed him. He needed a smarter way.

Dinner's last bite was a mix of everything, ham swiping the plate clean. Asher rose to stand at the window, cooled by the night, chewing on what his future might be.

CHAPTER 9

The man on fire stood before an open furnace, rubbing his hands together. He looked Asher straight on, as if to say, Yes, I am with you in this place too. I am with you everywhere. Asher awoke coughing.

In the atelier after breakfast, his gloves remained on the ground, right where he'd dropped them the day before. Bending with a groan, Asher took them like an ox accepting the yoke. Already the gloves had begun molding to the shape of his hands. His sweat had softened them. May that be a metaphor for the day ahead, he thought.

Asher studied the logs, their geometry. There had to be an easier way. The first time he bent, his back and shoulders ached. By the time Etienne had begun the burn, though, and the nameless man had thrown larger chunks atop the kindling, Asher's body was loosening.

Already he had learned that morning was easier, that the real demand came later—when he was feeding two fires, plus shoveling into the crucible. He was aware of Marc and Henri in the back, but there was no time to learn what they were doing. Patience and curiosity are enemies.

Water was his friend, however, and he paused to drink every five trips. Once the furnace was roaring, Etienne approached with the shovel.

"Time to put the kettle on to boil," he said. "And we'll need lots of material. We have two crucibles cooking today."

"Why won't the other fellow tell me his name?"

"A complicated story, in which he is not the hero." Etienne waved his long fingers at the bins of chemicals. "Let's get shoveling, shall we?"

Right away Asher knew there would not be enough. The potash bin was nearly full, but the limestone bin held no more than a quarter, and the sand even less. Still, he did as he was told, alternating bins till he took a water break.

The nameless man stood rubbing his beak. "You are attempting a third day?"

"Sorry not to conform to your prediction."

"The week is young. Twenty more shovels of each bin now."

"That will empty them."

Turning to go, he spoke over his shoulder. "Leave thinking to those with brains."

Asher lowered the ladle into the bucket, hoping that moving slowly would reduce his desire to do something quickly. He was outside loading himself with wood when he felt a tap on his shoulder. He dropped everything and spun with fists raised.

Marc stood square, smiling. He held a piece of green glass. "You startle easily."

Asher's reply was unguarded. "War will do that to a man."

"So I see." He stroked his beard. "We need to chat."

Asher waved a glove at the door. "They're expecting me to keep up."

"They'll be patient when they see you're speaking with me." Marc waved at the bench where Asher had parked to cool down the day before. "Please."

He sat, but from there he could see the main kiln's chimney issuing gray smoke into the day. By then he had learned about the ovens, how they devoured millions of his kind, and he would never look at smoke the same way.

"Everyone who comes here gets this lecture, so bear with me."

Asher pulled his attention away from the chimney. "Lecture?"

Marc remained standing. "The enemy drove us out of here early in the war, to use this château as a command post. We're lucky they did not destroy it on the way out, like some other places. But they did cut the electricity, and ruin the gas lines. The wires I was able to repair, with Henri's help. Gas requires a professional, however, and there are none hereabouts. Thus the need for wood, and I apologize."

"I wouldn't have known any differently, sir." Asher wiped sweat from his nose. "And I'm glad to be earning my meals."

Marc studied him before continuing. "The goal of this place is not what you might assume." He flourished the green pane in his hand. "It's not about glass."

"No?"

He shook his head. "Every person here is wounded. Whatever subtractions the war made from your life, someone else here lost more. Whatever deeds the imperatives of war required you to commit, someone else here did worse."

Marc held the glass up to the sun, making his skin green. "Our goal is healing. Glass is only a means to that end."

"I think I understand."

"This château operates on a contract." He lowered the pane. "Treat each person with respect and compassion—whether they deserve it or not—because each one is at a different place in his healing journey. Some may not merit respect or compassion at all, nor will they reciprocate the goodness you show to them. Do it anyway. Fail to meet that standard? We will send you off without ceremony."

"Bondurant provided an instructive moment," Asher conceded.

"You're paying attention." Marc gestured at the separated stacks of wood. "And doing good work. Since it seems you'll be staying for a time, what is your last name?"

The question came so unexpectedly, Asher stuttered. He had not said his last name in years; there had been no need, and it was so obviously ethnic, to do so now would reveal his religion instantly. His former religion, his uncertain religion, but still not the faith of this fervent man.

Asher again noticed the piece of glass in Marc's hand. "*Verte*, sir."

With a puzzled look, Marc glanced at the pane too. "Green is your last name?"

"Yes sir. Asher Green."

"Hmm." He kicked a knot of wood toward one of the piles, then gave a smile. "Welcome, then, Asher Green. Welcome to Le Château Guerin. Work hard, pray always."

Asher was not being fired or cast out. He drooped with relief. "Yes sir."

"Now, don't let those gaffers get too far ahead." Marc wagged a finger, then passed through the doors and back into the atelier. The whole way, he held the pane close to his face—maybe, Asher imagined, to examine it for bubbles or impurities. Or maybe to see what the world would look like if everything were green.

Collecting the wood he'd dropped, Asher toted it inside. The nameless man threw his arms in the air. "Where the hell have you been?"

Like a river reaching a dam, the surge of anger in Asher's blood came up against the conversation he'd just finished with Marc, and he buried the emotion in work.

The next two hours were crazed, no time for rest, but the bins saved him. He approached Etienne, shovel in hand, to deliver the news. "We're out of sand."

"Okay." Like a fire-crazed witch, he stirred the boiling soup with his steel pole. "Get ahead on the wood."

A dozen trips later, Asher was staggering. But the interior woodpile reached as high as room allowed, he'd supplied the annealing furnace as well, and he shuffled outside for a break from the heat. Suddenly arms as strong as rope seized him, hoisting him high in the air, though he kicked his legs to break free.

"Throw him here," he heard, and, craning his neck, Asher saw the big-toothed grin of Euclid. "I'll rip off his arms and drum on his head."

"I want to eat him first," Pascal growled from below. "Nom nom nom."

Instead, he lowered Asher with care, and brushed dust off his back.

"Hello, my giant friends," Asher said, hand on his chest. "May I thank you for not killing me?"

"Don't," Euclid said. "We will probably kill you soon anyway."

"Don't," echoed Pascal. "The people here are only fattening you up for us."

"But you found a way in," Euclid said. "Despite our predictions."

"Our discouragements," Pascal added.

"Lucky timing." Although Asher was frightened of these men, he also felt a strange affection. "Bondurant lost his temper one time too many."

Pascal shook his head. "An angry man. One time he hit me with a shovel."

"What did you do?"

"Bopped him on the head, is what."

"He did." Euclid banged his own pate with a fist. "The man crumpled like a puppet with the strings cut."

Asher laughed. When had he last laughed? "I've slept two nights in his bed."

"Well done." Euclid gave him a clap on the back that launched him forward a step. "And now you're the one to receive our deliveries?"

"Apparently."

"Well, here we go." Pascal grabbed the shafts of a cart behind him. With no sign of exertion, he spun it in place, raising the bars to dump a load of lime. Dust rose in a cloud. "Delivery number one. It's fine stuff today."

"It is." Euclid pinched the powder between his fingers. Wiping his hand on his tunic, he left white lines. "Nearly talc quality."

"What am I supposed to do with it?" Asher asked. The mound rose in a cone.

Euclid smiled. "Move this pile into the bins, so it's handy for the kiln."

"Yes, but how?"

"How?" Euclid looked around, as if he were searching for something. One odd result of his size was that certain motions made him look like a toddler still growing accustomed to the mysteries of gravity and balance. "With a shovel. How else?"

"A shovel." Pascal pantomimed digging with an imaginary spade. "You tote this pile inside while we go away, and return with sand, which goes inside too."

"A shovel?" Asher gave them a skeptical look, in case they were teasing. "It will take hours to move this pile twenty steps."

"True." Euclid nodded. "But our cart cannot fit through the door."

"True," Pascal said. "But we'll need that time to fetch delivery number two."

"This was Bondurant's job?"

"And now yours." Pascal clapped him on the shoulder as hard as his brother had. "Congratulations."

The giant men tipped their hats, grabbed the cart's shafts, and, now that it was empty, towed it effortlessly out of the delivery area, clattering to the lane and away.

A breeze passed through, spiraling some of the powder upward, floating toward the gardens. "Barely arrived, and already leaving," he said to the pile of lime. Adjusting his gloves, Asher went inside for the shovel.

Etienne strode over, steel pole in hand. "We can't have peaks and valleys. We need a stable temperature."

"Of course."

The moment Etienne left, Marc appeared. "Be a good fellow and feed our furnace first. Once we're up to temperature, you can concentrate on the gaffers again."

"Of course."

"Hey, lazybones," the nameless man called. "Lime in the crucible. Come on."

"Of coooouuurrrse," Asher said, jogging outside with his shovel. And over the next hour he left a white trail on the ground, waste from his haste. But the main furnace was nearing its red line when Brigitte appeared.

"Apologies," she said. "I managed to find some beef."

She bustled outside, while Asher stood stunned. Actual beef? How might she prepare it? In a rich stock? With black peppercorns?

"Come on," she prodded, passing with her first armload. "Let's catch up."

Lacking so much as a wheelbarrow, he hurried outside to plunge the shovel into the mound, half ran with it to the bin, and dumped it in before scurrying back.

Soon the fires ran high and steady. Brigitte had unfastened her smock, chest shining. He brought her the bucket, holding it waist-high so she could fill the ladle without bending forward. She did it anyway.

"You're a saint." She took deep gulps, one trickle escaping to run down her throat. Again he looked away. That droplet's course was not his affair.

She tossed the ladle back in. "I believe our human lorries are back."

He reached the rear delivery yard in time to see the trolls backing their cart up to a patch of open dirt. They prepared to tip it.

"Wait, wait, wait," Asher called.

"Gladly," Euclid said.

"Happily," Pascal added. Like horses, their barrel chests were heaving from the effort of pulling the load uphill. The sand was a dun color, with the occasional glint of crystal.

Asher fetched an empty bin, and set it by the cart. "This will be much faster."

"Very clever," Pascal said. "But not clever enough."

"I doubt any three people could carry that container full," Euclid said. "Even us."

"Because we are so weak," Pascal added, which made both brothers laugh.

Asher smiled. "As soft as flowers in a hailstorm. But I have an idea."

"Ideas are terrible."

"And always wrong," Euclid added. "Tell us what it is."

"Allow me to show you instead." Asher arranged poplar logs side by side on the ground, as snug as the children in a poor man's bed.

Yet the line of them at his feet brought back a horror of a memory. Why had Asher looked? Levi warned him. Why hadn't he listened?

It happened two days after Asher executed the major at his breakfast. Three other officers ordered a roundup of thirty local people—men and women, young and old—and conducted a mass execution. Four days later, when Levi and others opened the grave, Asher ignored their advice to look away, and it seared into his mind forever the image of decaying bodies, lined up like so many pieces of wood.

Soon he reckoned with those three officers. They were among the nineteen. War was a blunt instrument, vengeance an insatiable hunger.

"Is this the part of the job where we stand loafing?" Euclid asked.

"While our minds wander off?" Pascal added. "It's my favorite part."

Asher shook himself, as if to fling the memory away. He set the empty bin on the logs. "Now dump your load in here."

"No." Pascal wagged his grain bucket of a head. "You won't be able to lift it."

"No," Euclid added, "there'll be no room left to put the rest of our load."

"Pour it right in, my behemoths. We'll have it inside in minutes."

Brigitte bustled out to fill her arms with wood, giving them all a stern look. "I would not object overloudly if you men were to hurry the hell along."

"Anything for you, my love," Pascal called after her. Asher turned, expecting to see the enormous man grinning. Instead, his expression was wistful.

"Suit yourself," Euclid said to Asher. "If you want your silly ideas to get tossed out of this place even faster than Bondurant's rage . . ."

"I truly believe this will work," Asher said.

"But reality," Pascal replied, "does not give a fruitful farting fig."

"Brother, what perfection you speak." Euclid laughed. "A fruitful farting fig."

Nonetheless, he took the cart's shafts in hand, wheeling it to the empty container, and lifted. The sand trickled, poured, cascaded into the bin until it bulged on all sides.

"Enough," Asher said. "The rest can go on the ground once this is inside."

"But here's the fig part," Euclid said. "How will you move this bin?"

"By remembering the bodies." With no more explanation, Asher moved behind Euclid, a hand on each shoulder, guiding him to the bin. "Push with me?"

"Only because I am embarrassed for you." He flattened both hands against the bin, and gave it a shove. It rolled forward the length of a man's arm.

"Now wait," Asher said, scooping the rearmost logs to place them at the front.

"Of course," Pascal said. "This is child's play."

"I want to do the logs part," Euclid declared.

"I want to do the pushing," Pascal answered. "In case Brigitte is watching."

With that, they shouldered him out of the way.

In minutes, a bin full of sand sat fat beside the furnace. As the brothers departed with a wave of their enormous hands, Pascal craning his neck for one more peek at the lady of the house, Asher carried in a load of logs. Brigitte came over, smiling. "First you divide the wood. Now you solve the puzzle of getting materials inside."

"I enjoy organizing."

"For two days in a row I am freed to make dinner. Extra beef for you."

Asher found himself unable to reply. She waddled off, hips swaying. If not for Pascal's ardor, he might never have noticed.

An hour later, both wood stacks stood chest-high, both furnaces raged, the crucibles were full, as were the bins. Marc descended from the back, the vein on his forehead bulging. "Why are you idle?"

Their friendly chat had worn off already. "There's nothing for me to do."

"I'll be the judge of that."

Asher gulped water while the man checked both woodpiles, investigated the bins. When Marc's inspection was complete, Asher offered him a full ladle.

He took a swallow. "At dinner you mentioned beliefs. Are you a believer?"

This was the question, wasn't it? In what did he believe? Not innocence, that had died with his family. Not religion, he'd abandoned that with his first assassination. Not prayer, he'd found himself grousing at the silence and hearing silence in reply.

"I used to be. The war changed everything." It was as honest an answer as he dared to make. "Now I no longer know."

"Maybe that is why you are here. To sort that out."

Asher studied his boots. Made with his own hands, they had outlasted all of his trials. "Your wife said nearly the same thing."

It was the first time he saw Marc smile. "She's smarter than me. You'd better stay awhile."

"Yes sir."

"But I don't want you idle. It will aggravate the men who are working. Next time you get ahead, come see me. We'll find things for you to do." Marc handed over the ladle, hopping up the steps to the back area.

Asher dropped the ladle in the bucket with a gratifying plunk. "Yes sir," he said, though there was no one to hear.

CHAPTER 10

At day's end Asher all but crawled up the winding stairs. In the hallway he paused, promising himself he would marshal the strength to descend again for dinner. The door to his room was open, as he left it, because there was nothing to steal. Everything he possessed he was wearing. On the bed he found a towel, and a whitish block of something soft. One sniff, and the scent plunged him into an ocean of memory.

He and Aube rode a small train south to the coast, arriving at night in Le Lavandou, hailing a rattletrap cab that zipped them to a remote hotel that smelled like heaven, like they were the final ingredients in some recipe for romantic perfection. The aroma gave them wild passions, lasting hours, followed by a sleep so tender it seemed they were having the same dream. None of it made sense until they woke—gazing out the windows at the surrounding fields, rows of purple from end to end, accompanied by a symphony of bees: lavender.

Examining his hand, the skin mottled, dirt hardened around his nails, Asher stuck his head out the window. "Soooooooooap. I have soap."

"I'm glad you like it." A voice to his right startled Asher into banging his head on the stone. He craned his neck and found that Etienne, grinning, had turtled out his own window. "Marie left several bars yesterday, and I cribbed one for you."

"Very generous of you."

Etienne shook his head. "It is a gift to anyone who sits beside you at meals."

Asher remembered the small retreat Marie had taken when they first met, the day she gave him apricots. Now he knew why. "Where can I wash myself?"

"Aside from the kitchen, the plumbing here is unreliable at the moment," Etienne answered. "Which is to say, this year. Therefore . . ." He pointed downward.

In the valley lay the river, winking like a flirt in the afternoon sun.

Where Asher found the energy, he could not say. Perhaps it came from the soap he held under his nose during the walk. But by the time he reached the flatland road to the river, he had shed his coat and vest, rolled up his sleeves, and leaned on a fence post to remove his boots and socks.

Barefoot in the dirt he ambled, relaxing more with every step. A copse of poplars congregated to one side, like senators before a formal occasion. He rounded a bend, and there the bridge stood basking.

The river was more than beautiful; it was independent, a complete being, possessed by nothing but itself. The fluid it carried, the path it carved in the earth. He stood in a deep calm.

Suddenly out of the depths a fish leapt incredibly, higher than Asher had ever seen before, amazing, seeming to hang in the air, while the fish saw the upper world in all of its immensity and light, snatching some morsel before plunging back, making rings that remembered where the leap had occurred, and, in their spreading, forgot.

There is no water great enough, Asher thought, to wash away my sins.

Following a narrow trail, pushing aside branches that seemed intent on scratching him, he found a secluded spot downstream of the bridge. Any task that left him defenseless made him uneasy, so he sought a place with concealment. Leaving his boots on the bank, Asher tucked the soap in his pocket and, still dressed, waded in.

His shirt revealed his ribs like a cat's scrawn when its fur gets wet. Squatting till the water reached his neck, Asher felt its muscular pull, and liked it. What was current anyway, but a river's desire to take everything away?

He began to remove his clothes, pants first, scrubbing them roughly with the soap, rinsing them plunge upon plunge. Had the river been clear, a plume of dust and sweat would have become visible downstream.

After cleaning each garment, Asher draped it on a branch to dry, attire for a family of ghosts. When he grabbed his collar to pull the shirt over his head, it tore shoulder to shoulder, shreds in both hands, strips on his back. How could he stay at the château if he didn't have a shirt?

Tossing the rags on the bank, and with careful steps, he treaded to deeper water. The river flowed like all things, from past into future. Time to wash himself.

At first it was about removing dirt, scrubbing and cleaning, but soon something else began to happen. A rediscovery of his body, a re-acquaintance. Asher could not remember the last time he had been naked. Bruises here, calluses there, all of it nearly weightless, and tendered by the current's steady caress. He scrubbed his knuckles and rubbed his thumbs, his chest like a cabinet, folds and functions between his legs, the cleft of his rear, and down both thighs. Balancing, he gave the arches of his feet each a soapy massage, and nearly cried out at the pleasure. It was an awakening, the parts of his person remembering themselves. Bubbles formed on the water's surface, a beard of white as he soaped his neck and face, lathered his hair clumped with sweat and oil, till it was fine and clear and light. He took a huge breath and plunged.

The world went silent, no sense of current, only the lightness of his bones and a reserve of air in his lungs. Hair floating, shoulders relaxing, Adam in his Eden.

Asher rose gasping and splashing, wiping his eyes, and realized he was no longer alone. The clop of slow hooves, a creak of wagon wheels.

He cursed, to be caught this exposed and without a weapon, and drew into cattails on the far side.

Into view, upstream at the bridge, came a single donkey pulling a cart. A woman's voice corrected the animal, who reversed his steps onto the roadside grass. There, indifferent to all but his appetites, the donkey bent and began to feed.

Asher was already gliding across the river toward his dangling clothes. But before he could reach them, she appeared.

Marie. In an olive-green working dress, bending at the water's edge, cupping a handful of river to rub it on her neck. Saying something more to the donkey, she tossed her hat in the grass and unknotted her shoes. Asher ducked behind willow branches, their leaves trailing on the river like a maiden's hair.

His clothes hung between him and the woman, whose attention fortunately remained fixedly upstream. Marie stood on the bank considering something, then decided, and began to open her chemise: top button, second button, third. Asher checked in all directions. Nowhere to go.

Marie fiddled with the last button, but when it continued to resist she pulled the shirt over her head. She wore nothing else on top, only tan skin and white skin and a woman's secrets. He looked away, but not for long. She had stepped out of her dress, and, wearing a thin white shift, she waded in. The fabric ballooned around her hips, floating as Marie waded deeper, her motions as smooth as a swan's, until the water reached her waist.

As Asher watched, concealed, she splashed water up one arm and the other. She ran a hand along her neck, and down between her breasts. In one fluid motion she removed the comb on her head, tossed it to the shore, and shook her braid loose. Nut-brown hair cascaded down her shoulders. Moving to deeper water, she took a breath and vanished. Where she'd been standing, the river smoothed.

Now was the time for Asher to dash forward, grab his clothes, and retreat into the brush. But if she surfaced at any moment, there he would be. He did not move.

Time passed, and Marie had not come up for air. He craned out from the leaves, to see if she'd swum upstream. The river remained unruffled. Still she did not reappear. He crept from his cover; had something gone wrong, should he attempt a rescue, might doing so frighten her—of course it would frighten her.

The woman burst upward, sucking in a huge breath as she flung her hair side to side. Asher sank till only his eyes and nose were above the water, an ogling crocodile. Still Marie did not look downstream. Her back was muscled and lovely. But then her shoulders began to shake, her head tilted to one side, and he heard strange sounds. Laughter, he thought, until he understood that, no, she was weeping.

Marie did not bend, though, but rather stood upright, facing the sun while she let the pain pour out of her. Asher searched left and right and there was no exit anywhere. He was forced to witness as her sorrow deepened, the woman sobbing now, with her whole body, till he made himself turn downstream. And still could hear her.

Eventually Marie's keening quieted. She wrapped her arms around herself, as if being hugged. After another deep breath, again she submerged.

This time she did not stay under long. The moment she surfaced, she strode toward shore like the champion of a race, water down her glistening flank, the shift clinging to her hips and legs like a second skin. Even with the river spangled by sunlight, the wet clothes showed Asher everything.

Before he could recover, Marie had stepped into her dress, pulled the chemise over her head, toed her shoes back on, braided her hair with fingers deft and quick.

"Come on, Pétain," she told the donkey. "Home and I'll feed you now."

His hooves clopping, they crossed the bridge and headed south, out of sight.

Asher realized that he had been holding his breath. When he released and inhaled again, he felt like a different man. Unclean for what he had seen, enthralled by her nakedness, reminded that he was not the only person suffering in this world. Some part of him had leapt from the river, flinging itself clear of the water for a brief moment, falling too soon back into reality, but newly aware that there was an entire world in that upper realm, alive and brilliant with sun.

Striding through the river to take down his garment-ghosts, all that he knew was resolve. He was not leaving this place. He was not going anywhere.

CHAPTER 11

By the time the leaves were down, Asher had vastly reduced the midnights that he thrashed himself awake. Frost whitened the fields. Sheep grew fat with wool.

He grew too. With three meals daily, and strenuous labor six days a week, his physique had become solid and strong. Undressing at night, he saw arms grown as hard as cables, and felt an unfamiliar pride. His body was healthy again.

In late October they were all at breakfast when someone pounded on the kitchen entry door. Marc was first up from the table, Henri at his heels, and Brigitte close behind. The others followed, crowding into the open space by the stove.

They waited, but there was no more pounding. Brigitte picked up a rolling pin, then put it down. Henri snatched a knife and offered it to Marc, but he shook his head, clasping the doorknob, taking a deep breath, yanking the door open.

A man lay on the stones, wrapped in blankets that were soaked with blood. At the sound of Brigitte's gasp, his eyes blinked open. "God in heaven," he rasped, "you answered my prayers."

Asher heard a snapping sound and Etienne was running up the lane, his hair untied and swinging with his motion, a straight razor open at his hip. It flashed in the pale autumn sun. Wishing he had a knife himself, Asher went out to investigate in the other direction: the gardens shriveled by fall, frost in the shade. His body entered a familiar alertness, the keenness of an assassin, though he beheld a world stilled and cold. But there was no one out there. Once around the courtyard to be certain, and at the door he found Brigitte blocking Etienne's way.

"It is not necessary," she was saying. "Give it to me."

Etienne held a fist in his pocket. "It is necessary. Right now."

"Look at Asher here." She gestured. "He searched too, but without a weapon."

True, Asher thought, though if I'd had one . . .

"I'm not saying no forever," Etienne insisted. "Just not this minute."

"Such a hero," the nameless man groused, loud enough for Etienne to take one quick step in his direction.

Brigitte stopped him with a hand on his arm. "You don't need it."

"Neither do you." Etienne attempted to pass, but she stood unmoving. "You are asking me to weaken myself."

"No." Brigitte smiled maternally. "I am saying that a man who carries a weapon finds a use for it." She held out an open hand. "Unburden yourself."

Asher had never seen Etienne so pained. With a grimace, he put the razor in her palm, and as she gave way, he trundled into the house.

Dropping the weapon into an apron pocket, Brigitte bustled through the kitchen. The others had cleared the table, and set the bleeding man down to examine him.

"I knew they would come for me," the man was explaining, one hand clasping a crushed blue beret. "And eventually they did." He grimaced as Brigitte unwrapped the blankets, yelped when she held his ankle to remove his shoes, and yowled when Marc touched his chest.

"Broken ribs," the nameless man deduced.

"I was mayor," he continued. "They saw me dine with an enemy officer. But eat with the enemy is not to become one. I believed by breaking bread together I might lead him toward mercy. I brought him to church too, little that it accomplished."

The man's lips were blue, his whole frame shivering. "But they are experts in cruelty. They beat me within an inch of my life, but left me alive as a warning to anyone else who might seek peace. They are animals, do you hear me? Animals."

"Who are?" Brigitte was bringing forth bandages.

"The Resistance," the man on the table gasped. "Who else?"

Asher was glad to be standing at the back, because it prevented him from speaking. He wanted to defend the principles of underground fighters, to describe their sacrifices and catalog their pain.

"The war ended eighteen months ago," the mayor said. "Still they seek revenge."

Not the people I served with, Asher protested inwardly. But he also knew: It was completely plausible that Levi would spill the blood of Nazi sympathizers. Eli might be awarding himself prizes far larger than a stolen bicycle.

So he said nothing. His role in the Resistance was another secret he would keep. How could his gratitude to these people be authentic, if he was always lying to them? How could he live with integrity when his life was built on deceit?

Ah, but he was not entirely alone. Out a window Asher spied Etienne, patrolling again, a mallet from the atelier in his hand, pushing back tree limbs and peering under bushes. Here was a man with soldiering still in his blood.

"Do you have whiskey?" the man on the table asked. "Or brandy? For the pain."

Brigitte went in search, the others moving out of her way.

"What is your name?" Marc asked him.

"I am Simon," he rasped, raising a hand to cross himself. "Named for the first apostle, child of God as are we all."

THEY LET HIM STAY. IN the first days he sat by the hearth, or on a kitchen stool while Brigitte made meals. His ribs healed first, with rest and trying not to cough. His ankle improved too, till he limped here and there in the atelier, and the nameless man complained about some people not earning their keep. Not until early December did Simon's mouth recover from the kicks that had knocked out two teeth. But then? The man proved to be a lecturer, a solicitor before the war who did not converse so much as give speeches as if to convince a jury. One afternoon Asher came to refill the water bucket, and found Simon before the fire, holding a stoup of port.

"Everything all right?" he asked.

Rousing, Simon sat upright. "I'm thinking about architecture and fire."

"Okay." Asher started back for the atelier.

"Coals have a way of collapsing, you see. Flames carve furrows on the log, eating away the wood at intervals, until it all appears like a spine, *vertebrae noir*. The clefts deepen, pieces fall like bricks without mortar—and why does this happen?"

Asher shifted the heavy bucket to his other hand. "It's burning?"

"Of course." Simon gulped from his glass of port. "But also, coals lack architecture. Some design to hold them in proper place. If nature had contrived a form for them, fires would generate more heat, and—"

"Pardon me," Asher said, raising the bucket. "Men are thirsty."

"In conclusion . . ." Simon continued, but Asher did not linger to hear the rest.

After a month of his lectures, no one visited Simon. He sat alone all day, accompanied at night by wine if any could be found—and he had a knack for finding it. Ultimately it was not health, but loneliness, that raised him from his chair. He ambled into the atelier, no longer limping. Marc took one look, and put him to work.

One December morning, Asher dreamed he was outrunning the man on fire, when he jerked awake to see smoke in his room. No, no. It was only his breath. The air was as chilly as a dungeon, frost on the glass. At the window he found powder on the sill, snow blanketing the valley. It was only the second time he'd seen snow. He felt like a boy, his heart playful. Asher shivered into his clothes and trotted downstairs. Who could he convince to go exploring with him?

"There the man is now," Etienne said as he entered the dining room.

Asher drew up short. "Is something the matter?"

"No," Marc said, stroking his beard downward. "But we have invited Simon to remain here, a resident of the château, so that his fervent faith may strengthen ours."

"Wonderful," Asher said, wary, all boyishness vanished.

"He will assume the job of wrangling the wood and feeding the furnaces. As he gains skill and understanding, he will advance to supplying the crucibles as well."

"Those are my jobs," Asher said.

"They *were* your jobs," Etienne replied.

He fell back against the wall. Twenty times he had observed their sabbath rather than his own. He'd had to guess when in autumn the High Holy Days came, and to honor them in secret. He'd grown well enough to dwell on the deaths he had caused, eighteen intentionally and one unavoidably. And now, after great care with his secrets, after curating their view of himself, it was ended.

"Didn't I work hard, and organize things?" Asher asked. "Wasn't I spiritual enough?"

"What are you talking about?" The vein had risen on Marc's forehead.

"I'm stunned," Asher continued. "You're going to put me out in the cold?"

"What?" Marc laughed. "We're doing nothing of the kind."

"Asher," Etienne interjected, "you're joining the gaffers. As an apprentice, of course, if you're willing. We're going to teach you to blow glass."

"I'm opposed," the nameless man announced. "We're already crowded."

"Nonsense," Marc demurred. "We must build inventory for the commissions that are sure to come."

"Nonsense," the nameless man muttered to himself.

Asher scanned their faces. "I'm going to be blowing glass?"

Marc inclined his head while Henri nodded emphatically.

"And I," Simon answered from down the table, "will pray for your success."

THE HARDEST PART WAS NOT the heat, savage though it could be, and frightening when he opened the furnace door and the fresh supply of oxygen made the flames roar. The hair on his arms was singed daily.

When his job had been hauling wood, Asher was not exposed to the furnace's truth. Now he knew: It was a living thing, with needs, hunger, a will. It never compromised. It warmed the whole atelier with the lust to enlarge itself, reddening every man's face, soaking every shirt. Either Etienne or the nameless man would open the crucible hole, inserting his blowpipe for a gather of lava, and blistering rage would fill the air. If heat was not hate, Asher thought, it certainly felt that way.

"There are three levels," Etienne had told Asher. "Hot, extremely hot, and permanent injury." He'd laughed, holding up a hand whose back was topographic with scars. "I try not to injure myself more than twice a day."

So far, Asher had not yet been injured. In fact, those months of meals and labor had rebuilt him, given him a strong and solid body. The furnaces did not care. His eyebrows had curled, his lips split, his hair parched into straw—mostly from tending the cauldron. Still, when certain jobs needed extra speed or attention, he was called upon to blow. That was the hardest part.

The blowpipe was a hollow steel tube as long as he was tall, made of heavy black iron, impervious to the inferno. Breathing into it, and partly breathing, and sometimes not breathing, Asher was somehow expected to express his most artistic thoughts and inspired intentions—though, except for holding his breath while swimming as a boy, he had never spent three seconds considering the functions of his lungs. When he flattened leather on a shoe lathe, did he inhale? Gluing a hide to a sole, did he exhale? When he oiled a finished boot to waterproof it, did he breathe faster or slower? He had no idea.

Instead, he watched Etienne work. First he made gathers, an orange glob on the blowpipe. He pursed his lips at the cool end like a trumpeter about to play, but instead of a note emerging it was a fat molten orb. Rotating the pipe with his long fingers, he one-handed a waterlogged wooden mold out of its bath by the workbench. As he closed the mold around the glass, steam hissed and rose. Again, Etienne blew into the pipe—but this time with closed eyes, using his mouth to feel the resistance, the limits of space inside the mold. He popped it open to reveal a long smooth sausage of glass.

Calling one word to the nameless man, who approached wearing thick gloves, Etienne pressed a cutting tool to the pipe's throat, spun it once more, and the glass fell into the nameless man's mitts. He held the prize waist-high while Etienne pulled out his scoring tool, ran it top to bottom on the balloon, and the nameless man pivoted.

"Hot glass," he called, quick-stepping to the annealer. "Hot glass."

Henri was there, holding the door open, as the nameless man set the orb on a shelf. By then Etienne had tossed the mold back in its bucket to steep like a giant pot of tea, and snatched his pipe to make another gather.

That scoring would crack the sausage as it cooled, the two sides parting, each side lowering like pages in a book, till they lay flat and hardened, like an idea becoming fixed in a person's brain.

The pleasure of witnessing this craft, Asher admitted, was also the reason he was intimidated by it. Such ease, so many skills, such indifference to potential injury.

"Plunge in." The nameless man was preheating his blowpipe's tip in the kiln before making a gather. "Leap. It's the only way to learn."

Asher sidled to his workbench, picking up his pipe as though it were a punishment.

The nameless man, stepping away with his new gather, waved his free hand at the furnace like a maître d' displaying an available table. "All yours."

WHAT FOLLOWED WAS FRANCE'S COLDEST winter in a century, no household receiving its allocation of heating fuel, blizzards stopping coal trains and preventing deliveries. The kilns made the atelier a comfortable place, except for Asher, who experienced a season of broken glass and scalded fingertips.

"You're a beginner," Etienne reassured him. "It takes time."

"You're a beginner," the nameless man scoffed. "Ignorant and unskilled."

But not at killing, bub, Asher thought, instantly appalled that the reply had come to mind. Being annoying was no reason to take a man's life. Meanwhile, Henri gave Asher pats on the back, Simon told him to have faith, and Marc ignored him altogether.

Christmas approached and the château prepared to celebrate, which Asher observed with the same religious outsider's puzzlement as he had in Bonheur. The candles, the gospel readings at dinner, the lower work tempo. Daylight hours became grimly short.

On December twenty-third, Marie arrived with a brace of rabbits. By then Asher routinely helped her carry in the delivery. By then he'd given up trying to figure out why she had been crying in the river. The image of her climbing out of the water—her top naked and the rest in a wet clinging shift—was vivid in his memory.

That morning Marie was dressed in forest green, with a wool bonnet that framed her face like a child's. She held the rabbits at arm's length, by their ears, hoisting them to the counter beside the sink. Shotgun wounds spotted their pelts.

"Look at these lovelies," Brigitte marveled. "A fine Christmas dinner, and they'll make fine gloves too. Join us for the meal, won't you?"

Asher stopped in the doorway, not concealing his eavesdropping.

"I wish I might," Marie replied. "But the doctor has no one, and you have one another. I'll be keeping him company that day."

"We'll miss you," Brigitte said, her eyes on Asher. "All of us." Immediately he went out for another load from the cart. Later, he criticized himself for not saying something nice about her bonnet.

Christmas itself was an easier day than he'd expected, because no one worked, the kilns stayed cold, people played cribbage. Simon was merciless, beating them all without effort and despite steady refilling of his wineglass. Marc led an hour of worship in which Asher seethed over his growing prowess at false prayer. The rabbits were splendid in a broth with onions, and for Brigitte's holiday dessert there were pears baked in cinnamon. The afternoon dozed toward an early sundown, the war still too close in memory to allow much celebration.

On New Year's Eve, Marc arranged a row of bottles on the side table, in a neat line like soldiers, and without a word or flourish uncorked them all.

"That's a commitment," Brigitte observed, while he filled glasses all around.

"I'm ready to do my best," Simon joked, holding Marc's sleeve so he would give him a generous pour.

Fire roared in the hearth, the wine drank easily. Etienne tried to teach them a riddles game that no one quite understood. Surrendering, he waved a hand in Asher's direction. "Tell us a story."

"Why are people always asking me to do that?"

"Because," the nameless man prattled, "we can see that you are already having a private conversation with yourself."

Asher marveled not only at how often he received this request, but also how readily a tale would come to mind. Just then, for example. "All right," he said, rising.

"Here, here," Simon said, shifting his glass, sitting up.

Asher felt the wine more than he'd expected. He laid one hand on the mantel, setting his glass there, taking command of himself.

"One year in Bonheur, there was a sunless December. Every morning without cease, we awoke to gloomy skies and a damp chill. For weeks, a harsh wind blew down the sea from the north. Bleak days, grim nights. By Christmas Eve, everyone was praying for sun."

"Very clever." Simon winked. "Christmas Eve, praying for the Son. Well done."

Asher continued. "I will never forget that day. The next morning the ceiling thickened, a shroud on everything, the world gray as dusk at ten A.M. Starting at noon, the clouds delivered flurries for an hour, like a flirtation, then grew serious and released a downpour of snow. It quieted the world, and kept falling. It cleaned all of creation, and did not stop. Left a trail where cats had walked the piers, and then erased those tracks. Covered every mess and any litter, and piled higher. All day the snow continued—a cleansing, a benediction. In late afternoon, people emerged from their houses and celebrations, wary like nervous dogs, investigating the storm until they wore toupees of white. Spontaneously the villagers gathered by the harbor to stand and marvel. Two fellows struck up with an accordion and fife. People danced on the cobblestones like vintners in harvest, though the wine that they made was slush. Eventually people's fingers grew cold, their feet got wet. In singles, pairs, and families, they returned home. As the people were calling goodbye, happy Christmas, their breath rose like so many souls momentarily set free."

Asher reclaimed his wine, treated himself to a generous gulp, and found his seat. He had only told part of the tale. He did not mention the presence, on that remarkable day, of his wife, Aube so newly pregnant they had not yet told her mother, how they had held one another while watching the people dance, how vaulting and immense was his love. In truth, that feeling was what he would never forget.

"A good enough story," the nameless man sniffed. "I suppose."

If not for his nostalgic mood, Asher would gladly have slapped him. Hard.

"It's a fine tale," Simon added, "full of innocence and virtue. The symbolism—"

"No lectures today," Etienne interrupted. "If you please."

"Fine." Pouting, Simon gulped his wine. "Never mind."

After a minute of quiet, Marc stood, fire casting his shadow forward on the floor, and in lieu of a story began a recitation. "The melting point of silicate is one thousand seven hundred and ten degrees centigrade. That temperature, if it were attainable from burning wood, would melt the mortar and collapse our kilns. So." He waved his glass, the wine nearly spilling, and Asher realized the man was swaying. "So, we add potash to serve as flux. This organic material reduces the melting point to as low as . . . well, depending on the composition and purity, as low as fourteen hundred degrees. Flux, an excellent word. And do you know?"

He leaned toward Asher. "Do you know why we add lime?"

"Actually, no," Asher said, his mind still on Aube. Tomorrow would begin another year without her. And Rachel. It was unbearable. He could kill another nineteen over it.

"To make the glass insoluble. Otherwise, it would be penetrable by water." One hand behind his back, like a sea captain inspiring his crew, Marc listed this way and that. "Without lime, if you put a pane of glass in a tray of water, it would dissolve. All you would have left is sand at the bottom of your tray."

Asher leaned toward Etienne. "Is this true?"

Marc raised his glass high. "Here's to the lime, which makes things permanent."

"To the lime," they answered.

Tilting his glass to drink, Marc overestimated, toppling backward. He might well have landed in the fire, but while the rest of them sat useless in their seats, Henri darted forward, catching him, preventing the fall. Marc pulled himself upright, chest high, glass higher. "Thank you very much, Heinrich."

"What?" Again, Asher leaned toward Etienne. "What did he call him?"

But Brigitte had rushed forward from her place at the door. "Not funny," she said, swatting her husband on the shoulder. "Not a good joke. Good night to all." She piloted him into the hallway. "Happy new year."

"I tell you, it's the lime that holds it together," Marc insisted, dragging his feet.

"And you are the lime of this atelier," she replied, leading him upstairs. Henri followed a few steps behind, continuing past them to the back stairs and up to his room, which, like the rest of the crew's, was in the garret.

"Marc said Heinrich," Asher persisted. "What did he mean?"

"Drunkenness." The nameless man cleared his throat. "Nothing more. But I can't believe a pane would melt into sand that easily."

"Seems implausible." Etienne slid his chair closer to the fire. "But a priest is rarely one to lie."

"A priest?" Asher said. "Who?"

"Marc," the nameless man replied. "You know that perfectly well."

"But I don't."

"Brigitte was a cook at the seminary he attended." Etienne used an iron hook to tinker with the fire, turning a log. "He broke off priesting in order to marry her."

"And to inherit her family's atelier." The nameless man raised his glass in salute. "A fair transaction, I'd say."

"There is no greater devotion," Simon declared, rousing in the corner, "than the wish to atone for breaking a promise to God."

"Well," Asher observed, "at least that explains all the praying."

The others laughed, while Simon swilled from his glass, then nudged Asher's boot with his own. "Come, now. You're slow enough at blowing glass. Don't fall behind in drink too."

IN THE MORNING ASHER AWOKE heavy-headed, dry-mouthed, and no less perplexed by the world, finding himself in a strange and unfamiliar place known as 1947. The château saw no more snow, but the weather remained bitter. Asher organized the workbench tools, mixed a reliable crucible, and developed a system for replenishing the bins. He also put the glass in order, arranging it by color. Weeks passed in light labor.

"It's cobalt oxide time," Marc announced at breakfast one day in early April. "There's not much supply, and the prices are banditry, so let's minimize waste, please."

It was the most aggressive *please* Asher had heard. It implicated him too, and his lack of skill. His mood lifted when he reached the atelier, because swifts had been building a nest in the rafters, and it was looking nearly complete.

Henri, using a ladder to spy on the nest, had held up three fingers, signifying the trio of eggs he'd found. Asher admired how the man managed to communicate so well. Rarely did anyone misunderstand him—and even less frequently contradict him. His skill in window fabrication made him subservient to no one but Marc.

"Does anyone know," Etienne asked, "how long a swift egg takes to hatch?"

No one did, though the nameless man offered an opinion: "Not soon enough. Those birds eat their weight in bugs every two hours."

Indeed, the pair of them, while assembling the foundation for their nest, had quelled an invasion of horseflies, whose bite Asher considered worse than a bee sting. That feat cemented their welcome in the atelier. One morning Marc approached the nest, broom raised, and every man present raised a complaint.

The latest pestilence was houseflies. That morning Asher waved away one circling his head. A swift veered. The bug made a sound as it hit the bird's open beak.

"Skilled, aren't they?" Etienne asked. He'd approached without his blowpipe, a signal to Asher that he'd come not for conversation, but for tutoring.

"They're my role models," Asher replied. He was standing before the furnace, suffering its heat, working up the nerve to try again.

"Let's get busy." Etienne handed him a blowpipe. Asher guided it into the glory hole, twirling it in the lava till a bright glob collected on the tip.

"Move quickly," Etienne coached. "Cool glass is reluctant. Hot glass will obey."

"I know." Asher backed away. Sweat on his forehead overran an eyebrow on one side, requiring him to use a bicep to clear his vision.

"You're slumping." Etienne pointed. "Roll it, roll it."

Asher's gather was dipping toward the ground. He rotated the pipe with his fingers, using gravity to counteract the bend. Already the orange hue had dimmed.

He returned to the furnace, but the nameless man stood in the way, making his own gather. He hopped foot to foot, knowing his glass was cooler every second. The moment the door was clear, he darted his pipe into the fire.

"Go slower," Etienne instructed. "Let the glass glue to itself."

He paused to watch the nameless man blow a perfect orb, lift a molding form from its bucket of water, and close it around his sphere. Swift and smooth and certain. Asher made the third gather, rotating his pipe on the way to the workbench. Etienne stepped aside while Asher lowered his mouth to the brass fixture and began to blow.

One part bulged, where the gather was thinnest, like a bullfrog's protruding eye. Asher's shoulders dropped.

"Too slow," Etienne said. "Reheat."

While Asher carried his oddity back to the glory hole, the nameless man came beside Etienne. "Fire him."

"Give him time."

"It's nearly summer and he's still hopeless," the man said.

"It is not even May," Etienne replied.

Asher withdrew his pipe from the glory hole, and the glob had fallen off. He held up the empty tip. "Sorry."

Etienne shrugged. "Did it land back in the crucible?"

Asher shook his head. "In the fire."

"Don't worry." The nameless man scoffed. "It's only cobalt."

ASHER WORKED BETTER WHEN NO one was looking. It had been true with his cobbling too: If a customer came in, or Aube visited with Rachel on her hip, he put his tools aside. People thought it was politeness. In truth, he did not trust work when it was done as a performance. The boot maker in Caen with whom he'd apprenticed loved an audience, flirting with women while he measured their feet, gossiping with horse-men while repairing their saddles. He'd developed flourishes, spinning the hammers or snapping leather to make it sound like a slap. The customers loved it.

Invariably, though, Asher found that work of lower quality. The next time he saw the woman on the street, her boot's arch would have a crease in its middle. Or he'd come upon the horseman and see that the saddle needed work again.

So he was relieved by the other gaffers' departure. By noon he had accomplished a dozen good gathers, yielding four clear spheres. He'd eased them into the waterlogged mold. The breath of steam when he closed the blocks sounded like a sigh of approval. Then would come the real blowing, the art of it, as he attempted to expand the sphere to fill the mold—a thing he could not see, only feel.

For three attempts, he opened the blocks to find one corner crum-pled inward. Henri happened by, two thumbs up till he saw the flaw. The fourth time, Asher felt the relief of being completely ignored. Everyone was busy, lunch break imminent, as he closed the wood blocks on his sphere. He blew into the hot tube, waiting for the feeling that the mold was full—like knowing when a screw is tightened as far as it should go.

And there it was: a fullness, a certain pressure. He lifted his foot, the mold popped open, and the result was a long surface, no gaps, no folds, a balloon of blue.

"Attention, people." Marc had come to the steps for an announcement, but noticed Asher's work. "Look at that." He held an arm out. "A gaffer at last."

"He overlooks the twelve I've made this morning," the nameless man muttered beside Asher. "If I, like you, were willing to kiss Lady Brigitte directly upon her—"

"Enough," Etienne interrupted, relieving Asher of his pipe. "Let's get that secure before any mishaps."

He laid the balloon on a sheepskin, rolling it with a file at the throat, till the glass broke free. From his tool belt he drew a cutter, running it the length of the balloon. "There," he said, putting the tool away. "Let's get this in the annealer."

"Absolutely." Asher donned a thick glove to carry the balloon, his bare hand raised protectively, and started toward the smaller furnace.

The donkey brayed. They all heard it, each of the men, because its protest reminded them that food was being delivered.

Except for one, for whom the sound had a different meaning, causing him to raise his head. In that moment of distraction, Asher stepped on a chunk of wood Simon had dropped, three steps away from the annealer—which was being fed for the day, door open, logs crackling. The chunk rolled, Asher lunged to stay upright, and realized he was about to collide with an open oven. There was nothing to do but fall, launching the balloon at the annealer, against which it shattered.

It did not matter how often the men heard that sound. None of them became accustomed to it. If anything, they grew sensitized to glass breaking, aware of what it meant and what had been lost.

Asher knelt amid the shards, blue reflected all around him. His right hand, in the glove, was unmarred, his left sliced down the meat of the thumb, bleeding hard.

Brigitte was at his side, examining the wound. "Do you need a stitch?"

"What I need is the feet of a ballerina."

"Or the attention span of a hunting dog," the nameless man said. "At least he keeps his nose pointed where it ought to be."

Asher shook his head. "I finally had a good one."

Henri held a whisk broom to his collar, playing it as a miniature violin with an invisible bow.

Marc frowned at the scene, that vein on his forehead rising. "Simon?"

He appeared with loaded arms. "Sir?"

"This was your error. Sweep this glass up after lunch. Every least bit, and it goes back in the cauldron."

Simon shied back a step. "Yes sir."

"Sweet wife, Asher here needs lanolin for his split lips."

"Of course," Brigitte said.

"Which Etienne should already have dealt with. Asher, wrap your thumb and I'll examine it after the meal. Now, people." Marc clapped his hands once. "The sooner we're fed, the sooner we're back to work."

"Congratulations, Asher." Etienne pointed at the floor, a dark red splotch on the cement. "Your first donation to the atelier."

Asher continued kneeling as the workers filed past. The room fell silent but the heat remained, whether radiating comfort or malice he could not say.

He was surrounded by shards, in the atelier and in his life. No doubt his position at Le Château Guerin was in danger. He was bleeding profusely. Meanwhile, the donkey had brayed again, and his opportunity to see the animal's mistress that day shrank with every second.

Yet he could not help noticing. All around him, the glass had broken into fascinating shapes: a triangle, a finger, and here by his knee a slice of moon as perfect as if he'd intended it. Clumsy with the thick glove, Asher picked up the still-hot crescent—raising it toward the window, playing the blue across his eyes—and beheld for the first time what glass he had made could do with the light.

CHAPTER 12

First he saw her shadow, cast on the courtyard cobblestones: balletic, slender, and graceful. The darkness bent and lifted, it carried odd shapes, it was full of intention. He paused to bear witness.

No longer was the person casting this image a stranger. Asher knew she was assured in her movements. Her forehead furrowed at the least consternation: a bluebottle fly annoying her hair, her apron somehow unknotting. Her smile was a surprise, genuine and bright.

"Good morning," she said, gathering root vegetables from the wagon. She wore a tan work dress, the color of milky coffee.

"Hello, Marie." Asher barely had time to bow in greeting before she passed with a basket of onions, potatoes, and turnips.

Of course it was infatuation, not so different from when he'd been young and unruined. Had that moment at the river merely revived his capacity for lust? Or had it also stirred his compassion? Was his interest in her a kind of infidelity, or a sign of recovery? Asher imagined himself near the bridge again, some warm evening, Marie beside him in the grass, while they talked about anything at all, and the fish jumped high again, reminding him to be alive.

"Can you believe the bulbs are up already?" She waved at crocuses along the courtyard wall.

"We're lucky to have such a skilled gardener," he said as Marie bustled toward the kitchen entry. Seeing her hands were full, he hurried to open the door and she breezed inside.

Actually, Asher rarely noticed the château's flowers. That was Henri's realm, going to the gardens each afternoon after he'd sealed the annealer. Rain or sun, wind or calm, the small man would be tending and weeding until Brigitte called him to dinner.

If anything, Asher avoided the gardens. Too much memory of Aube in her domain, and her admonition for him to keep out. He obeyed, but remained near. He enjoyed seeing her mood ripen inside that area fenced against the bunnies, humming an aimless tune while bare-bottomed Rachel patty-caked the dirt. Sometimes after gardening, Aube asked him to help wash her hands, and as he made them slippery with soap they could not help laughing at how erotic it was. The memory brought him equal portions of delight and sorrow.

"How is your day?" Marie said, gathering another load.

Asher shook himself like a dog drying off, trying to shed the past, and followed her to the wagon. "I made you something."

Marie paused. "You did not."

"It was semi-accidental, but still." Injured left hand behind his back, Asher held forward the right. In his open palm there sat a slice of the moon in royal blue.

"Why, Asher," she said, surprised. He enjoyed hearing her say his name, especially in a tone so warm and pleased.

Marie tucked her hair behind one ear, tilting the crescent side to side. "In all the time I've delivered here, this is the first piece of glass I've been given." Her eyes darted at him, a glint of light and away. "Thank you."

"It's not annealed, so I don't know how long it will last." He leaned on one foot like a schoolboy. "But you're welcome."

"I need to hurry, though," she said, recollecting herself, dropping the crescent into her pocket. "The doctor in the village wants his lettuce early today. Forgive me."

"He can wait," Asher said. "All men's stomachs are equal."

She leaned over to select some hothouse beet greens. "Any man who pays double the price deserves special treatment." Arms full, she hurried away.

Asher eyed the rest of the cart's contents. She'd taken the vegetables from a pile on one side, so he assumed that stack was for Le Château Guerin. Gathering a flourish of garlic and loose potatoes, he entered the kitchen.

"What's this?" Brigitte looked up from a large black pot. "What are you doing?"

Marie called from the pantry, "He's helping me, the angel."

Brigitte stirred her wooden spoon. "Devils can carry potatoes too, you know." But she was smiling.

"Not this many," Asher replied, rolling them onto the counter, where they rumbled like wrestling boys. "I'd put them away if I knew where anything belongs."

"Gaffers belong in the dining room," Brigitte said, snatching up one of the fresh heads of garlic and plucking off two cloves. "Or they'll miss lunch. Today Pascal was kind enough to bring a creel of fresh-caught trout."

Through the open door, Asher could see the men at the table, passing around a platter heaped with fish. His stomach growled.

"Pascal? That man is half in love with you," Marie chirped from the pantry. She stood on tiptoe to reach a high shelf. Asher noticed the strength of her calves.

"Better not let Marc hear that." Brigitte mashed the cloves with her thumb, tossing their meat into the pot and sweeping the skins away in one sure gesture. "The giant would wind up only good for the job of vegetable delivery assistant."

"Could be a high calling," Asher said, grinning, "depending on who you assist."

Brigitte looked up from the pot, and sure enough Marie had heard. Half out of view, her blush was visible nonetheless. Brigitte's smile vanished, as she pointed her wooden spoon at Asher. "Mind well what you pick up," she growled. "People are not potatoes. And some things can't withstand dropping."

Her tone humbled him, and Asher backed away. His thumb still hurt from the cut. "I'll carry everything carefully."

But when he'd returned to the cart, he was no longer sure which things were meant for them, and which for the doctor. There was a robin too, perched on the wagon's side slats, that had flown up as he came out. It scolded him from above, in a tree that arched over the lane.

"Don't you lecture me too," Asher said. "I don't tell you how to find worms."

Gathering the last onions, he spied a wide-mouthed jar to one side. It held some sort of sliced leaves, white and stringy, in a brine with caraway seeds. He'd never seen this type of food before, and wondered if opening the jar for a sniff would ruin it.

"Don't touch that, please." Marie rushed forward, taking the jar from him. "That's special. That's . . . for the doctor."

"I'm sorry. I only wanted to help."

"You're bleeding." She pointed to where the rag bandage had fallen from his thumb. "Did you get blood on everything?"

"No, no," Asher said. "The wrap only came off just now. This second."

"Don't touch any more of this, all right?" She waved an arm over the wagon's contents. "I know you want to help. You're the first one who has lifted a finger for me. But blood? Just . . . just don't."

Asher stood stupefied at how many mistakes he had made in so short a time. "Of course. I'm sorry." He reached his good hand forward to arrange the remaining goods.

"No, you don't need to—"

"Have a grand afternoon, Marie." Brigitte waved a rag from the kitchen door. "Asher, leave the woman alone now. You've helped enough for today."

"He certainly has," Marie said.

Stung, Asher found himself speechless. He felt supremely awkward, worse than when he'd dropped the blue balloon fifteen minutes before. And now they performed a classic dance, which felt thoroughly juvenile given the hardships he'd withstood, the gavotte of embarrassment. He stepped away, downcast. She gave his wrist a reassuring squeeze. He stiffened as if receiving an electric shock.

"Marie," he whispered. But she had already released him, climbing onto the wagon, snapping the reins. Hooves clopped down the dappled lane.

The man raised his bandaged hand in farewell, but the woman did not look back. Exasperated, he looked up into the tree that arched over his head. The robin had watched the whole mortifying episode. Now that it had ended, the bird returned to his business—threading through the branches, quick-winged and away.

THERE WAS STILL TROUT LEFT. Asher took a generous serving and raised his fork.

"Don't forget to say grace," Marc chided.

"Of course." He lowered his head and counted to twelve. That was how long the others' mealtime prayer typically lasted. A woman in his Resistance cell had a name for Jews who hid their faith: U-boats. An insult as barbed as a thorn, but sharper because it was accurate.

Asher had no idea what he believed. The war had crushed all solace out of the old rituals. The death of his family brought God's existence into question. The only contradictory evidence was the world, its beauty and generosity. For example, trout for lunch.

"Amen."

The nameless man cleared his throat. "Two guesses what he prayed for."

"Does it involve a dress?" Etienne asked.

"Leave me alone." Asher started wolfing the food.

"Apparently romance," the nameless man observed, "gives a man appetite."

Amid the laughter, Asher did not look up from his plate. Rather, he ate like a bull, scuffing his boot under the table as though preparing to charge.

WHEN WORK ENDED THAT DAY, Asher wandered out to the courtyard. Hyacinths stood in colorful array. Henri paused in his weeding to give a two-finger salute. Asher ambled along, down the long exterior wall—until he noticed, snug against the stones, the jar of white leaves. So well hidden, a person would have to know where to look in order to find it.

Not for the doctor after all. Why would Marie lie about such a thing? Asher gazed up the empty lane. Something told him to leave it as it was. But that night in bed, he pondered it. She must have returned later to hide the jar. There was a whole world of people's deeds and intentions about which he knew nothing.

Then again, how much did anyone know about his deeds and intentions? He had hidden them all.

A clock's hands move at their own pace, revealing nothing about the works within. When Asher checked the next morning, the jar was gone.

CHAPTER 13

The following weeks in the atelier were worse. Asher's glass skills seemed to decay. His thumb bandage made rotating a pipe awkward. His efforts with the mold kept producing orbs too small to merit loading in the annealer. One after another he lowered them back into the crucible, where they melted like good intentions repeatedly thwarted.

"Keep the material moving." Etienne demonstrated, pulling his gather from the furnace, and spinning it nimbly. "The glass won't know which way is down."

Asher decided to do the next dip by imitation. A good gather, but the glob grew wrinkles. As he brought the blowpipe to his lips, bumps formed on the lava's exterior.

The nameless man shook his head. "Pathetic."

"You were a beginner once," Asher answered.

"My first gather was better than your fiftieth." He lowered his pipe into the crucible. "You are genuinely the worst at this work I have ever seen."

Asher assessed the wrinkled glob, and imagined what it could do to human skin. The agony, the scars, all from one touch he could later claim was an accident. There was no suppressing his violent thinking.

The nameless man, after a small puff into his own pipe, put his thumb over the mouthpiece. "First, you're taking too much material. Make small gathers. Second, you can eliminate bumps by adding air, because it will press outward. Third, don't rotate the pipe with jerky motions. Make it smooth."

As he spoke, the heat of the pipe was expanding the air he'd already blown in, forming a little clear bulb on the tip. As if the glass were making itself. Asher stared at the floor, ashamed of his impulses. He had forgotten Marc's welcoming lecture, and the requirement of compassion.

"Don't be a burden." The nameless man rotated his pipe. "Improve or leave."

THE CREW SAT TOGETHER AT lunch: baguettes so fresh they were still oven-warm, early asparagus, thin strips of beef slathered in sautéed mushrooms. The scent of Brigitte's cooking had been a torment and the men ate like dogs, heads down. She held court from one end of the table, the chair at the other end empty. Marc arrived eventually, but remained standing behind his seat. That was enough to quiet the men.

"My love." Brigitte put down her utensils. "How did we do?"

"Good news and . . . well, some challenging news. First, let us pray."

The men put down their forks and bowed their heads, Asher included.

"Heavenly Father, we give thanks for the food on our table, the skill of our colleagues, and good work to keep our minds and hearts moving toward you."

"Amen," they said as one, save Henri, as usual.

"We have been awarded a commission," Marc said. "The timing could not be better. For a year, the Vatican has been funding the restoration of the cathedral in Clovide. Now we are charged with building new rear windows. If the bishop finds our result satisfactory, we'll become eligible to do more. Either there, or at additional churches."

Clovide again. Where that woman had asked if he was a priest. Asher recoiled at the memory, at how dark his heart was in that time—

until he remembered that hours later he met the huge brothers, who fed him dinner and told him about the château.

"The cathedral of Clovide is where France crowned its kings," Etienne observed. "But I say that Marc deserves a crown himself, for winning this commission."

He waved off the praise. "Those walls contain ten centuries of sacramental grace. So we must pray as we work, that we make windows worthy of the years to come."

"Amazing," Etienne marveled. "To think that generations will see our work."

"Asher." Marc looked down the table. "You're quiet today. What do you think?"

That his circumstances at the château had never been more precarious. That he was incompetent at blowing glass, and ignorant of all things Christian. How important was a bishop? What did the word sacramental mean? What was a Vatican?

Everyone faced him, waiting. The longer he remained silent, the more the moment tightened. But as he opened his mouth, as if on cue a donkey brayed outside.

The men burst out laughing. Brigitte put one hand over her mouth, failing to conceal her amusement.

"Hilarious," the nameless man snickered. "The smartest thing you've ever said."

"She's late today," Marc observed.

"She changed the order of her deliveries," Asher replied.

"What do you mean?"

"There's a doctor in the village uphill." Asher swallowed, though his mouth was dry. "He wants his goods earlier in the day. For this, he pays much higher prices."

"We pay our fair share," Marc said. "And will again, thanks to this commission."

"Each person here has an expertise," the nameless man intoned at Asher, nose lifted. "Yours is the habits of the vegetable girl."

Etienne studied his plate. "I thought that there was no doctor for miles."

"Perhaps someone has come home from the war," Brigitte said.

"Perhaps we all have."

The statement had come from Simon, who—feeling chastised for his lectures—was speaking at the table for the first time today. And his comment brought a pause.

Asher looked around. The château housed a collection of oddballs, no doubt, but he was well fed. A gruff crowd, but he had a soft bed. When he was thirsty, Etienne appeared with a bucket and ladle. When he fell sick, Brigitte brought hot broth to his room. Asher no longer spent his days bewildered by hunger. He hadn't yet made a decent piece of glass, but neither had he stopped trying.

Twice Marc had announced that a priest would be visiting to perform Mass, putting a weight of dread in Asher's gut, but both times he had not come. Asher could fake grace at meals, but he did not know how much further he could go.

"Wrap up whatever you've been doing by end of day tomorrow," Marc was saying. "Henri will design the right-hand frame, I will do the left, and you"—he gestured in the nameless man's direction—"will join the two of us for the center nave."

The nameless man bowed. "I'm honored."

"Etienne, I'll rely upon you for a steady supply of glass." Marc held the back of his chair. "Simon, that means keeping both fire and crucible well supplied. Asher, I'll need you to assist Henri and me. An apprenticeship in assembly."

"Great," he answered, relieved that his lack of a response was forgotten. Relieved that he could learn something other than blowing. "Thank you."

When the donkey brayed a second time, Brigitte stood. "Excuse me."

"Perhaps Asher can help," Etienne said, though the laughter was weak that time.

"Mr. Marc," Simon ventured, "you said you had challenging news too."

"Our supply of materials," he replied. "We sent a considerable sum to Danzig, to replenish our color coffers. An expensive proposition, because the war absorbed manufacturing capacity. In a moment of ambition, I included a large request for red."

"I don't understand," Simon said.

"For centuries," Etienne explained, "Danzig has been the world's center for the chemicals that color glass. And red is made using gold. Actual gold."

"Months ago we sent an advance payment." Marc pulled back his chair, finally coming around it to sit. "The materials have not arrived. I've sent repeated posts, with no reply. We can't make windows out of clear glass."

Suddenly Asher saw Marc differently. Etienne and the nameless man might be expert gaffers, Henri might assemble skillfully, Brigitte might provide glorious meals, but all them combined did not equal Marc's work to sustain the whole enterprise. Sloped in his chair, he looked as exhausted as a flat tire.

"Yesterday I visited Clovide," Etienne said. "All the talk is about the flood of people into Paris. There is no housing, yet they arrive by the hundreds every day."

"It was bad enough already," the nameless man said. "I don't miss the noise."

Etienne rotated his goblet with his long fingers. "Apparently the black market for wine and produce is insane. Perhaps the fine and promising Vincent Auriol, our brand-new president, will demonstrate how nimbly the government can respond."

Asher thought: We have a new president? For years he had tracked every least change of course in national politics. Now there was a president he had never heard of.

"However Auriol's government acts," Marc said, "it will not help the likes of us. Banks and factories will be the beneficiaries. Landlords, perhaps. Art always comes last, and religious art is the tail of the dog." He stroked his beard. "We are on our own."

There was a sober silence. From the kitchen they heard Brigitte saying something in a bright voice. The reply was piping and cheerful.

Asher rose from his seat. "I'll see you all back in the shop."

The nameless man snorted. "And yet, he never returned." A chuckle went around the table, but it died young.

ASHER NAVIGATED PAST THE STOVE, where something in a giant pot roiled as if for witchcraft. Early-season scallions lay half-diced on a chopping board. Brigitte poked her head out from the pantry. "I think you've missed her for today. But if you hurry—"

He did not linger to hear the rest.

Outside, a rabbit darted from the lane out of sight, and Marie popped up from the wagon's other side.

"Good afternoon, Asher." Her dress was the same bright blue as the sky.

"Hello," he said, suddenly feeling as interesting as a toadstool.

"Is your glasswork improving today?" Her voice was singsong as she packed something away in the wagon.

"Anything that doesn't leave me bleeding or burnt is an improvement."

"I'm sure you're being modest."

"I wish that were true."

As she straightened, he saw that she'd been putting away the jar— empty. Whoever those white leaves were for, it was a secret she wished to keep.

But then she regarded him directly. "I wanted to show you what I did with it."

"It?" Asher said.

"This, of course." She opened the top two buttons of her dress, pulling them wide. He was speechless. It was the singularly most erotic thing a woman had done in his presence since Aube was alive.

There, below the knobs of Marie's collarbones, his moon of glass hung by a leather lanyard, its blue made deeper from lying against her skin.

"I thought drilling a hole might crack it," she explained. "So I built this sling."

"Beautiful," he said.

She smiled. "A gift from you would be."

He stood straighter. "I mean it's beautiful on you."

She stepped closer. "I owe you an apology for rushing away the other morning."

"I owe you one, Marie, for not stopping when my bandage fell off."

"Are you better? May I see?"

Asher held out his thumb, a large and tender embarrassment. She unwrapped it, examining the wound. The angle of her body caused the moon to fall forward, dangling, light passing through it. Which caused him to notice the elegance, the grace, of her throat.

"Does it hurt much?" Marie straightened, continuing to hold his hand. The moon darkened, coming to rest against her body again.

Asher shook his head. "Not anymore."

CHAPTER 14

Brigitte was glaring at the plates piled on the counter, as if that would inspire them to clean themselves, when Asher bounced in, light on his feet.

"Well, look at you," she said, corking the sink's drain. "The human daffodil."

"Isn't that great news, about the cathedral commission?"

Brigitte turned on the water. "I doubt that's the cause of your sunny mood."

"Among other things."

"I've told you already to be careful."

"I can be trusted." Asher grinned away. "I won't break anything."

"I hope not." Brigitte tested the water, adding a little cold. "But do I need to point out that Marie is not the only person involved here?"

"I'm not worried about her."

She picked up a pan, the roux inside having dried into cement. "You're not listening."

"Here." Asher rolled up his sleeves and brought plates to the sink. "Let me."

"You're needed in the atelier." She took the plates and put them aside. "Marc said everyone should finish their current work today."

"I'm not good enough to have current work," Asher replied. "The others will accomplish more with me out of their way."

"I hear you disparaging your glass every day." At the stove, Brigitte lowered the flame under the pot of boiling broth. "Please stop. You've organized the wood, the raw materials, saving time and reducing waste. You earn your keep just fine."

He stood back a moment, considering. The view down her top, when she bent forward, was almost totally revealing. "I know what." He snapped his fingers. "Let me borrow your smock."

"It's fetching, I know," she said, straightening, "but not your size."

Asher held out a hand. "Give it to me anyway."

She gripped the lapels as if she were preparing to fight him for it. "What dastardly plans do you have for this poor innocent garment?"

He laughed. "To alter it, so when you're working by the kilns you can cool off without needing to display yourself to half the population."

"What if I like being displayed?" Brigitte laughed. "And receiving the attention of men?"

"I don't believe that."

"Perhaps you should. Besides, isn't thread work a woman's domain?"

"If you counted the hours I've spent sewing leather, it would amount to years. This cotton shouldn't pose too great a challenge."

Brigitte gave him a sideways study. "I don't have time to help in the atelier today anyway. I suppose I could temporarily withstand a regular apron."

"See? It's halfway to finished already."

"Wait here." Brigitte shut off the running water, marched into the pantry, and he heard the sounds of things being moved on shelves. Reappearing with an apron knotted at her neck and waist, she carried the smock and a sewing basket—spools, needles, scissors. "I am trusting you."

He put the smock and basket in the crook of his arm. "I know."

"One more thing." Brigitte stared into the sink. "I encourage you to consider displaying your happiness . . . tactfully."

He switched the basket to his other arm. "Why would that be necessary?"

"Most people who come here never attain the status you have reached."

"Me?" Asher laughed again. "I'm barely one step from the bottom rung. What status could I have possibly attained?"

She wristed back a stray hair. "Beginning to heal."

"WHAT WE DO HERE," MARC said, waving a hand around the warren where he and Henri worked, "is design"—he held up a sheet of paper so long the bottom curled on itself—"and assemble." He tapped on the half-built window on the table.

Asher sat straight on a stool, a swift swooped over their heads, snatching a bug before veering back toward the kilns.

As Marc flattened the curled paper, Henri plunked an ingot of gray metal on each corner. Together they placed a half-finished window atop the design, careful to match up the lines. Asher leaned over: a bird with a branch in its beak, lines beaming away from it like light from the sun.

"Today we're making the medallion for the top of the window. The Holy Ghost, bearing an olive branch of peace."

"Of course," Asher replied. The holy what?

"Every image is a collection of shapes." Marc held a square of dark green glass up to his ear, tapped it, and nodded as if to say he approved of the tone. From the tool rack he selected a glass cutter. "The discipline is to build the window precisely as designed. Not art, discipline."

Aligning the pane with the stencil, Marc worked the cutter in the design's lines. He poked the glass with one finger, and out fell . . . a leaf.

All at once it was simple for Asher, after all the sweat and danger of the kilns, to see this material cut much as he had worked leather. He'd thought all links to his past were gone, but here was a direct connection—with that little piece of green. "This is the most interesting thing I've seen since the war ended."

"It's just a leaf," Marc demurred. But then he saw that Asher was moved, and made eye contact with Henri. "Aren't we blessed to have this role?"

Henri nodded as Marc handed him the leaf. He slid it in beside other leaves on a branch, notching it into a groove of dark metal that separated the pieces of glass. Lastly, he took a short nail and, with a small hammer, tapped it in against the leaf.

"Horseshoe nails secure everything, until we can seal it with solder and cement. That's how a window shrugs off rain and wind for hundreds of years, affirming the people's faith, and inspiring them to greater devotion."

Asher's attention remained on the design. For such lofty language, the bird seemed crude, almost rudimentary. "Faith and devotion."

Marc slid his stool back. "Do you feel God's presence in your work?"

His stomach clenched. "I'm busy trying to do a good job. And not burn myself."

Marc picked up the pane of green, a neat square with the leaf shape removed. "I know that you struggle with your faith."

Asher gulped. "You do?"

"I see your hesitations when we pray. Working here may help."

Henri patted his chest with an open palm.

"Yes, this man found his faith strengthened here." Marc prepared his tool and green glass to cut another leaf, but set them down. "Gentlemen, let us give thanks."

He bowed, Henri following that example. While they prayed, though, Asher studied the design. The dove and sunbeams were made of identical shapes, cut the same size. Everything appeared blocky, like a woodcarving. The bird looked square, though everything about actual birds, breast to wing to tail, was curved.

"Our corner is badly lit." Marc crossed himself in conclusion. "So we can't see our work as it will appear. Once we hang a window, though, once actual light shines through?" He raised his hands, as if conjuring a cathedral. "A living biblical lesson."

Absently, Asher touched the window's edge. "Can I ask one thing?"

"It's the only way to learn."

"What if you put that leaf going the other way?"

Marc stiffened. "Excuse me?"

Asher waved a hand over the assembly. "See how all the leaves point in the same direction? That's not how branches work, of course. Leaves go in all directions."

"It's a matter of form," Marc replied. "Of discipline. In time you'll understand."

Asher reached over, working the nail free, and the leaf. "If you put it this way," he said, placing it in the opposite direction, "it looks like a real branch. Right?"

Henri raised one hand to his mouth.

Marc glowered, the vein in his forehead bulging. "Do you think so?"

Asher pointed. "You could have leaves alternating sides all the way down."

"I value your enthusiasm." Marc took a deep breath. "But you should know the first rule of window etiquette: Never touch another person's work."

"Oh. Oh, I'm so sorry." He hurried the leaf back as it had been.

"Not to worry." Marc patted his hand. "No harm done."

"I wasn't thinking." He slid the nail toward Henri. "I don't know anything."

Henri stood the nail on its point and raised the little hammer. But he paused, and, reaching with both hands, put the leaf back the way Asher had suggested. Raising his eyes at Marc, he smiled.

Asher felt a thrill of recognition. This man did not need words to express opinions, or kinship.

"I'll tell you what." Marc brushed the stencil with his hand, as if there were dirt to remove. "There is a certain naturalism to your idea. We'll give it some thought."

Asher was not sure, but it seemed Henri had winked at him.

"Meanwhile"—Marc collected a handful of ingots—"you must learn the discipline of forming lead."

SWIFTS ZIPPED IN AND OUT, feeding above the three men. A battered cast-iron pan sat atop a dirty flame, ingots melting. An older man poured the softened flow into a form, then cranked it through a press. A black goo came out the other side. A younger man did the same, but dripped sweat into the pot, which caused the hot metal to spit on his arm. His yelps frightened the birds away.

When the swifts returned, he was working the press, while the others fussed over something on the table as colorful as a flower, but hard as a wall and impossible to eat. The heat of the melting, as usual, drew mosquitoes into the shed. The humans worked and prattled, mindless of the fact that directly over their heads, for those who dart and swoop, there flew an incomparable feast.

CHAPTER 15

For the first time in years, Asher worked all night. It was a habit from his cobbling days, which annoyed Aube but sometimes was the only way to clear a backlog of boots whose delivery date was near. One dusk-to-dawn uninterrupted work session—with none of daytime's sense of passing hours, as shadows crossed the floor and the cat's napping places progressed from one end of the room to another, just the calm steady lamplight of night—and in the morning a line of handsome boots would be pieced and sewn, ready for the first buff of polish.

"Charge more," Aube said, baby Rachel clinging to her like a monkey.

"We have enough income."

"Charge more and you can work less," she said, her jaw set like a cornerstone.

He had no answer. How could he explain that she was beautiful when she was annoyed with him? How could he explain the pleasure of working till dawn?

Asher's ability to remain awake proved valuable in war. A man was easiest found in his home, was most vulnerable in the dark, and rarely held a firearm while he slept. Of his nineteen, Asher had dispatched nine in a manner that meant the body would not be found till morning: knifed in bed through all of the linens, strangled on the toilet with his shame still in the bowl, poisoned in the kitchen clutching his guts, shot in an overstuffed chair before a fire—the man's uniform neat but tie loosened, his glass of port on the side table unfinished and unspilled. By the time of gentle dawn's discovery, the assassin was long absent, trying to sleep, facing his nightmares.

Nothing so grim involved Asher on that particular night. He'd borrowed a lamp with the intention of doing a single task in his room. Lacking a supply of fabric, he scissored the smock's lower end away, fashioned a new hem, constructed a collar closer to Brigitte's throat. Flattening the smock on his bed, he tested different locations for the buttons until he was satisfied. One by one he anchored them in place. The job required barely an hour.

But when he sat in the calm of accomplishment, he noticed that a silence had come over the atelier. A feeling of sanctuary. Most nights he was first to bed, so this was a new experience. Completing the smock seemed hardly an exhaustive use of the night's small hours, an insufficient spending of the luxury of solitude.

Asher stuck his head out the window. Night birds called to one another, an owl across the heights asking, *Who cooks for you?* And another owl, from a hedgerow in the far fields, replying with the same inquiry. *Who cooks for you?* In his nighttime mind they were rabbis, supervisory and wise. He could picture them flying through the air toward one another. With voices melodic and soothing, they would nevertheless render pitiless judgment upon him, kindly pronouncing the damnation he deserved.

He had done terrible things. The deaths he'd caused did not come from the panic of seeing a charging line of soldiers, nor in self-defense against a flood of fire from a machine gun nest. They had been intimate, each one, men looking him in the eye as they died. Some fought or cursed, which made the job easier. A few, realizing their predicament, became strangely resigned. Those men were frightening, because Asher knew he was ending a person's life during a genuine spiritual moment.

At first he'd accepted an assignment as assassin under duress, knowing it was a test of his commitment to the Resistance. Rage beforehand, and the feeling of accomplishment afterward, meant that the second time, he volunteered. Soon it became his profession, while the others disrupted fuel deliveries, dismantled rail lines, collected information or provided it, hid fellow resisters, snipped communication wires, tainted military food supplies, sabotaged bridges, buried colleagues. Whenever he finished an assignment, the group always had a meal waiting for him. At some point his motives surpassed vengeance, and became a way to keep himself fed.

By the summer of 1947, however, he had not killed in more than two years. Marc and Brigitte kept him fed and housed. When he tore his shirt that time, washing in the river? They'd immediately given him another to wear. He spent no time stalking people, learning their habits, and finding the best moment to end their lives without losing his own. Instead, his thoughts were about glass: how to make it, how to make art with it. What's more, life was energized by his fledgling connection with Marie, which was small, yet full of promise.

Like the château that night, the whole world had grown quiet. When the war first arrived, noise was part of the violence. The terror of mortars, the panic of a bombing raid. On the morning the Allies arrived to deliver liberation, their aircraft bombing and warships firing and soldiers spending all the ammunition they possessed, it may have been the loudest day in history. Now there were birds. Winds that rustled the leaves. One afternoon he'd heard a dull droning, craned his neck, and at the peak of the roof spied a cone of gray paper, an army of wasps building its fortress. A day might contain the creak of a wagon wheel, the scrape of a shovel as it is plunged into a bin of sand, the rumble of a furnace devouring oak, the grunts of one man's exertions to keep the fire fed, a pot bubbling in the kitchen, splashes from down the hall as Henri shaved. The universe might rumble and roar, but with the war ended, it seemed to whisper.

What if he were to put it down? The grief, the hunger for revenge, the guilt over what war had required him to do. What would happen if he put it all down?

These questions made Asher restless, and he left the window. Grabbing the altered smock and the lamp, he headed for the back stairs. In the hallway he heard night's metronome, the other men snoring. His shadow descended ahead of him. Reaching the dining room, he folded the smock and set it at Brigitte's place. That was when he heard other noises. He was not the only one awake after all.

The sounds came from the atelier. Asher blew out his lamp and crept through the house, floorboards creaking, moonlight spilling onto the floors. He kept to the shadows. The noise continued, louder, no effort at concealment. Reaching the workroom, he pressed against the stones and poked his head around.

The fuel door to the main furnace was open, orange light dancing in madness on the far wall. A form came out of the darkness, it had many arms, an octopus fire demon. But when the monster reached the fuel door, its tentacles proved to be pieces of wood, which went one by one into the fire. Flames flared, the sound of crackling, and Asher realized this was how the kiln could be at full temperature every morning when the crew arrived. Someone fed it at night.

Now the remaining creature had two arms, which used a shovel to close the fuel door. As darkness filled the room, the fire feeder stood in profile.

Marc. While everyone slept, he worked. They all took the kilns for granted, and he never said a word. No wonder Brigitte adored him. He paused, hands together in prayer, then strode out of the atelier—passing inches from Asher, but so intent on getting to bed he did not notice. The man smelled of wood and exertion.

Alone in the foundry for the first time, Asher felt like an intruder. But his eyes adjusted to the moonlight. Here was a blowpipe, a workbench. It was familiar, a room he could navigate at night. Some of the tools' handles had been smoothed by his use.

Eventually he went to the assembly table, but it was too dark, he

couldn't see glass nor stencil. That was when he had his second idea of
the night, revisited the kitchen to fetch the lamp, and began the project
that would keep him working till daylight.

"WHAT IS THIS MESS?" MARC swept his shoe through sawdust. "Asher?
Asher."

He hurried over from the lead-melting forge. "Sir?"

"We can't have this. People will slip. Organic material will taint
the lead."

"Yes sir," Asher replied. "When I finished last night, I couldn't find
a broom."

"Finished what?" The vein rose on Marc's forehead. "What reason
could there be for you to be doing carpentry at night?"

"I couldn't do it while you're assembling. It would interfere."

"What would interfere? And that grin is not persuading me of anything."

"Yes sir. May I show you?"

"I'm out of patience." His face pruned with consternation. "Show
me what?"

"You told me you couldn't see the designs in here," Asher said.
"Only when they were installed." Striking a match, Asher lit the lamp
he'd used the night before, and slid it beneath the assembly table—a
clear glass surface on a wooden frame. Light streamed through, revealing Marc's half-finished medallion.

"What in the world?" He leaned over.

While Henri left what he was doing to come see, Asher lit another
candle. "Now you can see your work before it's installed."

"Interesting." Marc sat back, marveling, then pointed. "The dove's
too small."

"Do you think so, sir?"

"The sunbeams overwhelm it. Better to see the flaw now than when
it's permanent." He clapped Asher on the shoulder. "By heaven, you've
brought the day into our work."

"The light table is all right, then?"

"All right?" Marc laughed, and so did Henri. It was the first sound Asher had heard the man make, guttural and raw. "Is it all right?" Both men guffawed.

"Such hard workers we have here today." Brigitte swayed her hips up the steps.

"Judge not," Marc replied, still smiling. "Mirth has its purposes."

"Pish. So does not working. We call them excuses."

Henri stepped forward, motioning with both hands at the display platform.

Brigitte caught her breath. "You can see the window before you've made it."

"That was the idea," Asher said.

"You built this?" She patted the smock. "And this table? You must have been up all night."

"Actually, yes."

"Darling, look." She presented herself to her husband, smock open at her throat. "I can cool myself without inadvertently offering to nurse the entire crew." She made a mock pout. "No more ogling."

"Asher." Marc gazed at his window design. "I am grateful for your inventiveness—on my behalf and my wife's."

Asher bowed his head. Praise was not his goal; security of meals and shelter were, along with getting to follow the pull that window assembly had on him. What came to mind, oddly enough, was an afternoon when he was twelve, and showed his father that he could swim on his own all the way out of Bonheur Harbor, and back against the tide, he was strong enough, and how he had stood on the dock afterward, shivering and panting and proud, while his father took out his pipe and repacked it, tried to light it twice before giving up, and took his son by one shoulder, saying, "Well done, my lad. Well done."

The braying of a donkey made Asher jump as though he'd been poked with a pin. "Would you all excuse me a moment?"

Brigitte chuckled. "If we said no, wouldn't you leave anyway?"

"Go, go," Marc said, half listening, while Henri swept both hands away with open fingers as if brushing him out of the room. Asher hurried past a browbeaten Simon hauling wood, the scent of alcohol undeniably coming off of him, past the furnace where Etienne was making a gather and the nameless man waited to go next, into the house. A wind blew as though he swam against the tide, out to the courtyard, where he would find Marie.

THE BOUNCE LEFT ASHER'S STEP the moment he realized that she was in distress. Marie knelt, dirt on her burgundy dress, wrestling something under the donkey, and when Pétain shifted weight she gave his rear leg a swat.

"Good day to you, Marie," Asher called.

"Not at the moment."

Asher hurried around to her side. "What's the matter?"

"It all gave out at once." Rising, she flipped a strip of leather, and he saw immediately how the traces had worn through. Instead of securing the donkey to the wagon's wooden breech, the strap dangled in the dirt. "Pétain has been pulling by his collar all day, and I thought it was laziness. So I've been chiding him and using the crop, and I feel terrible. Plus, the harness looks beyond repair."

"May I?"

She threw her hands up. "See what miracles you can perform."

Starting on the donkey's good side, he followed the straps to see how they worked correctly, then examined the broken side. "The leather's pretty much finished."

"I'm glad the château is my last stop today. If the doctor didn't already get his delivery, he'd have had a fit."

Marie sounded sour, but Asher liked that they were having regular conversation, they could talk about any old thing. Sliding his hand between the girth strap and the donkey's belly, he felt no blisters. "Pétain is fine, at least. Not even a hot spot."

"I'm relieved. And I still feel guilty for scolding him."

Asher went to the rear of the wagon. "I bet he'll forgive you as soon as he's out of the breech." He brought a small carrot, which he held beneath the donkey's snout. The animal wrapped his thick lips around it, and ate it with the crunch of his big teeth.

Marie patted Pétain's flank. "You are sweet to show concern."

"I can repair the trace," he said. "But it won't last. You need new leather."

"Fine, but what do I do about tomorrow? When things in my garden ripen, I need to deliver them. Otherwise, they spoil."

Asher scratched his scruffy jaw. "I could fix it. By tonight, maybe."

Marie put a hand on her hip. "Don't you have responsibilities here?"

He had planned to sleep, to recover from his night of work. But his mind was already solving the problem, slicing excess leather from the collar and back straps to make temporary traces. "I can try. Walk your donkey home, and take an afternoon off."

"I wish. My greenhouse and fields always need more care."

"I imagine they do." Now he felt awkward, as if she did not appreciate the work he was offering. Had he misstepped? Pétain nosed his hand, which Asher held open to show it had no more carrots. "I'll bring the wagon as soon as I can."

"How?" Marie was smiling, but her question was a challenge.

"I'll pull it, I suppose. Shouldn't be too bad."

She continued to smile, her head tilted in such a winsome way that he felt himself lightening. As if her improving mood somehow gave him more oxygen.

"How about if I promise to bray and complain every chance I get? And I'll lean out of line to gobble any blossom I pass."

"Perfect." Marie's eyes twinkled. "But you don't know where I live."

"Which means either you tell me, or I spend the rest of my years wandering the earth, a lost pilgrim pulling his wagon, an undaunted saint—"

She laughed. "We can't have that."

"There are worse fates." Asher marveled that he could joke about wandering when he had done it for so long, and in such misery. Perhaps his time of pain was coming to an end. Perhaps he could put down the past. Not yet, but someday.

"Hello, all," Brigitte called from the kitchen door. She smoothed the smock on her chest. "Asher, I don't believe I properly said thank you."

"You're welcome, of course." He stepped nearer to Marie. "I am finding, this morning, that I can be useful. Please allow me to help you too."

She put a hand on her hip, and he felt that she was assessing him in some way, frank and skeptical, until her expression calmed. She had made a decision. "Do you know, down in the bottomland, where a bridge crosses the river?"

Asher grinned, private memories coming to mind. "I know it well."

"Cross there, then take every left you can till you see the metal windmill. That's my well pump. Come for a meal, please."

"Honestly?"

"A small repayment." She shifted her stance. "But listen."

Marie surprised him by reaching up, placing her hand on his scruffy cheek. Asher froze in astonishment. It was a caress, yet a thunderbolt: the touch of a woman, the stunning realization that his body's starvation for human contact was as severe as his hunger for food had been.

"Marie, I am definitely listening."

Lowering her hand, Marie met his eyes with hers. "Bring smooth cheeks."

"MAY I BORROW YOUR SEWING basket again?" Asher was speaking before he'd entered the kitchen.

Brigitte paused, her chopping knife poised over cubed sweet potatoes. "Shouldn't you be making glass? Don't Marc and Henri need you?"

"You know I worked all night. I earned some rest today."

She eyed the leather straps in his hands. "Doesn't look like rest to me."

"Besides," he continued, "the task I want to finish will benefit you."

"Oh really?" Brigitte waddled toward the pantry. "I am the benefi-
ciary?"

"Among others." He sniffed the soup simmering on the stove. Savory broth, sliced carrots tumbling like orange coins. "By the way, I
won't be here for dinner tonight."

She returned, handing him the basket. "Asher, please use caution."

"Of course." He started for the door, but Brigitte held his arm.

"You're moving away from pain, which is a glory to behold. But be
careful."

Asher searched her face, trying to understand. "I'll use a thimble."

As he hurried off, she spoke to the roiling soup. "If only thimbles
were enough."

MAKING ANYTHING WORTHWHILE ALWAYS TOOK longer than expected,
and the traces were no exception. The pieces Asher carved from the
collar and girth had different thickness and uneven wear. Brigitte's
needles were for household fabrics, and bent against leather. Asher
threaded two together, and they were firm enough to poke through,
but it was tedious work, and besides, Brigitte's warning replayed in his
head. What was she trying to say?

By the time he'd finished, so had the atelier's workday. Etienne and
the nameless man trundled up the stairs, Simon and Henri soon after,
with the heavy footfalls of the exhausted. Asher went visiting. Finding
Etienne's door open to draw the breeze through, he knocked on the
doorframe.

"Nobody home." Etienne lay flat on his bed. "Unless it's dinner."

"I wonder if I might borrow your razor."

The lanky man opened his eyes. "My razor?"

"You're always clean-shaven. If you wouldn't mind."

Etienne sat up. "This could be entertaining."

"I don't follow you."

Etienne rose and marched past. "Then do so."

In the water closet, Etienne filled the basin with hot water. On a shelf above sat a mirror the size of his palm. "Go ahead," he said. "Soap up, and I'll get you started."

"This is so kind of you." Asher scrubbed himself, his scruff softening.

"Perhaps," Etienne said, long fingers reaching into his sack. "Here is your razor."

What he handed over was a triangle of yellow glass, as thick as three windows, with a keen edge honed on one side. The other sides were wrapped in cloth, to protect the shaver's hand.

Asher eyed the glass skeptically. "Does it work?"

"It takes practice, I'll warn you." Etienne leaned against the wall, hands in his pockets. "But you've seen me every morning, smooth as a baby's bottom."

"Shouldn't be too hard." Asher glanced in the mirror, the memory strong of Marie's hand on his face. *Bring smooth cheeks*, she said. Drawing the glass edge to his throat, he took a breath for nerve, and began to scrape.

The first thing he did was cut himself. He winced, and Etienne laughed.

"All right," Asher said, a thin streak of red descending. "I'll be more careful."

Gradually he mowed away the scruff under his jaw, over his upper lip, around the knob of his chin. Etienne observed in silence, his expression as fixed as a monument's. Asher splashed the yellow glass in water, clearing it for the next stroke, while he watched himself grow younger with each salvo, less the vagabond.

At the end he wiped his face and looked down at the basin. There in soapy white floated the red evidence of his hopes.

CHAPTER 16

Henri knelt in the garden, leaving a trail of pulled weeds on the cobblestones.

If he continued in the same direction, Asher estimated, he would reach the jar in an hour. Every delivery, either Marie left a full jar for someone, or someone left an empty jar for her. Asher felt as if he had happened upon an illicit correspondence. He could have asked Marie about the jar any number of times. Instead, Asher's silence enlisted him in the conspiracy.

He took up the wagon's wooden slats, and set out down the dappled lane. The cart rolled more easily than he'd expected, and soon he reached the fork, where going right would take him up to the village. Someday he meant to explore up there. Maybe he'd introduce himself to the doctor. Maybe he and Marie would dine at a café.

"Maybe this wagon will grow wings," he groused, steering left and downhill.

Instead, Asher felt it pushing him. Gravity grabbed it and took charge. When he tried to stop, it dismissed his weight like a locomotive sweeping a tree limb off the rails. The braces veered and the wagon drove itself into the ditch, pitching Asher headlong.

He rose laughing, shaking dirt from his hair. The right brace jutted into the ground, but the wagon appeared unharmed, and so was he.

But he also realized his predicament. How easily the wagon's bulk could overpower him. The brake, positioned for the driver's convenience, was well out of reach from the braces.

Shoulder against the frame, driving with his thighs, he pushed Marie's cart back. It cooperated, and he angled the wheels to hold it steady.

Instead, the braces swerved, slapping him backward into the ditch. It was a hard landing. This time he rose in a rage, driving the wagon out with a roar. The moment he stopped pushing, though, it veered, bounding into brambles across the road.

Asher's resolve vanished. After all he'd survived, all he'd withstood, this would be an absurd defeat. He flumped down on a boulder to think.

All he wanted was to roll this wagon down to Marie's house. To be the hero of a broken harness, nothing more. Temptation came readily: to abandon this nuisance and return to the château for dinner. He wanted to beseech the cart—I lost my family, I lost everything, I am nowhere near whole—as if wood had the power to show mercy.

Rising, wiping dirt from his brow, Asher measured the descent, gauging it: the steep immediate pitch, four lesser switchbacks, then the broad flatland beyond. A distant glint from the river, where one day there had been a fish, whose great leap out of the water had told Asher that he too might rise above the past.

If the château had only fed him a single meal, it would have been enough. If he had spent the winter there, warm and laboring while the gray days shrank and then lengthened, but in spring was forced to leave, it would have been enough. If he'd had the company of others for some three hundred dinners, it would have been enough.

But now he was on the cusp of so much more: assembly, recovery, Marie.

She might have warned him about this slope. He imagined Pétain complaining each time they came this way. And there he found the solution: the donkey.

Asher untied from the braces, instead sliding his neck inside the donkey's collar. It had the pleasant earthen stink of all work animals. Using his thighs, he backed the cart out of the ditch, and with his feet slapping the road and his knees all but buckling, he guided the wagon down like a good, dependable beast.

He nearly careened at one switchback, but stood tall in the harness like Pétain, and the wagon obeyed. Laughing with relief, Asher imitated a bray—strained, but containing a note of jubilance.

At the river, he felt the sting of sweat where the coarse razor had cut him. He set the brake and trotted to the water's edge. Splashing his cheeks, wet fingers through his hair, he stood to catch his breath. The light had begun to lean toward evening.

Yet he paused there, considering. Marc's design was too formal, too rigid. Asher knew nothing about designing windows, but he knew that creation was not made of squares and triangles. Everything—the river, his fingernails, the cart's wheels, the road, the sky—everything was curved.

Which made him think of Marie, and how the day was waning. Asher ducked back into the collar and trotted the empty cart along at a rumble. He took all the lefts as she'd instructed, till he arrived at an intersection where there was no left turn.

It was either go right, or go straight. Had he passed Marie's without noticing?

From behind he heard a cheery ringing. Craning in the yoke, he saw a young girl approaching on a bicycle. He would have called to her to ask directions, but it occurred to him that he did not know what to ask. He didn't even know Marie's last name.

Besides, although she was barefoot, her hair streaming out long, the girl was pedaling in earnest, as if delivering medicine or late for dinner, speeding past him with a wisp of tailwind.

She had a companion: a rough mutt, mottled and lean, who chased along as if urging her homeward. Another dog that somehow had survived the war, it matched the girl's speed, and at the intersection they went straight without hesitation. In a few seconds he saw the girl's head farther along, above the grass, showing that the road soon bent left.

That was all Asher needed to take up his yoke and follow. Yet when he rounded the corner, the girl and dog were gone. They'd vanished.

He spied a metal fan on a set of rusty stilts, Marie's windmill. Beside it stood a stone bungalow, bearded in vines. In the dooryard sat a chair with an umbrella fixed to its back. Asher simultaneously felt the thrill of arrival, and doubt about his appearance.

He noticed a lily in bloom at the roadside, its bright cup like a yellow bell. "Perfect," he said, sliding out of his gear. The flower's petals arced away from the center in beautiful curves. How could Marc render such a thing in his blocky style? And when had Asher become a person who thought in stained glass?

He pinched the flower off at its base, taking it in hand. Pétain brayed in recognition of the cart, and Marie emerged from the house.

"You made it," she cried. "I'm completely impressed."

Yellow she wore, like the lily, a light summer dress. It favored her tanned skin, made her eyes seem brighter. Asher extended the flower toward her.

"Ah," she said, taking it in both hands. "Who knew you were a gallant?"

"I—" What did she mean? What did that word mean? "May I show the repairs?"

"Please." She was smiling, the flower beside her cheek.

Asher led her to the cart's near side, showing where he had repaired and reinforced, but he felt duller than Brigitte's sewing needles.

"You need to buy new leather soon," he concluded. "This material will not last."

"I will. Because of you, though, I will not miss one day's deliveries." Marie rested the flower on each of his shoulders, a royal bestowing knighthood. "Thank you."

All shyness was gone, he could feel her confidence. He noticed too the blue crescent of moon on its leather lanyard, below the notch of her throat. "It was my pleasure, mademoiselle. And I like your chair." He pointed at its umbrella.

"For those rare times when I get to read in the sun. Perhaps twice a year."

A tearing sound caused them both to turn their heads—Pétain was eating the grass outside his fence. He snorted and continued chewing. Beyond him, near the house, an orange blur leapt from the bushes and into an open window.

"Who is your furry friend?" Asher asked.

"Clementine." Marie led him down the walk. "Sweet, but very shy."

"Where could she have learned such ways?" Asher teased. "And what is that smell? It's lovely."

"Geranium," she answered. Bending, Marie grabbed a leafy plant beside the walk. She crushed a few leaves, and waved them under his nose.

"That's it exactly," he said. Until then, he had not noticed the delicacy of her wrists, the elegance. He nearly said so, but she lowered her hand.

"It occurred to me on the walk home"—Marie rested the lily on her shoulder like a parasol—"that you might have difficulty with the hill. Pétain always protests."

Asher laughed. "It was nothing."

"Really? Nothing?"

"Aside from getting thrown to the ground repeatedly. And losing my temper."

Now it was her turn to laugh. "I hope you've regained it."

"I have," he said. "I think I might be in Eden."

Quick as a starling, she spun and kissed his cheek. "Come in," she said, backing toward her house. "Please come in."

DINNER WAS A FEAST OF freshness, by the light of two small lamps. Vegetable stew from her garden, a wine so clean it might have been water, and a feeling in his head like getting more air with every breath. The room was tidy and cool, each thing in its place, a deep stone sink, a curtain at the back.

Briefly Clementine visited, making figure eights between his feet, but the moment he bent to pet her, the cat bolted away.

They chatted about weather and the season, Henri and his weeding. Asher told her about the cathedral commission, everyone's excitement, how he wished he knew more so he could participate, and the hours passed.

Courting was entirely strange. Asher had known fewer than twenty words when Aube was born in Bonheur, three streets away. Their families attended the same synagogue. One summer day when he was twelve and strolling the beach, he heard someone humming a Hanukkah song. Amused by the tune out of season, he followed it to discover a girl in the sand, contentedly digging a well of seawater, with a gothic dribble castle on its edge. Asher watched, spellbound. When water from below caused the wall to collapse, and the castle tipped, she finished the job with both fists and the sound of imagined multitudes being crushed.

He did not see her again till the marionettes. More years passed before they wed, more still before she bore Rachel into the world. Then the war came, swift as a harvest, but instead of crops gathered it was lives destroyed. And notions of devotion obliterated, because until her death he had never known that love contained such pain.

Here was this woman before him now, the shadow of her cheekbones deepening as the sun set, and he wondered what she had been like as a girl. She'd put his flower in a slender vase. Riverbank trees, she explained, were primarily poplars, whose cotton seeds fell in May like snow, or black willows, which grew like weeds but fell over from inner weakness, and both woods were no good for building or burning.

One of the oil lamps fluttered and went out. A bell might as well have tolled. Asher rubbed hands up and down his thighs. "Time for me to head back."

"It's farther in the dark," she answered.

"I'll have the moon to guide me."

As he stood, Asher realized he'd neglected to ask about her family. They'd chatted so easily, but the past could be a dangerous topic, given how thoroughly the war had spread its ruin. People generally kept their conversations in the present tense: the wagon, her delivery customers, the dwindling supply of glassmaking materials. What he did not know about Marie could fill an ocean.

Too quickly he found himself at the door, his awkwardness returning as he extended a hand to her. "I don't want to go yet. Work starts early, but I—"

She grabbed two of his fingers, the incompleteness of it somehow interrupting, silencing him, and she gave them the slightest tug.

"What do you mean?" Asher was surprised to find himself whispering.

Marie drew him close. The room fell away, there was only the still, quiet place where they stood. As she put her hand on his smooth cheek, Asher bent forward, and they kissed. He flinched: It was a different mouth, not the one he remembered, not the one he had kissed for years, morning and night, in passion and indifference, in their wedding ceremony and at the moment of her death. But as they continued, the warmth, Marie's breath, their touching bodies won the day. She tasted leather, he tasted wine.

He pulled away, needing a breath. "Marie—"

Her expression was resolute. She still held two fingers, pulled on them frankly while her eyes revealed neither fear nor hesitation, and he followed. From the table she took the remaining lamp, ducked under the curtain, and led him to the small room in back. Richly it smelled of lavender—that scent again, the memories—bundles of it, dry and hanging from a rafter. One small window, a rag rug underfoot, and Marie steering him by the tiller of his hand till he came to stand, astonished, beside her bed.

From a hidden corner the cat appeared, ducking past them, dashing away while Marie presented her back to him, the buttons on her dress as orderly as a procession of nuns. "Would you please release me?"

At first, no, all he could do was caress her shoulder, kiss her neck. But she pressed back against him, their bodies making contact, and years of hunger awakened.

Asher pulled her around, swept by the impatience in his blood. Her willingness made him a wagon racing headlong down a hill, or perhaps a fish leaping free of the river's will, and he kissed her throat and mouth.

In a minute they were naked, embracing, groping. Lamplight made a contrast of shadows: the luster of her tanned skin, the whiteness of everywhere else. Asher, who'd thought arousal was gone from him forever, felt it surge like the sea. Was this infidelity or freedom? Did this moment dishonor his wedding vows or accept that he'd been faithful to a ghost? The urgency of desire swept away all questions and concerns.

Marie tumbled backward onto the bed. Asher hesitated, amazed, taking her in. "Look all you like," she said. But he couldn't, the waiting was unbearable. Standing, his thighs against the bedside, he pressed harder, her knees parting, until their bodies aligned.

"Do something for me?" she asked.

He was surprised by her voice. "Anything."

"To the hilt," she said.

"I'm sorry?"

"Don't worry." Marie pressed her lips into a thin line. "As deep as you can go."

Aube had never been so frank, so bold, and it thrilled him. Asher raised himself, anguished and proud, and plunged. Marie cried out, her face wrought by pleasure. And yet in the next moment, she squeezed her eyes closed tight.

CHAPTER 17

He woke before dawn to the cat clawing his feet. Mostly Clementine used her pads, concentrating on his foot that stuck out of the covers. But there was that one little hook of nail, like a warning, pricking the softness of his arch.

Lying on his stomach, Asher felt Clementine climb his legs, pausing to knead his bottom, right paw and left, right and left, before ascending to the place between his shoulder blades, where one leg at a time she settled herself, and began to purr.

In his sleep the man on fire had been chasing him, screaming as loud as a foghorn. Now Asher did not move beyond opening his eyes. Cloth draped over the window, tangled bedding, Marie's face—which did not wear an expression of repose, but rather of consternation. Of concern. This woman worried in her sleep.

Amazed as he was to find himself in that place and time, Asher felt no sense of conquest, no manly bravado. This was the second woman he had slept with in his life. Her hand, curled under her chin, was tender in the mild light. He rolled over to pet the cat, who dodged his hand and thumped unceremoniously on the floor. But when Asher crept from the bed, Marie did not stir. He paused there, stooped under the low ceiling, to look once more: hair strewn, pale skin, one breast exposed. Untangling the knot of their clothes, he separated his things and stole into the other room.

Clementine eyed him as he dressed, cleaning one paw indifferently, till Asher reached to scratch her ears. Darting away, the cat trampolined off the little dining table and out the open window. He considered waking Marie, decided against it, and closed the door behind him with care.

Mist lay low on the fields, a foggy S snaking above the river, and in the pink light before dawn he took a moment to see the property he'd had no interest in the night before. Perhaps a sprig of mint would cure the sourness in his mouth.

Tools leaned against the bungalow like workmen on a break—hoes and shovels and rakes—but on rounding the corner he discovered a garden of easily a thousand lilies: red, orange, and, yes, a whole carpet of the same yellow as the one he'd given Marie. The lily he picked had probably escaped from the bounty that lay before him, carried by a rabbit or squirrel. How humiliating, that his gift was so small. How generous she had been to show gratitude for it anyway.

Beyond the lilies grew all manner of vegetables, beanpoles and climbing peas, tomatoes in frames to bear the weight of their fruit, hoop houses full of greens. Zinnias, daisies, and flowers he did not recognize flourished to one side. He remembered Aube's modest household plot, and the scale of Marie's gardens humbled him.

Yet Marie had pulled on his fingers. And he'd been unable to resist. Brigitte warned him to guard his heart, but all he'd found was kindness and warmth. And—heaven above—pleasure. Was delight allowed, in a world still in pieces?

Two minutes out of her bed, and already his thoughts were tangled rope. Pétain sneezed in his paddock, kicking one back leg, but giving Asher an idea, a way to clear his mind for the day's work ahead. The river. Perhaps sometime he would learn why Marie had wept, the day he unintentionally spied her. Perhaps he would see the fish leap to see the world again. Perhaps he had just done that himself.

ASHER PAUSED TO FEED THE goats. So many times he'd hurried past them on the way to the château, but he felt lighter, as if that morning contained extra time. At the fence of their pen, he waved dandelions he'd picked. The animals trotted stiff-legged over from the water trough, a stump, the roof of a discarded shed. His hair was still wet, his clothes clinging. Early sun glimmered through the trees.

He offered the flowers, the animals jostling, their narrow mouths open. One smaller goat was not getting any. Asher stretched his arm over the others for that one, to keep things fair. When they fought and butted each other, he found another clump of dandelions, tossing the flowers in the air.

The goats tossed their heads, searching him for more treats. When he held his palms open, one snorted while the others went back to their business.

"At least you're honest," Asher said with a laugh.

His optimism lasted all the way up the slope, but at the fork in the lane, he felt a darkness waiting. He'd been enjoying leaf shadows on the road, considering what shapes would portray them best in glass. Now something was off-kilter. He raised his head like a curious bird, and then knew: The metallic smell, the scent of the kilns, the first thing he had noticed about the château. It was missing.

With the sun clearing the horizon, he expected the atelier to be primed and busy, breakfast devoured, furnaces roaring. Asher had been preparing himself for the ridicule he would receive for being away all night. He resolved not to appear too proud about it.

He paused where he had once eaten a tomato and wept. The past lived barely an inch from the present. What was ravaged and broken lay right beside what was growing and green. Asher could not imagine returning to Bonheur, to boot making. Too much destroyed, too many wounds. There on the leafy lane, he allowed himself to acknowledge his desires: For this sanctuary to persist and his recovery to continue. He wanted to see Marie again, to know her, to couple with her in the new pleasure of her bold manner. To learn how to make windows that used colors and light to help people have faith. He wanted noisy dinners with opinionated men, including the one who won everyone's friendship without speaking a word, and the queen who reigned from the foot of the table. Noise was the companion of life.

Yet he proceeded into a morning that was eerily quiet. Where Henri had been gardening lay a clump of weeds. Odd. Asher checked, and the jar was there, full.

The kitchen door remained closed, no scent of bread baking, no banging of pots and pans. Even the chickens remained closed in their hutch.

Asher used the courtyard entrance. In a moment he would know. Not war again, please God. Not any of the hundred terrors his imagination supplied.

At the table the nameless man sat alone, spooning berries into his mouth. On his plate a heel of bread, a slab of cheese, and before him an open book. Eyes on the page, he gestured at the mug steaming by his bowl. "I had to make my own coffee."

"Where is everyone?"

The nameless man shrugged. "Still at the doctor's, I suppose. Perhaps keeping a vigil makes them feel less helpless. But I saw no point in it."

"What are you talking about?"

"You don't know?" The nameless man licked his fingertip and turned a page. "Did you work all night again?"

"Something like that." If the man could not be bothered to reveal his name, Asher felt no obligation to tell him anything.

"Well." He blew on his coffee, he sipped. "I can't imagine what place I'll grace with my presence next. But this temporary oasis is probably dried up."

Asher started pacing on the other side of the table. The nameless man was not going to volunteer any information. "Why would this place be finished?"

"It was in decline anyway, with the raw materials running out."

Asher stopped. "Please. What are you talking about?"

"The silicate, you dolt. And coloring chemicals. Haven't you been listening? The shipment from Danzig hasn't arrived."

"Of course I know about that. I mean, why would this place be finished?"

"As dim-witted about the château as you are about blowing glass." The nameless man put down his mug, tapping a finger on its rim. "Where have you been?"

Asher gripped a chair back with both hands. "Tell me what's going on, or I will wring your neck."

The nameless man flipped a page again. "It's not my fault no one informed you."

Asher started around the table.

"It's Marc, all right?" He raised both arms as a shield. "It's Marc."

Asher gripped the man's shirt with both hands. "What about him?"

"Yesterday, not an hour after you left. He had a stroke."

CHAPTER 18

That afternoon, Asher was waiting in the courtyard when Marie arrived. Wearing a peach-colored dress, she was still seated on the wagon when he told her.

"The doctor is my next delivery," she said. "I'm glad to know now, instead of being surprised."

"Also, I need to thank you," he said, offering a hand to help her down. "For a night I will remember a long time."

"I should be the one giving thanks." She leaned toward him. "I can still feel you."

"Well." Asher blushed, her frankness amazing him. "Even though I'm an idiot?"

"Why do you say that?"

"I saw your gardens this morning. Only a fool brings flowers to a gardener."

"No." She placed a hand on his chest. "Only a generous man."

"May I visit you again?"

"Of course." She bent to set the wagon's brake. "But I have a rule. Only one, but it's important. You may come only when you have been invited. If you ever appear at my house without an invitation, you will never be welcome there again."

"That rule sounds ironclad."

She smiled. "It is."

"Well, then please promise that you will invite me."

"Asher." Marie stood upright, as calm as he was excited. "You want to make love with me again."

"Of course, but not only that. It's as though we leapfrogged. I want to listen to you. I want to share more meals with you. I want to know you."

She fiddled with the crescent of glass at her throat. "Those ideas, I will consider. As for the coupling, I say yes."

Asher was too disarmed to reply.

"Now." She stepped around him to the back of the cart, surveying its contents. "What should I leave today? Quick things, I suppose, since Brigitte will be busy caring for her husband."

NO ONE RETURNED FROM THE village all day. Asher found a blowpipe in the middle of the floor, glass hardened on its tip. Someone had set it down hot, risking severe injury to anyone who stepped on it. He scanned the room, trying to reconstruct what had happened.

The sun was low when the rest of the château's residents trooped down from the village. They barely greeted Asher. Brigitte went straight to the kitchen, and made something that involved many whipped eggs and a mound of diced vegetables, mixed and poured into floury pie-crusts. Henri stood by, helping and slicing. The others idled in various chairs throughout the house, more fatigued by a day of worry than by one of hard work, while the château filled with the aroma of baking.

When everyone was seated at the table, Henri raised his hands and pressed them together, a call to prayer.

Brigitte rubbed his arm in gratitude. "I'm not Marc, and won't pretend to be. But let today's grace be a prayer for his survival, for his recovery."

"For all our sakes," the nameless man added.

"*Our* sakes?" Etienne growled. "What the hell does that mean?"

"You curse during grace?" Brigitte said.

"It means," the nameless man backpedaled, "so that we may continue the Lord's work here. The world needs it."

"I apologize." Etienne bowed toward Brigitte, but when he lifted his head Asher saw that his jaw remained flexed. "To Marc's healing."

"Amen," Asher blurted. It had come involuntarily, and felt immediately false. He too wanted Marc to be well for his own benefit. Yet he did not feel hypocritical. He had simply expressed hope in their language.

"Amen," the rest of them echoed.

They set to, chowing on both sides of the table. Henri took charge of washing the dishes, the nameless man assisting, which was out of character but perhaps a sign of penitence. Brigitte went upstairs to change out of clothes she'd been wearing for two days. Etienne remained in his chair.

Asher had waited hours for that opportunity. "What happened?"

Etienne looked him in the eyes, seeming eager to tell. "Marc was coming down the steps from the warren when he started to stagger. I was holding a hot pipe with the day's last gather. He collapsed faster than I could put it safely aside, and he fell on the cement. I lifted his eyelid and its irises had gone north. Brigitte came from the kitchen so quickly, it was as though we'd sounded an alarm. When she shouted his name, Marc did not respond."

Etienne sighed heavily. "We used Henri's wheelbarrow to carry him to the doctor, but he was too heavy for the climb. We could have made it with Mister No-Name, but he could not be troubled to accompany us. Luckily Pascal came whistling along, and saw the situation. Waving us aside, and after giving condolences to Brigitte as formally as an admiral in the navy, he pushed Marc the rest of the way. We could not keep up, and caught him as he was pounding his massive fist on the doctor's door."

"What's he like? Does he seem able?"

"The doctor? He's younger than I expected. But he served in the military, and flinches at nothing. When we arrived, he was treating a patient with a lacerated eye."

"I didn't need that image in my mind, thank you."

"This afternoon Marc was awake, but confused. His eyes kept dart-ing here and there. The rest of him might as well be a statue." Etienne sighed. "We're low on materials, we have a commission deadline, and our leader cannot move."

Asher felt dinner coagulating in his belly. "What will we do now?"

"Close the damper on both furnaces, until we know the situation better." Etienne went to the window and stared out into the courtyard. "It's time to put the fires out."

DESPITE SUMMER'S ADVANCE—LUXURIOUS SUNSETS and the late lingering light, dew on the morning grass as if the world were freshly washed—lack of work made the atelier a cold place. Asher possessed no talent for being idle. Nor, apparently, did the others. Simon built an elaborate platform of logs beside the furnace, attempting to nap on top with his old blue beret over his face, but daydreaming instead. Once, as he waved one hand side to side in the air, Asher came near, smelled wine—how did the man always manage to find it?—and asked what he was doing.

"Conducting a choir, of course."

Henri melted and molded lead until there were piles of it. Etienne scrubbed the cauldron. The nameless man read, or wandered down the lane, only to return to his books. Asher peeked at one, and the title was in Greek. He went to his window upstairs, hoping to see Pascal or Eu-clid pulling a loaded wagon up to the château. But there was no potash to mix with the sand, much less Marc to order a resupply. Days passed like missed opportunities. Nights, the man on fire opened his mouth to scream, but what came out were flames.

Then it rained. A string of days, gray and damp. The château, with-out furnaces to heat and dry the air, grew chilly and bleak.

One afternoon, wandering among the empty rooms, Asher found a study with the door ajar. Inside there were shelves of books all cob-webbed in place, a window frozen half an inch open, a chair so dusty it was clear no one had sat there for years. But on the desk there were several rolls of the same paper Henri and Marc used for making designs. Alongside, there sat a box of pencils and charcoals.

For a moment, the world seemed to slow. He picked up a chunk of coal, blacking his fingers, and nostalgia beamed upon him like sun into a glade.

In his young days, when his mother had dinner to make or his brothers needed her for some reason, Asher's grandmother would hand him paper and pencil and tell him to go somewhere and sketch. Hours passed, till his mother wondered where he'd gone and his brothers were annoyed he had not come for supper when called.

His grandmother loved Asher's drawings. "I'm a vain old woman," she declared, sitting as stiff as a bristle-brush while Asher drew her portrait over and over. Cleaning the morning kitchen, reading to one of his brothers in the afternoon sun, resting by the hearth at night. He became an expert in her cheekbones, her chin, the worry wrinkle across her forehead. Yet the drawing his mother loved best was of her hands: full of shadows, twisted like apple boughs in winter. His grandmother said the picture was cruel, however, and shuffled away looking wounded. Asher put his pencils aside.

Till now. Rolling the chair to the desk, he wiped it with his sleeve, and sat. Asher considered the room, looking for a place to start. There: an umbrella stand in the corner, in whose shadows and shape lay all of life's complexity. Before the rain had ended, Asher saw the château with new eyes. The world provided an encyclopedia of subjects, as if every object existed to be seen, and studied, and rendered on paper: his hand, a lamp, a vase of flowers.

"What are you wasting time at now?" the nameless man needled on the way past a chair where Asher was working.

He did not look up. "If I'd been drawing all this time, I would have made better boots."

The nameless man snorted in disdain, but Asher did not hear. He was busy finding something else to sketch. His compulsion lasted one day into the next, as he repeatedly unrolled a fresh surface of paper, took hold of the coal, and set to work while the weight of the atelier's quiet burdened him not in the least.

How could it, when the supply of perspectives was infinite? His foot from above, bony and pale. A tree from below, the leaves' green and many-fingered canopy. The dinner table from a corner, looking down the plane of it as a farmer might regard a field before beginning to plow. Hours could go by, half a day. No thoughts of violence, of weapons or mortality. Time did not pass as much as cease to exist.

"I was wondering where you'd vanished," Etienne said one morning, on his way to the winding stairs. "Perhaps you are rewriting the Bible?"

Asher lay on the floor, sketching the shadow cast by his bed. "On the first day God made light, and said that it was good."

"Coming to breakfast is also good," Etienne replied.

"I'll be right there."

But Etienne had eaten and left for the village before there was any sign of Asher downstairs.

He progressed to more complicated images. A rack of blowpipes in the atelier's dark corner, steel-gray against black. The stack of wood on which Simon dozed, its logs rough and raw, while golden light poured in the open doors.

One day, perhaps it was inevitable, he looked in a mirror. The one on a shelf beside the sink, with which he shaved daily for Marie. But the mirror was small; he could only view pieces of himself at a time.

The higher hairline? His father. The narrowed jaw? His eldest brother, Albin. The eyes, however, were like no one's. They had witnessed things none of his kin had seen.

Page by page, a sensation grew in Asher that drawing was more than a pastime. Something about it might be important—if not what he drew, then what he saw.

"I said clear the street," the soldier barked at him, waving his gun at Aube's body. "Remove that garbage or you will be next."

Staggering with grief, gasping, Asher rolled his wife over, revealing Rachel beneath, and the soldier flinched. He must not have known the woman he shot was holding a child. Asher saw that. Hurrying Aube into the house, he laid her on the threadbare couch, where her tongue lolled out to one side. He saw that too. Returning for Rachel, whose hair had spilled over her face, a rose of maroon bloomed among the flowers on her frock. He saw that as well. The blood of them both on his shirt, his hands, he had seen that, a permanent stain upon his memory.

By the time he thought to grab Rachel's beloved Dolly, troops were marching up the street. He stood at the window, trembling with rage, as they passed. Asher creaked the door open. There lay Dolly, trampled, button eyes broken. He saw all of that.

Oh, and the vengeance he had wrought as retribution for those sights, the calculated spending of that anger, the discovery that fury was a form of love, and as a result with these same eyes he had witnessed nineteen deaths—including the one who did not need to die, the one he hadn't intended. Asher saw and saw and saw.

Yet when he finished with the mirror, pencil down, the drawing he laid on the bed did not reveal any of that hideous history. Instead, it showed a man remarkably ordinary: decently fed, skeptical but alert, enlivened perhaps by the exhilaration of a new lover, though so far it had only been the one time. Asher's darker truth remained as concealed as his religion. To his eye, the portrait was a lie.

On he worked, though, the atelier empty while dust motes floated in the air, his pencil in motion like a spoon stirring perpetual soup. His window, a candle, a feather curled on the ground. A basin, his bed, the CHÂTEAU GUERIN sign.

The nameless man looked over Asher's shoulder. "I can tell, that's the wall there." He pointed. "But what is that silly outline across the page?"

"My shadow," Asher replied. "The shape of my head when I started drawing. I'll add another one when I finish too. This picture will contain the passing of time."

The nameless man moved away. "Simpleton."

Asher found the gardens, which provided a chaos of shapes, lines, colors. The natural world was the most interesting subject possible. A single peony blossom, with its byzantine petal folds, held his attention for the better part of two hours.

Henri tapped him on the elbow, startling Asher from his reverie.

"Hello, my friend," Asher said. "Is it time to go back to work?"

Henri shook his head, an exaggerated mournful expression, but he tapped the drawing and clapped his hands.

"This?" Asher scoffed. "Too crude for applause. But I do have one I'm fond of."

He flipped back in the roll, and there was the tulip, late for the season, each petal a simple, finite shape. "This one here."

Henri made both hands into fists, and shook them.

"You approve?"

He held his hands out. Asher passed him the paper and pencil, and Henri made additional marks on the page. He paused to think, then scribbled more before passing it back. He had redrawn the flower, but changed. Each petal was divided into triangles or squares, with heavier lines between them.

Asher studied the drawing, trying to understand, until Henri ran his fingertip along the darker lines. "Ah," Asher said, "this is the window version."

Henri nodded with enthusiasm, pointing again. This square he outlined, that triangle, identifying each piece of the image. It made a rough approximation of the flower, but only if it were made out of blocks.

"Very nice," Asher said. "But what about the roundness? What about this?"

With the pencil, he drew his own breakdown of the tulip: one color of glass for one side of the petal, a darker one for the other half, and the tip made of two curved pieces that resembled the actual flower's shape.

Shaking his head, Henri drew heavier lines where the curved pieces would meet.

"It would take too much lead?"

Henri made a circle of his arms, and staggered around with stutter steps.

Asher laughed. "Making the window too heavy?"

Henri smiled, then rubbed his fingertips together.

"Also, too expensive?"

Grinning, Henri clapped him on the arm.

"How is it that I am completely won over by you, my friend?" Asher was smiling too. "When you have not said a word?"

Henri made a muscle pose, his arms raised and flexed, before leaving for his garden.

Asher reviewed the paper. He knew nothing about assembling stained glass windows. But he was certain: the detailed drawing looked better.

CHAPTER 19

S ome men are better than others at boredom," Brigitte observed, kneading dough on the cutting board. "You look like a rank amateur."

"I had my own business before the war," Asher replied. "Anytime I wasn't working, my family was still getting hungry for the next meal."

She paused, blowing a dangle of hair out of the way. "The difficult part for me is not knowing. How long till he is well? How long till we have sand?" She shoved the dough aside, tossing flour on the board and kneading again. "Someday we'll have a working telephone again. I will call those strong galoots and order their next delivery."

"I could probably find them with a day or two of walking."

"Thank you. But that would be like raising the sails when the captain's not aboard." She flattened the dough with the heels of her hands. "We have to wait."

Asher wandered out to the courtyard. He gazed down on the valley—animal pens, croplands, the serpentine river—and allowed himself a memory. The roof of their home in Bonheur needed a costly repair, so he'd done an all-night work session. By midmorning, he was starving.

Asher went home, expecting his wife and ten-month-old Rachel to be at play, chirping like birds, or perhaps the baby in her high chair gumming a wedge of apple while Aube worked in the kitchen. Instead, the house was silent. They were always in the house when he was there, so the stillness felt unfamiliar. His body tensed. Slipping off his boots, he picked up a piece of firewood. Aube's boots by the door, Rachel's pink jacket on its hook, meant they were home. But it was too quiet. Log at his shoulder, he slid in his socks across the snug kitchen and sitting room, and crept up the stairs.

They were on the bed, in light made milk-blue by a thin curtain that the breeze raised slightly and let fall. Aube lay bare-breasted and splayed, her legs under the blanket, so that she looked like a mermaid. Rachel, also naked, her adorable tiny bottom upward, nuzzled against the mother-warmth. Asher's arrival did not wake her, though she made an unconscious sucking sound with her mouth.

He lowered the piece of wood. What a thing to discover, standing there: How he had climbed the stairs ready to kill. How instead her tiny lips, shaped like cupid's bow, held a thread directly to his heart.

"Why don't you come with me?"

Marie stood at the courtyard gate. It took a moment for him to register. She wore a dress the gray of a dove, with large white buttons up the front. Wrenching himself from that memory felt physically painful. "Excuse me?"

"Brigitte said the atelier has stopped." Marie came closer. "Why don't you join me?"

Asher looked around, confused. "To your house?"

"Naughty boy." Marie smiled. "Maybe, if there's time. But I meant on my delivery route. No village stops today, no doctor. It's all Clovide. Keep me company."

"I haven't been to Clovide since the day I first saw you."

"You look better now." She tugged on his shirt. "Less vine, more tree."

Asher considered the château, its smokestacks issuing nothing. "Why not?"

"Exactly." Marie backed away toward her wagon. With a last glance at the place where he'd been standing, remembering, mourning, Asher followed after her.

PÉTAIN PULLED THE WAGON SEEMINGLY without effort, down the hill, past the river, and across the croplands. All that time Asher barely spoke. The landscape looked different, because he no longer saw with the eyes of a starving man. They were going to Clovide. He searched around his seat, wishing he had a club, a knife, anything. But what he found? Lilies. Cucumbers.

Marie did not try to draw him out. Pétain's muscled rump rolled them through a tidy vineyard, vines cultivated up their posts, to a bridge. The wagon was nearly across before Asher recognized it.

"Wait a moment," he said, squeezing her reins hand.

This was the bridge where he had met the brothers cooking a stolen chicken. That vineyard had given him hope. The row of damaged houses stood as before, but two had been restored.

"You've been here before," she said, climbing down from her seat.

"It feels like a century ago." The repaired houses, he saw, had glass in the windows, clothes drying on a line. "I'm glad to see a few homes in better shape."

"That's France. One small fraction rebuilt." She tugged Pétain's bridle and he ambled along with her stroll.

They arrived at a bank, a man emerging at once. He wore a stiff shirt with sleeve garters, and his hands fluttered like worried birds. "I was afraid you weren't coming."

"M'sieur Francois." Marie smiled. "When have I ever failed you?"

He pulled a watch from his vest pocket. "But you're late."

Asher gritted his teeth. In the presence of a flighty man, he did not like being without a weapon.

Marie strolled to the rear of the wagon, though, as easy as a breeze. "M'sieur, you've been winding your watch too tight."

Francois followed, hovering till she gave him a look that made him step back. Reaching into the wagon's bed, she lifted out a giant bouquet. "Will this suffice?"

"Lilies." He reached out, but she held the bouquet away to one side. He took a shallow breath, lowering his hands. "My beloved Alix loves lilies."

"Doesn't everyone?" Asher asked, his voice low like it was not a question but a challenge. Or at least a reminder that he was present, and watching.

"I hope she is pleased, then," Marie said, giving him the flowers.

Immediately his hands stopped shaking. He heaved a great sigh, then tilted his head toward Asher. "Your sweetheart?"

"My servant," Marie replied.

"Business must be good, if you have a hired hand."

"A successful farm is the least I can do to honor my husband's memory."

"You've landed a good job," the banker called up to Asher. "The boss walks while the servant rides."

Asher did not know how to answer. Her servant?

"Only for the moment." Marie laughed. "It's the same as how President Auriol imagines himself with the French people. He works while we roll along."

"In his dreams," the man replied.

"M'sieur Francois, my friend was noticing that a few houses by the bridge are inhabited again. Could you please tell him how that is possible?"

Holding the flowers in one hand, the banker put the other behind his back as if he were addressing an assembly. "The latest national tally I've seen said the war destroyed one and a half million structures. Schools, churches, hospitals. Homes."

"And tell him how a few manage to get rebuilt."

He wagged his head. "It's certainly not due to our loan business, which is pathetically slow."

"What is it due to, then?"

"The economic engine of this region stalled with the war. Now it's running again, not fast but at a low idle. Families who own those businesses are first to rebuild."

"What businesses are they?" Asher asked.

The banker rolled his eyes melodramatically, as if the answer were everywhere, in all directions. "Champagne, of course. We stand in the very heart of the Champagne region. And the world is celebrating again. A dozen families own the vineyards, cellars, and so on." He shrugged. "The repairs are a sign of family wealth, not a result of government largesse."

Marie nodded. "So, our president has work to do?"

"Like every man and woman in France, yes."

"Exactly." Marie climbed into her seat. "You'll put the payment in my account?"

The banker sniffed the flowers as he departed. "For lilies, I will add a gratuity."

Asher kept an eye on him until he'd gone back inside. "I don't trust him," he said. "People who are nervous usually have a reason."

"Very astute," Marie said. "A week after the war ended, 'my beloved Alix' caught him in a flagrant celebratory adultery. Every Wednesday, as atonement, he gives her flowers. One week I was ill, and she assumed he was having a new affair."

Asher exhaled with relief. There had been no danger in the banker, only an ugly domestic fear. "And the gratuity?"

"His guarantee of my discretion. And punctuality next Wednesday."

"I hope his tip is gigantic, to cover the expense of employing your servant."

She gave him a swat. "I had to say something, or the gossip would reach Paris in an hour. Which is bad for business. Everyone wants to help the poor widow."

"Beloved Alix must be an intimidating person."

Marie laughed. "A house of a woman, with three thick black hairs on her chin."

Asher laughed along. "Now I'm frightened of her too. Maybe the president can help." Not knowing better, he parroted what Etienne had said at dinner a few nights before. "He seems like a fine and promising man."

"You must be joking," Marie snapped. "The man is a walking compromise. It's the opposite of leadership."

"Is that right?"

"Auriol is a blank. A null. A twit, who prefers casting for trout to governing."

She tossed the reins to urge the donkey along.

Asher did not dare to reply, the only sound coming from Pétain's shoes, clopping up the road. "Once I entered the château," he confessed, "I stopped following politics."

"I'm not interested in politics either." Her tone was still sharp. "But I am acutely interested in the well-being of our country."

They were passing a street parallel to the cathedral, and Asher leaned in his seat for a look. "But you are a vegetable farmer. What can you do about any of it?"

"And you are a laborer at a glass foundry," Marie answered. "But if we do nothing, then everyone is allowed to do nothing. So I stay informed, and look for every opportunity to make even the least difference."

"Is every delivery day like this? Gossip and tidbits?"

"From here forward, it's more than gossip."

Their route veered away from the cathedral, Asher craning his neck as they passed. Scaffolding latticed its exterior, men working away. Then the wagon rounded a corner and his view was gone.

THE GROCER WAS SLOVENLY, HIS apron stained and beard haggard. But he greeted Marie waving both hands and giving a great belly laugh. As the wagon stopped, he stretched a hand up to Asher. "Jean-Jacques, *à votre service, m'sieur.*"

"Asher. A pleasure to meet you."

The man's grip was strong and unhurried, while he made unapologetic eye contact, and in those two seconds of assessment Asher felt a bald aggression.

"I have something sweet for you," Marie said, climbing down from her seat.

"*Ma cherie*, nothing could be sweeter than your presence."

"You are a terrible liar," she parried.

The grocer followed her to the wagon's stern. "Wait till you see," she teased, hoisting out a small basket with a cloth covering.

"Let's make a game of it. Can I identify this thing by its smell?"

Marie held the basket forward. "Be my guest."

Jean-Jacques leaned forward and took a deep, somber sniff. "Too easy, mademoiselle. Those . . ."—he circled a finger over the basket—"are peaches."

Marie whisked the cloth off the basket. "Correct, as always."

"I did not come to the pinnacle of my profession by having the snout of a hog."

The man winked at Asher, as if to say, What pinnacle? His manner was so winsome, Asher suspected it was phony. There was some larger game.

"Keep the cloth for now," Marie was saying, "to discourage fruit flies."

Jean-Jacques bowed. "I will return it in immaculate condition. But first—"

As the grocer reached behind his back, Asher recognized the high singing that a sharp blade makes as it leaves its scabbard. He stood, snatching up Pétain's reins, ready to snap them on the animal's back if they needed a quick escape.

The grocer placed the peach on the knife's upturned blade, rolling it once around so that two neat halves fell into his palm below. "Let us break bread, so to speak."

"No, thank you," Marie said. "It is for you, and your customers."

"Ah well." Jean-Jacques reached up to Asher, half a peach in his open palm. His other hand held the knife, but also the rest of the fruit. Any attack would take two steps, and he could be gone before the grocer had finished the first one.

Asher took the peach half, making a quick bite. "Delicious," he said, sitting again. "I'm grateful to you."

Marie reached into the wagon for the rest of her delivery, the picture of nonchalance. "What do you hear of the world these days?"

"Good things."

"The cucumber count is wrong here. One moment." She stepped onto the tailgate and tallied them one by one. "What have you heard?"

"I am always amazed when a woman shows interest in affairs of state," Jean-Jacques observed, wiping the knife on his apron and sliding it away behind his back.

"It enlivens the day," she said, still counting.

"*Et alors.*" The grocer took a healthy bite of his peach. "This man named Marshall, who is America's foreign secretary, gave a speech last week at the university of Harvard. In which"—Jean-Jacques held one finger aloft—"he pledged billions of dollars for the reconstruction of Europe. Not only France, but Britain, Belgium, Poland."

Marie straightened from her task. "Billions? I don't believe it."

"I heard it on the radio news." One more gobble, and he had finished his half of the peach. "This Marshall says France is on the verge of economic collapse. Instead of having currency reserves, our nation is two billion dollars in debt. Aside from Paris, where people drink and screw and stay out listening to jazz till the sun comes up, the rest of the country is barely surviving. He wants us to rebuild, with American money."

"Amazing." She handed him an armful of cucumbers, so many he had to juggle them in his arms. "Do you believe it?"

"Ah, who believes anything these days?" He waddled to a bin by his shop's door, dumping the vegetables in. "The radio news also interviewed a professor at the Sorbonne. He said the goal is not to improve our lives, but to reduce political danger. A stronger France is less susceptible to communism, which the Yanks hate even more than Hitler."

"Well." Marie pulled out a bag of garlic cloves. "Let them have their politics, so long as it helps us to eat."

"They think . . ." Jean-Jacques laughed, enjoying his joke before he had spoken it. "They think the French people are excellent chefs. They do not understand that this is only so because we are excellent eaters."

While he guffawed, Marie's eyes met Asher's and he relaxed his defenses. She trusted this man. Climbing aboard, she noticed Asher was holding the reins, gave him a quizzical look, and he placed them in her lap.

"*Au revoir, mes amis.*" The grocer waved them goodbye with both hands.

The next deliveries were all business: a shop that wanted zinnias, a family whose basil had a blight so they were buying it this year, a little boy who followed the wagon till Marie reached down and handed him a peach all his own.

"This is the last," Marie told Asher, as they stopped outside a low-roofed shop. Painted on the large front window: LA MEILLEURE DE COIFFURES.

"Agnes?" Marie called as she climbed down. "Are you busy?"

"Always," came the reply from inside. "Give me a moment."

Marie lay a hand on Asher's jiggling leg. "I know it's tedious, so thank you."

"This is the longest daylight time I've spent with you."

She paused in her climb down from the seat. "It's also the longest we've gone with our clothes on."

Asher smiled. "Could we visit the cathedral on our way back?"

"We'll be approaching the bridge from a different direction." Her faced pinched in calculation. "Let's see how the time looks."

"Who's this one?" A big, brassy woman barged out of the shop, her hair pulled high in curlers. A metal spring slapped the door closed behind her. "Your bodyguard?"

Marie was grinning. "That's exactly what he is."

Agnes was holding scissors, Asher noticed immediately. Once in the war he had seen Levi use scissors to execute a man, the commander of a tank unit, by closing the blades and stabbing them straight in under the jaw, the gush as his brain emptied, a mess all the way down Levi's arm. Now Asher kept his eyes on the woman's scissors, ready to pounce if she raised them one inch.

But in the next moment she tucked them in a pocket and sniffed at Asher. "Looks too peaceful to be a bodyguard. Couldn't protect you from a ten-year-old terror." Her expression changed to concern. "Or certain ten-year-old terrors, anyway."

"Speaking of which . . ." Marie dug in her pocket, handing over a small glass jar. "The doctor gave me this for the infection. He must take one at breakfast, one at bedtime, until they run out."

Agnes raised the jar, examining it. "These tiny things will stop his fever?"

"And swelling, and suppuration." Marie smiled. "I know this doctor, and I trust him."

"Oh, they're all quacks." But she tucked the jar away in her apron, which seemed to have dozens of pockets. "How many today?"

"Thirty-six, if you can."

"You'll empty me out. And I should hurry, there's a customer waiting." She opened a container in the shade, removing eggs and nestling them in a straw basket.

Marie went forward, seeming to examine Pétain's braces, though Asher could see that it was a pretense. "Did you hear about the Marshall idea?" Marie called.

"I did. The whole filth of it."

Next she checked his bridle. "Billions for rebuilding? What filth could there be?"

"It will also fund the rebuilding of Germany." Agnes spat. "A pox on them all."

"Impossible." Marie stopped her pretense of preoccupation. "After what they did to this continent? And an entire race of people? I don't believe you."

"Go ahead, close your eyes and be the fool." Agnes went back to counting eggs.

"This is your devotion to communism speaking again," Marie said.

"Without doubt or apology. Who defeated Hitler? Russia, that's who."

"There were the beaches," Asher ventured. "I saw that with my own eyes."

"True," Agnes said, addressing him. "And congratulations on surviving it." She rested on her hip a hand that held a small brown egg. "I'll grant the Yanks their splendid invasion, with my thanks and a five-franc tip. But it was primarily a diversion, pulling Hitler's forces west so Russia could storm in from the east, fight the real war, and bring the actual defeat."

Again, Marie caught Asher's eye. "Agnes, you have a creative view of history."

"Do you understand how diabolically clever this Marshall Plan is?" She bent back to the egg bin. "If Russia marches, Western Europe will be the battleground again, while the Yanks sit on the far side of the Atlantic and throw parades to celebrate a war they tell themselves they won. The tragically misled people of Germany will have to form an army and fight, because they'll have become so deeply indebted to the Americans and their ruthless, calculating Marshall."

Agnes caught her breath. One of her curlers had come undone, and she coiled the hair back into place. "There." She handed over the basket. "Thirty-one is all I can do."

"You'll add them to my tally?"

"I'd starve otherwise."

"I hope your boy is running around making a nuisance of himself in no time."

"So do I. Meanwhile I've left someone under a dryer, and should get back to her." She kissed Marie on both cheeks. "Again in two days, my dear?"

"As sure as the sun rises."

Agnes went back inside, the door slamming behind her. Asher sat like a lump, lost in confusion. "Is she right?"

"Agnes and I often disagree. But in the haystack of what she says, there is often a needle of truth." She gave the reins a snap. "Whatever that is these days."

THEY WERE RIDING IN SILENCE toward the bridge when Marie spoke out of the blue. "The contractor for the cathedral's stonework is on the take," she declared. "Everyone knows he's robbing the church but the docent, who cannot be bribed. So they paid his wife to form a children's choir." Marie steered around draft horses pulling a hayrick, their chests like barrels. "Money for hymns, yet people are starving."

"You would have made an excellent Resistance agent."

Marie shook her head. "I had to stay on the farm. Away from town and soldiers."

"But your authenticity would have helped. Farmers often had significant roles."

"Not a chance, I tell you."

There was a commotion ahead, and Pétain slowed. "Why not?"

"Because"—she drew the reins to direct the donkey right, away from the noise—"I would have been raped a hundred times."

As they drew to a stop, the hubbub neared, voices shouting just off the square.

"I don't like this," Asher said. "Pull into the alley."

"It's only hooligans," Marie replied. "Afternoon drunks, nothing to worry—"

"Into the alley, damn it."

"Since when are you in charge of the driving?"

Asher jumped down from the seat, darting around in the search for a weapon. All he could find was a cobble, a square road stone broken loose, which he seized as the shouters spilled into the square. He peered at them from behind the wagon's bed.

Five drunk men tugged a sixth along by a rope. One held a sheet of tin, which he drummed with a piece of wood, *bang bang.* If the clamor was supposed to raise a crowd, it had the opposite effect, the square empty but for a bronze statue of a rearing horse.

The man being dragged seemed dulled. Either he was drunk too, or numbed to what was happening. Meanwhile, one of the men—he wore a sword on his hip and seemed the most sober—climbed onto the statue and threw a length of rope over the horse's extended foreleg. Only then did Asher see that the rope's other end was a noose.

"Poor Antoine," Marie said, still in her seat.

"You know him?" Asher felt his heart thrumming: the electricity he had known so well. All day it had been idling, and now he was galvanized.

The drunkards kept shouting, as if their quarrel were with silence. The man in ropes was not speaking a word in his own defense.

"He owns a dry goods store. He was a customer of mine, but no more."

Alertness passed through Asher's limbs, a reawakening. "Why not?"

"Cheap as a miser on holiday. He'd be a few coins shy when I delivered, a trivial amount, but it happened every time. Agnes suggested I keep track one month, and when I added it up, he had cheated me the cost of a full delivery."

"That's hardly a hanging offense."

"I'm sure he's done nothing that merits execution," Marie said. "Antoine is far too careful about protecting his self-interest."

"Then what is this about?"

"Frustration." Marie's voice was flat with indifference. "Someone's business fails, or wife leaves, or rash won't stop, so he gets drunk with similar types and they find some poor soul to declare a collaborator, or spy, or whatever that week's blame is."

"But to hang him?"

"Don't forget we're in the land of the guillotine."

Now the men were jerking Antoine forward, bringing his neck nearer to the noose. But he did not go willingly, squirming against his restraints.

"Can we leave?" she asked. "I don't want to see a man executed without a trial."

"Neither do I." Asher emerged from behind the wagon, gripping the stone in his hand. He marched toward the group of them, growling, "Let him go."

The men all wheeled, looking as surprised as children caught stealing cookies.

"Who are you?" the sober one asked. "Who put you in charge?"

Asher did not slow his stride. "Let him go, or I will kill all of you."

Then they reacted, some shouting, some laughing, until Asher grabbed the one in charge by the throat and tossed him against the statue's base.

"Ow." He grimaced, rubbing his lower back. "You hurt me."

"There will be no execution today."

"Maybe we'll hang you too," said one of the others, swaying on his feet.

Asher whirled on him, brandishing the stone. "Just you try."

The man with the sheet of tin responded by striking it louder and faster, *bang bang bang bang bang*. Asher drove the stone into the middle of the metal, caving it in like an old hat, the drummer tumbling down.

"You fools don't even know how to hang someone." Asher began untying Antoine's bonds. "If you managed to get the rope around his neck, how were you planning to lift him? Much less drop him down?"

They fell as silent as scolded schoolboys. With Asher's help, Antoine twisted out of the last of his knots and slipped off like a fish unhooked.

"You let him get away," the sober one seethed, though he was still down.

"No," Asher said. "I set him free. You're the ones I'm letting get away." He glared at each of them in turn. "You deserve far worse, and next time you'll get it."

He spun on his heel, headed for the wagon. In her seat, Marie perched as straight as a bobbin. "I thought your hiding was comical. I had no idea you would— Look out!"

Asher spun, and the sober one was charging him with the sword high. He made a quick dodge, but the man slashed him on the upper arm, blood blooming on his shirt.

The wound sent Asher into a rage: He tackled the man, wrenching the sword away, and throwing it to clang on the cobblestones. Three blows to the face, and the man stopped resisting. Twice he grabbed the man's hair and slammed his head back against the stones. Asher dragged him rag-doll over to Pétain, where he grabbed the leather reins and spun them three times around the man's neck.

"Say one word, I'll swat this animal, and you'll be the one who gets hung today."

"No." The man began blubbering. Tears and blood streaked his face. "Please."

Marie bent down over Asher's shoulder and whispered, "Do it."

"What?" Asher spun his head. "You want me to finish him?"

"If hanging is his idea of justice?" She looked down from her seat. "Give him a dose."

Asher had eased his grip on the reins, and the man tried to wriggle away. He yanked the leather tight again. "I really ought to."

"Please," the man begged. "I have a family. Three children."

Asher leaned in to his face. "You disgust me."

"I am sorry. I am so, so—"

"Do you promise never to hang anyone again?"

"I promise," he blubbered. "Of course I promise."

Asher unwound the reins. The man staggered back, a hand to his throat. His compatriots had already fled, and he stumbled off after them. Marie hopped down, examined the sword with a critical eye, and tossed it in the back of the wagon. When Asher gave her a look, she shrugged. "I'm certainly not going to return it."

"IT'S DULL TO THE POINT of worthlessness," Marie said, returning from giving Pétain his dinner. "Like they practiced with it on rocks. That sword would have to be reforged to be of any use."

Asher sat at the small table in her kitchen, his shirt unbuttoned, gingerly peeling cloth away from his wound. "Oh, it was of some use, all right."

"Yes, but if it had been sharp he might have taken your arm off."

Wincing, he sucked air in through his teeth. "Lucky me."

Marie crouched beside him, pushing his hands away to examine the cut herself. "Ideally we should stitch this."

"No, thank you."

"Let's clean it first." Pouring warm water on his sleeve, she was able to ease his shirt the rest of the way off. "I have some questions about what happened today."

"We had a nice friendly round of deliveries in Clovide," Asher joked. "And we managed not to meet the dreaded 'beloved Alix.'"

Marie did not smile, only went away, and returned with some soft cloths. "All this time I've thought you were a glass artist. Today I saw someone else."

"A man with a temper?"

Marie dipped a cloth in the water and pressed it gently on his wound. "You are a soldier, trained and experienced."

"Not really. I just felt badly for the man about to get hung."

She paused. "Let's not waste our lives debating what we both know happened, shall we? You disarmed a man with a sword, beat him nearly unconscious, and were seconds away from killing him."

"Well, and you seemed somewhat excited by it."

"I was." She dipped the cloth and dabbed it against the injury again. "I am."

"It saddens me."

"It thrills me." She gave a little growl.

Asher stared away to one side. Clementine was watching them both from beside the bedroom curtain. "I've been struggling with it. How to stop being a soldier. And how to stop treating everyone as a potential enemy."

"That explains your behavior earlier in the day."

"You noticed?"

Marie's tone was sharp. "You took the reins when I was off the wagon. It could easily have run me over."

"Those men had scissors and knives."

"They always do." She rinsed the cloth in the bowl, water reddening, but with each swipe she revealed the cut to be smaller. "This isn't looking as bad as I expected."

"It hurts, but nothing terrible."

Marie rose, emptying the bowl and returning with iodine and bandages. "Did you see the man from the château?"

"Who do you mean?"

"The noisemaker you knocked down." She swabbed the cut with iodine, purpling the skin around it. "You know, the one they tossed to make room for you."

"Bondurant? I didn't recognize him."

"Is that his name?" She arranged gauze over the cut, then wrapped cloth around his upper arm. "I always called him Toadstool."

"We only overlapped for half a day." Asher winced as she tightened the cloth. "They expelled him for uncontrolled rage."

"He's still raging, I'd say. Bigger too, heavier." She put her medical kit aside. "And you were being methodical, as if you had a plan. Outnumbered five-to-one, yet you did not hesitate. That's how I knew you were trained."

"We all had to survive the war. And after."

"There is a difference between a survivor and a warrior."

"I know. I'm trying to be one and not the other."

She taped the end of the cloth firmly to hold it secure. "Is that why you hesitate to couple with me roughly?"

"I—" He had never conducted such a conversation, not in all his time with Aube. They had taken years to learn one another, and to learn themselves, and always gently. In fact, sometimes as her moment of crisis approached he would hold back, until the ache of desire caused her to plead. Then he would give, and she surrender, and there would come a frenzy they both rode like a wave of incoming tide. After, they kissed on the mouth and pretzeled their limbs, in ardent hopes that they'd made another child.

"No need to reply," Marie said. "Your silence is answer enough." She sat across the little table from him. "Tell me one of your stories."

"Honestly? I'm kind of sore."

"Today I learned something important that you've concealed from me. I deserve to know the hidden Asher."

"You didn't see enough today?"

She made a face. "Would I be asking for a story if I did?"

Asher tilted his head back, scrutinizing the house's snug ceiling. "Remember, as a little girl, when you learned the Ten Commandments?"

"Of course."

"Thou shalt not kill. It's right there, the sixth one, short and clear. As a boy I had read about various wars, always wondering—what about the sixth commandment? Thou shalt not. A law of society, and the law of God. Yes?"

She folded the spare bandage cloths. "Yes."

"War arrives, uninvited. I joined the Resistance. Because so many Frenchmen died in the Great War thirty years ago, most Resistance leaders were women."

"I didn't know that," she said. "Interesting."

"They were bloodthirsty: Blow this bridge, burn that building. Kill this person."

"It was combat, Asher. Lives were lost."

"Because of things I did." Asher rose from his chair. "What you saw today? Playtime. You cannot imagine the horrors I perpetrated. Now we're back in a world in which the commandments exist again. Those times I broke the law . . . they haunt me."

Marie was organizing the medical supplies in a neat stack. "That's what I want, then. Tell me one of the stories that haunts you."

"Are you sure?"

Marie sat back, her eyes suddenly bright. "I dare you."

"All right," Asher began. "There were three of them." His breath caught, but he calmed himself and continued. "It happened this way. A soldier was ordered to clear the streets, and in his haste he . . . well, he shot some harmless people. In response, he was assassinated. In retaliation for that, because this is the way of war, three enemy officers ordered something truly vengeful. They had troops gather dozens of people, men and women, children and aged, thirty in total, all of them innocent of the soldier's death. At gunpoint they forced the people to dig a hole, narrow but long and deep. It took all day. When it was finished, they made the people stand at the edge of the hole, then unceremoniously gunned them so that they fell into the grave of their own making. When the killing was finished, these three officers stood at the lip of the hole, and pissed on the bodies. Lastly, they ordered men to bulldoze the dirt back on all of it."

"What savages we humans are."

This was the woman who had told him to do it, to hang the man with the donkey's reins. Savagery takes, savagery gives. One of the lessons of wartime. "Days later, I received an assignment, the next act of vengeance," Asher continued. "Back then, if I told you about it I would have been shot."

Marie pulled her chair closer. "It's now, Asher, and I'm the only person here."

"I was ordered to kill all three. It was a simpler assignment than most, because of their overconfidence. Most nights they went to an officers' canteen. I saw them enter. I heard a piano, men singing. I snuck down, and wired their staff car, an old roofless one with open seats. As they drove away, the wire would break, detonating a bomb I'd secured under the gas tank. I hid in the trees and waited."

She sat forward. "This is a story completely beyond my experience."

Asher stretched his wounded arm out partway, then cradled it close. "Hours later they emerged, singing and staggering. I was furious. I knew some of the people they'd pissed on, and now the officers were anesthetized. I had wanted them to feel the complete pain."

He picked up a cloth she'd used on his arm, a streak of red in the cotton. For a moment he dangled it at his side, shaking it, till he felt tugging on it. This was how to win over Clementine. After a skirmish, he let the cloth go. The cat scurried away across the floor, worrying the rag like she'd caught a mouse. It was time to tell the hard part.

"The officer who was driving backed directly into a clump of bushes. The other two, in the back seat, laughed uproariously. When he tried to pull out, and stalled, they roared, and he refused to drive. They began to argue. A corporal happened along and they yelled at him too. From the canteen's outside lights, I could see that he was young. Maybe seventeen? A corporal, nonetheless: no stripes on his shoulder, a V on his sleeve. The boy pointed up the road, which I interpreted as him saying he was expected somewhere. I thought, Yes, let the baby go, don't make him chauffeur. But the man in the driver's seat snarled, pointed at the aluminum braid on his shoulder with its bright gilt star, and slid over onto the passenger side. The corporal took the wheel, started the car, and with one more shout from the back seat, off they went."

Asher stood, crossing to lean against the windowsill, eyes down.

Marie waited a long time for him to continue, but he only stared at the floor. "Did the bomb work?"

He raised his head. "Perfectly. The gas tank exploded in a fireball. The car flipped upside down and burst into flames. But the difficulty . . ." He paused, hesitant. "The problem was that one person did not die in the explosion. He wrenched himself out of the wreck, the entire back of his body on fire, and ran. By chance he stumbled in my direction, so

I saw his face, the agony on it. I smelled the smoke coming off of him. For eight steps he fought his fate. Until, mercifully, he fell."

"The corporal?"

Asher cradled his bandaged arm to his chest. "Men poured out of the canteen, firing their sidearms drunkenly into the woods. I did not stay any longer."

"You can live with the officers' deaths," Marie said, "because they killed your friends and defiled the bodies. But that corporal . . ."

"Exactly. That man is on fire for the rest of my life."

She rose and came to his side. When she spoke, it was her quiet voice, the one he knew from after lovemaking. "That experience led you to prevent a hanging today. You saved a life."

Asher shook his head. "I cannot turn my killings into good deeds."

"You have that exactly wrong," Marie said, her voice still soft and close. "They were good deeds when you did them, and they are good deeds now."

"That would be a convenient thing to believe."

After placing the lightest kiss on his bandage, she took his other hand and drew him away from the window.

"Where are you leading me?"

She continued pulling. "I am taking the warrior to bed."

CHAPTER 20

Morning light beamed through the dining room windows, everyone squinting till the nameless man yanked a drape across the glass. Brigitte was breakfasting with the men for the first time since Marc's stroke: cheese, berries, slices of cold chicken. She wore an old smock that day, a more revealing one. The men noticed, but said nothing about it. They spoke only to ask someone to pass a platter, or the salt, until Asher broke the peace. His arm hurt and he needed distraction.

"Give us some news," he said. "Please."

Brigitte lowered her spoon to the plate. "Telling you will make it real."

"It is already real," Etienne answered.

Brigitte looked up at the men, their hunger for news. "It's his left side," she said. "Marc's arm and leg are paralyzed. And not improving."

"I'm sorry," the nameless man said. Asher glanced over, surprised to hear him express sympathy.

"His swallowing has made progress," she continued. "Yesterday I heard him recite the Lord's Prayer. The doctor remains optimistic. But without his left side, I don't know how he . . ."

Brigitte trailed off, rising and bustling back into the kitchen. When she reappeared she wore a hat, and held a basket of food. "I'll see you at dinner. Pray."

She was gone—and, seemingly with her, the month of July. Some days Henri accompanied her. Etienne also visited often. Asher kept quiet, his arm mending more slowly than he'd expected. Meanwhile, Simon, when he could not find port or wine, would amble into the atelier seeking someone to lecture, and if there was no prey, fashioning himself a better place to nap. The nameless man read in his room, at the table, anywhere he pleased. Some days Asher spied him stretched atop the courtyard wall. He'd used a little wooden ladder, which he pulled up after himself.

"What are you reading?" Asher asked one afternoon.

"Virgil." The nameless man closed his book on one finger. "The *Aeneid* is as superior to the *Iliad* as Latin is to Greek. Lyricism, imagery, human universality of theme. And you have no concept of what I'm saying."

Asher squinted up. "Do you like being up there? It doesn't look comfortable."

"Privacy is a luxury superior to any upholstery." Reopening the book, he held it up like a barrier.

Anger simmered in his belly, and Asher imagined yanking the man down. But his arm was sore, and then a donkey brayed.

SHE WORE WHITE, UNDER AN apron with a pattern of green apples. Bold as she was in private, at the château Marie could behave as shy as a dove. "How is Marc today?"

"Brigitte said his speech is better. Yesterday he prayed."

Asher hovered, helping her carry vegetables, asking after her gardens, a puppy at her heels. At departure she might pause, on days entirely of her choosing, stepping partway up onto the cart's seat, causing the dress to drape away from her leg—her shift lifted, her bare calf visible—to lean forward so that the glass crescent dangled away from her skin, and whisper, "Come to me tonight."

"You know that I will."

As Pétain pulled Marie away, the wagon swaying in the rutted lane, he might spin on one foot like a top. He might clap his hands many times.

ONE NIGHT HE DREAMED THE man on fire had found Marie, and with one touch on the hand had set her arms ablaze. Jerking awake, Asher saw her sleeping beside him, in fact with a calm brow instead of her usual concern. As day dawned, he noticed a book at her bedside, a worn edition with pages folded over, which he opened to a blank page at the front. Rising to dig in his pants on the floor, he found a nub of pencil. Leaning naked against the dresser, he outlined his lover asleep on her side. The rise of her hip, the ease of her arm, the pool of shadow between her breasts.

Clementine began fussing with the bedclothes, her claws tugging the fabric, so he pulled on clothes and went outside. Taking a seat in the chair with the umbrella—for some reason Marie never wanted him to sit there, but it was placed invitingly right in the morning light—Asher added details, imagining how many curves of glass her shape would require.

If only he had drawn Aube, perhaps her face would not be fading in his memory. The feel of her bones, her voice, the scent of her hair—they were all weakening. Perhaps time was being merciful, but it saddened him. If only he had sketched her, naked and asleep. If only he had drawn his wife before the soldier drew his gun. Rachel would never have sat still long enough for him, but if she had, if he possessed a drawing of her, would he stare at it constantly? Or put it away, too painful to behold?

Marie's beauty was a harder kind. Forged by war. His pencil paused as he realized: She was not growing closer to him. Despite the passion, the few confessions of vulnerability, she had maintained her remove. That did not make an easy path for love. Sun broke over the trees across the field, spangled beams and the glint of dew. He wished she'd been there to see it. Heading back inside, Asher left the book on the kitchen table, a teacup to hold it open to the drawing, and set off for the river.

THAT NIGHT AT DINNER ETIENNE tapped a fork against his goblet, *ting ting*. The men fell silent immediately. "Last week I wrote the bishop to inform him about our situation," he announced. "Today I received a reply."

"Are we out of business?" the nameless man asked.

Etienne shook his head. "No. The bishop will honor the cathedral commission. Meanwhile, Marc was well enough this afternoon for us to have a frank conversation about the project. Not surprisingly, he has been giving the matter deep consideration."

Etienne paused, arranging his silverware in a straight line.

"It's all right." Brigitte stood in the kitchen doorway. "You're doing fine."

"Thank you." He cleared his throat. "First, new duties. Henri, you'll continue with your side window, assembling according to the original plan. Asher, you apprentice with Henri on the other side window, as his assistant." He gestured at the nameless man. "You and I must make glass for them. All we can produce with the supplies on hand."

"Are you telling me that this witless novice"—he waved a hand at Asher as though he were swatting a fly—"this trifle of flagrant inexpertise, will be making a window before I do?"

"Allow me to finish," Etienne said.

"Oh, this is rich," the nameless man said. "Please, carry on. I cannot wait to hear what other brainless ideas you and our newly minted idiot have concocted."

Etienne's expression soured. He tapped two fingers on the handle of his knife, and Asher wondered what the man had done during the war. Soldier? Commander? But Brigitte caught Etienne's eye, and he lowered both hands into his lap.

"We have silicate, thanks to our muscular friends from the valley, but the potash is nearly gone," he said. "The supply of color chemicals is likewise low. Production of new glass will cease sooner than we would want. At that time"—he gestured at the nameless man—"your task will be to design and assemble the central window."

"I will what?"

"It's yours. That's Marc's decision. The main one." Etienne took a deep breath. "Asher and Henri will serve as your assistants, while I . . ." Again, he looked to Brigitte, a palm flattened on her chest, who nodded. "I will supervise site preparation, and the windows' installation, as well as manage the château's finances."

Simon shifted in his chair. "What happens when the windows are done?"

"One of the bishop's lieutenants will review our work, to confirm that it is satisfactory. Presuming he approves, we will receive payment, enabling us to remain here until the next commission comes, or the materials from Danzig arrive."

"Let us pray for both," Brigitte interjected.

"If he does not approve, the funds for operations here will run out faster than the sun goes down, and Le Château Guerin will be put up for sale."

"Pray to heaven that it never happens," Simon said.

"I want to understand this clearly," the nameless man interjected. "I will be designing the main window? Marc has entrusted that task to me?"

"Yes." Etienne stared at his plate. "And not to me."

"This is excellent. Wonderful. This window will be a piece of history."

"Yes," Etienne murmured. "The first cathedral in France with repaired glass."

"It will hang for a hundred years. No, hundreds."

Henri laid a sympathetic hand on the shoulder of Etienne, who remained with his head down.

Etienne patted Henri's hand, then stood, shoulders back. "So. Time to fire the furnaces, men. Let's get back to work."

CHAPTER 21

She invited him often. After the thwarted hanging, it was twice a week or more. Also, she kept his drawing of her sleeping on the bedside table. She said it made her feel beautiful. Often they went directly to the back room, barely speaking until afterward. Other times they conversed in the dooryard, or in the kitchen as she scrubbed dirt from her hands, or while undressing on opposite sides of the bed.

Nearly always, at some point she would command him to be rough. "Harder," she'd say. "Make me feel it."

Asher obliged, though his arm was not all the way healed and he had to strain. Of greater importance to him, sometimes the roughness created distance between them, brutal in the way of horses breeding, almost unkind. He had not made love with Aube that way, even at their most passionate. While he enjoyed giving Marie what she asked, he wished he had the nerve to speak as plainly, to ask that they be tender just one time.

Always during the act—always—she closed her eyes. That was what made speaking to her difficult. Once he did summon his courage, and asked her to look at him. She blinked open for a minute, eyes locked on his, and he thrilled to the audacity of it. The electricity of shared understanding, what they were doing and feeling, revelation of the deep wound within her that he was maybe somehow helping to heal, it was real and true. Then she closed them again, retreating to her inner world.

Clementine continued to stalk him, to clean herself just out of reach. When they made love she sat at the foot of the bed, facing away in disdain. During meals she insinuated between his feet, but if he reached to pet her, she sprinted away in a drumroll of paws.

"Give her time," Marie said. "She'll be snuggling with you soon."

"It's not *her* snuggling I desire," he replied.

If they were dressed when he spoke like that, Marie would kiss his throat. If half-dressed, she would bat her eyes and sway her hips—"Want to draw me again?"—and scamper away. If already naked, she would clasp his manhood without a flinch, aiming it toward herself, and the moment he responded she would close her eyes.

Once, their intimacy came by surprise. For days Marie had been making deliveries elsewhere. Asher was busy molding lead—a gritty job that left a metallic taste in his mouth. On the fourth day he grabbed towel and soap, and hiked for the river.

An August afternoon lay basking at his feet. The dappled light made such shadowed shapes on the road, he could imagine a hundred drawings, thousands of pieces of glass. He reached the river before realizing that someone was already there.

The donkey dozed in the shade of poplars by the bridge. Asher stopped, letting himself feel the anticipation, the desire. He had never forgotten that vision of Marie in the river. The right moment to confess had never presented itself. Perhaps voyeurism was like infidelity: the offender must always carry the misdeed privately and alone.

In the wagon he saw celery, peppers, peas. A separate box held tomatoes to the brim, so ripe, so packed with summer sunlight, the fruits had splits in their skins. With the hiss of river and stink of donkey, he followed the path to the water.

There were her clothes in the grass, discarded here and there as if she'd disrobed for bed.

"You," Marie exclaimed, her head bobbing as she wiped under her eyes. "Wait."

She dunked again, then rose—water cascading from her face, shoulders, glistening breasts. Her smile seemed perhaps forced. "What a perfect surprise."

It was like the time he'd spied on her, but this time permitted. Asher was out of his clothes before she'd taken three steps. They met in the shallows, kissing madly as if they'd been apart for months. He pulled away to dive into the river, spinning like an eel, wiped himself up and down, then surged out of the water to hoist her toward the grass banks. Her arms around his neck, Marie's smile now looked sincere.

"You are a piece of heaven," he panted, as they tumbled to the ground. She opened her legs, guiding him. "You're not ready," Asher said.

"Just shove it in," she growled. "Just take it."

As he did what she asked, Marie gave a wild love cry, then squeezed her bright eyes shut.

SHE WAS DOZING ON HER side. The imprints of leaves on her skin filled Asher with tenderness. Making love outdoors, beside a summer river? Could this be the peace everyone had promised would follow victory? Two people at a time, one quiet hour at a time, might this be a taste of it?

"Tell me a story," Marie whispered.

"I didn't know you were awake."

"A good story," she replied, snuggling back against him. "You've calmed everything in me."

"All right." Stalling, he kissed her shoulder blades. Here was the opportunity he had wanted for telling the truth. Steeling himself, he embarked.

"One time in my first week at the château, I came here feeling dirty and desolate. I stood on the bank, looking the place over, when a fish jumped, right over there."

He pointed vaguely toward mid-river. "This was not some insignificant hatchling, but a fine fat one, the size we'd keep to eat. He'd seen his share of seasons and dodged his quota of hooks. Lurking on the bottom through winter starvation, then spring times of abundance, when bugs skimmed on the surface for easy eating. No fool, this fish. Yet his leap was so high, so extravagant, I stood here thinking, he did not do that only to catch a fly. He wanted to see. To find out what goes on up in this roofless realm. I've admired this fish ever since, his optimism and ambition, and what the world must have looked like to him: all the greenness, the vastness of possibilities, the brilliance of the sun. And there on the bank, also, he saw a human animal watching it all dumbfounded, as if he had lost the capacity to be aware of the world, to be astonished by it. And what a tragedy that must be for him."

He kissed her shoulder blades again. "He fell back with a slap, and darted off. Yet, in a way, that fish changed my life. He told me that's all we get: a leap from the unknown into this nonstop miracle, before we plunge back into unknowing. I began to notice the world again. Now I am drawing it. With every mark of the pencil, I am rediscovering."

She wiped her nose on her arm. "Good story."

"Thank you." *That was also the day I saw you,* he continued in his mind, *when you were sobbing and beautiful and bare, and it changed my life as much as any leaping fish.* But he did not voice those thoughts, only grimaced at his weakness.

"Asher," she said, "before the war, I was married."

He lifted his head. "You were?"

"His name was René."

"Was? What happened to him?"

She remained on her side. "An enemy soldier shot him. Who knows why? There may not have been any reason at all. The best man at our wedding brought me the body in a wagon."

"Will you tell me about René?"

"You already know a great deal."

He sat up. "I do?"

"Who built my wagons? Who trained Pétain?"

"I had never stopped to consider."

"Why would anyone." Her voice was flat.

Asher studied the curve of her shoulder, slender but strong. With one finger, he outlined its shape on the water. "How else do I know him?"

"My gardens. They're actually his. René planted them, built the fences and beds." She rolled onto her back. "I continue what he began."

He began to draw her face on the river. A memory of Aube came forward, an intrusion, but there was her stern jaw. He'd wanted to invite her parents for Rachel's second birthday and Aube was opposed, not out of hostility toward them, but rather a desire to assert her adult independence. Asher did what he nearly always did when she set her expression in iron—because it was a facet of her beauty, and because it communicated that she was an excellent mother—and capitulated.

Returning to the present, he began drawing Marie again. "Do you miss him?"

She sniffed, rubbed her nose, motions too fleeting to sketch. "René is buried in a corner of our land. I ache for him every day."

Asher went still. "Does our lovemaking help?"

Marie waited before answering. A grasshopper landed on her thigh but she did not move until it leapt away. "I could couple with a hundred men and still grieve."

"What a thing to say."

She did not reply. This was the moment to confide his secrets. He felt sympathy with Brigitte, when she said talking about Marc's illness would make it more real. If Asher entrusted Marie, the sorrow and horror would move from being his burden into being their burden. Would that poison their romance? He had no way of knowing. But she had told him about René. If he did not tell Marie, he could not tell anyone.

"Well." He picked a bit of grass from her knee. "Remember the corporal on fire?"

"I will never forget him."

"His death, and those three officers' deaths, that whole sequence of retaliations began with an event I witnessed. It started with one soldier, and the innocent, unarmed woman he killed. He shot her in the back as she was running away. She was carrying a little girl, a toddler, and the bullet killed her as well."

"Asher." Marie sat up. "What a horror."

He avoided her eyes. "There was one redemption in what I saw."

She took his hand. "How could there be?"

"When I lifted the woman to remove her body, and the soldier saw the girl underneath, he flinched. And I felt sympathy for him."

"But he had just killed those people."

"That is why I made some vows there, standing in the bloodied street, some dark and brutal vows. The war kindly gave me an opportunity to keep them."

There. He had partly confessed. Asher could have said more, could have told her about all nineteen. He could have confessed that he was not Catholic like everyone else at the château, but rather a Jew in spiritual confusion.

"I know what that flinch meant." Asher wiped the water as if clearing a slate. "Somewhere deep in that boy, under the arrogance of his uniform and weapon, despite the madness and savagery of his government, there remained a fraction of humanity, some sliver of conscience. He killed two innocent people, yet he was not all monster."

Marie scooted her bare bottom closer till her legs were woven with his. "Your wife," she said. "Your daughter. What were their names?"

CHAPTER 22

As summer advanced, so did rectangles of gold across the atelier's floor. Sunbeams reached into the assembly area, where Henri was finishing the first side window, while Asher drew designs for the second one.

The light caused him to lift his head. End of day was approaching, the tempo of work already eased. The nameless man sat at his workbench, smoking a cigarette of pencil shavings, looking as cool as a winter pond. Simon sat too—on a stool, dipping a ladle into the drinking bucket, pouring the water slowly back.

Asher felt no such lassitude. His arm was nearly healed. After a ten-day lapse, Marie had invited him for that evening. Eagerness about their reunion made him feel young. With luck, he would have time to shave, and bathe in the river. Whenever he arrived with wet hair, she cooed like a dove. He could picture the moment, her two-handed grip on his locks, steering his head this way and that, while he undid her buttons one by one by one.

Etienne appeared from behind the main furnace with a glowing glob on his blowpipe. It was small, though, less than a child's fist. Flopping down at his bench, he stirred through the bin of tools, selecting long-nosed pincers.

Shifting upright, he rotated the pipe, while the tool tweezed the glob at intervals. He ended with a flourish, a twist of the wrist, and suddenly it was clear. He'd made a flower, its petals clear and curved, supported by a slender stalk. One more spin with the pincers, and the lily dropped into his glove.

Etienne raised the crystal flower in the afternoon light, angling it this way and that, prisming a rainbow around the room, then put it on a shelf beside the annealing furnace. With that, he clapped his bare hand against the gloved one.

"That's everything, gentlemen," Etienne announced. "The very last of it."

Henri straightened from his work. The nameless man, on a break, squinted as he drew on his cigarette. Simon straightened on his stool. "Last of what?"

Etienne tossed the glove on his workbench. "The last of our supplies. No more raw materials."

The nameless man blew a veil of smoke sideways. "How am I supposed to build the main window now?"

"We have made a good inventory of glass," Etienne answered. "As generous supply as a person could want. We are depending on you to make it into something timeless."

"Could be a fool's errand," the nameless man replied.

"Or the opportunity of a fool's lifetime," Etienne countered, hulking past him on his way out of the atelier. At the last second, instead of stowing his blowpipe in the rack as usual, he flung it like a javelin into his workbench. The loud clang when it hit the floor made all the men jump.

He kept marching, right out the door. The nameless man ambled over, bent to pick up the pipe, held it out so they could all see that the tip was bent. "Ruined."

"EVERYONE?" BRIGITTE SANG OUT THAT evening from the château's central hall. She craned her neck up the curved rear stairs. "Everyone, please?"

Normally she rang a bell, or the men gathered for dinner based on the clocks of their stomachs. But that was an hour away at least. Now they hurried down from their rooms. There they drew back at the sight: Marc in a wheelchair, attempting to smile.

"Doesn't he look excellent?" she said.

To Asher? No, the man looked beaten. His beard was unruly and hair unkempt, his left hand frozen in a kind of palsy, his left leg flopped as if it had no muscles.

"Better than ever," Etienne said, coming forward to lift Marc's right hand from his lap and shake it. "Welcome home, sir. I am so glad this day has come."

"What d—" Marc contorted his jaw, reddening with effort. "What did I . . . miss?"

"Not a thing," Etienne boomed. "It is we who have missed you."

He caught Henri's eye and waved him forward. The small man scurried up, pumping Marc's hand up and down, doffing an imaginary cap. So that was the game. Asher went next. "Great to have you back," he said, somewhat frightened to realize that Marc's hand was not gripping his in return, was as flaccid as a dead fish. The others gave the same performance, as awkward as horses running sideways, while Asher stood apart. He'd expected Marc to recover, to take control again. Instead they were out of materials, and he could neither move one hand nor grip with the other.

Asher wondered: How long before he was on the street again? Would Marie take him in? Not likely. Perhaps tonight they should discuss it—after they made love.

He heard a strange sound, a high cheery ringing that perplexed everyone but Brigitte, who clapped her hands. "There's our other surprise."

"This place has a doorbell?" Etienne asked.

"To celebrate Marc's recovery," she explained, "the bishop did us the honor of sending a priest. For the first time in years, our chapel will host a celebration of Mass."

"This place has a chapel?" Asher asked.

Brigitte laughed, light as a lark. "What do you think?"

Etienne squatted beside Marc, their heads at the same height. "It has been a long time since I received Communion."

"Yes." Asher's mouth had gone sawdust-dry. "Me too."

THE PRIEST WORE A COAT although it was August. As he slid it off, Brigitte stepped forward, folding it over one arm to prevent wrinkles. It seemed as if the priest knew someone would be there to take it. Asher noticed with some pride that her blouse was buttoned to the throat. In fact, there was a general air of formality.

"Thank . . ." Marc stalled, paused, took a breath. "Thank . . ."

The priest bowed. "Shouldn't I be thanking you?" Under the coat he wore a black shirt with a stiff white collar. Black pants, black shoes as polished as a private's belt buckle. "Isn't it always an honor, to perform the Holy Sacrifice of the Mass?"

"Shall I lead you to the chapel, Father?" Etienne stepped forward.

"Why don't we all proceed there?" He took his satchel in hand. "And, lady of the house, could you please bring us a bit of wine?"

Etienne backed away, the priest following. Henri took charge of wheeling Marc's chair, with the nameless man and Simon close behind. Asher remained in the entry, in a knot. If he left now, there would be questions. If he stayed, there was no way he could conceal his ignorance of their rituals. He certainly knew that something called Mass existed, though he had never experienced it. Most of his neighbors in Bonheur attended—from the part-time saints of Christmas and Easter to the daily piety of the aged. A secret revealed meant an Asher ejected.

"Don't wait for me," Brigitte told him.

"I don't mind."

"I'm going to hang this"—she patted the priest's coat—"and attend to dinner. You run, and I'll be right along."

There did not seem to be any alternative. He followed the sounds of the others' voices into the chapel he had never seen. It was a small stone

room, cool and dim, rows of benches with an aisle between, a stone altar
at the front. The windows to either side, with clear glass, struck Asher as
a missed opportunity.

First the priest placed a crucifix on a table behind the altar. Asher
wanted to run, his sense of not belonging was so acute. But Henri pulled
him in to share a bench. The priest lit candles, opened a fat red book,
flipped pages to find his place. Brigitte arrived with a bottle, a bit of lace
pinned to her hair, and an apology for keeping him waiting.

"Under the circumstances," he replied, "shouldn't we all be infor-
mal?"

From his bag he removed other items: a silver cup and a little pitcher
into which he poured the wine. He touched the fingertips of his hands
together. "Shall we begin?"

One summer when Asher was a boy, a traveling fiddler had come
to Bonheur. He was fork-bearded, sun-bleached. He slept on the beach
and ate seafood raw. When he played, crowds gathered, and fed coins
to his upturned hat. At dusk he drew families from their homes, nearly
the whole village, everyone dancing. In Asher's imagination, the normally serious adults seemed to levitate, floating over the houses—his
grandmother, schoolteacher, parents—not ghosts, but spirits musically
elevated.

Then came the evening, with humidity as oppressive as a bitter
mother-in-law, when the man's instrument would not stay in tune. He
started with his usual toe-tapping songs, but often had to pause to crank
a peg on the neck, tightening his highest string again and again—
until it snapped. Cursing with the filthiest words, and no regard for the
women and children present, the man announced that he owned no
extra strings. By the time he tucked his violin into its case, the crowd
had dispersed and the summer of dancing had ended. The fiddler was
gone by morning.

Now Asher felt like that string, there were so many things putting
him out of tune. He wanted desperately to confide in Henri: Wounds
to his heart, pain in his conscience, a body slowly healing, the promise

of a lover, the uncertainty of his housing and next meal, the pressure from continuously deceiving people who deserved better, doubts about what he believed in, the delight of designing windows—each of these forces winding him tighter and tighter, and now he was in a room of high spiritual humidity. One more crank of the peg and he might snap.

But then the priest did an astonishing thing: He turned around. Between the benches and the altar, facing the crucifix instead of them, he began to chant—in Latin. Asher understood some words, they resembled French—father and son, father and son—but he could not assemble them into sense. He released a long sigh. A priest's back would not see Asher faking a prayer, or fumbling as the others sat or knelt. High rose the man's hands, and his voice, for an hour, until he tore bread into pieces, lifted the wine goblet while invoking the sky, and Asher's string did not break.

The priest ate and drank with reverence. To Asher, the room seemed to fill with expectancy. When the priest raised his head, the men stood. As Asher watched with a choke in his throat, they filed forward to kneel on a row of pads by the altar. Repeating an incantation, the priest moved from one to the next, giving them bread.

Henri nudged him forward. Asher stepped aside to let his friend go, but the short man bent low and he had no choice but to proceed.

They were saying something in reply to the priest, but what? Henri poked him from behind. At the front, Brigitte knelt to his left, Henri settling on the other side. Asher folded his hands in imitation of theirs. The priest spoke his prayer, Brigitte mumbled something Asher thought he heard correctly, then opened her mouth. The priest fed her and stepped along. Asher waited till he had said his words again.

"Thank you," he said, and opened his mouth.

"Amen?" the priest replied. When Asher gave him a quizzical look, he responded with a bewildered face, for only an instant, then showed an expression of keen intelligence. Eyes narrowed, he leaned forward. "Amen?"

"Oh yes," Asher said. "Amen."

The priest placed the bread on his tongue, moving on. If Henri heard the mistake, he gave no sign. Chewing the bread, Asher wondered if he had fooled anyone.

After the service they filed into the hallway, and Asher felt an awkwardness among everyone, quite unlike the gabby vestibules of synagogues. As if they were embarrassed, to be seen openly with something so private. Perhaps no one had deduced his secret simply because they were preoccupied with their own travails of faith.

"Is the man of the house fatigued by all the fanfare?" the priest said, joining them. "Shall we put him to bed with a blessing?"

Henri guided the wheelchair down the hall, Etienne hovering nearby. At the foot of the stairs, as both men lifted Marc up, the priest made the sign of the cross over the rest of them—with a frown in Asher's direction, unambiguous, as precise as an arrow.

Afterward they milled in the courtyard, chickens investigating underfoot.

"He had a decent singing voice," the nameless man announced, rolling another cigarette of wood shavings. "Most priests sound like tortured cows."

"How do you know what a tortured cow sounds like?" Asher asked.

"I think this priest was one of the truly holy," Simon replied. "I felt it." He pulled his beret from a pocket and put it on his head.

Henri noticed weeds among his flowers, and knelt to pluck. Asher wondered if he could start toward Marie's, or would leaving while the priest was still there draw the wrong kind of attention? To settle the matter, and his rattled spirits, he fetched his roll of paper, and sat against the courtyard wall. With a pencil he recommenced a sketch halfway done.

The nameless man gazed over his shoulder. "What in God's name is that?"

Asher squinted up at him. "I'm sorry?"

"That scrawled line." Cigarette in hand, he wagged his fingers over the drawing. "Aren't you too old for scribbly child's play?"

Asher flattened the paper in his lap. "This is the roofline of my hometown. The view from my childhood bedroom window. The memory of it comforts me."

"Roofline? Pray tell, then, what is a fish doing up in the sky?"

Asher couldn't help smiling. "He's flying, of course."

"Waste of time." The nameless man took a long drag, exhaling smoky words. "Complete waste of time."

"Asher?" From the doorway, Brigitte crooked a finger at him.

Spinning the paper onto its roll, he rose from his seat. "How may I be of help?"

"Bring this to the clergyman." She held out a basket. "Dinner. He asked for you."

"Ah." He gulped. "A pleasure to do it."

"I'll hold your drawings," she said. "He's parked where Marie normally goes."

As soon as she'd left, Asher felt a boiling in his thoughts. What would the priest say? Would he issue his reprimand privately, or had he already told Marc?

Worries were moot; here came the reckoning. As Asher moved along the wall, he saw the mysterious jar in its place, empty for now.

"Is this the man I seek?" the priest hailed him. "Has he brought my supper?"

It was a fine small open carriage. In the braces, an immaculate quarter horse stood unmoving, well fed and handsomely groomed.

"Sir." Asher bowed slightly. "The lady of the house asked me to bring this."

He held up the basket, but rather than take it, the priest rubbed his chin. "Do you know that it is a mortal sin for the unbaptized to receive Holy Eucharist?"

Although Asher already expected damnation for his deeds in the war, he found himself stammering. "I . . . I can explain—"

"Can you?" The priest narrowed his eyes, as he had when Asher said thank you. "Is this matter between you and I? Or is it between you and your Creator? If I may speculate, is your deceit of these people, despite their many kindnesses to you, a consequence of the war?"

Asher opened his mouth, and found that he was unable to answer.

"Ah." The priest drew himself up. "Young man, do you bear unhealed wounds to your immortal soul?"

Asher staggered back two steps; the arrow the priest had launched earlier hit its mark. Survival had required so much of him, the war had demanded so much. All of the lies—to his friends, the people who housed him, the woman who had taken him for her lover—felt like self-defense, a necessity. Meanwhile, the priest awaited an answer.

"I have a great deal of work to do," Asher said at last.

"Don't we all?"

The priest reached out an arm, with supreme confidence that Asher would assist him into his carriage, which, to his own surprise, he promptly did. Settling himself in the seat, its springs creaking, the priest leaned over with an almost jovial expression.

"Thank heaven we worship a merciful God, who loves all of his children." The priest took Brigitte's basket, setting it primly beside him on the seat. "*All.*"

An expert flick of his wrists sent a curl down the straps on the horse's rump, and the handsome animal trotted off. Asher watched them progress down the lane, till the fork where one route led up to the village, the other down to the river. There, still facing ahead, and correctly confident that Asher had not moved an inch, the priest raised a hand to wave, and descended out of sight.

But not entirely: Setting sunlight dappled through the trees, casting the buggy's shadow upward. The lower the priest rode, the taller his shape climbed. As if the man were lifted by faith and forgiveness, elevated by reluctance to judge what he did not understand. As his buggy wobbled down, he also sailed over the land and away.

Asher remembered the time the cows' calls had echoed off the stones, and his imagination made the animals fly. He recalled the night the owls became rabbis and spoke with the power of the prophets.

Those moments felt similar to this one. Something in those daydreams made a higher sense, something surpassing reality.

Asher waved goodbye as well, though by then the gesture was empty, a farewell to nothing. The man had gone down his road, no one to witness but the shadow, which faded as quickly as it had appeared.

CHAPTER 23

I told you it's all right," she said, uncorking a bottle of wine. "I made do."

"What does that mean?"

"Are you jealous?" she teased. "Perhaps I have another lover? Perhaps two?"

"I don't know how you could, between your work and my visits."

"There is always time for mischief."

"I just couldn't get away." Asher shrugged. "You know I wanted to. But that priest was looking right through me."

"He must be skilled." Marie poured claret into two glasses, its deep red matching her long pleated skirt. "Because you are not the most forthcoming person I have met."

"I tell you stories."

"Each one wrapped with a bow." She set a glass before him on the table. "They're not the same as conversing. You choose what to tell and what to hide."

"I'm not hiding things from you," he protested.

"How many times did we make love before you told me you had a wife?"

"The exact same number as before you admitted you'd had a husband."

Marie raised her glass. "Touché."

Asher took a sip, expecting something acidic and refined. Instead, it was earthy, rustic, with sediment at the bottom of the jar. "This tastes like biting into a grilled fish."

"Amazing, isn't it? A friend of mine calls it sandwich-in-a-glass."

"What friend is that?"

"No one you know." Marie went to the counter for a platter—cheese, bread, crudités—which she also set on the table. "A customer in Clovide. Now you will tell me one of the things the priest saw in you. Something you have not confessed."

"I will?"

"If you want to bed me tonight, yes." She crowned a crust of bread with cheese, popping it into her mouth.

Asher laughed. "Aren't you the smug one?"

"I learned it from her," Marie said, pointing her chin at Clementine, who sat on the windowsill—just out of petting reach.

"All right," he said, breaking a piece of bread in two. "Marie, I think I may be in love with you."

She drew back. "I advise you to use that word carefully."

"Why? If I tell my heart's truth, the risk is to me alone."

"You underestimate the danger. I do not know one person who has today what she loved yesterday."

"The past is not the future."

"Yes, it is." Marie sipped her wine. "Now tell me a story."

Asher stood. She wanted to change the subject. Did not want to talk about love. He reached toward the cat, but it darted away, an orange blur. Suddenly he knew exactly the story for her to hear.

"It's one of my first memories. Remembered as if in dim light, when I was four or at most five years old. It was a sweltering day, the house stifling, everyone complaining. My grandfather took a bowl of carrots onto the roof to eat in the shade. Normally he was as serious as a funeral, dressed all in black, and strict as a judge about rules and religion. I was frightened of him, though I believe I loved him too, as a child does. We heard his shoes overhead. He was having fun up there, I could hear him calling out to anyone passing by. I went outside and peered up at him from the walk. He waved and hallooed as if I were half a mile off. I can still see the old man's immense beard, pure white against his traditional garb."

Asher was surprised at how amused he felt, what lightness there was in telling this memory. "When he came back down, there were bits of orange in his beard. It was funny to me, sidesplitting really. Tiny bits of carrot in the white. Of course, I tried to hide it, holding both hands over my mouth. But I was afraid to say anything. It might be considered criticism when I only meant to be helpful, so I held back behind the door. But my grandmother also had noticed. She went right over, stood in his way, and picked those bits out without comment. Every one of them. Then she took the bowl and brushed him along on his way."

What Asher did not say was that this was the love he wanted for his life, where affection was as ordinary as the air. He had no idea how his grandparents accomplished it. The chemistry Asher felt with Marie was powerful, propelled by desire and the wish to heal. And here she was, listening to every word. Yet it was nothing like picking carrot pieces from his beard.

"That's your story?"

Through the cottage window he saw the gentle afternoon, heard a warbling birdsong. "It is."

"Then I should tell one too. About a different hot day."

"What a treat." Asher returned to the little table. "No one ever answers me with a story." He sat like a king, palms on knees. "Please. Go ahead."

Marie moved into the same position, but leaning closer. "I bore him a son."

"What? What are you saying?"

"Gabriel." She shook her head. "When I was eight months along, big as a house and as nimble as a concrete block, I paused my deliveries one day in Clovide because of the heat. I was afraid I might faint, so I sat on a fountain to rest. It was in view of some officers, but all I did was sit, and splash a little water on my face. A soldier who wanted to impress his superiors decided what I'd done was unacceptable. He swaggered over, called me 'a fat blight,' and jammed his rifle butt into my big baby belly. The next day in the early afternoon, my son was stillborn."

"Marie, I am so, so sorry—"

"The last heir to my husband's surname. I named him Gabriel. He's buried beside his father. A little wooden cross for a boy who never opened his eyes."

"I cannot imagine—"

"You regret your killings." Her eyes flashed. "But even as I lay in the dirt by that fountain, convulsing in pain, I memorized that soldier's face. Branded it on my mind. If I saw him now, I would know him. And without a blink I would slit his throat."

"If you did that," Asher replied, "however justified, it would remain with you."

"Like your burning man."

"Exactly. It's no way to live."

Marie sat back, pushing up her sleeves. "I would rather have a lifetime of guilt than a lifetime of grief."

"If you could choose, that is."

"Come." She rose and pulled his arm. "I have something for you."

There was a message in her tug, and at first Asher thought she was drawing him to the back room. An odd choice at that moment, unless it was to comfort each other. But she stepped into her clogs. "It's a short walk, fifteen minutes."

"Are we going to their graves?"

"Never," she snapped, then softened. "No, that's for me alone."

Asher followed Marie outside. The chair with the umbrella attached stood in his way, he had to hop around it. She continued bustling along. "Shall I tell you another secret? About the nameless man?"

"You want to gossip about that awful creature?"

Marie scooped up his forearm to pull him faster. "If you mean am I deliberately changing the subject? Yes."

The way she gripped his arm, the urgency, again made Asher imagine she had something erotic in mind. A private field, a grove of trees, a bed of moss. "Fine," he said. "Do you know his name?"

"I know his story."

"Even better," he said, though in truth the topic was hardly seductive.

"He was master of a boys' school in Roubaix, near the Belgian border. He taught Latin, Greek, mathematics, and calisthenics. He was famously strict, teaching self-discipline to young men. For naughty lads from wealthy families, he was the antidote."

"This is all entirely believable."

"Until the war. One morning during lessons there was a bombing raid. The local protocol was to shelter in a basement or stone structure, but the school had no such thing. Only an old cistern, with barely room for one."

"Uh-oh."

"Yes." She was speaking faster. "As the bombing grew nearer, he ordered the boys to read aloud a favorite passage from the *Aeneid*, all of them at once. Amid that noise and chaos, the students' noses in their books as they struggled to pronounce, our man dashed away to hide in that cistern. And do you know what happened?"

"Suddenly this gossip is not very much fun," Asher said, slowing.

"A bomb hit the school. Twenty-four children died. Twenty-four boys."

Asher stopped. "This is terrible."

"A few survived to tell the tale. The master's name became a local synonym for cowardice. That is why he will never tell it. He holds himself as superior, but he carries those boys on his conscience. A greater burden than you and I put together."

Asher kicked a stone away. "Pathetic bastard."

"And those poor kids."

"How did you learn all this?"

She pulled him along again. "The best sources of gossip must remain secret."

"He must have confided in someone. A person at the château he could trust to keep his secret ironclad. Except that this person told you." He slowed. "And I have confided so many things to you . . ."

"Here." Marie pointed past him. "We're headed that way. You'll like it."

A field of timothy, stems chest-high with purple seed heads, and a bluff rising on the far side. The lilt in her voice, he could hardly contain himself.

Marie gathered up her skirt and broke into a trot. Her hair had come undone, flying behind her. "Come on," she called. "I want you to see before it's dark."

The sun did sink lower as they climbed the bluff, entering a grove where the trees stood like sentinels. It was like entering a theater, the hush before a performance. Marie came around behind Asher.

"Trust me." She cupped her hands over his eyes. "I won't let you fall."

They stumbled forward, bodies bumping, till they emerged from the grove.

"Are you ready?" she asked.

"Completely."

"*Et voilà!*" She snatched her hands away.

Asher took in the view with a puzzled expression: A giant field of vehicles, parked in orderly rows. Personnel carriers, trucks, halftracks, sedans, motorcycles with sidecars. Green, black, or brown, their paint sun-bleached or pocked with rust. And every one of the vehicles—on the doors, the hood, the roof—bore a swastika.

"I don't understand."

Square buildings stood at the front like generals addressing the troops—a mess hall perhaps, a barracks, all of them charred, black stains rising from every window. And really, Asher thought, you could not fault anyone for committing arson here.

"What is this place?"

"Come see." Marie plunged pell-mell down the steep bank.

Was this where she wanted to make love? In the presence of enemy equipment? Asher lingered at the bluff's edge. "Can you please explain this to me?"

Marie reached the bottom before shouting up to him, "What is that line from scripture? I'm sure you remember it."

"I don't know scripture." He started down. "I wasn't schooled in it."

"You know the commandments. This one starts, 'Ashes to ashes . . .'"

"Dust to dust?" He was watching his footing, legs flexed against the incline.

"See? You do know."

"What about it?" Asher reached the bottom, confused but still game. He slipped his hands around her waist.

Marie spun away, though, her claret skirt blooming. "Dust to dust, do you see?"

Now that he was down there, all of the windshields were purple. Were they somehow stained? Raising his eyes, he saw that, no, they were reflecting the clouds overhead, painted by a sun that had just finished setting. Stained glass made by nature. What did this have to do with dust? "In fact, I don't see."

She waltzed up, pinching his cheek. "You're looking right at it."

Asher jerked his head back. "Please. You are being quite annoying right now."

"Honestly?" She skipped off, waving at the rows of trucks. "I give you this gigantic gift, and you say I am annoying?"

"What gift? I'm telling you, I don't understand."

"Asher." She stopped, facing him. "What are we made of? Our bodies, I mean. What is our raw material?"

"Water, mostly. And some chemicals."

"Dust, right? We are made of sand?"

She was playing a game, as if to be clever but actually agitating him. Aube had been iron-willed, no doubt, and when her jaw was set there would be no negotiation. But she did not tease him like this, did not withhold till he was out of patience. "I suppose, yes."

Marie spun in a circle. "And everything becomes sand again, right?"

"Is this supposed to pass for an explanation?"

"Look at these machines." She rapped on a headlight. "All of them have glass."

"I can see that," he shouted. "Goddamn it. Stop playing with me."

Marie's expression changed at last, from enthusiasm to calm. "All right," she said, coming back to him in small steps. "All right." She took his hand, and drew him to the nearest row. "This place is an abandoned Nazi motor pool. The vehicles are worthless. They've already been stripped of anything valuable."

"I'm listening."

"This is the junk that is left after a war, after starving people scavenge what they can. It has been decaying here, baking in the sun, probably full of rodents by now."

"Okay." Asher calmed as well. "And why is it important?"

"You said several times that you're almost out of raw material. You said the château can't do the cathedral job because it doesn't have enough glass."

"All true, yes."

She patted the hood of a truck. "Here's a supply for you. For the whole château."

"I still don't understand."

Frowning, she lowered her voice. "I overheard one day at lunch. Marc and Etienne were talking, and I thought you were there. But Asher?" She slowed, trying again to soothe him. "They were describing how to reuse glass. Grind it down and heat it or something, I don't know. The important part is that you can make it into fresh glass all over again."

Understanding washed over him like a wave. Asher's shoulders dropped from around his ears. Her intent had not been romantic. Nor had it been to torment him. It had been kind. Asher had become furious while Marie was trying to be kind. She didn't know how to do it directly, though. Only through a kind of elusive game—even if it frustrated him into anger.

"Windows, mirrors, windshields," she continued, rapping on the headlight of the truck where they stood. "You take them out, you melt them down. You make it all into stained glass."

"I get it now." His voice was small, humbled. "Sometimes, Marie, you are too rough on me."

"I am beginning to learn that."

He lowered his head till it rested on her shoulder. "Also, sometimes I am an idiot."

"Yes." She snickered, clasping his shirt with both hands. On tiptoe, she kissed his neck. "Yes, you are."

CHAPTER 24

Asher needed Simon's help to carry a windshield, but Euclid handled one by himself, balancing the heavy curved glass on his head as he ferried it to the wagon. Henri kept the men occupied, using a stepladder to climb onto trucks' hoods, angling a pry bar to break the windshields' seals, then working them free for loading on the wagon.

They were using two, actually: the brothers' battered delivery cart, and one Marie had loaned them. While the crew filled one, Pascal pulled the other across the valley, over the bridge, and up to the château. There he rested while Etienne and the nameless man unloaded, stacking windshields on one another like glass spoons. Then back in the harness and on down the hill.

"Hum hum, bah bah bum-bum." The crew heard Pascal's singing over the rattling of an empty wagon. He came to a full stop, sweating but smiling.

"Did you see the beloved?" Euclid called, sliding a windshield atop the others.

"No luck." Pascal ducked out of the harness. "But I sniffed something splendid coming from the kitchen." He chef-kissed his fingertips. "What a flavorful woman."

"Flavorful?" Asher asked. With a chisel, he was working a door window free. "Such a poet you've become."

"Don't test my patience, rascal." Pascal wagged one fat sausage of a finger. "I'll tear your arms and legs off."

"Is that so?"

"Yes, and put your legs back where your arms used to be, and your arms back where your legs used to be, and you will have to open your mouth to pass wind."

All of the men laughed, Henri rapping his knuckles on the hood of a transport truck.

"Brigitte must be making something truly delicious," Euclid said, "to inspire such a savory threat."

"She did bless me by wearing one of her old smocks." Pascal cupped his imaginary breasts. "Perhaps I will kill this Asher anyway. For sport."

"How is everything else at the château?" Simon asked.

"No-name man and Etienne were arguing. Threatening with tools at each other."

"I know whose side I would take," Asher said. "What did you do?"

"Threatened to bop them both on the head. Wham and bam and story over."

Euclid laughed. "Anything else?"

"I put a blowpipe on the floor between them. Anyone steps across, I kill."

"Did they obey?" Simon asked.

"Etienne offered me water. I had him hold the ladle while I drank from the bucket. The belch I made startled the birds out of their nest."

Again all of the men laughed, so Pascal took a bow. Then he slid into the harness of the other wagon, beginning the next trip up to the château.

"May the heat of the kitchen cause Brigitte to open her buttons," Asher called, to which Pascal replied with a high wave of his cap. His gait was steady, with the deep momentum of a millstone.

"Ah, the steadfastness of love," Euclid said. "But he will never forgive you."

Asher was concentrating on the window removal. "What do you mean?"

"For making that modest smock." Euclid hoisted a windshield. "Half the reason we're underpaid is that he considers a glimpse of her bosom to be part of our wage."

Asher smiled. "I must apologize to your brother for my thoughtlessness."

"I suspect too that being gazed upon is a piece of her recompense."

"You think she enjoys being ogled?"

"I am certain of it." Euclid hoisted a windshield to his shoulder. "How else could my brother have been seduced?"

They returned to work, each in his own task—removing a headlight, shucking a rearview mirror from its housing like an oyster from its shell—till they heard a hard knocking down the row. Asher raised his head, but didn't see anything amiss. The knocking continued, faster and harder.

Simon came strolling down the column. "You fellows hear that?"

The knocking grew urgent, and Asher laddered down from his perch. Ten trucks away, they found the source: Henri's hand was snagged under a half-freed windshield. Somehow one side of the glass had refused to release. When he slid his hand under, it pulled back, and he'd been caught. Three of his fingers trapped inside the windshield's pinch. He was writhing, rapping the hood with a pry bar.

"God in heaven," Simon said.

"One second, friend." Asher opened the truck's door to clamber out on the hood. Simon did the same on the other side. They worked their hands under the windshield's open end.

"On three," Asher said. "One, two . . ."

They gave a hard heave. But unlike on the other trucks, the glass would not budge. Henri was sweating, his body curled toward the trapped hand. What could they do? Through the glass Asher could see that the fingers had gone white.

"Again," Asher said, as they took fresh grips on the glass. "We'll get it this time."

"Move," they heard from below. Euclid held a boulder overhead, his giant arms trembling. "Move."

The men slid away, Henri squeezed his eyes tight, and Euclid tossed the boulder. It struck the windshield dead center, shattering the glass. A million shards and pieces scattered on the truck's interior.

Henri rose to his knees, holding his freed fingers high, and blew Euclid a kiss.

"No need," the giant replied. "If we left you pinned, crows would eat you, and we'd be dealing with their guano the rest of our days. It was a favor to myself."

Henri slid across the hood, his feet tapping around the ladder till they found its rungs, which he descended while holding the sides with one hand and one wrist.

"We must be more careful, my friend." Asher rubbed Henri's shoulder. "We do not have any spare hands."

AT DAY'S END THEY TOOK a break in the shade of the burned-out buildings. Henri had limited himself to mirrors and headlights. Some were stubborn, so he hit them with a hammer—held by his thumb and uninjured forefinger—the shards falling in a bucket.

By reflex, the men always spun at the sound of breaking glass, to see what had happened. So, after each hammer blow Henri began to make faces—ears pulled back, tip of his nose pushed up, eyes crossed—which made them laugh. Pascal arrived again, shrugged out of the harnesses, and lay on the ground.

"Men," he said, "I have one more pull left in me today. I offer to spend it toting you up to the château, my labor for your rest, with one condition."

"I can't wait to hear it." Asher was leaning against a truck. Avoiding the hike would be luxury indeed.

"You convince Lady Brigitte to invite me for dinner."

"All of us?" Simon asked.

"All of you," Euclid answered.

"All of you," Pascal echoed. "One time in my life, I want to experience the honor of sitting at table with the most beautiful woman in the Champagne-Ardenne region."

Asher coughed. "You know, my powerful friend, that there are other beauties? Unmarried ones who—"

"Again you trifle with my temper," Pascal interrupted, rising up on one elbow. "Brother, remind me why I have not already swatted this mosquito into oblivion."

"Sloth," Euclid said. "You mean to kill him, but you are always too lazy."

"But brother, you suffer from the same affliction."

"True, and think of the opportunities we've missed," Euclid replied. "The mosquitoes we might have slapped."

"Also, this one here? Somehow he always rescues himself with a story."

"Also true," Euclid replied. "In fact, he's going to tell one right now. So that I don't have to kill him for you."

"I am?" Asher asked. "But I'm exhausted."

"You are," the giant brothers answered as one.

"Make it about your faith," Euclid added.

Asher felt his chest clench. "My faith?"

"Yes." Pascal cracked his knuckles, methodically and with evident satisfaction: all the fingers of one hand, including the thumb, and the other hand with equal thoroughness and gratification. "Or you die."

While by then he knew there was little actual danger, Asher nonetheless felt the presence of risk, to him and to his standing at the atelier. Especially on faith, which waited like a stubborn windshield to trap him. Henri, cradling his hurt hand, moved closer so as not to miss a word.

Simon too came to sit in the dirt. "Stories of faith are my favorite kind."

"Faith." What tale could he tell, to satisfy them and not reveal himself? One word about the temple and he'd be unmasked. Asher studied his blistered hands. Nothing. The rusting vehicles. No idea. The cloudless sky, afternoon dozing toward evening. The hunger in his belly. Nothing, nothing. The stain of his sweat on the dirt. The bridge they must cross on the way home. The river.

"Yes," he said. "Yes, I have a story about faith. Faith and water."

"I like it already," Euclid added.

"It happened at a river when I was nine years old."

Pascal let his arms flap out to the ground. "Proceed, and save your skin."

"It was not my skin that was saved. Someone else's."

"Salvation, plus a river?" Simon said. "It hints of baptism. Tell away."

Asher sat on the bumper. "In Bonheur where I was born, everyone's lives were shaped by the sea. The rich lived on bluffs with ocean views, inland shopkeepers and tradesmen could hear the surf day and night, and even humble homes like ours could smell when the tide went out."

He leaned forward, forearms on his thighs. "For some odd reason, though, one July day my parents took us all away to a river. Some tributary of the Seine? I don't recall. Four brothers I have—or had. They all obeyed the orders to board the train, and I don't know who of them survived the war."

He sighed. "Anyway, they were all older than me. Stronger too, and none more than Albin, the eldest, named for my grandfather, who was named for his grandfather. He was seventeen, and as the youngest I saw him as a tree of muscle, an encyclopedia of knowledge. That day we hiked through the woods till the trail opened beside a place of waterfalls. We'd never seen anything like it. A long sequence of basins and spills, accompanied by the sounds of a continuous splash. My parents gave us strict instructions about which pools were allowed and which were beyond our abilities. The one farthest uphill was strictly forbidden."

Simon raised a finger. "Did you all know how to swim?"

"My brothers, strongly. Myself, barely. But I didn't mind. The current was mild, there were warm pools and gentle cascades. One had a calm hideaway behind its shower, safe from the pounding water, a secret spot snug against the rock."

"I want to go there now," Euclid said.

Henri nodded too, his pinched fingers now tucked into the opposite armpit.

"A long walk from here," Asher replied. "But we were playful, and glad. As time passed our courage grew, we explored rougher downpours and faster currents. Naturally the uppermost basin held the most appeal, because the water fell the greatest distance. It also had the virtue of being forbidden. Albin waited till my parents were busy assembling our picnic lunch on a flat rock. He scurried up to examine the big one for himself. A certain little spider scampered after him."

"You both drowned, didn't you?" Pascal growled. He was still on his back, staring at the sky. "Drowned your poor selves dead."

Asher ignored the question. "Albin was too fast for me to keep up. I was distractable anyway. Near the upper falls, I noticed how their spray, with the sun high behind them, made a prism. There was a rainbow in the air. It stopped me in place."

Asher stood. "Then they were shouting, everyone shouting at me. My mother, my father up on the ridge, of course they yelled, I'd disobeyed. But my three other brothers shouted as well, all carrying on." He began to pace. "They were well back from the cascade, while I stood right beside it, secure on a kind of platform rock, and with the din of the falls I could not hear a word they said. I had never seen my mother so distraught, though, and I wondered what I had done to enrage her so severely. I hadn't even touched the water. All children have the sense innately, I believe, that in a fair world, the punishment fits the crime."

Asher paused. He had forgotten how strong this memory was, how deep its effect on him. His brothers would be scattered all over the earth now—if they were alive. Loss was a kind of waterfall, waiting for its chance to flood your heart. He stopped pacing, and leaned against the truck. His father, who went early each day to the synagogue to pray for his ancestors, sometimes returning with a loaf of black bread. His grandfather, on the roof eating carrots. His grandmother, picking out the orange. They were all gone.

"Come on, man." Simon could not contain himself. "Why were they shouting?"

"I didn't know." Asher extended one hand. "Finally, Tomas, my next-eldest brother, pointed behind me. He shook his arm and gestured again. I followed his aim, and there was Albin, suspended in the pool beside me, amid the thick of the waterfall's splash. Not an arm's length away. His limbs were pumping like the strong swimmer I knew him to be. But his face was not clearing the surface. As if he could find no purchase in all the churning white. After a few seconds I realized he was not in actual water. He was trying to swim in foam, and could not rise enough to get a breath."

Asher paused, aware of his own breathing, and the men were keen for his words. "Already Albin's arms were tiring, he was seconds away from drowning. And the only person in my family who might help him in time was me, the littlest, too weak to save anyone from anything, yet all the others could do was point and shout. I knew too that if I did it wrong, he would pull me in, and our family would watch us both die."

Asher held his arms forward. "I took two steps out on the platform, set my feet, and reached into the foam. There was a confusion, a flailing, but when I found my brother's wrist I grabbed it with both hands, and yanked for all I was worth."

"You saved him," Euclid proclaimed. "You saved your brother's life."

"By doing almost nothing. We were on our backs, he was gasping, coughing up water. My parents were cheering. Albin recovered swiftly, but I had a gash on my back. We were not punished, and my father carried me to the car on his shoulders."

"I love this story," Simon said.

"For years, Albin told anyone who would listen that when he was seventeen his baby brother had saved him, and one day he would repay the favor. For all I know, Albin is still alive today, somewhere, still hoping to keep that promise."

Pascal cleared his throat. "Whereas you are about to be silenced forever, plus three eternities, because this story has nothing to do with faith."

"You are mistaken sir," Simon said. "Everything in it is about faith."

"I'll kill you too," he said wearily, "in a minute."

"Hear me out." Simon pressed his hands together. "The trip to the river, for a seaside family, is an act of parental faith. The pools are life's pleasures and challenges, of varying strength and hazard. The safe place behind that one waterfall, that is church. The brother climbing into danger, that is temptation. The little one following, that is angelic guarding. The foam is sin. The yelling people are gospels, words to keep us on the right path. The rescue of his brother, that is the promised salvation. You see? Every word in this story is about faith."

Pascal frowned at him. "In my world, the smart ones die first."

"Do you know," Simon said, "what is the greatest act of faith today?"

"Enlighten us," Euclid said, "and after, shut up entirely. You tire my brain."

"This." He spread his arms toward the rows of vehicles. "By removing glass from these instruments of death, and making it into church windows, we are committing the opposite of war. We are transforming our enemy's hate into something sacred."

No one spoke for a minute.

Finally, Pascal sat up, groaning. "I can't bear another word." He staggered over to the wagon, wrapping its harnesses on his shoulders. "Remember our bargain, men. Set me a place at the lady's table tonight, or, certain as I breathe, I'll slaughter the lot of you."

CHAPTER 25

The crew did as they'd promised, and asked Brigitte to offer Pascal a seat at supper. She surprised them by saying yes, if they all washed their hands. Asher found himself last in line, behind Pascal, who plunged his paws into the water, scrubbed with abandon, and left it clouded and black. Considering the basin's dark contents, Asher decided that going unwashed would be more sanitary.

Once Etienne had wheeled Marc to the head of the table, the rest of them took their seats and dove into serving themselves. Roasted pork tenderloins, in honey and mustard and herbs. Pascal studied the others' plates before taking a modest portion.

"May I offer you some bread?" Brigitte held a wooden bowl toward him.

"I be enchanted to accept," Pascal growled, the bowl looking tiny in his hands.

Euclid did not join them, begging off for having overeaten earlier in the day. He remained outside to doze in the wagon and ignore his grumbling belly.

"How was your day of removing the glass?" Brigitte asked Simon.

"I believe Pascal can answer you best," he said, winking at him.

The huge one straightened himself, unavoidably crowding the men on either side. "When we finished our labors, Asher told us a story about faith." He nodded at them all, his head moving like a bull considering which cow was next. "It were uplifting."

"It was indeed," Simon affirmed, and the meal was off and running.

Pascal proved himself so well mannered, sipping from his goblet with a pinkie extended, that what began as comical behavior in a man so large became a kind of rough gentility. He was full of pleases and thank-yous, and caught himself before he'd completed uttering a threat to kill someone.

Finally, Marc, who had remained silent, coughed emphatically, one hand raised to beg the group's patience. "Have." He shook his hand. "H-h. Have him . . ."

Brigitte beamed from the table's other end. "We're listening, my love."

Pascal saw her expression: pain, certainly, but unflinching affection as well. It stopped his chewing. He put down his fork altogether.

"Again." Marc coughed. The vein bulged on his forehead. "Have."

"Take your time, my love. We are in no hurry."

Seeing her, their connection miles deep, Pascal clutched the front of his shirt.

"Have." Marc shook his head with frustration. "H . . . have him again."

"Why, of course." She smiled at Pascal. "You are welcome to dine with us again."

The giant man blinked at her several times. "Thanks to you for the inviting. But I would not want to impose."

She placed her small hand atop his thick forearm. "Someday you must. Please."

Pascal lowered his eyes. "Amen."

HENRI STOOD OVER THE LIGHT table Asher had built, one hand with splinted fingers, his face downturned like a waning moon. Before him lay the first side window, nearly finished: a huge gray hammer, raised by a pink but muscular arm, about to come down with full force on a black nail already stabbed into another man's palm, pinning that hand to the brown wood behind it. In the background, a blood-red sun. The image was full of foreboding, a horror about to occur.

"Grim as an execution," Etienne observed. "Which is exactly what it was."

"Anyone seeing this window," Simon said, "will realize the magnitude of our Savior's sacrifice."

"Does anyone care to get any work done today?" the nameless man bellowed from his corner.

Etienne rolled his eyes for the others' benefit, before marching back to the bins of broken glass. As he shoveled shards into the crucible, they floated on the boiling soup, icebergs in an orange sea, until they melted into the heat.

Later, the nameless man condescended to come see the window. "Could you two possibly go any slower?" He stood with his blowpipe upward as a knight might hold his lance. "It will be months before I can assemble my wedding."

Asher finished the cut he was making in a pane. "What are you talking about?"

"Jesus's first miracle, you dolt. Water into wine? The wedding at Cana?"

Asher blinked at him blankly. If he did not reply, he could not be caught.

"Writ large in glass for generations to see," the nameless man continued, "an uplifting refreshment after your ghoulish portrait of human savagery."

"Right." Asher bent to continue carving a dark blue shape, for the robe of a Roman centurion.

"Have you two decided what the other side window will be?"

"Henri thinks we should finish this one first."

"To here." The nameless held a hand at his sternum. "I will have grown a beard to here before you two finish, and the important part of this commission can begin."

Henri had been bent over the table, soldering the intersections of lead, but now he sidled around sideways, aiming his backside in the nameless man's direction.

"Fine," he huffed, toting his blowpipe away. "But I'll get old waiting for you."

IN HIS DREAM AUBE WAS furious, her eyes flashing with indignation. The man on fire was attempting to embrace her, which somehow was Asher's fault—until he woke and saw real flames on the wall. Which wall? Then reality returned, the whole château, and he found himself with his head out the window. In the distance there were fires.

Often he felt that the only reality was there in the atelier, and everything outside was an abstraction. But here was proof that the world continued, was in fact quite busy with itself. There were flames near and far in the lowlands.

"Must be a battle of some kind," the nameless man declared.

It startled Asher, who scanned the long high wall; Simon had his head out too, beret on even at night. Henri and Etienne had come across the hall to see as well.

"One fire is a mishap," the nameless man continued. "A clogged chimney, a lamp kicked over in the barn. Two fires is a coincidence—and an unhappy one, because most towns haven't rebuilt a single fire squad, much less two. But three fires?"

He lit a cigarette, shaking out the match before he dropped it in the dark. "Three means arson. Fires to inflict damage or conceal deeds. Strike, counterstrike, retaliation."

Henri knocked quickly on his shutter, pointing with a straight arm. A fourth burn had just begun, just beyond the one on the right.

"Anyone who thinks this war is over . . ." Etienne said.

"Lucky us," Asher said, "that we don't have combat here."

"We don't?" The nameless man laughed, one harsh bark, before drawing his head back inside like a turtle retreating into his shell.

Asher stayed at his window an hour or more. He would not have said it out loud, but flames in the distance had a kind of beauty.

DAYS LATER, THE NAMELESS MAN sat at the dinner table long after the dishes were washed and dried, and shelved according to Brigitte's iron-clad methods.

"I volunteer to scrub the pots," he'd called to the kitchen, "if I can work longer at my window design."

In truth, the page before him was blank. He had found his own roll of drafting paper, but, as if to refute Asher's method, he'd spent the better part of a night cutting it into pages, hundreds of them, marking a few with scribbles but nothing substantial.

That evening he was trying to draw clay vases in a corner. But under his pencil they looked flat. No one would be inspired. It was ironic that he had chided Asher for simple drawings, when his own looked cartoonish.

Asher came from the kitchen, drying his hands. "How's the wedding coming?"

"Neither bride nor groom has appeared yet."

"Have you left room at the peak for Marc's medallion?"

The nameless man froze over his paper. "I had forgotten."

"If you're tight for space, we could include it in the other side window."

"No," the nameless man all but shouted. He calmed himself, though, realizing that a medallion at the peak relieved him of part of the design. Now all he had to do was draw wedding guests, a banquet table. "Marc's work belongs at the peak."

After Asher left the room, the nameless man scrubbed the clay jars away with a rough eraser, his page blank again. "I'd rather be reading Cicero."

And there were still those pots to be scrubbed.

A WEEK PASSED WITHOUT A delivery. Marie made one stop so brief, Pétain did not have time to complain—Asher's usual alert—and was gone before he'd known. He assumed she was busy, but as the stretch of days grew, he wondered. The jar remained empty in its hiding place; more than one person would be feeling her absence.

He took to lingering after lunch, clearing the table, refilling the water bucket. Brigitte, chopping carrots, watched him with a wary eye. "Hovering will not help."

Asher set a stack of plates beside the sink. "What are you talking about?"

"She'll come when she comes. When she has things to deliver."

"I know." He collected silverware to one side. "Marie said everything is based on when things ripen."

"Poor boy." Brigitte went back to her chopping. "I worry about you."

Pétain brayed from the side yard, and Asher's eyes lit up. "See? Things ripen." And he hurried outside.

Marie—dressed in a smock colored the pale green of new leaves—was examining the donkey's braces.

"Hello, Marie," Asher said.

"Good afternoon," she said, following the leather strap around and under, till she stood on the animal's other side.

"Are those repairs holding up all right?"

"Just checking, yes. The replacement gear has been slow to arrive."

Asher stood across from her, Pétain between them. "I've missed you."

"That's very sweet."

Marie glided to the rear of the cart, selecting vegetables for her delivery. Asher met her there. "I've craved you."

She paused, her lips pursed. In that moment without words, Asher felt himself suddenly poised at the edge of an abyss. She kissed his cheek like he was her elderly aunt, and whisked her first load of greens away into the house.

Asher stood stunned for a moment, the bed of the wagon looking like a litter of green. He stirred the vegetables, considering how to help, before slinking around to the woodpile entry, to put himself back to work.

THE TANTRUM WAS IN FULL force before Asher knew it had begun. Absorbed with studying an orb he had blown unevenly, he did not raise his head until he heard shouting. Etienne was barking at the nameless man, who was throwing tools right and left. All at once he grabbed a blowpipe he'd left in the furnace's glory hole for who knew how long.

"Careful." Etienne held both hands out and low, as if telling an oncoming driver to slow down. "Be careful with that."

Asher could see a third of the pipe glowing, and he was impressed that the nameless man could bear to hold the other end. But as he registered that thought, the man had come to the back area's steps and poked the glowing part in his direction.

"Calm down." Asher jumped out of his chair, snatching a lead-cutter knife. A familiar thrill coursed through his veins. If this was the moment, he was ready to draw blood. "I'm just trying to work over here."

"Interfering," the nameless man seethed. "Delaying. Being inexcusably bad." He swung the glowing pipe in an arc, wildly, its tip nearly touching Asher's chest.

"I said be careful," Etienne called, but the nameless man remained keyed on Asher—who already had a plan: kicking the water bucket over for distraction, and when the nameless man turned to see, plunging the knife in his unguarded ribs. Meanwhile, the hot tip made small orange circles in front of him.

The wood supply door swung back, Brigitte entering with an armload. She needed only an instant to see the situation. "Now, now. Everyone calm down."

She dropped the wood and opened her smock—the modest one Asher had made—to display her collarbones. "There's no need for this."

"Stay out of it," the nameless man growled.

Without a blink of hesitation, she strode straight toward him. "It is not necessary," she said. "It is no longer necessary."

His face contorted. "But it *is*, though."

Brigitte shook her head. "Not anymore. Not here."

The nameless man retreated a few steps. His eyes were pressed closed. Asher thought it was the opposite of Marie—who closed her eyes to feel more, while this man did it to feel less.

"That pipe's too hot for me to touch," Brigitte said. "Please put it down."

"This life." The nameless man opened his eyes. "How do we bear this life?"

And he released the blowpipe, hanging his head as it clanged on the concrete floor. Brigitte stepped over the pipe to put one finger under his jaw, bringing his face level again. "Your pain is strong at this moment, but only momentarily," she told him. "Your genius is stronger, and it is permanent. That's why I believe in you."

He melted, falling against her, and Brigitte hugged him, his arms hanging, till meekly he brought one hand up to her side. The aloof man was permitting human contact, the solace of it. As long as they were touching, no one in the atelier moved or spoke. The nameless man pulled away first.

"Look at you," he said, "all of you."

Asher scanned the room: Etienne by the furnace, Simon feeding it fuel, Henri at the annealer's open door, an orange glow behind him.

"All drawn to the heat," the nameless man continued, "as if it could heal what you have done, and what has been done to you. As if fire were some kind of truth." He toed the blowpipe, rolling it away. "The only truth here is that if you get too close, you burn. Yet we cannot resist getting closer. And I'm as much a fool for it as all of you."

He started to leave, but paused in the doorway. "We think we're artists here, but no. We're only . . . we're only a society of moths."

And he was gone. Using gloves, Brigitte picked up the blowpipe, slid it in the rack. "War is made by army after army. Peace is won one soldier at a time."

As she left, Asher remembered the cutter in his hand, and dropped it in a toolbox. "What the hell was that?" he asked the room. "Why did he come after me?"

"We were working along in silence," Etienne answered. "I have no idea."

"He hugged her," Simon marveled, coming forward from the furnace. "He actually gave her a hug."

JUST BEFORE DINNER, HENRI SAT back on his stool, and nodded at his window for a solid minute. Asher, brushing away bits of solder and lead, did not notice right away. Accustomed to the silence of his partner, he somehow had learned when a gesture was meaningful and when it was Henri's equivalent of saying, *Um*. But when he saw Henri continue nodding, unease came over him.

"Nearly done?" he asked. "Checking for finishing touches?"

Henri was panning his gaze corner to corner, top to bottom, inspecting seams and edges. He reached a bandaged hand over and rested it on Asher's shoulder.

"Do you think it's finished?"

Henri replied by smiling ear to ear, and Asher's discomfort worsened. Yes, in one sense the window was complete. All spaces filled, metal supports in place, fulfilling the original design. The image—a hand about to pound a nail into a hand—contained dread any sinner could see and be chastened by.

"Spectacular," Simon crowed on his way past, arms full of wood. "It is the sacrifice, you see. God sacrificing his son."

"Yes," Asher murmured.

The problem was not his ignorance about Christianity. It was that the window looked primitive. The raised arm, about to drive a nail into the heart of believers for centuries, contained no tension, no hint of the thinking and feeling body attached to that hammer. Nor did it convey the pain of the man whose palm that nail would sunder, pinning him to a plank until he died. The fingers were as flat as slices of herring. Above it all, like a giant cliché, there hung that blood-red sun.

"Do we want to give this another day? In case anything else occurs to us?"

By way of answer, Henri came around the window to lean against him, bumping him sideways with his head like a loyal old dog.

Asher patted him on the back. "Well done, my friend," he lied. "Well done."

Henri put both arms around him, a fierce hug, then stepped back crimson-faced. With his uninjured hand he held up two fingers, pointed at the finished window, and waved them back and forth between himself and Asher.

"We're doing the next one together?" Asher asked.

Henri bumped Asher's shoulder with his fist. Then he crossed the atelier, waving and gesturing, inviting the others over to see. Asher backed around behind the annealer, out the doors, where Simon was sorting wood.

Sweating, he looked up from his labor. "You need anything?"

"Air." Asher continued past him. A fluster of goldfinches sprung from the ground, darting into the trees like daytime fireflies.

By habit he checked as he passed, and yes, the jar was replenished. Someday he would ask Marie all about it. If she ever invited him again. For the moment he needed to relieve his claustrophobia, the enclosed feeling as he contemplated making another crude window. He had watched Marie arrange flowers in a vase: different colors, different heights, though the blooms would not last a week. These windows would hang for generations, yet they did not equal the art in her flowers.

What had become of her lately? There was a distance he did not understand. He arrived at the fork in the lane, the road rising to the village or descending to Marie's. Knowing better than to break her one rule, Asher returned to the courtyard—where he heard cheers of celebration.

"Oh-ho!" Marc cried, his voice booming unstuttered over all the others. "Oh-ho!"

Henri must have brought the window into the house for him to see. After the pop of a cork, another round of cheers went up.

Asher knew that his secrets kept people at a remove. But he thought everyone was that way. Now, in the courtyard, he understood. He was the true outsider. No one else had held his daughter as her breathing stopped. No one else had killed people with his own hands. If they had, he would have seen evidence. These were destinations of the heart from which no traveler returned. So the second side window would also be dull, between them would hang the nameless man's uninspired wedding, and none of it would say anything about the world, or faith, or even light.

Asher navigated around the woodpile into an atelier that now was empty. Finding his roll of paper, his box of pencils, he crept up the stairs undetected. Let the others drink and celebrate. That night his dinner would be drawing.

CHAPTER 26

The next day, everyone was muted and dull. At breakfast Etienne complained about a trove of *pommeau* Marc found in the cellar, an apple brandy three times stronger than wine. They had downed every drop of every dusty bottle.

"Couldn't we have stopped at three?" he moaned, head in his hands. "Why did Marc keep opening them?"

"It's going to be a beautiful day," Simon answered, bright as a new penny.

"How . . ." The nameless man sat flummoxed. "You drank more than anyone. How are you not catatonic?"

"Tolerance," Simon replied with a shrug.

"Experience," Etienne corrected.

Asher noticed the nameless man's drawing paper on the table, but all he could spy were vague scribbles.

Henri was not at breakfast, but Asher found him later at the light table. Ingots held down a sheet he knew contained a rough design for the second window. He already had a different idea, drawn in minute detail, left on his bed.

Henri gazed at him with bleary eyes. He exhaled a sour plume of alcohol, and Asher fanned the air in front of his face. "You indulged last night too?"

Henri nodded, rubbing his forehead.

"I suppose some celebration was called for." Asher sidled over. "Are you sure you want to start the new window today?"

Henri waved Asher closer. There was no evading it; he had to look.

A lion and a lamb, lying beside each another. A beatific sky, angels and beams of light. As cheery as the other window was dour.

But the design was horizontal, when the window was vertical. To fit the lion and lamb beside each other, Henri had reduced them to miniatures, leaving a large gap of plain glass between them and the angels. Henri swallowed audibly, awaiting a verdict.

"I like the idea," Asher said finally. "But if we put the lion above the lamb, or the other way around, we can make them both larger and reduce the open space. The animals will be big enough for people seated away from the window to recognize."

Henri pressed his pencil on the lamb, then the lion. He held bandaged fingers to the lamb's head and tail, then moved them to the lion's head and tail.

"They're the same size," Asher replied. "Yes, I see."

Henri smiled in his usual way, then threw down the pencil, spun to the nearest trash bin, and vomited.

BY NINE A.M. HENRI WAS back in bed, as were Etienne and the nameless man. Marc did not come down at all that day, his wheelchair parked by the stairs. In the kitchen Brigitte slumped on a stool, staring into space, while Simon wrestled the woodpiles, sorting and separating as though it were play.

All of which meant that Asher was alone in the warren, working on the lion and lamb. The idea itself was inspired: natural enemies who had found peace. The France that Asher knew—the broken, divided, hurting place—needed an image of healing.

But Henri's lamb was too small. It should convey vulnerability, so members of a congregation would see their own worries and fears represented. The mane of Henri's lion, a circle of outward-pointing triangles, made the king of the jungle look harmless, incapable of so much as a roar.

Lunch was a bowl of plums, hard-crusted farm bread sliced and fanned on a plate, a crock of salted butter, a stack of salted carrots, a platter bearing thick slices of fatty ham, and no sign of Brigitte.

"I imagine she's tending to Marc," Simon said, the only other one at table. "He's the one who drank hardest."

"I can hardly blame him," Asher replied.

"I've completed my work for the day." Simon contemplated a carrot before biting it in half. "I may march down to the river and give myself a good bathing."

Asher could not help smiling. "Be careful. I hear those waters are enchanted."

Simon shook his head. "Not a worry for any sincere believer."

"I envy you that," Asher said, not thinking.

"Is your belief less than sincere?" Simon sat forward, suddenly attentive.

Asher realized he had been too casual. "That's not the problem."

"Tell me, tell me, tell me." Simon was as alert as a squirrel.

Asher fiddled with the bowl of plums. What was the risk in confiding in him? "Things I saw in the war, and things I did, put holes in my beliefs."

"Your first priority must be to restore that faith." Simon put down the carrot. "Nothing else matters. You must dwell on those moments in scripture that contain great displays of faith. Moments when God tested his people, and they responded with such fervor that it brought redemption and salvation."

"Good idea," Asher replied. But platitudes did not help. The man might as well have been speaking German.

Simon pressed his hands together. "Will you pray with me?"

Asher felt claustrophobia pressing in again. "I will," he conceded, "in silence."

"God will hear you." Simon closed his eyes, and his lips began to move.

Asher did the same, his mouth in counterfeit motion, while his mind flittered like a hummingbird from flower to flower: Marie's curtained bedroom, the steady river, a night of drinking he had avoided, the challenge of making a second window worthy of the cathedral. What scripture did he know about unbreakable faith?

All at once, he had it. Like when his stories arrived, he knew what the second side window should be. Eyes popping open, he stood.

Simon looked up with worry. "What is it? Are you all right?"

"I am magnificent." He reached over the table to clap the man on the shoulder. "Prayer is exactly what I needed."

"The Holy Ghost works in many—"

"Yes, the Holy Ghost." Asher went to the door. "Have fun at the river."

"It wasn't me who helped you. It was—"

Asher had already left. Simon contemplated the empty table. Afternoon stretched before him, as lazy as a cat in the sun. Why not? he thought, drawing the bowl closer, and selecting for himself the ripest plum.

THE DRAWING REQUIRED LESS TIME than Asher expected, because he had Henri's first window as a model. The château remained quiet, upstairs and down. In the atelier, sunlight made its arc across the floor while he worked. Sometime before dinner the nameless man appeared, toting his pencils and stack of papers. He sat at a workbench and, with sighs Asher could hear across the room, labored over a drawing too. When Asher next lifted his head, the man had left—who knew when—and abandoned his papers. Unable to quiet his curiosity, he ventured over.

One earthen vase. It was a good drawing, excellent even. A shadow slanted left to right across its brim, indicating where the source of light was. He tried to feel sympathy for the nameless man. But he'd been working on the wedding window for three weeks, and as Asher flipped through the pages, the total result was one vase.

Asher felt his pride, and knew it was unmerited. He was a beginner, a novice's novice, a maker of boots, and a taker of lives. Having never blown a sheet of glass successfully, having mixed crucible contents only under supervision, having seen only two sets of stained glass windows in his life—both in synagogues—his criticism was thoroughly unschooled. Still, he was full of opinions. A lion's mane was not made of triangles, any more than a wedding could be conveyed by a single vase.

He raised the ladle from the water bucket, draining its contents in one pull. After, Asher did not pause until evening, when he had to light the lamps. The design was rough but sufficient. From the racks of colored glass, he collected panes in various hues—earth tones for the lower portion of the window, brightest yellow for the sun—and brought them to the light table. There, with no hand to guide his cutting, Asher began to build his first window.

In less than an hour he saw the flaw. Henri was correct. All the small pieces he wanted, to make the image more natural, required too much lead. But if he used larger pieces of glass, the design would fail. Asher left the desk and paced.

Both furnaces were cold. Normally at night they idled at a menacing glow. This time they were dark, doors ajar like an opened shotgun.

There must have been more to that night of drinking than celebrating one side window. Marc's return? A drowning of sorrows? France recovering too slowly?

For the first time it struck him: Maybe the three officers had not gone to the canteen that night to celebrate their deeds, but to mourn them. Maybe they were tormented by conscience, desperate for alcohol's numbing. Stupefaction achieved, they climbed into their car to get home and sleep it off, but instead sent themselves to whatever hereafter awaited.

Asher wandered to the doorway. Time for invention. In one hand he held a length of the lead he'd been using to secure the glass, and in his other, the lead cutting tool. Laying the metal on its side, he shaved half of it away. The slot to hold the pane was half as deep, but that also meant less lead to blacken the image.

Next Asher dismantled what he had built. So quickly did his hands move, he dropped one piece on the floor and it shattered. Leaving the shards for later, he began shaving all of the lead he'd used. When it dulled the blade of his tool, he went from one workstation to another, grabbing every cutter he could find.

At the table, he spilled the tools with a clatter. Asher was neither tired, nor hungry, nor cold. The notion of working all night gave him a sense of abundance, an expanse of time uninterrupted.

"Now," he told the design before him. "Now we can do it."

HE DID NOT REST TILL the smallest hour, when his lower back hurt from bending over the table. Asher took a lamp and drifted out to the woodpile.

Henri would be upset. Others could be angry. Asher's design might reveal his religion and bring his expulsion. But it was the right image, a perfect companion to the other side. The problem was not that the window might cost him his place at Le Château Guerin. It was that he missed God. Could not find his God.

What had they been doing in the street that afternoon anyway? He himself had heard the soldier ordering everyone inside. He'd come to the door assuming his wife and daughter would be waving from the window of some neighbor's house. No, they were running up the middle of the street, the last ones by whole minutes. The soldier lost patience. Why had they taken so long? He would never know.

Before Aube's and Rachel's bodies had hit the ground, Asher's beliefs were gone. No deity could permit such a thorough wrong. And so in war, when anyone might call on heaven for support, Asher could not do it. *Dear God, I am on my way to kill someone, please protect me so I don't get caught or shot.* That prayer would have been cold-blooded blasphemy.

A puff of wind swept over the woodpile, wavering the flame in

Asher's lamp. It sent him back to work: Cut glass to a curved, natural shape. Tap it free of the pane. Nestle it into the lead. Make everything snug. Make another cut.

Wasn't Asher's design also a story of lion and lamb, but with God as the lion and humanity the lamb? Weren't Aube and Rachel a pair of lambs?

All at once he drew back, thunderstruck. He'd been assembling the face of a boy, Isaac. But now Asher realized whose portrait belonged in that place. The child he had known from her first birth cry, the one he carried in his arms and wrapped in blankets and cherished whenever she fell asleep. Here was an opportunity to give her life again—not growing up, not learning to read or cook or become a parent herself, but with her face honored at least, seen by generations of strangers with reverence.

Unrolling his paper to a blank spot, Asher sketched the changes to his design. In a fever he began removing the boy's features, as if the idea might escape him. Tears fell from his face onto the colored glass. He wiped them with a chamois cloth and continued to work.

HENRI FOUND HIM ASLEEP ON the floor, among shards of glass, lumps of lead, discarded lead-cutters. He examined one, and the blade was notched and dull, as if Asher had stayed up all night hacking at something. Henri checked another, and it had the same damage. He scratched his head.

One by one the others arrived. Etienne told Simon to fetch kindling, it would take half a day to fire the kilns back to working temperature. The nameless man arrived at his workbench, scanned his drawing of a vase, and stuffed it away in his coat.

They were all sober, ate a good breakfast. A proper team, back to business, except for one up in the warren, sound asleep, his hands prayered into a pillow.

Henri, chastened by the day lost to a hangover, went to refresh his memory of the window he had made. The start of crucifixion, under a cold red sun. A draped sheet, as thick as sailcloth, fell away like a model's robe in drawing class, revealing his masterwork, it would hang in the cathedral for a hundred—

The sun was yellow. Bright beams streamed from it in all directions. The red was gone. The blood of sacrifice had been removed. Someone had changed his window.

Hands shaking, he raised his head as though the atelier were now a foreign place. The other men were busy with their tasks. Henri carried the window over toward the kiln. But the nameless man stepped around him, showing only annoyance. He was busy recovering the lost day.

Brigitte arrived in her high-buttoned smock. "That's right, men, back to it."

Henri marched toward her with the window, but she dodged him. "Yes, it's beautiful. Now we need to start the next one."

She bustled out to help Simon with wood. Henri stood stunned in the middle of the room. After a moment, and resting the window against a side wall, he went to the assembly area and slid out a large clear pane of glass. Holding it horizontally, waist-high, stepping over Asher so as not to wake him, Henri waddled down the steps to the center of the atelier. No one paid any heed when he raised the pane over his head, as if sacrificially, and flung it down on the concrete floor.

It was sacrilege, he knew that. But the impact exceeded his expectation, an explosion and splash as the pane shattered. Henri hopped back, shards spraying from woodpile door to kiln to warren steps.

As a way to gain the people's attention, he could not have succeeded better. Everyone spun to see the small man with his bandaged hand outstretched. Etienne left his workbench, the nameless man came with a shovel, Asher jerked awake, and Brigitte charged forward in a rage.

"What in the almighty has come over you?" she shouted, waving her arms in all directions. "Isn't it hard enough here already, without you wasting something that took hours to make?"

Crunching his way over broken glass, Henri toted his finished window, poking at the bright yellow sun. He shook his bandaged fist overhead.

"I told you I love it," she answered. "We all do."

Henri stomped his foot, poking his thumb repeatedly against the yellow sun.

"The poor fool," the nameless man said. "He's gone mad."

"No, he hasn't." Asher cleared his throat. "The sun is different."

Henri nodded like his head was in danger of falling off.

"You're right," Etienne said, coming closer. "It was red."

"Wait a minute." The nameless man rested the shovel tip on the floor. "Who would know how to change the color of your sun? Much less have the gall?"

While everyone was silent, Henri stood rigid with righteousness.

"I did," Asher said. "I took the red out and put in yellow."

"Asher." Etienne stomped his foot. "I've told you about this. Never alter another person's work without permission."

"You've completely changed the meaning," the nameless man crowed. "A sunny crucifixion? Does heaven smile on this tragedy?"

Brigitte faced Asher. "You have violated the principles of artistic integrity and respect that are the foundation of this château." After glancing at the other men, as if she were taking their votes, she elevated her head. "I must ask you to leave. Now."

CHAPTER 27

"Wait." Asher stood, working a sleep kink out of his neck. "Let me explain."

"No." Brigitte's face was flushed. "Henri is my husband's right hand."

"We must discuss this." Asher put aside the canvas tarp he'd slept under. It remained semi-upright, like an abandoned ghost. "There will be discussion."

"Who are you to say such things? This atelier has been in my family for four hundred and twenty-four years."

"Then surely you will not begrudge me ten seconds, to come and see."

She waved her arms this way and that. "I am needed at the kiln. And the woodpile. And the kitchen. We're behind. All of us missed an entire day of work."

"Not all of us." Asher remained as imperturbable as a stone. "While you all were ruined by drink, I worked day and night. Ten seconds is all I ask."

"No." Brigitte stamped her foot. "You have offended all proper—"

"Not ten? After all this time, I haven't earned that sliver from you?"

She faltered, exchanging a look with Henri. "To see what?"

Asher waved a hand at the light table.

"What trickery are you up to?"

"You may dismiss me anyway." Asher backed away, making room. "But it should not be for disrespecting Henri, who is my honored friend."

They paused, like a wagon on a hilltop before gravity pulls it down the far side. Henri hitched up his trousers and shuffled forward. Brigitte followed, as the others gathered at the steps. She saw an assembly on the table. "Whose work is this?"

Asher removed a soft cloth. In that dim corner, the image was not visible.

"Is it yours? When did you build it?"

Asher struck a match—amid the tension it seemed unusually loud—lit a candle, and placed it below the window. With slow deliberation he moved, less to prolong the suspense than perhaps to delay the moment of his expulsion.

A second candle glowing, he placed it in the opposite corner. They leaned closer. Was the image a tree limb? A golden seal?

Not until the third candle was flickering could they see what he had made: an arm, raised in a pose identical to the one in Henri's window. But instead of a hammer, the hand held a knife, and instead of a nail about to receive the blow, it was the chest of a boy. Meanwhile, the large yellow sun dispensed its beams on everything, its size and shape the same as in Henri's window, in the same optimistic yellow.

"*Voilà*," Asher said.

Brigitte put her hands on her hips. "How does this excuse your change of Henri's work?"

Asher appeared surprised. "They both have to have the same sun."

The nameless man shook his head. "If you are trying to make some clever artistic point, you have chosen the wrong method. Especially for a person so utterly inexperienced. You're barely one step above being the boy who hauls the wood."

"Excuse me, please." Simon stepped forward, brushing chips and splinters off his chest. "Since at the moment I bear that noble responsibility, and I have not been a boy in decades, permit me to say that you are missing the point. Every one of you."

"*Quidquid praecipies, esto brevis*," the nameless man replied.

"I'm sorry?" Simon said.

"Whatever advice you give, be brief." He snorted. "I find myself less disposed than ever for one of your lectures."

"It won't take long, and having your mind changed doesn't hurt much." Simon squeezed through the group of them. "You have misunderstood."

Brigitte crossed her arms on her bosom. "Explain. And to the point."

Simon climbed the steps to stand beside the light table. "Asher's window comes from the Old Testament. The Jewish part of the Bible, you might say, long before Christ. One day God told Abraham to bring his only son, Isaac, to a mountaintop, and sacrifice him there like a lamb."

"We know the story," the nameless man said.

"Here we see the arm of Abraham," Simon continued, "his knife raised to do the Lord's will. Here is Isaac, obeying his father, who appears to have gone mad. Here, from above, is the golden light of mercy, God's angel sent to stay Abraham's hand."

He smiled at Asher. "Like we discussed at breakfast. A test of faith, wasn't it?"

Asher pressed his lips together. "It was."

Simon lay a hand on Asher's shoulder. "We must have the same sun in both windows. Otherwise, we would not have the same loving God in both scriptures."

"Oh my dear," Brigitte said.

The rest of them were silent, studying one window, and then the other. Simon raised a finger. "A final thought, if I may?"

The nameless man frowned. "Why must you always exhaust our patience?"

"Look at the precision of this window. See that arm so expressive of human anguish, and the boy's face clouded by fear. Asher's workmanship is undeniable."

Etienne climbed the stairs to lean over the window, eyeing it from side to side as if reading a page. "Sweet God in his heaven."

"What do you see?" Simon asked.

"Excellence," Etienne said. "I see an unorthodox but astonishing craft."

"The window *is* beautiful," Brigitte said. "I'll grant you that."

Asher felt a knot untie in his belly. Perhaps he would not be evicted after all.

"Forgive me," Simon persisted. "But beauty is irrelevant. Imagine these two windows, in a church, side by side—"

"Surrender the pulpit," the nameless man interrupted. "We've heard enough."

"Well, I . . ." Simon shuffled aside.

Henri climbed the steps and stood over Asher's window, though he only inspected it for a few seconds. He showed more interest in the waste to one side. A green shape, for instance, like the top of an old wizard's hat—there were four pieces of glass in nearly identical cuts. False starts for the sunbeams too, pieces that cracked in the cutting. All around the workbench lay curls of lead, where Asher had honed the metal to a thinner gauge. Alongside lay half a dozen lead cutting tools, all of them blunted by hard use. So much waste, it was staggering. If Marc were present, there would be a fierce dressing-down. Measured by materials, Asher did not know what he was doing.

Yet he had made something sublime. His first window surpassed all the ones Henri had made in his life, and everyone was cooing over it. Suddenly the work area felt crowded. Henri descended the steps, taking his window and leaning it against the side wall, once again draping a cloth over it.

"Absolutely not," Asher said, trotting down to him. "Not you, my brother in glass, who taught me everything." He removed the cloth, bundling it in his arms. "I was wrong to touch your work." He spoke thickly, his voice strained. "I am truly sorry."

Henri considered him, his tone of voice, how the cloth looked like a swaddled infant. He leaned sideways, pressing his head against Asher's chest.

While the others scrutinized the new window, the nameless man gave it only a glance. Instead, he went to the workbench by the low window, where he picked up the roll of Asher's drawings and began to unscroll it. His face looked as bitter as if he were chewing on an aspirin.

Etienne bent over the window. "This crease down the middle of Abraham's bicep." He drew a finger along it. "It expresses his anguish, his struggle. You have not only said something about glass, you have also said something about humanity."

"Simon fed the fires that made this possible," Asher replied. "You blew the glass. Marc taught me design. Henri taught me assembly. Brigitte fed me so I could heal and work. Everyone made this window."

"What a sweet thing to say." Brigitte beamed.

On they chattered, while the nameless man looked and scowled. The drawings were childish, and rough. First? A fox, poking its nose in from off the page. Next, boots: tossed under a table, paired by a door, left by a workbench with one on its side. He would have called the drawings pedestrian, but for how quickly their quality improved. The nameless man unrolled more paper.

Some of the images he recognized: A man wielding a knife. Whatever had become of Bondurant and his anger? A buxom woman in an unbuttoned smock, he could have predicted it. That fox again, but now it held a pencil. A man feeding logs to a fire, sparks rising like dandelion seeds. A man shaving before a triangle of mirror. A man on fire, flames climbing his back. "What is this nonsense?"

Other images had a winsome simplicity. A bird peering down on a conversing couple. A naked woman wading in a river. Who was she? Dogs: on a beach beside an old woman, chasing a ball toward a cathedral, running beside someone on a bicycle.

The deeper the nameless man ventured into the roll, the stranger the drawings became. An indifferent cat cleaning one paw, while a donkey danced on its hind legs. A man holding a tomato and weeping. A woman at a gate, looking back over one shoulder. Cows flying through a starry sky. Men flying too—with great long beards, and the wings of owls. A furious waterfall, and a boy reaching into the torrent.

Strangest of all, there was a fish. It appeared in nearly every drawing. At first it swam normally. But soon it leapt in the air, high above the water. Sometimes it was concealed—in the folds of a woman's smock, in the tangle of a man's beard. In a tree, watching a man drive his buggy down a lane while his shadow loomed beside him. Flying over a bridge, holding a single lily.

The sketches possessed an undeniable tenderness, and the nameless man swallowed the hurt they were causing in his throat. Yet as he unrolled more paper he also felt an anger rising, a recognition of talent that he could not dismiss.

Eventually he arrived at the last drawing, the most recent, and it left him stupefied. The tip of a blowpipe poked in from one corner, making a glass orb that contained the whole page. And inside that orb was a great sea craft, a big-bellied wooden ship, with animals of all kinds crowded in pairs along its gunwales, and with the fish again, yes, making an appearance in one low corner—but more importantly, diagonally opposite, in the far upper right, there flew a dove.

He bent closer. Beyond dispute, it was a composition of balance and poise, precision and grace. As a window, it was challenging but attainable.

Clutching the paper, putting a crease in it, the nameless man all but gnashed his teeth. White rage boiled in him as fierce as any crucible, and only with real effort did he suppress his impulse to rip the drawing in two.

Straightening at last, he saw that the others had not noticed. They were still crowing about the new window. With impeccable care, he rolled up Asher's paper, wedging it securely against the bench so it could neither fall nor unravel. Passing the group, he took Etienne's arm and drew him down the steps.

"What is it?" Etienne said, pointing up the stairs. "We weren't done speaking."

The nameless man led him farther, leaning close to whisper in his ear. All conversation stopped. They could not see the nameless man's expression, but they witnessed Etienne's reaction. "Are you sure?" he said.

Head bent nearer, the nameless man continued with his whispers.

"Of course," Etienne replied after a moment. "But are you certain?"

The nameless man glowered at them all before bustling out of the atelier.

Brigitte came to the top step. "What just happened?"

Etienne indulged in a long sigh. "A change in responsibilities. The man with no name will be forging the windows' framework at the cathedral, and supervising their installation."

"How will he find time," Asher asked, "when he is building the main window?"

"He has abdicated that role."

"But he was so fervent," Brigitte protested. "He's been slaving over the design."

"Yes." Asher stood beside her. "If he doesn't build that window, who will?"

Etienne blinked at him, and smiled. "You."

CHAPTER 28

This time there was no celebration. No drunken dinner, no lost day. Supper was solemn, in an atmosphere of fragility. Brigitte made a mountain of eggs in black pepper. Asher hesitated to ask the nameless man to pass the bread.

After the meal, he went back into the atelier to decide what his central window should portray. Moses receiving the Ten Commandments? Eden, with man and woman innocent in the Garden? Before he'd made a rough sketch, he knew why these ideas wouldn't work. Did any of them say anything about wartime? How a nation rebuilds? How a man recovers? Did any biblical episode answer questions like those?

The atelier quieted, swifts in their nests, the furnaces ticking as they cooled. Asher pulled out his roll of paper, thinking that drawing might ease his mind. First, he chose to scroll through old ideas. Memories, sights, surprisingly little of Bonheur. He chuckled to see how often his leaping fish appeared.

Then he arrived at the ark. It was not a skimpy sketch, but a realized image. It brought back a memory that reappeared like an old friend.

He had not wanted to go, his mother made him, and there on the grass outside the synagogue, those marionettes and their art had captivated everyone. Later, after the troupe drove away, his seventeen-year-old self was left alone with a young woman he would come to hold above all others, and from her a child he would gladly have taken the bullet for, had there been a means.

The ark might possibly represent a nation attempting to rebuild. After a flood of deaths, forty days and forty nights of deprivation lived forty times over, here was a vessel brimming with life, ready to revive and repair and repopulate. Here was a bird carrying in its beak an olive branch, the symbol of peace, and a harbinger of dry land not far away. And here a rainbow, promising that no such flood would ever happen again. Here was the loss, and the hope.

AT BREAKFAST ETIENNE ORDERED AN inventory of glass on hand—how much, which colors. He sent Simon to fetch Euclid and Pascal, who arrived hungry and said so. While Brigitte fed them liver and beans under a mountain of steaming onions, Pascal complimenting every forkful extravagantly, and Euclid shaking his head at how even a behemoth can be enfeebled by love, the nameless man instructed them on how much steel he would need for the cathedral installation—enough anchor screws and wedges to secure windows against any wind and all weather, for the next three hundred years.

He had done the calculations, writing them out, and referred to them repeatedly, until Euclid interrupted to suggest he try other methods for remembering the numbers.

"We are strong as trees in many ways," he said, "but not overmuscled in the uses of papers and such."

Henri and Asher were instructed to clean the assembly area, while Simon removed furnace ash till his shovel scratched the brick. By the time everyone finished, the atelier's entire supply of glass was leaning against the walls. The room spangled with refracted sunlight, and a person walking from kiln to annealer would seem to pass through several different races—most of them nonexistent.

"Asher." The nameless man inspected the supply. "How is your color plan?"

Over at the design desk, he raised his head. "Excuse me?"

"You don't know what that is, do you?" The nameless man leered at the rest of the men. "He doesn't know."

"Instead of singing an opera," Etienne replied, "why don't you explain it to him?"

He rolled his eyes, then spoke to Asher as if he were addressing a child. "First you make a cartoon. That's a life-sized version of your design. That way, you'll know how much glass you'll need, and of which colors. You assemble it with lead, you paint it sometimes, you solder any gaps in the lead, you stabilize the whole thing with cement. But none of it happens without a color plan."

"Don't worry," Etienne added. "I'll show you how."

Henri poked his chest with both thumbs.

Etienne smiled. "Of course, you should teach him too."

"Why don't we open a little schoolhouse?" the nameless man huffed. "We can invite cowherds from down in the valley. Cows too, since they might be smarter. I'm sure the bishop will be very appreciative." He left the room with a parting sneer.

Simon paused in his shoveling. "It's uplifting to see how the new duties have improved his humor."

The others laughed, except for Asher. "Schoolhouse," he mumbled to himself. "An odd suggestion, coming from him."

ON THE WAY TO DINNER that night, Asher was passing through the main hall when Marc rolled his wheelchair into the way. "T." He tilted his head, angling his eyes. "T." His cheeks rounded, as if he were about to spit. ". . . Titanium," he barked at last.

"Excuse me, sir?"

"Saw . . . saw your Abraham and Isaac."

"Yes sir."

"Well done. Now, an ark is made of w . . . wood. You'll need." Marc took a long breath, held it with his eyes closed, released it slowly. "Need brown."

"Etienne tells me we have a good supply on hand, sir."

"Not enough. You n . . . need strong brown to withstand God's rains." The last words caused Marc to spit a little. He wiped his mouth, but his lips still glistened.

"T . . . titanium makes yellow-brown." The vein on his forehead bulged. "Co . . . co." He shook his head. "Cobalt for blue. Manganese for purple. Ars." He rubbed his thumb back and forth on the chair's armrest. "Arsenic for white. Nickel for black."

"Apparently it's red we've run lowest on."

"S. Sss . . ." Marc strained, reddening.

Asher squatted beside the wheelchair. "It's all right, sir."

"Selenium," he blurted, eyebrows high as if he'd surprised himself. "It gives you pink. But ruby hues, or cranberry? Requires gold. V . . . very expensive."

"I'll make a design that avoids ruby or cranberry."

"No." Marc pounded the wheelchair. "No compromise because of materials."

"Well." Asher smiled. "It seems all I have to do to help you heal is continue to say stupid things. They make you articulate."

But Marc did not smile. "N," he replied. "No compromise. Because windows are the p . . . the poor man's Bible."

"Yes sir."

"We'll receive new C." He shook his head. "C. C." He huffed for several breaths, blinking. "New chemicals from Danzig any day now."

"If you say so, then I'm not worried."

Marc reached up, poking Asher's chest with a bony finger. "Poor man's Bible."

And there they stayed—Marc recuperating from the conversation, Asher remaining at his side out of manners—a long and awkward frieze. Brigitte rang the dinner bell, the spell broke, and they heard men stirring upstairs.

Asher piloted the wheelchair toward the dining room. Marc's

difficulty, somehow, reminded him of how he'd struggled when he arrived at the château. How fortunate he had been, ever since. The welling of emotions made him pause.

"Thank you for letting me live here, sir." Asher spoke with tightness in his chest. "I'm honored beyond words to make the main window. Thank you for saving my life."

Marc turned in his seat, craning his neck. "Which one are you, again?"

"Uh." He took a step backward. "I'm Asher, sir."

"Right." He hammered on the chair's arm. "Asher. I've been m . . . meaning to tell you something."

"Yes sir?"

"T . . . t." Marc extended one hoary finger and shook it at him. "Titanium."

AT BREAKFAST THE NEXT MORNING, Etienne had more announcements. "First, we're out of sand. So today we will break down the windshields from the motor pool."

"How do we do that?" Asher asked.

"There's only the one way," the nameless man said. "Hammers."

Brigitte passed through, bringing a tray upstairs to her husband. Etienne moved out of her way, fiddling with a folded bit of paper.

"Second," he continued, "is a greater concern. There are no colors."

"What do you mean?" Simon asked, his mouth full of bread.

Etienne consulted the paper. "Cobalt is nearly gone. That's a problem if you want ocean. Titanium? Low as well, and Asher's design calls for an ark of it." He folded the paper again. "We have no gold. None."

"So, we'll make a window with clear glass?" The nameless man bristled. "Brilliant. How unique it would be. Uniquely dull, that is."

"We'll be fine," Asher interjected.

"Pray tell," the nameless man scoffed. "How will clear glass be fine?"

"I discussed all of this with Marc last night."

"Let me guess," Etienne said. "He spoke about Danzig."

"Where he's done business for years, yes. He told me he'd placed an order—"

"Pardon me," Etienne said. "Pardon, but there is no polite way to say this."

"Lord have mercy," Simon moaned from the table's far end. "What?"

"If that order exists, it would have arrived months ago. He has told me repeatedly that he placed it the day after we received the cathedral commission."

For a moment no one spoke. Asher's brow furrowed. "I don't understand."

"Perhaps the company no longer exists," Etienne replied. "Perhaps his payment was misused or stolen."

"Whatever the explanation," the nameless man said, "it means we are embarked on a folly. You can't make stained glass without stain."

The old dread washed over Asher like a wave smothering a beach. Two days into his window-making life, was it already ending? How long could the château survive without income? Was this postwar life, every advance followed by a retreat?

"What alternatives do you recommend?" Etienne said.

The nameless man shrugged. "Inform the bishop, so he can find someone able to do the job? Close the atelier and declare defeat?"

Etienne folded the paper away. "Can anyone offer something besides sarcasm?"

Simon raised his hand. "Is Danzig far? We could go there and buy directly."

"Thank you, Simon." Etienne's tone was soft. "Danzig sits on Poland's easternmost edge, on the Baltic Sea. Presuming we could find a safe route, it would be two months' journey each way."

"We could minimize waste of colored glass," Asher offered. "We could commit to a design that will not exhaust our supplies."

At that Henri stood, his chair trumpeting on the floor as it slid back. He had been following the conversation closely. Now he left the room; they could hear him clomping up the stairs, stomping back down. He returned carrying Asher's roll of drawings.

Shoving away plates and bowls, Henri unscrolled the paper to a fresh space. Spreading it on the table, he grabbed a candlestick and banged it on one corner, louder than necessary. He took Simon's empty goblet and banged it on another corner, as if he were beating a drum. The other candlestick he pounded at the top of the sheet.

"What are you doing?" Etienne asked.

Henri was off again, back moments later with Asher's bin of colors and implements. He tipped it over, spilling colored pencils out on the table, sorting through them heedless of the mess he was making.

The nameless man raised an eyebrow. "What foolishness has come over you?"

Henri swept up all the implements but two—a thin black pencil and a square of charcoal—dumping the rest back in the bin. The remaining two he slammed down in front of Asher, rapping the unrolled paper with his knuckles, *one, two, three.* With that, Henri stood back, arms crossed like a prison guard.

"No colors." Asher sat forward. "You want me to do it anyway?"

"We all do," Etienne said, with a glance at Henri. "I think."

"A fool's errand," the nameless man replied.

Henri knuckled the paper twice again. Then, sweeping his hands like a broom, he shooed everyone else away. They filed out, the nameless man grumbling on his way.

At the door, Henri paused. Already Asher was working on the scroll, pencil in motion, drawing with his head over the paper, as if nothing else existed.

ON A BREAK THAT AFTERNOON, Asher found himself wandering down to visit the goats again. Each time he found something to pick along the way, and regardless of what he chose they were ravenous for it. That day he'd gone to Brigitte's herb garden, behind the kitchen, and helped himself to many sprigs of mint.

"Take all you like," she said, bustling by. "That plant wants to take over the whole garden."

So he'd arrived at the goat pen with an armload. This time he made sure each of the animals received a good share. He'd never been more popular with them. Wiping his hands off, he turned to get back to work, but noticed something on the road below.

A woman on a wagon, pulled by a donkey, crossing the bottom-lands at a slow pace. His first thought was that the sight was beautiful, Marie was beautiful, looking like something from a century ago. But then he was struck by her solitude, the degree of her isolation, with no other wagons or cars or trucks on the road, how enormously alone she was. The wagon passed beneath the poplars by the bridge, and he could not see her any longer.

The alpha goat butted him mildly through the fence. Asher held his palms out for sniffing, to prove he had nothing left to give. Then he looked back down at the valley.

"Funny thing," he told the goats. "I thought I was the only one."

THE GIANTS WERE PLAYING WITH IRON.

It lay piled akimbo in the courtyard, hard metal beams as red as clay, unloaded from a wagon they had muscled uphill to the château. There the nameless man had built a makeshift forge: a brick firebox, coarse mud for mortar, a bellows fashioned from two planks sewed to a goat hide. Euclid hoisted a beam nearly as long as he was tall, and as broad as his forearm.

"Oof," he said, giving his brother a devil's grin. "She's a beefy one."

He stepped up to the courtyard's edge, coiled at the waist, and heaved. The rod arced over the wall, clearing it with room to spare, be-fore plummeting out of sight—a calamity of sounds below as it crashed through branches and brush.

"Bull's-eye," he crowed, and both of them chuckled.

"That will be hard to find," Pascal said. "But this one will be harder." With a grunt, he lifted a similar beam, spun himself to gather speed, and launched the rod over the wall. For a moment they heard nothing. Then it clanged against the road, way down the slope, chimed off of something else, and clunked against what they could only assume was a tree trunk.

Both of them roared with laughter, bending at the waist.

"If someone had been traveling," Euclid guffawed, "you would have cut their wagon in half."

"Or tooken some poor pilgrim's head off," Pascal replied, sending them both into another convulsion of laughs.

"That's all we need," the nameless man said, arriving with an armload of kindling. "An accidental killing for the sake of juvenile amusement."

"I don't know what juvenile means," Pascal said, "but you make it sound like an illness."

"It means happiness," Euclid replied, "which this smart fellow is allergic to."

"Like me and cats?"

"And ragweed."

"And enemy soldiers' boots."

They burst out laughing again, as loud as a pair of roosters. The nameless man stood with closed eyes.

"Gentlemen," he said at last, opening his eyes to see the two of them sobering, or attempting to. "Please retrieve the rods you threw. With the cost of iron, I'm sure you understand that we did not order any extra."

They looked at one another, their expressions so identical it was as though one bearded man were facing a mirror. "Yessir," Pascal said. "We'll fetch them right up."

"My father was a farrier," the nameless man explained, holding them a moment. "He traveled the countryside making hinges, repairing wheels, shoeing horses." One boot on the makeshift forge, he looked into the distance. "He elected not to take an apprentice to perpetuate the enterprise. Smithing was pleasant work, he said, but paid too little and made life too itinerant. Therefore, he insisted on my schooling, for which I am forever grateful. Still, on occasion his jobs required an extra set of hands, thus I learned. If you would collect your toys now, please." He toed the stack of metal on the ground. "We can bend this iron to our purposes."

Euclid made a small bow. "Indeed, sir, we will."

Away they scampered, trying to pinch each other's bottoms, yipping like pups.

"Please." The nameless man beseeched the sky. "Have mercy."

THE MOMENT ASHER ACCEPTED THE hammer from Etienne, he felt a pang of nostalgia. How many hammers had he owned in his boot-making days? One mallet for shaping the leather to a last, its rubber head wrapped in felt. One tack hammer, sharp-nosed for upholstery, though he found it ideal for securing soles. He'd borrowed a neighbor's hand sledge to drive the posts that held the chicken wires protecting Aube's garden. Once, in the hands of a friend who did bodywork on cars, he saw a brass hammer, which could pound steel pins without breaking them. A lifetime of hammers.

At that moment he held a classic carpenter's tool: a hard flat head on one side, a nail-removing claw on the other. It was well made, the handle smooth from use. He imagined Marc pounding nail upon nail as he maintained Le Château Guerin over the decades.

"We don't often insist on goggles." Etienne handed primitive eye protectors to the men. They'd moved the workbenches back, and now ten windshields lay on the open concrete. "This is dangerous, though. Fragments will fly."

The nameless man stood on the atelier's other side, scowling as though his hammer smelled bad. "I detest this task. Where is Simon?"

"In bed," Asher answered. "A stomach something."

"He looked ill at breakfast," Etienne added. "That means more work for us today. We're going to do fifty of these, so pace yourselves. When they're reduced to pieces smaller than a penny, we'll shovel it into a bin and start round two. Questions?"

The nameless man adjusted his eye protectors. "Fluent in Latin and Greek, yet I am required to be a pugilist."

"If it's any comfort," Etienne said, "with goggles on, you are unrecognizable."

"A most welcome costume," he replied, squatting, and tapping the nearest windshield on one corner. A piece broke away, flat to the floor, where he hammered it twice, reducing it to slivers.

Asher had more working room, so he knelt on all fours, lifted the hammer, and struck his first blow in the center of the windshield. *Bang.* It made a spiderweb of cracks, but no pieces broke loose. Rather than work from the edges, he hit again in the middle. *Bang.* The glass broke into five fractions, the nearest of which he drew closer and banged all around its perimeter. Shards spilled away with every blow.

In a way it was heresy. Any other day, the least sound of breakage would cause every man to stop what he was doing. What masterpiece had shattered, whose work was wasted, what was lost?

Yet Asher found demolition oddly gratifying, as he wielded the hammer again and again. Droplets of glass rose as if in splashes, reminding him of that day each spring when he and his brothers would first venture back into the sea, meaning only to cool their bare feet, but inevitably someone would start splashing, and in seconds they'd all be flinging water on one another, hooting and laughing from the icy torment.

This was not play. Arm lifted, he thought about Abraham raising the knife against Isaac, about the soldier in Henri's window preparing to drive a nail. The room filled with shattering clashes as though some kind of monster were gnashing its teeth.

Gradually Asher's method improved. He began hitting harder, making more pieces with fewer blows. *Bang* was the bomb that caved in his work shed. *Bang* was the bulldozer that flattened his house. With each strike he felt stronger, more purposeful. *Bang* was his synagogue that someone had set on fire. *Bang* was the family he had loved and lost. A frenzy took hold of him, a need. *Bang* was whatever had happened to his brothers. *Bang* was the kick his friend Levi gave to the feet of the enemy soldiers. *Bang* was the person he had been before he began killing. *Bang, bang, bang*—Asher counted the next burst of blows all the way to nineteen.

And he stopped. Panting, heart drumming, he'd reduced his windshield to sparkling dust. Sweat fell from his brow inside the goggles.

He looked around. Henri made quick but fierce taps around the glass, popping its edges away. Etienne's hair had come undone, hanging around his face like a shawl while he hammered methodically, a machine, glass rising in silvery fountains.

And the nameless man? Lost in a passion, gone. He'd picked up the hammer meant for Simon, and now was pounding with both hands like a timpanist gone mad, shards and dust around his windmilling arms. Every other blow he would grunt like a mating horse, until the noises became one long growl. Glass flew from him like an eruption.

Finally, the thunderstorm passed. He sat back on his haunches, hammers resting on his thighs while his chest heaved and he gulped for air. At that, all of the men paused, their first round complete, ten windshields, one-fifth of the job.

Asher watched the nameless man regain himself, and wondered if the tantrum had helped. Briefly he contemplated going over to check on him, but the man's expression soon reassumed its regular contempt.

Only then did he notice that Simon had appeared after all, by the main furnace.

"Feeling better?" Asher called to him.

"I've been watching." Simon wore an expression of complete incomprehension. "What in the world happened to you people?"

CHAPTER 29

The shoveling screeched like fingernails on a blackboard. At first, when the shards were inches deep, it sounded like cleaning up sand, and no one minded. But when Simon scraped the last of the wind-shields off the floor, the scrape of metal blade against concrete floor drove everyone away. Even the nameless man, who never refilled the drinking water bucket, was driven to grab it and head for the kitchen. Etienne hurried out the woodpile door. Henri led Asher by the arm, up to the assembly warren.

He pointed to a stool by the light table, where Asher dutifully sat. From a shelf, Henri brought four pieces of green glass, all shaped like a wizard's hat. First he held them up to the finished window, where a similar piece came to a sharp point. Then he placed the four inferior ones in front of Asher like a gambler revealing his hand.

"I know," Asher repeated. "It took me five tries."

Henri wagged the four pieces back and forth, pointing them at the bin where Simon was emptying the last shovel loads of glass.

"We have too little material to waste any." Asher smiled. "You don't have to shout about it."

Henri smiled too, patting him on the back.

"I would use less if I knew how to cut better. It was late, and you were asleep."

Henri held one finger up, as if to pause with that thought. Reaching into the tool bin, he found a glass cutter. Bending so that his nose almost touched the glass, he cut each of the four into a sharp point.

Asher held a glass cutter to his chest. "How can I possibly learn well enough, fast enough, for the whole center window?"

"You answered that with your thanks yesterday," Etienne said in passing. "Don't do it alone."

"One thing I know," Asher said to Henri. "You are a master of glass cutting."

Henri tilted his head, but took a small bow.

"What if I design, you cut, and we share the assembly work?"

Henri seized Asher's hand and pumped it up and down.

BY LUNCH, ONE WAVE OF windshields remained to be broken. Asher's arms were tired, his hand blistered by the hammer handle, but Brigitte had made bean and potato soup, using a wild boar pelvis for the stock. Three servings he bolted down, wiping the bowl with pieces of baguette. From the kitchen came a familiar voice, and he jumped from his seat.

The nameless man moaned. "Must you behave like an infatuated teenager?"

"I would rather be exhilarated by life than annoyed by it," Asher replied.

Henri banged his goblet on the table, and everyone looked at him.

"What?" Asher asked, but Henri stared off to one side and did not answer. "I hope you're not getting Simon's stomach bug." He took his bowl into the kitchen.

"Well, hello," Marie hailed him. "There's a stranger."

"We haven't seen you here in a century," Asher said. "It's like the sun came out."

She wore a beige dress with thin green stripes, like a garment of mint. "The château has been buying fewer vegetables lately."

Brigitte bustled in carrying an armload of carrots. "We need to economize."

"As if I would not feed you people on credit," Marie replied.

"No charity here, thank you."

"Charity and credit are not the same thing," Marie said. "One is a gift, the other I get repaid with interest."

Brigitte leaned back from behind a cabinet. "Another reason to say no, thank you."

Marie shrugged, but the moment Brigitte vanished again she grabbed Asher's shirt. "Come to me tonight," she whispered. "I'm aching for you."

At first he stammered; so much time had passed. He deserved an explanation. But he answered in a whisper too. "You know I will."

Releasing him, Marie noticed white powder on her hand. "What's this dust?"

Asher smiled at her. "Windshield."

TO SHORTEN SIMON'S SHOVEL SCRAPING, Asher swept the dust into a pile. And there on the floor, a memory was waiting: helping Aube clean the kitchen, using a whisk broom and dustpan, and Rachel toddling over to help.

"Here you go, princess," he had said, handing her the broom. But it was longer than her arms, and she had a hard time holding it. So he gave her the dustpan, which she held securely while Asher swept in crumbs and dirt. When he'd finished she stood, proud as a field dog that caught a quail, dumping everything all over her front.

Immediately Rachel cried, smacking her lips from the dust. Aube scooped her up, wiping her face in the sink, cooing that she'd been a huge help. Asher put his arms around them, sandwiching the girl between her parents as the tears quieted.

Aube leaned against him. "I am the luckiest person alive."

"No." Asher squeezed them both. "Me."

"Hello?" Simon tapped his shovel blade on the floor. "Asher? Anyone home?"

"Sorry," he said, sweeping the small pile into the shovel. Leaving that memory caused him physical pain—even if he couldn't say exactly where.

"People?" The nameless man appeared at the woodpile doorway. "I've managed to find us a ride to the cathedral." Indeed, they could all hear the chugging of a truck. "They're not waiting, though. We need to leave at once."

"Too much for me here," Etienne replied, "melting the new material. Go on ahead."

Asher started toward the exit, but paused when he felt a flutter. He had no defenses, no weapon, not so much as a stick.

"What's the problem?" The nameless man shifted a bag of tools on his hip.

"The world," Asher said. "Last time I was out there, it was not a safe place."

"That's why we're investigating. How will the unwashed masses react to a new window? They might pray before it, they might put a rock through it." The nameless man stepped aside, giving Asher a way. "There's only one way to find out."

The truck had sprung shocks, jarring them on every pothole. Men huddled in the back, laborers who nodded hello and otherwise kept to themselves. Engine noise prevented conversation.

When they reached the bridge, its boards rattling under the truck, Asher could not help sitting up, to see the place he came to wash and to think and, one time in the summer grass, to make love with Marie.

But the sight left him with an unexpected feeling: attachment. The first time he'd crossed that bridge, he'd been starving. Next he was filthy, preparing to depart, only to be inspired by the leap of a fish, and hooked by the sobbing of a naked woman. Now he wondered whether he could ever leave this place. Was the château where he belonged? Yes or no, Asher could not conceive of living anywhere else.

On a hilltop outside the city, the truck pulled over and the crew tumbled out. Somehow Simon had found a fellow with a flask to share, to whom he tipped his beret in parting gratitude, while Henri applauded the men in back. Waving an arm, the driver rattled off.

Asher did not say goodbye. He was captivated by a road sign, new and intact: CLOVIDE. Recalling the broken one he'd seen, Asher heard the peal of church bells. They had not tolled when he was there before.

"Many encouraging signs," Simon said, "including a welcome from God." He grabbed one of the nameless man's tool sacks, and set out.

Their moods soured soon enough, when they encountered the stench of rotting trash. Rats dug through piles of it, scampering and quarreling, chased here and there by stray cats. Henri held a cloth over his mouth.

"Next time," the nameless man told the crew, "we'll find a better route."

They reached the square where Asher had seen the boys with their dog, and the ball that showed him where to go. "I recognize this place," he said. "I know the way."

"You've been here before?" Simon asked.

He was already hurrying down the cobblestones. In minutes they rounded a corner, and there lay the plaza of the great church. Someone had planted new rows of sycamores, as gangly as teenagers. Gardens bloomed red and white near the front door. But the cathedral itself was most striking of all, the statues beside the entrance repaired, the giant doors intact, the rubble removed.

"I have a good feeling," Asher declared. "Good, good."

Inside, it was as dark as a cave. Before, openings above had let sunlight in. But now they were roofed with bricks the color of tombstones.

"It's like a crypt," Simon said. Henri nodded in agreement.

"Imagine how welcome our works will therefore be," the nameless man said, his gaze craned upward.

Asher did not remember the room having such a lively echo. "Aaahhhh," he sang, the note continuing long after he'd stopped. Smiling, Henri clapped his hands, *bop-bop, bop-bop*, like the hooves of a trotting horse. That too echoed, the clops multiplying.

A man emerged from a side chapel, skinny as a candle wick but holding a shotgun. "What in the name of the blessed Almighty is going on out here?"

"Easy, friend," the nameless man said. "We're unarmed and no danger."

"No friend of mine disrespects the house of God," the skinny man said.

"We meant no disrespect," the nameless man replied. "Those were sounds of appreciation."

"Not what my ears heard, mister."

"Permit me to make introductions." He held an arm out to one side, like a salesman highlighting his wares, though what he displayed was three men in ragged clothes, carrying canvas tool bags. "We are from Le Château Guerin, a stained glass atelier uphill of the Marne tributary. We have a commission from the bishop to provide new windows for behind the altar. Today our work begins."

"It does not." Slowly the skinny man lowered his shotgun. "Them window-making folks was due here six weeks ago. They must have took the money and absconded or such."

"There seems to be some confusion." The nameless man folded his hands together at his waist. "Six weeks ago we had barely received our commission papers."

"Not my concern," the man said, fishing out a pipe, using his thumb to pack the bowl with tobacco, and producing a match as well. The shotgun, hooked over his elbow, did not cause the least encumbrance. "Either way, the bishop's emissary will be here in nine days, and I don't see anybody carrying any windows."

"Nine days? Why, that's impossible."

"Not really." He struck the match on the stone of an archway, hovered it over the pipe's bowl, and sucked the flame downward. "Around here, one day follows after another pretty dependably."

Asher stepped forward. "Who are you, sir, may I ask?"

"Denis, the docent." He took a deep draw on his pipe. "Keeper of this holy place, reporting to the emissary until such time as we have a proper monsignor. Which I am not hardly holding my breath about."

As though to emphasize the last phrase, he let out a long exhale, a cloud of fragrant smoke, and two of the men were stunned by it.

For Asher, scent connected to memory, he had smelled that particular tobacco before, and it made him stagger away. While he leaned on a pillar larger than a tree trunk, to keep himself from falling over, in his mind the cathedral had ceased to exist. He was lurking behind a juniper bush, stiff from crouching because his target was two hours late. At last, the officer arrived—a lieutenant colonel, the highest rank Asher had been assigned—a corpulent fellow who grunted from the exertion of opening the door to the veranda, pulling a metal chair from the table, and sitting. While he caught his breath, Asher straightened, flexing his knees, waking his body.

The officer produced a bag of tobacco and a calabash pipe, curved in the manner of Sherlock Holmes. He packed the bowl with care, and tucked the bag in a pocket. Flame over the bowl, he sucked in pulses to light the leaves. Asher pulled out a knife.

"Mmmm." The officer smoked away. But the guillotine blade was already lifted.

Three days prior, pausing his staff car on a rural roadside to relieve himself, this lieutenant colonel had discovered a secret sty: nine piglets overlooked by the soldiers who came periodically to confiscate whatever food they found. Summarily the pigs were roasted, the farmer was shot in the belly, and his wife, as punishment for lamenting too loudly, was also shot in the belly—several men of low rank later complaining that haste had deprived them of certain pleasures they might first have enjoyed—making three children into orphans.

Though Asher did not smoke, he considered stealing the bag for Levi when the job was done. But the smell would be a giveaway, a telltale to any passing enemy soldier. Instead, while the lieutenant colonel enjoyed the final pleasures of his life, Asher gripped the knife and stepped out of the trees.

Levi had taught him: to make it quick, stick the knife below the ribs and drive upward. That meant coming around in front of the officer, who inhaled with surprise as Asher rushed him and struck. With a shudder of realization and horror, the officer released a huge breath of smoke into Asher's face, which caused him to jam the knife deeper. The lieutenant colonel grimaced, teeth yellowed by a lifetime of tobacco, and froze into the position he would maintain until he was found.

Weeks later, though Asher successfully washed the blood off his sweater, he could not bear the lingering scent. He gave it to Levi. The yellow teeth too remained with him. Now Asher noticed his hand on the pillar, the same hand that had held the knife. Would he ever be free of thoughts of killing?

Meanwhile, the other person stunned by the scent had become fawning. "God in heaven, what is that sweet ambrosia?" the nameless man cried.

"A blend," the skinny docent said, sucking on his pipe. "It's foreign."

"What would you accept in trade for a pinch of that fine stuff? I've been smoking garbage for years."

"Not for trade nor sale." Puffing away, Denis shook his head.

"Where did you buy it? We'll be back tomorrow." He patted his pockets, finding a few coins. "I'll bring hard cash. Who is your supplier?"

"Back off, mongrel," Denis barked. "Take your thieving ways elsewhere."

"Thieving? I just said that I would pay."

"You all." He waved the pipe in an arc. "Don't you be worrying about my tobacco or this bishop or that monsignor. Get your dang selfs to work. You've got nine days, best put them to use. And respect this church while you're at it."

Denis pivoted to go, the shotgun low, and only then did they see that one of his legs was locked in a metal brace, as he limped off into the gloom.

Simon again took up a tool bag. "I'd say you found his tender spot."

"I will smoke that man's tobacco before this job is done." The nameless man struck out for the rear of the church, the others in tow, footsteps echoing. Asher came last, still trying to shake the memory.

The window openings in the back—one large archway in the middle with a smaller one on each side—were bricked up.

"The first step," the nameless man said, unzipping his tool bag, "is to open these spaces again." He pulled out a long-handled sledge.

"Another hammer," Asher moaned, gazing down at his blistered right hand.

"This is going to hurt," Simon said.

Toting the hammer, the nameless man clambered onto a stone window frame. "You poor tender lambs."

Pulling the sledge back, he let it swing of its own weight, a pendulum, punching a neat rectangular hole in the brick. Through the opening poured the light of day.

BY THE TIME ALL THREE window frames were clear, Asher's hands felt like ribbons. His thumbs burned. When he dropped the hammer into the tool bag, and the handle stuck out, he moved it into place with his foot.

"That mess of bricks in the rear courtyard," Denis whined. "What about them?"

The nameless man drew up. "Tomorrow we'll bring shovels and wheelbarrows."

"And what I am supposed to do about it all overnight?"

He shrugged. "Hope someone steals it." He shouldered past with two tool bags, which he toted to the altar and slid underneath out of sight. As he straightened, Asher passed by walking sideways. "What are you being strange about now?"

Asher ignored him. He was concentrating on the crucifix in the center of the altar. At one time he feared it, and the brutality it portrayed. But he had grown accustomed, with crosses on so many walls in the château. Marie even had one over the bed in which they committed their rapturous sins. This one was large, and gold, and, despite the cathedral's dim light, radiant.

"Henri," Asher called. "Do me a favor? Walk to the center window?"

Henri, half-dozing in a pew, rustled himself and shuffled to the back.

"Just climb up into the frame." As Henri complied, Asher backed away from the altar, into the center aisle. "A bit to the left."

"We need to get marching, if we want to eat dinner," the nameless man said. "There's no jitney for the return trip."

"Now can you raise your arms, and hold them wide?"

Henri stretched his arms out like he was preparing to give the whole world a hug. As a joke, he puckered his lips and made kissy-kissy sounds. Asher held a hand toward the nameless man. "Do you have a tape measure?"

"What are you up to?"

"If I tell you," Asher said, "you will oppose it, as you always do. So please answer me. Tape measure?"

"I object to that characterization."

"All right." Asher took a step closer. "You are in charge of the installation, and we obey your every command. Even though we're working without protective gloves." He raised his hands, displaying the flesh red and raw. "I am in charge of the window design. While I won't go so far as to ask for obedience, because I know I won't get it—"

"Because you don't deserve it," the nameless man interrupted.

"—it is nonetheless fair . . ." Asher struggled with himself, fighting his anger. "Fair to expect you to help me fulfill my responsibilities. Now, do you have a damn tape measure or not?"

The nameless man did not answer. He looked left and right, seeking alternatives.

"God in heaven," Simon said, unzipping the bag and digging. "Here." He tossed a measuring tape to Asher—who caught it, wincing at the impact with his palms.

"Thank you. Henri, arms up again, please."

As the short man raised his hands, the nameless man glared at Simon. "Whose side are you on here?"

"Give me a coin," Simon replied.

"I beg your pardon?"

"A coin." He held out one hand, also blistered and raw. "I saw you had some."

He looked surprised. "Well, I do, but . . ."

"Please," Simon said.

The nameless man dug in his pocket, producing a handful of them, which Simon poked through before taking one. "Thank you." He walked off, toward the area where votive candles sat in racks, a few lit and the rest dark.

Asher stretched the tape to Henri's head, his chest, his feet. "If this works," he said, "we will have done something remarkable."

"What are all of you people doing?" the nameless man shouted, his voice echoing. "I need my dinner."

"Me too," Asher said, tucking the tape measure into a pocket. "It's a long way, and I'm starving."

Henri hopped down, rubbing his tummy.

Asher approached Simon, who lit one votive candle, then another, then slipped the coin in the slot of a little lockbox, where it landed with a musical clink.

"They look pretty," Asher said. "What is it you're doing?"

"This candle is a prayer for Pamela, that one is for Michael." He crossed himself. "My parents, lost during the war."

"You have to give money to offer a prayer?" Asher blurted, before considering how it might reveal his ignorance about churches.

Simon pulled his beret back in place. "Pennies like mine," he answered, "are how the church pays for new windows."

Henri had reached the front entrance, where he clapped to urge the others along.

"Coming," Asher called.

"Finally," the nameless man groused, striding up the aisle.

Denis poked out from a side room. "When will you people learn some respect?"

CHAPTER 30

Day after day she invited him, though in the past he had never visited her house consecutively for more than two nights. Night after night he went to her.

"Why are you around the château so much lately?" he asked. "Not that I'm complaining."

On the second night, Marie paused while unbuttoning her dress. "Brigitte is concerned about not paying me." It was a work garment, dark brown like wet soil. "I want to prove to her that I don't care. I have the produce, you people need to eat. We can sort money out later."

She resumed disrobing. Asher remained in his seat, fully dressed, watching.

"Besides"—Marie itched a bare shoulder—"the doctor insists on overpaying me."

Her dress fell to the floor in a puddle. Asher rose from his chair.

The third night, they wound up on her small sheepskin rug. As they strove together, its scent rose, and with it, memory. Aube had loved his workshop's closet, where he stored leather ready to be used. She said it smelled like an immaculate barn.

At Marie's house the scent was distracting, too full of the past, and Asher stood. "Come to bed," he said, the aggressor for once, and she clasped his outstretched hand.

Later that night the man on fire came to her house. He had been more intense lately, louder and more surreal. But Asher recovered from him faster when he slept beside Marie. He spooned her, his face pressed against her back. Without waking, she hooked her feet between his.

Normally there might have been difficulty with him staying at her house so many nights, but now the château was too busy for anyone to notice. The nameless man fired his forge. Simon tended the furnaces. Etienne wrought windshields into high-quality glass. Henri built what Asher designed.

One afternoon Etienne left the kiln, hovering in the warren till Asher raised his head. "What's wrong?"

"Our coloring chemical supply," Etienne replied. "Even with the economizing you suggested, it's dire."

Asher looked sideways at the assembly before him. The image stretched out like a map. How could you make a stained glass window without stains? A memory arose: prisoners in olive uniforms, marching away from the Bonheur fountain, the seats of their trousers lightened by the marble dust they'd sat in.

Asher lifted his head. "From now on, make glass with degrees of color intensity."

"What do you mean?" Etienne said. "Blue is blue."

"Start with a weak mix," Asher replied. "Then blow some pale glass, like robin's eggs. Add color, and make the sky. Then go full strength, and make night."

Etienne could not help smiling. "How many shades of blue do you want?"

Asher studied the window design. "Eight. And three of yellow: sunrise, then daffodil, then breast of a goldfinch."

"And for the ark, a whole range of browns?"

"Exactly." Asher took a chamois cloth and wiped the assembly. "Meanwhile I will invent something for the glass that will have to be clear. Something to make it interesting anyway."

Etienne ambled off. "I cannot wait to see this window."

In the château that night, after the man on fire woke him, Asher lit a lamp, took up colored pencils, and began drawing on his bedroom wall: dark, strong colors, surrounded by tones that grew lighter and lighter with distance from the center. Like ripples in the surface of a river. Once he began, he did not stop till daylight.

MARC SEEMED STRONGER EACH DAY, wheeling around the atelier to monitor furnace temperatures or call for firewood. There were moments when he forgot himself, his thoughts wandering where none could follow. Brigitte had keen eyes for those incidents. She would take his hands and invite him to rejoin everyone.

But the immediate problem was Henri, who had caught Simon's stomach bug and taken to bed. Asher missed his optimism, and worried about what he would do if the illness grew serious. Then he hoped for another invitation to Marie's, his mind keen on things he wanted to do with her, for her, to her.

AFTER DINNER EVERYONE SCATTERED: ETIENNE to the courtyard, Simon to wherever he'd hidden his drink, the nameless man to his forge: Pumping the bellows till the embers pulsed, he heated a length of iron, pinched off a piece, and made a chime as he hammered it into a shape. Sparks flew, demonic and possessed.

Before bed Etienne checked the atelier, and Asher was working by lamplight. "You didn't work enough today?"

Asher looked up from his design. "When else can I make the design?"

"Well," Etienne said, "I earned a night's sleep. So good luck."

Asher was already concentrating again, head down.

The next morning, Marie offered another invitation. He was exhausted, overburdened. Between the cathedral work, the design, and the assembly, there was no free time, day or night. He said yes.

That night, and the ones that followed, she had been insatiable. Each morning he thought she must be content, yet it seemed almost the opposite: waking him in the dark hours, reaching for him again in the morning. It was as if the more she ate, the hungrier she became. Frequency was not helping, passion was not enough. There was some place Marie needed to go, to arrive at, to accomplish. Each coupling brought it nearer, which made reaching there all the more urgent.

Asher felt himself striving too, toward a thing that also refused to exist. No woman could substitute for Aube, if only because of the span of years she had possessed his heart. But Marie was more frankly intimate, which he'd thought would lead more directly to love. A shorter path to a stronger bond. It was not happening. They felt one another's longings, their yearning. Perhaps if one of them arrived at the destination, the other would as well.

So he tried to help her, night after night, though sometimes he needed to pause and eat something. Or gulp water. Or breathe deeply, while she lay panting, fevered and feral, shameless and splayed, before pulling him close again.

It might have gone on indefinitely, this exertion toward a thing Asher could not see but whose imperative he felt continuously, until a night when he felt tired, bone-tired, exhausted like during the time of wandering, the fervor in bed not bringing them closer, but actually creating a distance he would not have imagined was possible between two people coupling, while she squeezed her eyes closed and grasped his flanks, saying harder, harder, come on, until he could bear it no longer.

"Enough." Asher withdrew, untangling himself to sit across the bed. "Enough."

"You can't hurt me," Marie said, stretching a hand toward him, hooking an ankle around his waist. "I know my limits."

Asher pushed her foot away. "How can I be brutal in an act of love?"

Marie pulled a pillow to her chest. "Perhaps it is not love."

"This is not love? Are we not making love?"

"Maybe a damaged version," she continued. "The broken kind that is possible after war has finished its business."

"What about affection?"

"You know how I feel," she answered. "Tomorrow I will make you dinner."

"And afterward, I'm to show my gratitude by leaving you bruised?"

"Don't you understand how small a bruise is? And how necessary, if it makes a person feel alive?"

"Pleasure is more than enough." He rose, searching for his trousers.

"Don't be ungrateful." Marie pushed the pillow away. "Sleep with me, at least."

Asher knew how chilly the night was, how long the trek to the château. After exaggerating his deliberations for a few seconds, he climbed back into bed, pulling the blankets over them both. "The point is that no. I don't."

"Mmm." She snuggled warm against him. "Don't what?"

"Understand."

BEFORE DAWN, THE MAN ON fire stood at the château's door with kerosene and matches, about to commit arson. Asher could not fall back to sleep. As a result, he reached the cathedral long before the others. When they arrived, a smiling Henri was among them.

"There he is." Asher patted his friend on the back. "Thank goodness."

"I didn't see you ahead of us on the walk down," Simon said.

"I wanted to see how this place looked in early light," Asher replied. "What sunrise would do with our windows."

"How fastidious of you." The nameless man raised an eyebrow. "Positively conscientious."

"The deadline." Asher shrugged. "It makes me a light sleeper."

The nameless man was no longer listening. He'd gone to the altar to retrieve what were now three bags of gear. Simon was hurrying to help, when they all heard someone in a side chapel conspicuously clearing his throat.

"What is it now?" the nameless man groaned. "We're busy. And expecting rain."

The docent took out his pipe, but did not pack or light it. "As I am a Christian," he said, "I must not lie to you."

That caught Simon's attention. "If you have told us an untruth, may it please be that the bishop's emissary is not coming in four days."

"No such luck," Denis replied. "It's about my tobacco."

"We don't care," the nameless man said, "unless you're willing to share it."

But Asher drew closer. "What about it?"

"I stole it." Denis scratched his chest with the pipestem. "From a German corpse. Either he served in a quartermaster's unit, else he was a thief, because he had a dozen pouches in his kit. Other folks wanted his pistol, his boots. Let them grab and quarrel, I took all the smoke for myself."

"Why are you confessing this to us?" Simon asked. "We are not your judges."

"I am not proud of robbing a dead man," Denis replied. "And I don't want to double my sin with a dang lie."

"When the emissary comes"—the nameless man hoisted a tool bag in each hand—"clear your conscience with him. We, meanwhile, have work to do."

He strode off, tilting from the bags' uneven weight. The others followed, while Denis put away his pipe, and limped back where he had come from.

THE HAMMERING WAS FINISHED BY noon, the installation frames secure on exterior shelves. The nameless man called for a mallet, reaching one hand back without looking, when Asher smelled that tobacco again. He jerked as if he'd been poked with a pin. The yellow teeth would never leave him.

"You again?" he snarled.

"Just watching," Denis said, drawing on his pipe. "Not talking nor anything."

"It is a talent," the nameless man said, taking the mallet Simon offered. "How without saying a word, you nonetheless manage to interfere."

The docent inspected his pipe bowl. "I was concerned, that's all. Whether you'd finish before the rains."

"We might." The nameless man grunted, shoving an uncooperating window frame. "If we can work without interruption."

Denis approached the base of the scaffold. "How do you make them windows stay put, anyhow? Sure gotta last a long time."

"You explain," the nameless man muttered to Simon. "I can't bear him."

Simon faced the docent. "This is my first installation, so I'm only repeating what I've been told. But there's a metal border around the outside of every window. It sits on a shelf." Simon pointed down the frame before him. "We put a hole in the stone on the outside, fix the border with a bolt, and there you go."

Denis scratched his chest with the pipestem. "So it's held from the outside?"

Simon pulled his beret snug. "With iron."

"We're all set here." The nameless man straightened, handing back the mallet. "Tomorrow we bring windows."

Asher looked up from below. "We're almost there, aren't we?"

"Pfff," the nameless man hissed. "Said the man who has never installed anything."

Asher weighed the hammer in his hand, then dropped it in a tool bag and stomped away.

ON THE WAY TO THE château, they heard a violin. The nameless man stayed behind, conversing with the docent, which Asher presumed was an attempt to beguile him out of some tobacco. The crew followed the music till they found the source—on a rooftop. A skinny musician in a top hat was playing from the peak of a house.

In the old quarters of French cities, streets often meet at odd angles. This square was shaped like a V, into which the roof of one house jutted like a ship's prow.

The men ran ahead, Asher following with tired feet. The building on which the fiddler played served as a barrier between two squares. Each had a fountain, rows of shops, and a crowd that was smiling and listening and sometimes clapping along. But no one moved from one square to the other. They all kept to their side.

The violinist was a wonder. Capering during frisky tunes, swaying when the tempo slowed, he leaned this way and that, up and down the crown of the house.

Asher spied an old woman on a bench between the squares, the musician's busking hat upside down near her feet. He leaned over. "Why is he playing up there?"

"To avoid a brawl," the woman warbled.

"Excuse me?"

She raised a wrinkled hand. "This side, people believe Stalin's communism saved us from Nazism, and is our future." She gestured the other way. "That side, people believe we should not place the interests of a foreign state above our own."

"I imagine it's hard to satisfy both audiences."

"Harder than dancing on a rooftop."

The musician was talented, Asher could tell. Every minute he changed the tune: a jig to a ballad, a hymn to a gavotte, all while matching his dancing to the song—romantic sweeps or hopping and spinning. Asher saw that the soles of the violinist's boots were desperately worn. It took balance and courage to perform with footwear that slippery. Poor fellow must have gone years without audiences, without being paid for his talent. What care he was showing too, to entertain both sides without favor.

Asher squatted beside the old woman. "Which group do you belong to?"

"You see me sitting on either side?"

The violinist came to the peak of the roof, where he stood on one foot, raising his right leg over one square. The people below applauded wildly. Switching to balance on his other foot, he held his left leg out. The other crowd roared.

She pointed with a bony thumb. "That man's not a musician. He's a diplomat."

A little boy trotted up to the hat, dropped in a coin, and dashed back to bury his face in his mother's skirts.

"It's very trusting," Asher observed, "to leave his hat in the street. Any passing lout could snatch it."

"He has a protector, I'm sure."

Asher scanned the crowds to see who it might be. There was no telling who held a weapon. The château's men were following the fiddler with their eyes, smiling, speaking asides to one another. Ever enthusiastic, Henri was tapping his foot.

Across the square, was that Bondurant? Asher squinted but could not be sure. A resemblance certainly, but stouter, strong, and well fed, yet sniffing around for opportunity like a small dog that smells sausage. It was reassuring to think that there was life after the château, but Asher did not want to speak with him. Besides, this man stood aloof, frowning at everyone around him. Kept a hand in his cloak as if holding a knife. Spat on the ground every few seconds. All around him people were dancing, while this man—Bondurant or not—ducked up a flight of stairs away from the street.

The violinist segued into "Alouette," a call-and-response tune— playing the first phrase to his right, the second to his left, back and forth until the chorus, "*Alouette, gentille alouette, alouette, je te plumerai.*" On both sides, the people cheered and sang.

"Isn't he deft?" Asher asked. The old woman's smile had more gaps than teeth.

Just that moment, it began to rain. Fat drops on the cobblestones made a sound like applause. The violinist stopped playing, arms beseeching the sky. As the crowds realized what was happening, he threw a coat over his instrument and vanished. The rain picked up, people rushing away. Crossing paths, they were as skillful at evading one another as fish in a school. The old woman was right too: a broad-backed fellow scooped up the player's hat, donning it as he dodged into an alley.

Asher sidled over to the crew, huddled under a canopy. "Half an hour at least for our walk back. No point in hurrying, if we're going to get soaked anyway."

"How about that fiddler, though?" Simon marveled. "*Alouette, gentille alouette.*"

They set out in the downpour, nothing to be done. Henri scampered ahead, his arms spread open to the bathing rain.

CHAPTER 31

Everyone went directly into the atelier, drip marks and footprints on the gray cement floor. The furnaces were stoked high. As the nameless man threw the doors open—drenched from his own, separate walk home—the others basked in the heat.

Brigitte emerged from the wood supply, carrying logs that she stacked by the annealer. Pivoting to pump the bellows, she saw the men all laughing and loose. Steam rose from their clothes. Her smock, the modest one Asher made, had several buttons open. "Hello, gentlemen," she said.

"H'lo," Asher replied. The rest ceased their conversation, moaning and ahhing in the kiln's warmth.

She gave them a wistful look, before leaving for wood—reappearing with a fresh armload and another button undone. None of them noticed.

Brigitte came near to check the kiln temperature. "You gents recovering a bit?"

"Getting there, ma'am, thank you," Simon said without a glance.

She dumped the logs at their feet, and stomped off for another load.

"Well." The nameless man sniffed. "Someone has a bee in her bonnet."

SOON ETIENNE WENDED BETWEEN THE men to make a gather. It broke their leisurely mood, spiraling them up the back stairs for dry clothes—

except Asher, who climbed into the warren and spread his drawing roll. Pulling out the nameless man's tape measure, he began moving angle by angle around the design, penciling a tally on the side of the sheet. The longer the list of numbers grew, the more he shook his head before taking the next measure.

Henri came up the steps, noticed the tape measure, and gave two thumbs-up.

"Yes, I kept it, for now. But we have a problem." He tapped his pencil on the page. "I wrecked fourteen lead-cutters making the side window, and we have four left. In about two days, we'll run out."

Henri reached into the tool basket, found a cutter, and ran his thumb across the blade. He tossed the knife back. Rubbing his chin, he looked around the assembly area, then snapped his fingers and trotted away.

Henri returned with a cast-iron pot so battered, it seemed to Asher as though its function was to be dropped down flights of stairs. He clanked ingots of lead into it, then thumbed his chest. With a finger, he tapped on the design paper and pointed at Asher.

"You'll solve the lead problem, while I keep drawing?"

Henri bobbed his head, hustling into the assembly area's dimmest corner.

"Did you notice those trees behind the cathedral today?" Asher called. "We should make them visible through the window."

The only reply was the clang of more ingots landing in the pot.

IN THE MORNING THE NAMELESS man rapped on Asher's door, entering without waiting for a reply. What he saw stopped him in his tracks. Every inch of the room was painted or penciled: the walls, the floor, two pillowcases that hung by the window.

There was a woman, flying all over the sky. That fish again, leaping across roads, snooping over walls. A large man with a huge beard sat on a roof eating carrots. And on the bed, an actual man slept on his stomach, atop the covers, in his clothes.

"This is the dwelling place of a lunatic," the nameless man said aloud.

Asher jolted awake. "What did you say?"

"How can you possibly live this way? I ask not as criticism. More out of appalled curiosity."

Calming, Asher rubbed one eye. "Live what way?"

"Amid chaos. I thought you were the one who brought order to everything."

"There's no time for cleaning." He noticed one of his hands was blackened by a drawing charcoal. "The windows come first. I'll tidy up later."

"Reluctant as I am to interrupt your beauty rest," the nameless man sniffed, "I've completed the frames for the side windows. The vegetable girl has loaned us her spare wagon, to bring them to the cathedral. Your muscles are needed."

"The vegetable girl?" Asher reached for a boot. "You don't know her name?"

"What of it?" the nameless man snapped. "At least I don't sleep in filth."

Downstairs, everyone had already eaten breakfast. Henri was not to be seen, though. "Better for him to sleep," the nameless man said.

"But not me?" Asher asked.

"Skills are rare, labor is cheap." He headed outside. Asher sat, opening and closing his fists.

Skipping breakfast, he went outside to see how he was needed. Brigitte was hovering beside Marc, who continued to improve every day. "Do you want to watch the loading, my love?"

"Watch? I want to s . . . supervise."

"Well, then." She wheeled him over to the loading area.

Asher followed, catching the end of the nameless man's instructions to Simon. "Iron is heavier than you think. Make sure you have a good hold first."

While he climbed into the wagon, Simon and Asher bent low, working their fingers under the frame of Henri's side window. "What if we drop it?" Asher joked.

"The w . . . the world will end," Marc said.

They hoisted the window. "Mercy," Simon wheezed. "This is a beast."

Once they were standing straight, they began to carry the window horizontally, like a tabletop.

"No, no," Marc cried. "Keep it sideways. K . . . keep it."

"Not that way." The nameless man jumped down to help them lift it to one side. "A window lying flat can't bear its own weight. It will shatter in your hands."

"A warning would have been helpful," Asher said.

"Experience is helpful too," the nameless man said, climbing aboard again.

One shove, Asher thought, and the window would knock him backward. An injury, for certain, but not enough to kill him. Maybe enough to humble him, though.

With a last heave, they set the window on the tailgate, sliding it in. The nameless man hurried to rope the assembly into place. They went back for the second one.

"This is a good day," Brigitte said, rubbing Marc's shoulder.

"It has been f. F. F . . . far too long since Le Château Guerin sent a w . . . window into the world."

Asher's side window loaded smoothly, and while the nameless man secured it, Asher whispered to himself, "Take good care of my beautiful Rachel's face."

As he and Simon strapped themselves in the wagon's harnesses, Henri appeared with a freshly washed face. Bows of apology, a wink to Asher, and they were off.

"Where were you?" Asher asked. But Henri could only smile and shrug.

HIS SIDE WINDOW INSTALLED EASILY, gliding into place. The nameless man tapped bolts in around the top and sides, each one attaching the assembly more securely.

All that time Denis stood by, attending so closely it seemed like he was trying to learn how. The skies threatened, but the rain held off.

From outside, it was hard to see what image the window made. Denis snuck away, though, using the cathedral's side door to go inside.

"Why does it gall me," the nameless man asked the crew, "that this odd duck is the first person to see the window with daylight passing through it?"

None of the men answered. They were tending to their sore hands.

THEY HAD CARRIED ASHER'S WINDOW halfway to the scaffold when the skies opened. This was not the gentle rain of the day before, however. Big drops fell sideways, with a wind that made the assembly harder to manage.

Simon slipped to one knee.

"Be careful," the nameless man barked. "You fool."

"Do you think he was not being careful?" Asher countered.

"Evidently not careful enough."

"Both of you." Simon worked his way upright. "You're not helping."

The nameless man jerked away. Asher glared up. His patience was running out.

His window slid nicely into place—on the left side. But the right edge did not fit. It scraped, resisted, would not move into position.

The nameless man pounded a fist into his palm. "*Aut inveniam viam aut faciam.*"

"Which means?" Simon asked.

"I'll either find a way, or make one."

"What's the problem here?" Denis had put on a slicker, keeping the rain out of his eyes with a duck-billed hat. "Can I help?"

"Please." The nameless man stared into the cathedral's stone exterior. "For once. Give me some peace."

Unflinching, the docent observed a while more before limping away. Asher and Simon hoisted the window out, sliding it into place again. Still the right side caught.

"I know anything I ask you will be an annoyance," Asher began.

"Then keep the questions to yourself," the nameless man answered.

"Could we have mismeasured?" Asher asked. "Is that possible? Can we gently tap the edge with a mallet? Or chisel out some stone to help it fit?"

"Which idea should I reject first? Shall I answer in order of stupidity?"

"I've heard enough." Asher gripped the scaffold, its metal cold in his hand. "You are the one who surrendered the main window. You made that choice, not me."

"I did not," he said. "There was no choice for me whatsoever."

"What are you talking about? We all saw you speaking with Etienne."

"You were born with so much natural talent, I had no alternative but to withdraw. Damn the fates that gave so huge a gift to a feckless buffoon like you."

"It wasn't about talent," Asher said. "It was about work. You took one look at my drawing roll and gave up."

"You listen. You listen for one minute." The nameless man was all but spitting, and stood nearly on Asher's toes. He ignored his clenched fists too, as well as the long fall to the cobblestones below. "I know about work. Every piece of this assembly gear I forged in iron with my own hands."

"That may be true, but—"

"I know what I'm doing here, and you don't. Admit it. Go worry somewhere else, while I do my best for a perfect installation—not for your benefit, you undeserving opportunist, but on behalf of the generations who will see what we did, what we were capable of doing while our nation was flattened."

"Opportunist?" Asher said. "Who the hell do you—"

"Try this, fellas." Denis had something in his hand. They looked down at him as if he were speaking a foreign language.

"Had an idea," he continued. "Might ease her right on in."

He tossed up a white object. The nameless man could not tell what it was until he had caught it: white and round and the size of his fist. "A candle?"

"Give a good rub on the side there." He pointed. "A big mess of it, like ham fat."

Simon leaned near the nameless man. "Be kind. This is a simple fellow."

"Simple?" He smiled. "He's smarter than all of us. Hold the window."

While they gripped it, straining against the wind, the nameless man rubbed the candle up and down the side, top to bottom, leaving a white smear the whole length.

"That's about right," Denis said. "Don't hold back."

Shoving the gouged candle in a pocket, the nameless man placed himself along that uncooperative edge. "Once more now, men. Simon, say your prayers."

The three of them heaved as one. The base slid in, the left side went snug like a belt buckling, and, with a pressure that made the candle wax ooze, the right side scraped its way reluctantly, firmly, irreversibly into place.

"Yes," the nameless man cried, slapping the stone, shaking his fists in the air. "Yes, yes, yes."

"There you go." The docent chomped down on his pipe.

Henri clapped, water dripping from his earlobes.

The bolts all but fell into place, ringing true with every blow of the hammer. By early afternoon the men were climbing down, oblivious to the rain, gathering their tools into the old canvas bags.

There, Asher told himself. The window is in, and you didn't punch the nameless man, nor storm off, nor say that his past cowardice did not justify his present nastiness.

Now the task was to finish the main window before the emissary arrived. Two days? Impossible. He should speak to Marc. A musical voice called out from behind them, and Asher pivoted to see what song had entered his day.

"Hello, gentlemen," Marie called, pulling her donkey's lead line, the animal and cart following. She wore a broad-brimmed hat and a dark navy work dress. It matched the crescent of glass dangling at her throat. "I've brought you lunch."

To a man, they dropped their tools where they stood. In minutes, they were inside the chapel, enjoying brie, baguettes, tomato slices steeped in basil and vinegar.

"A feast," Asher declared, filling his plate. He hovered near Marie, offering to help. She was having none of it. The only person she paid any attention to was Henri, serving him food, declaring that she hoped he was back to full strength.

Henri nodded, wearing a huge grin, and beat his chest with both hands.

Marie laughed, bright-eyed. "I bid you good afternoon, gentlemen. Pétain and I have customers waiting in Clovide."

When she had gone, the nameless man sniffed at Asher. "I know the name of her horse. It's Pétain."

"It's not a horse," Asher scoffed. "It's a donkey."

"And you," the nameless man replied, "are an ass."

Asher felt the surge of anger strongly enough that he was glad there were no weapons handy. "I'm leaving," he announced. "I have better things to do."

As he rose, Simon and Henri did as well, preparing for another trek uphill in the rain. The second time did not feel at all freeing like the first.

"Take the wagon with you," the nameless man ordered.

"Why should we?" Asher snapped.

"Because I have work to finish here. And I can't pull the damn thing by myself."

Asher stood with hands stiff at his sides, chastened but not relenting, wrestling with violent impulses, before marching out the cathedral door. He slammed it so hard the latch did not catch, and it wobbled back open after him. After nineteen in wartime, how easy number twenty could be.

CHAPTER 32

By the time he'd dried and warmed himself and changed his clothes, Asher lost track of Henri. In a thorough search, he'd found Etienne in the atelier, Simon in the chapel, and Brigitte in the kitchen, and still no Henri. Upstairs, he nearly collided with Marc, who sat by a window, gazing at the rain.

"Hello," Marc cried out from his wheelchair.

Asher stalled, interrupted in his search. "There's the man himself," he said.

"I've been thinking," Marc said, wheeling backward slightly. "About you lads installing in this w . . . in this weather."

"Rain is the least of our problems."

"Let me guess." He stroked his beard. "Our friend without a name."

"He has been unbearable."

"Have you f . . . ff . . . forgotten our first conversation? In which I discussed patience and compassion, because everyone here h . . . has suffered?"

"But I know his story. I don't think it entitles him to treat me like dirt."

"You couldn't possibly." Marc steered the chair using his good hand.

"At best, you have gossip and shallow speculation. You have no idea what motivated him, what c . . . causes, nor what enormous efforts he is making toward redemption. We give this man more latitude than most, because he has more to overcome."

"The man constantly tests my patience. He brings out my worst self."

Marc smiled, his eyes squinting.

"I confess I did not expect you to be amused, sir."

"I'm sorry," he said, still grinning. "You should have seen him when he arrived here. He would curse us d . . . day and night. In Greek."

"For someone so smart—"

"This man is skilled and he works hard. He n. He n . . . never asks anything for himself. More importantly, he thinks hard every day about how to heal a terrible w . . . wound to his soul. How to live with a mistake he can never repair. If he of all people can find a means to recovery, a sense of strength and p . . . strength and purpose, it will benefit this atelier, all we make and do. It benefits all of us."

"You make him sound noble. I don't know quite how you did that."

Marc rolled his chair to the window again. "Patience and compassion."

Asher had started away down the hall, when he paused. "Sir, I have something else to say to you."

"You can't f . . . can't finish in time."

"That's right. How did you—"

"You will, though. I have total confidence."

"With two workdays before he arrives?"

"There's no alternative. No d . . . no delays when a bishop's emissary is traveling to see our work. You'll f. You'll f." Marc took a deep breath, in and out, his shoulders lowering with the exhale. "You'll finish on time, simply because you must."

Asher had no reply. Marc had given him nothing to challenge or dispute.

With his good hand, the old man waved him along. "Better get going."

"THEM ARE SOME FINE WINDOWS you folks have made," Denis said.

The nameless man frowned. "I was enjoying a quiet moment with them."

The docent, missing the hint, sat beside him in the pew. "And getting a break from your crew."

"You can tell that we have conflicts?"

"Someone has to be the wax to get everything into place. Your job, is my guess."

"I'm not sure it's possible."

Denis dangled his hat from a finger. "Hear me out a minute about something?"

The nameless man heaved a sigh. "Do I have any alternative?"

"Won't take long."

He held his hands forward. "Be my guest."

Denis pointed with the hat's bill. "That right-hand window, the crucifixion? It's awful good. Plainspoken, like a sermon all the folks will understand. Looks almost carved, you know?"

"I do. He mostly uses block shapes."

"You ask me, it works. Now, that other one, on the left, it's not so easy."

The nameless man lowered his head so as not to see it. "I know."

"It's genius, of course. Looks like a painting. And I'll say this. I cannot look at it without thinking about my soul. My immortal soul, I mean, and being a sinner, and knowing I am tiny, tiny, tiny compared with God almighty."

"You see all that in one window?"

"And the big one isn't even here yet. So. My suggestion?"

Again the nameless man sighed. "What is it?"

"Cover 'em up. Don't let anyone else gawk like I did. Hide them till the whole idea is up there together and finished. Plus . . ."

"Yes?"

"Don't mean to put anybody down. But this emissary, I've known him forever plus a week. He's dramatic, likes to make a big occasion of everything. An unveiling would about do the trick."

"How about that?" the nameless man responded. "Those are both good ideas."

"Got one more for you. It's bigger, though. Very big."

"You have my attention."

"Come on." Denis tugged his hat on. "I want to show you something."

ETIENNE CLOSED THE ANNEALING FURNACE door with an accidental clang. "Sorry."

Startled, Asher jolted up from the assembly. "I didn't know you were here."

Etienne sidled over. "We can't let a lack of glass slow you down."

"Thank you. But lack of skill is a bigger worry."

Etienne leaned over, examining the window taking shape. "That dove looks elegant. How are you going to do the rainbow?"

"I don't know yet."

"With two days to go." Etienne laughed. "Perfect." He seated himself on Henri's work stool. "Are you still able to find time for nights with Marie?"

Asher went still. "You know about that?"

"Asher." Etienne picked up a lead ingot. "My room is across the hall from yours."

"Right." He sat back a moment, hands in his lap. "Do you know everything here?"

"Only Marc does. That's how he decides that Simon can stay despite his drinking, because somehow it doesn't hurt his work. So." He weighed the ingot in his hand. "Is it a genuine romance with Marie?"

Asher rubbed the cutting tool up and down his leg. "First date, her house for dinner, I brought a flower so as not to be empty-handed."

"How gallant."

"Sure, until I saw the nursery behind her house, with hundreds of flowers. Thousands. I thought, This woman has abundance. This is how I will get well."

"Has that come true?"

"We're drawn to each other, powerfully. But it's like we're each building a bridge over a river, and we didn't line up first. Her half is over here"—he held up his right hand—"and mine is over there." He held up his left. "We miss."

Etienne rose, heading for his workbench. "Don't go away."

"Not much chance of that." Asher picked up the pane he'd been about to carve. Pale yellow, it would represent part of an animal's soul.

"I haven't known what to do with this till now." He handed Asher the flower he'd made of glass. "I guess I was saving it for you."

"I don't understand."

Etienne smiled. "This came from the last of our sand. Give it to your lady love. I guarantee she will not have another, much less thousands more."

Asher twirled the flower. "I don't know what to say."

"That's fine. Imitate this guy." With a thumb over his shoulder, he indicated Henri, who was just arriving.

With care, Asher placed the flower in a cubby, where it was unlikely to get bumped or broken. "It's beautiful. I'm touched."

"Better than melting it down for the cathedral, don't you think?" Etienne trotted back down the steps. "And now I'm done for the day."

"Thank you," Asher called.

Henri climbed onto his stool, giving a little wave of greeting. Asher saw that his hair was dark, plastered to his head. "Have you been out in the rain?"

Henri smiled, bobbing his head side to side.

"I've needed you," Asher said. He angled the piece of yellow glass into its lead channel. "We're tight on time, and you disappeared. Skipped dinner and everything."

Henri shrugged, looking off to one side.

"I'm down to the last lead-cutter." Asher lifted a worn-down knife. "You said you would take care of this part. But I'm about to run out of lead."

Henri held up one finger, shaking it in the air.

"What is it?"

He trotted into the warren, hauling back the battered cast-iron pot. With an *oof* he hoisted it onto the stool, and lifted out a handful of window-making lead, dangling like a pirate's necklace.

"I don't understand," Asher said.

Henri dropped the clump and fished out a single strand. Placing it on the table, he picked up the nearest piece of glass. In two seconds he had slid the pane into place.

"You made thinner lead?" Asher asked.

Henri jogged away again, bringing two more buckets, straining under their weight. He lifted another clump for Asher to see.

"We still don't have enough time," he said. "But you just eliminated the biggest obstacle."

Henri took a deep bow.

"But I have one more idea. Can you make me lead with a wider groove?"

First Henri spread his arms apart, then held two fingers close together.

"How wide?" Asher held up two pieces of glass together. "Two panes thick."

Henri's eyebrows went up, parachutes above his eyes.

"I know. We're changing the game, aren't we? Making new rules."

Henri banged his chest with both fists. He emptied one of the lead buckets on the table and hurried off. To any question, the answer was work.

"THIS PLACE WAS MADE FOR storing champagne." Denis panned his torchlight over barrels and bottles. "Chalk floors, chalk walls, chalk ceilings. Something about temperature, humidity, I don't know."

"I'm not much for champagne, myself."

"Nor me. In the war, the church hid Jews down here till it got obvious. Too much food going into a cathedral every day."

The nameless man did not like this dark, how complete it was. If the flashlight went out, they would be lost underground with no vision at all.

Also, the light's beam wobbled from Denis's limp. "Kept troops here too, late in the war. But that's not why I brought you." He led into a smaller cavern. "Main worry was that I might die, and nobody would know. They'd be lost maybe forever."

"What 'they' are we talking about?"

The way was blocked by a pile of broken barrels, the ends staved in.

"Them barrels are better-made than you'd think," Denis said. "It was a dang pile of work to break them up." He set one barrel upright, arranging his light on it, and began tossing others aside. "Wife was furious. I smelled like wine for a week." Denis bent into the light so the nameless man could see him grinning.

"Forgive me if I'm not seeing the humor just now."

"You will. And sooner, if you lend a hand."

The nameless man waded into the broken casks, and soon they cleared a path.

"Now keep snug to the wall." Denis panned the light over broken glass lying everywhere else. "After all this time, you can't imagine how exciting this is."

"You're right." Creeping forward, the nameless man made no effort to conceal his skepticism. "I can't imagine."

They entered a new room, he could feel open air overhead, and Denis stopped abruptly. "Well, then. Imagine this."

Casting the beam across the cavern, he revealed an array of rectangles on the far wall, all of them reflecting light.

"I'm not sure I . . . I don't quite—"

"Awful dusty now, sure. Gave a right colorful reflection when I hid them."

"What am I seeing right now?"

"Windows, of course." Denis chuckled. "All the ones I could salvage."

"These are the original stained glass windows of the cathedral?"

"From the side walls, yup." The docent shook his head. "The others would have required scaffolding, which of course soldiers would see right away. Still." He panned the light back and forth. "Twenty-eight of them survived."

"This . . . this treasure," the nameless man stammered. "Do you understand what you have saved?"

"Oh sure. Half of them, the west side, was stations of the cross. The east side, all portraits. Saints, popes, some kings who was crowned here."

"Priceless, simply priceless."

"Never wrote down what order they were in," Denis continued. "Didn't think I'd have to remember for so long. I barely recall my wife's birthday."

"But they're undamaged. It's incredible."

"Not even the bishop knows yet. So far, in the whole world? Me and you."

"But this is serious. You need to get these back aboveground. Have them properly cleaned, repaired. And, by God, installed again."

"The diocese sent two window teams before you folks, you know." Denis sat back on a barrel. "Rank amateurs. But I've had a good gander at your crew. How exact you are, how you protect the window. And there you go."

"What do you mean?"

"I spent half the war working for this bishop. We still communicate directly, none of this middleman. He'll about wet himself when I tell him."

"I imagine he will."

"Pay handsomely too, I figure. For cleaning and fixing and such."

"What a project," the nameless man said, marveling. "Historic."

Denis took out his pipe. "For a smart guy, sometimes you don't savvy much."

"Why? What do you mean?"

"All this work." He aimed the flashlight at his other hand, which held a bag of tobacco out like an invitation. "Who you think is going to do it?"

HOURS LATER, WHEN A CANDLE had puddled in its dish and burned out, Asher paused to find another and realized that Henri was gone. Had he waved good night, his wordless farewell? Or had he slunk off into the dark, unwilling to explain where he'd been earlier?

The world was quiet, the house still. Dawn was hours away, yet time raced. If there were spirits afoot or afloat—flying cows or speaking owls or stars whose arrangement in the sky made the shape of an immortal fish—now was not the time to attend to them. The window lay unfinished before Asher like an unsatisfied lover. Be it making boots or committing murders, working alone, and being alone with his conscience, was a circumstance he knew all too well.

CHAPTER 33

The din of heavy rain surrounded the château that morning. It drummed on the roof, spilled on the cobblestones, washed the gardens and grass. The cows, milked and driven to pasture, made their usual morning complaints, but invisibly, behind falling shrouds.

Day upon day it had rained, the scent smothering all others. Rain hissed and seethed. It puddled the lowlands. It crossed the fields in sheets, like ghosts made of water. It drained from the gutters like a tin drum hit constantly on the same note. It teemed like a fog insisting on some quiet idea. It softened the paths and draped branches. It bent garden flowers as though they were ashamed. It made a washing sound, as if the trees were perpetually repeating the word *wish*.

The nameless man, finding Asher asleep on the atelier's floor, stepped over him to assess the progress. The main window contained three panels, each of them the size of a side window, with Marc's medallion at the top of the center panel. That portion was completed, and rested on its side against the wall. On the assembly table, the second panel appeared complete, but not yet sealed in solder and cement. Of the third and final one, there was no sign.

"And the bishop's emissary arrives tomorrow," he said. "How reassuring."

Asher jerked awake, sitting up with clenched fists. "What time is it?"

"You've missed breakfast again, if that's what you're asking."

"No, I was asking the time." He rubbed his head as though he had a hangover. "Precious minutes."

"Why do you always wake with a start? What a horrible way to begin a day."

"You would too, if you'd slept in some of the places I have."

The nameless man picked up a lead-cutter, scowling at its dull edge. "Tomorrow may prove more entertaining than I'd imagined."

"You keep imagining," Asher said. "And I'll keep working. Is that rain I hear?"

"It will never stop."

"Will you install the center panel today anyway?"

"I would do all three if they were finished."

Asher stood, patting his pants as if trying to remember where he put something. He'd fallen asleep with a lead-cutter in his pocket. "You keep giving answers to questions I haven't asked."

The nameless man sniffed. "I depart in fifteen minutes. Whatever work you have completed, I will transport with care and install with precision."

"I'll be there." Asher scanned the assembly. "To make sure nothing goes wrong."

"How would you know whether that was happening? From your vast experience of this week's two side windows?"

Asher spread a cloth over the panel in progress. "Most people, when they're waking someone who worked all night, say something different than you."

"Please educate poor ignorant me. What do 'most people' say?"

Asher brushed past him on the way out. "Good morning."

RAIN FELL INTO THEIR FACES on the way down. It had potholed the road, slowing the trip, making more work for those whose turn it was to pull.

But the other challenge was wind. As the crew loaded Asher's first panel on the wagon, a gust nearly tipped it over. They held it in place with both of their hands for the whole ride down.

When the crew reached the cathedral, Denis scuttled around despite his bad leg, nagging them not to track mud inside, and mopping after them when they did.

"We have to collect our tools," the nameless man explained.

The center panel of the main window did not fit well. It scraped on the lower left, stuck on the upper right, and at one point was so wedged they could not move it in or out.

"Asher, I need your help with something," the nameless man called.

He was working below, holding a crowbar, preparing bolts. "What now?"

"Under the altar you'll find the remaining tool bag, which contains a hammer and a pouch of nails. You'll also see a large canvas tarpaulin."

"All right. And?"

"Conceal the windows. When the emissary arrives tomorrow, he will expect a proper unveiling."

"My window is stuck, and you want me to go inside?"

"Now would be an ideal time."

Asher squinted upward, into the rain. "What if I say no?"

The nameless man stared squarely down. "Let's be frank. If I climb down from here and you climb up, do you sincerely believe you will have a better method, and better success, at installing this window without damage? Honestly?"

Asher looked down to see that he was standing in mud. His loyal boots, intact after all that time, were still waterproof. He was expert in footwear, not windows.

"All right," he said, leaning the crowbar against the scaffold. "I'll hang the tarpaulin."

Denis greeted Asher at the door, with a whiff of tobacco that all but stabbed him.

BY NOON THE RAIN HAD lulled, but the wind stayed moody. Canvas hung and windows concealed, Asher went back outside to find the main window's center panel snugly in place.

"Looks tight in there," he observed.

"They'd better not ever crack a pane," Simon answered from above. "This thing is never coming out." As he leaned back to admire the installation, his beret toppled off, floating down like a parachute, inexplicably hooking waist-high on a piece of scaffolding. "What luck," he yelped. "Not in the mud."

From the lane they could hear an argument approaching, a woman telling someone to leave her alone. All of the crew turned, except the nameless man, who was securing a bolt along the panel's upper frame.

"All I want to know is what you mean by it," a man shouted.

"I don't have to tell you anything," she yelled back. "Stop bothering me."

Marie's voice. Asher moved toward the cathedral's rear churchyard, Henri two steps behind. Around the corner she came, in a long gray dress, its hem darkened by the rain, leading Pétain and the wagon, and wearing a harried look.

"It's a fair question," the man behind her insisted. He was large, wearing rough work clothes. In one hand he held the lead line to a well-muscled mare, with bundles on either side of her saddle. Though a thick beard hid his face, the man seemed familiar. "By giving your animal that title, are you paying homage or giving insult?"

"It's just a name," she said.

"No," he barked. "It's either/or. Either you praise the victor at Verdun, a champion of the Great War and prime minister of the Vichy government, or you insult a hero convicted of treason in a show trial, and sentenced to life in prison despite pleas from leaders the world over."

Now, from the voice, Asher knew who it was—and the man was

still angry. Marie stayed five steps ahead of him. "Maybe I named him to annoy people like you."

"Maybe," the man growled, "I should snap your little neck."

"Bondurant," Asher said, approaching on the cobblestones. "That's enough."

"You stay out of this, weakling who stole my place at the château. You too, you . . ." He waved his fingers at Henri. "You ant."

Hackles up, Asher assessed what weapons were within reach. Bondurant had nearly doubled his weight since his days at the château, so he'd be too big to choke with donkey reins. The mallet might serve, with its gray iron head. But it lay on the ground too close to Marie, and he did not want to risk any fight coming near her.

He had no problem with there being a fight. He relished the idea of taking Bondurant apart, of using his belligerence against him. But he also knew that with any tussle, so much as one punch, he would not stop until the man was dead. Whatever horrors were necessary, whatever gore the others saw, whatever evil they learned about the window maker in their midst, none of those considerations would stop him.

The crowbar, that was the answer. It leaned on the scaffold where Simon's beret had hooked. Asher pictured spiraling the hat in the air, Bondurant watching it float as all fools will, while he seized the crowbar and plunged it into his throat.

Killing was no longer a skill. It had become a way of being. Let the bastard gasp, clutching the bar in a vain attempt to withdraw it. Let him fill with dread and regret. Let him bleed in the street.

As Asher lifted his gaze, he and Marie made eye contact. She wore a look of complete understanding, giving a nod so subtle, he could only interpret it as granting him permission. She alone knew what he was capable of, and how bloody the outcome would be. It was the strangest form of intimacy he had known.

But then he saw something more surprising: Henri, hand behind his back, had stepped closer, and he was holding a knife.

It was excellent too: military-grade, a long steel blade with a forged blood gutter, and jagged teeth on the upper part of the blade so that withdrawing the knife would tear flesh. At one time Asher had coveted such a weapon. He found his whole estimation of Henri shifting.

"Tell me now." Bondurant leaned in to her face. "Whose side are you on?"

"Leave her alone," the nameless man called from above. "She can name her animal whatever she chooses. And she certainly doesn't answer to a failure like you."

Bondurant jabbed a finger upward. "Shut your gob before I shake your scaffold to the ground. No one asked your opinion."

"You need to go," Asher said. "Now."

"Or you'll do what?" Dropping his horse's line, he pushed up one sleeve. "Come on, coward."

"Don't you use that word," the nameless man growled from above.

"These two?" He waved at Asher and Henri. "Cowards." He gestured at Marie. "Such a coward, she won't say why she named her own donkey. And you, trembling up there instead of coming to her defense?" He sneered. "Coward, coward, coward."

Asher had the strangest sensation then, it came over him like a rash: How he could have turned out this way, like Bondurant, but for a few different choices and a few lucky breaks, and now there was a vast chasm between them. He had people, he had a lover, he had company in his troubles. He was making things of value and he felt his efforts were worthwhile. The man standing before him was stronger, perhaps, and as angry as ever, but all it was going to earn him was his death.

The nameless man started climbing down. "Where is Denis with his shotgun when you need him?"

"No ammunition," Denis answered from the rear doorway. He'd come to see what the commotion was about. "It's all bluff."

"We could use a good bluff right now," the nameless man said.

"Look here," Simon said, also descending. "Nothing is proved by fighting."

"The war we just won proves you pretty damn wrong," Bondurant bellowed. "And now my fists are going to prove me pretty damn right too."

As he advanced, Asher began moving toward the crowbar—he could see the whole episode, three or four seconds and the man would be dead—just as Pascal and Euclid came rolling around the corner, laughing and slapping one another on the back.

"Well, now," Euclid cried out, drawing up. "What have we here?"

"A big tough guy," Marie said, "when it comes to women."

"And cowards," Bondurant growled.

"Really?" Pascal sidled closer. "You mean, like a guy spoiling for a fight?"

"Begging for it," she said.

"Not afraid of it," he boasted.

"Wait. We know this fellow," Euclid exclaimed, coming up beside his brother. When they stood shoulder to shoulder, they were a barrier the length of a cow. "Didn't you bop him on the head one time?"

Pascal shrugged. "Some people need two bops."

"It's unfortunate."

"Sad," Pascal said.

"Wham and bam and end of story."

They stood arm's length from the man, completely at ease. Of all things, Henri swaggered forward beside them. Asher was tempted to make a joke, but the knife's blade was too good.

"You talk tough," Bondurant said, "now that you outnumber me. But suppose I come back here at night and smash all your damn windows. How about that?"

Euclid winked. "I will tear off your head and make dirt on your neck."

Pascal gave a loud laugh.

"But you won't know it was me. Anyone with a rock could have done it."

Euclid shrugged. "That would make me no less eager to punish you."

"You'd better hope no one else does it," the nameless man called from above.

"Maybe we've just found a night watchman," Euclid said, not taking his eyes from Bondurant. "What do you think, brother?"

Pascal considered a moment. "I want to eat his horse."

Euclid chuckled. "Mares are delicious. And it would hardly be a crime, under the circumstances."

"I'd practically be eating the animal in self-defense," Pascal said.

"How long do you think it would take you?"

Bondurant shook his fist at them. "Are you two lunatics?"

"To eat the whole thing?" Pascal stared into space, as if engaged in some complex algebra of the appetite, before giving them all his toothiest grin. "A day."

Euclid guffawed, Asher laughed, Henri's shoulders shook.

"So what if you guys are big?" Bondurant said, setting his weight. "I'm not the weakling I was before. I've spent all this time moving stone, and it makes a man hard as iron. If we go at it one at a time—"

A strange noise interrupted him, made him pause, caused all of them to go still. A quiet sound, but strong enough to catch their attention. Coming from the cathedral—what was it? As odd and unexpected as bombers had been some years before, buzzing out of nowhere and unloading their burdens of death. This was the opposite, somehow, and every person in that courtyard wore a puzzled expression. No one spoke, not even to ask what it was they were hearing.

Simon was first to head for the rear door. One by one the others followed. The pull was magnetic.

Voices. Singing voices. In the cathedral's gloom, the sound paused for a moment, some woman snapping her fingers, hissing at two girls to stop fooling around and pay attention. She raised her arms, counted down, and it began again.

A children's choir. They were working on a hymn, an even dozen of them: ten girls and two boys. The woman conducting seemed exacting, making exaggerated arm motions of support or sharp cuts to abbreviate a note, while before her stood four rows of three children each, angels practicing their hallelujahs.

It was Asher's first music since the day Aube and Rachel died, but for some reason he did not cover his ears, did not run. He remained in place, tendrils from his bones insinuating between the cathedral's giant floor stones, probing the earth beneath, the compacted soil, the depths beyond, gripping, taking hold, his roots digging deeper as their voices chimed higher. He and the planet had a grip on one another.

The conductor sang a snippet of melody, her clear soprano ringing in the nave, and half of the children repeated the notes, in voices smaller, quieter, and unspeakably dear. The woman sang another snippet, and the choir's other half repeated after her. Lifting both hands high, she counted two, three, *and*—

All twelve children raised their voices, half and half, and the two snippets she'd sung made easy harmony with each other, floating high and echoing into the lofty space. It was like hearing water, the pouring of clean water. Young voices rang, while the adults listened in a huddle by the rear chapel, muddy and stunned.

"First choir here since the war," Denis whispered. "Kids hate it, but my wife insists. I'd bet they—"

"Shhh," Simon said, because the children were singing again. Some simple melody, nothing fancy or dramatic, but their voices were high and innocent, and the men and Marie stayed where they were until the song was finished.

Asher stood flummoxed. Something had shifted. These children were completely defenseless, and no one seemed to mind, or worry, or even keep watch.

Instead, the director told the children which song was next. One of the boys dropped his hymnal, the other kids laughed, and the spell was broken.

"I gotta get back to work," Bondurant said. No one answered, nor did he add anything more. He left the door open as he exited, and they could hear the clop of his horse's hooves on the cobblestones.

Peace would not come from an army, Asher realized. Nor in a command from a president or king. Twelve children could be enough.

Only then did the nameless man come inside, peering into the cathedral, keeping in the shadow. Imagine being that damaged, Asher thought, that your misdeed with children in the war meant you couldn't bear to hear them now. Asher's contempt for the man, he had to admit it, diminished an iota.

While the conductor instructed the children for the next song, the nameless man called from the doorway. "Could we recommence work now, people?" he pleaded. "The emissary comes tomorrow."

The choir began to sing, the crew went still again, and he ducked back outside.

ON THE WALK BACK TO the château, Henri affected a bit of a swagger, his knife concealed again, as though he personally had trounced Bondurant. Marie had gone on her way, continuing deliveries, but Asher couldn't help wondering. Was Henri infatuated with her? He could hardly blame the man. Another way they shared a kinship of the heart. The difference was that he knew the shape of her ankles. The strength of her hands. The demands she made with her eyes closed.

"Pardon, sir," said Pascal, he and his brother pulling the wagon with ease. "May I ask a question?"

"As long as you never call me sir again," Asher replied. "Or I'll have to kill you."

The giant men gave him a puzzled look, then burst out laughing.

"Well said." Euclid chuckled, then poked his brother. "Rip his legs off."

But Pascal had already fallen serious again. "Do you think, Asher . . ." He pointed ahead. "Do you think they are still husband and wife?"

"What?" He eyed the road. "Yes. If anything, things are stronger between them."

Pascal wagged his huge head. "But can he husband her, I mean? Is he able? I cannot stop wondering."

"This question does not flatter you, brother," Euclid said. "Brigitte is married."

"Do you think I have a choice?" Pascal snarled. "As long as I lay eyes on her, I will desire."

"I am truly sorry for you," Asher said.

"Not that I would do anything wrong, not the least thing. But"— Pascal pressed a hand to his heart—"strong as I am, the longing is stronger."

The brothers continued pulling the wagon upward without saying more.

"DO YOU WANT TO KNOW the truth?" the nameless man asked. Everyone else, their dinner done—chicken in hot mustard, early apples baked in cinnamon—had already left. He and Asher had been working later, though, one at a window and the other at a forge, so they lingered in separate corners of the table to finish eating.

Asher looked up from his plate. "Truth about what?"

"Your side window. No one has leveled with you."

"Isn't it moot?" He put his fork down. "It's already installed."

"Yes, it's completely irrelevant, if you intend never to make another window. Otherwise, you might consider that the completion of one does not mean you possess all expertise."

"By all means, then." Asher sat back. "Level with me."

"Well, quite frankly, it's junk."

Asher went still in his chair. A serrated knife lay inches from his fingers. "Junk."

"The technique is clever, of course, despite all the attention it draws to itself. Quite show-offy. And the small pieces of glass imply a kind of ugly naturalism, however much it is mannered and contrived."

Brigitte was cleaning pots in the kitchen, banging away. She wouldn't see or hear a thing. "Ugly naturalism."

"Exactly. Despite everyone's excessive praise, there's really only one thing in the window worthy of note."

After the incident with the nameless man swinging the hot blow-pipe, if Asher claimed he'd been attacked again, and had to defend himself, no one would doubt it. He remembered the power Levi had felt, knocking that soldier's boots back with the yardstick, and he could feel the same dark pleasure in his veins. A calm, cool certainty. Perhaps he didn't have to suffer this abrasive human being any longer. Perhaps this moment was not an insult, but an opportunity.

"Please," Asher said, clasping the knife. "Enlighten me." His thumb came to rest on the base of the handle, so he could drive the blade deeper. "What is the one thing worthy of note?"

"The face of the boy." The nameless man wiped his plate with bread. "It's excellent. Masterful."

"What?"

"I have to admit it. So accurate and human, I half expect the boy to breathe."

Asher's eyes flooded before he could hide it. "That face was modeled on someone I knew."

"Oh God. Don't turn dewy on me." The nameless man stood, taking his plate to the kitchen. "I promise. The rest of the window is still garbage."

The moment, to Asher, felt similar to when the heavens had stopped Abraham from killing his son. He sat a long time before realizing he was still holding the knife. Shoving it away, he too rose to go back to work.

"YOU WERE VALIANT FOR MARIE today," he told Henri hours later. He was completing the main window's second panel. All that remained was to solder the places where lead met lead. "I noticed."

Henri shrugged, a soldering iron and wire in each of his hands. He held the heating tool over the notch, melting the wire to drip into gaps in the lead.

"I hope she noticed too." Asher did the same on his side. "So she can thank you."

Henri gave him a long look, his lips pursed.

"Sometimes I would love to know what you are thinking."

Henri nodded his agreement. Then, with each of them easing away, scanning one last time to make sure they had not missed any intersections, the second panel was complete. Asher set the iron aside, and sat back.

"Look at that, my friend. Look what we've done."

Henri was beaming.

"Did you just wipe a tear? Did I catch you crying?"

Henri shook his head, but slid down from his stool and looked away.

"I'm terrible," Asher said. "Just help me move this beast out of our way."

Henri positioned himself at the upper end, Asher at the lower. They leaned the window on its edge, heaved it up, and muscled it down the warren's steps. Grunting, they lowered the assembly to the floor.

"There," Asher said. "We are champions."

Henri clasped his hands together and shook them on each side of his head.

They returned to the light table, Asher spreading design sheets for the main window's final panel. "The first one took us four days," he said. "The second one, two and a half days. For this last one, we have tonight. Assemble and seal. That's not counting the time to haul these panels to the cathedral, and install them."

Henri made a show of rolling up his sleeves.

AN HOUR LATER, ASHER SAT back to stretch his lower back. "Can I tell you a story?"

They were surrounded by candles, the château as quiet as snowfall.

The rain must have paused. Henri looked up from his assembly and nodded.

"I'm glad. I always worry that people will tire of my stories." Securing the new piece, he worked a dull lead-cutter back and forth.

"I grew up in a harbor town." Asher reached for a piece of yellow glass. "Our house was well back from the water. My four brothers and I shared a bed, but we did not think of it as poverty. It was the way of the world, and that must be how all families lived, right?"

Henri shrugged, and Asher paused. "It occurs to me that I don't know anything about your background," he marveled. "You might be an only child, or one of fifteen. Maybe dirt-poor, or the son of a baron. Well, it's enough to know you now."

Henri made the slightest bow, and they both went back to work.

"As a boy, I loved to watch the ships come in. Slow, but full of momentum, needing large spaces to stop. Each one used its highest mast for the flag of the nation where it was commissioned. But most ships flew smaller ones too. My brother Jacques told me they sent a message—to the harbormaster, to other ships. Isn't that great? An international language, in flags."

Asher used a felt mallet to tap a piece of glass snug. "I never learned what the flags said, but I made a game out of guessing. If a ship rode low in the water, I decided it was signaling, *I'm overloaded, I won't be nimble at the docks.* If one came in fast, I thought the flags said, *The captain can't wait to see his children.* That sort of thing."

Absently Asher ran the meat of his thumb over the edge of the next pane. "One day the harbormaster's son started explaining to me what the flags meant. A red square in the middle, with a white square around it, and a blue square around that, meant the ship needed medical aid. A flag like France's, but with the colors red, white, and blue from left to right, that meant keep clear, stay back."

Asher shook his head. "I made him stop. Learning the signals ruined the fun. I realized: not knowing created an openness to many possible meanings."

Again Asher reached for the lead-cutter. Driving his weight downward, he was able to slice the lead to proper length. Again he reached for the next piece of glass. "Which brings me to you, and the purpose of this story."

Henri interrupted his own work to sit and listen.

"I don't know what your signals say, any more than I did the ones on those ships. But I trust you to understand me, and trust myself to understand you, and somehow it always works."

Asher put down the knife, the piece of glass. "Henri, you are an immensely skilled artist. I'm aware of it because I feel much less confident when you are not here to help me. But you are also a splendid human being. Splendid. I am proud to know you, and honored to work with you. That is my story for tonight. The end."

Henri blinked at him, bashful. But he reached over the window and grabbed Asher's arm, holding him firmly, and they grinned at one another.

"To repay you," Asher continued, "now I'm going to teach you something."

Henri raised his eyebrows, and Asher smiled. "Yes. How to work all night."

CHAPTER 34

Etienne waited to wake them till the last possible minute. He found both men under a tarpaulin, lying spine-to-spine to share body warmth. Without the furnaces lit, the atelier's air was as cold as its concrete floor.

"Good morning gentlemen," Etienne said, squatting beside them. "I regret to say that it is time for you to rise."

Asher bolted upright. Barely one second before, in his dreams, the man on fire had been holding him by the neck. "What day is it? Are we too late?"

Henri blinked awake, making a sour face, and scanned the room as if trying to figure out where he was.

"Not yet," Etienne said. "It is six fifteen, and we have enough time for everything. If you tell me, please, that the last panel is complete."

"It is." Asher rose, climbing to the warren as if to reassure himself. "What happened to the second panel?"

"The nameless man and Simon removed it before sunrise," Etienne said. "I promised to throttle them if they woke you. They took it down on the wagon and by now they're probably installing it."

"How will we move this one, then? Without a wagon? I wish people had thought this through."

"My worried friend," Etienne said, "we did. The doctor loaned us his truck, so Marc can witness the unveiling. First we'll use it to carry this panel to the cathedral."

Asher's shoulders came down. "We might actually make it."

"It will be tight." Etienne straightened. "Part of the reason we'll have Marc there is to stall the emissary."

Henri, listening to the whole conversation, stood and nodded at them. Holding one finger in the air, he bowed slightly, and left the room.

"He'll be right back," Asher translated.

"Let's not wait. Brigitte has food for you. Let's get that panel on its way."

THE TRUCK WAS ACTUALLY AN ambulance, and an antique. The engine chugged as though it had only one cylinder. But the rear door opened far enough for Etienne and Asher to slide the window in diagonally.

"There's not enough room to stand it up," Asher said. "We'll have to keep it at an angle."

Etienne leaned down, pondering. "How about you and Henri crawl under the window, supporting it from below? I'll drive slowly, and avoid every pothole—"

Asher rubbed sleep from his eyes. "I'll fetch Henri."

"Do me a favor and hurry," Etienne said.

The dining room was empty. In the kitchen, Brigitte worked alone at the stove.

"Good morning," she said, waving a wooden spoon. "I'm just preparing tonight's celebratory. See you in church."

Upstairs the rooms were empty, save Marc at his desk, dozing in the wheelchair. Asher called through the château and Henri did not answer. Lastly he checked the atelier. Not only was Henri absent, but the place was melancholy. No one firing a furnace, no one making gathers or blowing glass, no one designing or assembling. Just a shed, some workbenches, a stack of wood. Strangely lifeless.

He ran back outside. "Could he have started down ahead of us?"

"I don't know why he would," Etienne said. "But we can't wait anymore."

Asher wriggled into the ambulance, curling under the panel. A fleeting thought: perhaps this was what a coffin felt like. Lying on his side was awkward because of the lead-cutter in his pocket, which he'd forgotten to leave behind. It jutted into his thigh. Etienne put the old machine into gear. "Here we go," he called from the driver's seat. "Slow and steady."

THE SECOND WINDOW WAS IN place when they arrived. The nameless man secured it on one side, Simon doing the other, both of them ignoring the rain. Denis stood in the rear doorway, under the little roof, inches from the downpour.

"How close are you to finished?" Etienne called up the scaffold.

"Depends on when you get that thing up here," the nameless man replied.

Asher squirreled his way out of the ambulance, while Etienne slid the last panel halfway out. As Asher took a position to grab the top, Etienne lost his footing on the wet cobbles, and fell.

"No, no, no," Asher cried. The panel banged against the stones, and rested on one corner. He could see the metal bowing outward.

"Lunacy," Denis cried, leaving his dry spot to rush over. Regardless of his bad leg, he raised the downward end to level. Etienne rose, favoring a knee and noticing his pants had torn. "Stand away, son," Denis said. "You're a mess."

Instead, Etienne scurried up beside Asher, and together they slid the panel the rest of the way out. "No one saw that, right?" He smiled, a streak of dirt on his cheek.

It took all of the crew to raise the final panel into place, Asher again hampered by the lead-cutter pressing into his thigh.

"Where the hell is Henri?" the nameless man barked. But no one replied.

He and Simon clambered to make the final installation, Asher and Etienne holding the panel steady. The rain intensified, a north wind gusting and cold.

"Tell me this is not biblical," Simon yelled. "When is the plague of locusts?"

"Calm yourself," Denis called from below. "I'll find towels, so we can wipe that window down before it goes in."

By the time he returned, the final panel was sitting in its permanent home. All it lacked was the array of bolts to secure it. Asher stood elbow to elbow with the nameless man, as Etienne tapped his arm. "We'll take it from here."

He wiped rainwater from his eyes. "Of all times, you want me to leave now?"

"You made the thing," the nameless man said. "Let us hang it."

Looking from one of them to the other, he understood that this was not like flags on ships, where not knowing was valuable. At that moment, knowing was everything. He had no choice but to trust them. "Please, please do it perfectly."

Etienne stepped forward, as Asher climbed down to stand beside the docent. Simon monkeyed his way down as well. Rain fell heavily, but they remained, watching the men struggle to drive the bolts.

"I wonder where Henri disappeared to," Asher said.

"No idea," Simon said, "but it's bad timing." He called up to the men on the scaffold. "I'm going to collect Marc now, all right?"

"As long as you hurry," Etienne said.

Simon slammed the ambulance's rear door and started the grumbling motor. Asher and Denis watched him drive away on the cobblestone road.

"Halloo?" Someone was calling from the cathedral door, which Denis had left open. A tall man in a long black coat waved one pale hand. "Halloo?"

"Sweet Mother of God." Denis slid in the slop as he limped over. "He's early."

THE EMISSARY WAS DRENCHED. AND freezing. "The rain I didn't mind," he told Denis when they were back inside. "But that wind was blowing right through me."

"Father, I'm relieved you made it here in good health," the docent replied.

"Just now I saw clear sky in the north. But I'm afraid it will take days to arrive."

"Wrong weather for unveiling windows," Denis observed.

"Whatever the Lord wills. But"—he checked his wristwatch—"I'm a smidgen early. I hope that won't inconvenience anyone."

"Not a bit," Denis replied, though sounds of scraping and grunting were clearly audible through the hanging canvas. "A few folk aren't here yet. Come sit a minute beside the heater in my office. We'll get your blood flowing proper again."

"Excellent." He patted Denis on the back. "I'd enjoy tea too, if you have it."

Denis held a hand toward a side hallway. "After you, sir."

Outside, Asher was pacing. It was too much, men muscling his work, hurrying an installation meant to last centuries. "Careful," he shouted. "Go easy with it."

Etienne said something to the nameless man, and climbed partway down. He called Asher over. "You've done your part here. I think it's best you go in."

"And miss this? Why in the world?"

"I don't trust Denis to stall the emissary. You're more useful there."

Asher considered what Etienne had left unsaid. His presence was adding to the pressure. He bowed wordlessly, and made his way into the cathedral. Wind slammed the door behind him, and the gigantic room echoed with the sound.

Denis popped his head out like a rabbit from his den. "What's that racket?"

"Beg your pardon," Asher said.

"You're a wet rat," Denis said. "Come dry yourself."

Asher followed him into a tiny office as warm as an electric blanket. Huddled by the heater sat a tall man in a clerical collar.

"Hello, sir," Asher said.

"Hello, Father, you mean," Denis corrected, handing him a towel.

"Of course I do." He forced a smile. "Father."

It was not funny, though. Asher was tired of the pretense, exhausted with being an impostor. Once again, today he would behave like someone other than himself, deceiving people who deserved better.

"A pleasure to meet you, my son." The priest gestured to an empty chair. "Come share the warmth."

Asher followed, but left the door ajar in case he needed to escape.

"So." The emissary lifted his teacup, pinkie extended, and took the daintiest sip. "Are you a native of Clovide?"

WITHIN THE HOUR, THE NAMELESS man announced that all was assembled. Inside, Denis gave him a towel, and the nameless man greeted the priest warmly. "Could we speak a moment, Father?"

"Of course." The priest smiled at Asher. "Would you mind?"

"Not at all," Asher said, already backing into the hall.

"So," he heard the emissary say. "Denis has told me about the hidden treasure."

Etienne entered the rear door, and Denis gave him a towel too. He wiped the rain from his face. "There's blue sky coming," he confided to Asher, "but painfully slowly. I'm sorry the sun won't get here in time."

"Damn it to hell," Asher replied.

"Shall we have a consecration?" The priest had come up beside Asher, but they appeared not to have heard each other.

Etienne rubbed his hands together. "The moment of truth arrives."

If only that were so, Asher thought. If only.

Limping, Denis led them into the cathedral. Brigitte was wheeling her husband down the main aisle—Marc fastened into the chair with the strap high on his chest, so that he looked upright.

"The director of our atelier," Etienne explained. "Recently afflicted."

"So I see." The priest advanced to meet them, with both hands raised.

The nameless man took that moment to pull Denis aside. "Our project," he whispered. "He approves. Provided he likes what he sees today, he approves."

Asher went still—in order to eavesdrop.

"Course he does," Denis replied, as loud as he pleased. "The man's no fool."

"Do you understand how gigantic that will be?" he continued whispering.

"Gigantic?" Denis shifted the weight off his injured leg. "How do you mean?"

"I'm no good for people anymore, you've seen that. But I'm still useful for glass. The windows you saved might just save me."

"*And so*," the priest declared, hands over Marc's head, "blessings from the Almighty for healing and acceptance." Then he held them above Brigitte. "Daughter of God, remember always: caring for the sick is one of the seven works of mercy."

The emissary had a grand voice, rich and resonant, his words echoing in the stone arch overhead. He smiled around at everyone. "Now that the praying machine is all warmed up, let's do the day's business."

The group filed forward, Asher bringing up the rear beside the nameless man. "What's this about a gigantic project?"

Instead of replying, he scowled. "We had no time to see what your final window looks like. But the stakes are even higher now. It had better not be awful."

Once again Asher felt his rage rise. But insecurity was close behind. What if he *had* made something awful? He'd liked each new idea and technique, but what if they combined to make a giant mess? It was too late for something as simple as seeking a second opinion. Asher ducked behind a pillar—just as Henri arrived, breathless.

"Where have you been?" Asher snarled. "We needed you."

Henri fluttered his hands in the air, shook his head.

"I was counting on you." Asher's jaw was clenched. "Where in hell did you go?"

Henri held a finger to his lips, pointing past him—at the priest.

"Gentlemen—and lady." He bowed to Brigitte. "There is no established service for the consecration of new windows. But let us enter into a prayerful spirit, remembering that we are merely instruments of the Almighty. And let us now—I confess it, I love this part—let us now have the unveiling."

No one moved. No one had thought to assign ceremonial responsibilities.

Etienne stepped forward, spying Asher behind the organ pipes. "Unless there is an objection to me doing this . . ."

Asher shook his head, a sickness in his stomach. Henri dodged away from him, into a pew near the others.

"D . . . do us proud, Etienne," Marc called.

Etienne gripped the first window's cover in both hands, and pulled.

CHAPTER 35

Asher's first thought was that the weather might be clearing outside after all. Hints of light glinted through the glass.

"Ah, the crucifixion," the priest said. "Scripture's most painful moment, and this is a powerful rendition. The nail about to pierce our savior. Brilliant."

Next Etienne removed the canvas from Asher's side window. The light seemed slightly stronger.

"Fascinating," the priest said, hand to his mouth. "Abraham and Isaac. Muscular, passionate. The light from above, staying Abraham's hand. An unusual style."

Asher knew there was no theatrical way for Etienne to uncover the main window. All he'd done was hammer tacks through the tarp into wood above the frame. Etienne tugged on the cover unsuccessfully until he realized how it was attached. At that, he gave Asher a look, and backed away.

There was no alternative. He crept forward and gathered the cloth in both hands. If it didn't come away cleanly, he would use the lead-cutter in his pocket. With a deep inhale, Asher tore the covering down in one full tearing sweep.

The room went silent. Rolling the canvas into a bundle, he realized: Everyone was looking up, above his head, and they were not speaking or

moving. He also went still. He also wanted to see. Not the windows—
he'd been staring at them for weeks, nearly every minute his eyes were
open, and sometimes when they were closed. No, he wanted to watch
the people, and gauge their reactions. In that way he witnessed something unexpected. Whether due to God, or the wind, or lucky timing,
after all those gloomy days the sun had come fully out, pouring its
beneficence on them all. Gloom retreated as the chapel filled with light.

Such bright, lively, interested eyes the people had, as the windows'
colors projected onto them: a green the color of spruce needles on Marc's
wheelchair, winter-sky-blue on Brigitte's chemise, tree-trunk-brown on
Simon's arm, goldenrod-yellow on Henri from his boots to his eyes,
wavy shadows on the legs of the nameless man and Denis, who stood
beside one another. And red—deep, brilliant, blood-red—on the face
of the bishop's emissary, who stood in the center aisle with his mouth
hanging open.

In fact, Asher observed, every one of them wore an expression of
wonder. But seeing this gave him a feeling much larger than pride. His
glasswork was nothing. The window's image? Nothing. These people,
they were the astonishing thing, they were the accomplishment. After
all they'd withstood and suffered and survived, somehow stained glass
made the misfits beautiful.

What a thing humanity was after all. Perhaps now, years after victory, hard years, the peace might truly begin. Asher stood amazed, all
from the light on their faces.

Simon broke the silence. He prayed, his hands together. "Glory be
to God."

The others burst into applause, even the nameless man. As the
fanfare faded, and people absorbed the windows, gradually they shifted
their gazes to the priest. From where Asher stood, nothing about the
man's expression indicated pleasure, or reverence, or delight. His forehead bore a deep furrow. His lips were tightly pursed.

"Good people," he said at last. "What can I say to you?"

The priest tugged on his chin. "I admire the sincerity of the right side window, and I see the intelligence and passion of the left. But the center work? I am baffled."

He tapped a forefinger against his lips. "I mean, you know your business. When you made this, you knew what you were about. But honestly."

He tilted his head back, consulting with the ceiling, before leveling it again. "I praise the image, of course. God saving his chosen people. Beyond that, I am at a loss."

From one of his pockets, he produced a prayer book. He flipped through the pages, finding the spot he wanted, reading, then shook his head.

"No. I need to speak plainly, and for myself." He tucked the book away. "The truth is, I don't like it. I don't. A stained glass window ought to educate. Inspire. This one is too busy, it has too many shapes. A correct window should . . . it should . . ."

Asher stared at the floor. He had been wrong. The lies, the work, the hope—it was all a waste. He should have told them from the beginning that he was Jewish, and either stayed to haul wood, or departed to muddle along on his way. For his deceit, this humiliation was a fitting punishment.

"I can appreciate," the emissary continued, "how unique the construction is, to use clear glass for much of the window. An interesting experiment, to which a congregation might become accustomed over a span of years."

Years, Asher thought. First, they would hate it for years.

The priest took out a rosary and fingertipped the beads. No one spoke. Asher thought he heard the church's main door open, but he could not see anyone entering. At last, tucking his rosary away, the emissary cleared his throat.

"The crucifix hidden in the ark's timbers?" He pointed. "That's quite subtle. I've never seen that technique before. But the ark is a tale of forgiveness and redemption, whereas that detail warns of a crucifixion many generations away. It is not the purpose of a window, to work on two levels like that. Not the purpose at all."

Reaching into a different pocket, the priest produced a set of eyeglasses, which he fixed in place on his nose.

Denis elbowed the nameless man. "Spectacles."

"I am capable of observation."

"There is an interesting effect," the emissary continued, "with yellow in each animal's chest—horses, deer, rabbits . . . all of them, I suppose. The color grows paler as it moves from the animal's heart." He raised a finger. "Very clever. To me it shows that all living creatures possess a soul, which radiates God's goodness and mercy."

Asher lifted his head. Had the man choked up for a moment? Definitely he was walking up the aisle, reconsidering the window. Meanwhile, Asher saw who had opened the cathedral's door: Marie, in a dress the color of cream. He pressed a hand to his chest. She pursed her lips.

"I'm not clear what that leaping fish is all about," the emissary continued, "down in the corner. There's no fish in scripture's ark story that I recall. And those slashes of color behind the bird, it suggests the rainbow of God's promise, but barely. Also in the lower right here, you have a row of, what? Fangs?"

He stopped walking. "But your *dove*. Heaven, do I adore your dove."

The priest raised both hands toward the bird rendered in white, a green branch in its beak, surrounded by a halo of stunning red.

"There is the ark's true lesson, yes? The great message of hope. After rain for forty days and forty nights, a bird was able to reach the people, and it carried an olive branch. This bird means that salvation is near."

Asher again took stock of the people before him. Simon's eyes were closed, probably in prayer. Henri and Etienne seemed restless in their seats. Marc was chewing on his lower lip. Brigitte stood behind him, tears shining on her face.

"What is most striking, though"—the priest was orating now, his voice gathering strength—"is the clear glass. The more I look, well, it has changed my mind. Even without color I see the shapes of owls, hawks, swifts, as a kind of shadow of the dove."

The emissary's eyes were alight. "We are not seeing the promise of hope in one bird. We are witnessing it in all creation. And all the wings you've made behind those birds, just wings, attached to nothing we can see? Are they not the sweet cherubim, the mighty seraphim, the heavenly host singing, 'Peace on earth'?"

The priest paused to collect himself, rubbing a finger under his nose.

"One last item." He was pointing again. "Just now I noticed the trees outside, waving in the wind. I have never heard of a stained glass creation anywhere on earth that included the world outside. This window has transcended its placement."

He strode onto the apron of marble around the altar. "Faith is an essential force in our lives and in the life of the Church. But it is also a power in the world. That is what seeing the trees says to me. What an excellent parable you artists have made."

Smiling now, the emissary beamed at the people seated before him. "I repent of my initial reaction, friends. It was premature. What the flock will learn here, what lessons. I am . . ."

Then he did choke up, closing his eyes, taking a moment. Asher held his breath, as with the owls that were rabbis, once again awaiting his damnation.

"I am so proud of you," the priest said, opening his eyes. "And all that you have accomplished in this battered corner of a broken world. It gives me great hope."

He strode to the pulpit, grasping it, standing upright. "The bishop will hear all about this masterpiece. If I'm able, I will bring him here myself. What's more, I hereby exercise my authority and approve your atelier to restore and reinstall the salvaged windows of this church as well. May they endure for centuries to come."

"The what?" Asher said. Marc leaned over to look at Brigitte, who shrugged.

"Later we'll address the basilica near here, whose rosette window was destroyed. Many other churches merit reconstruction, to assure congregations that they are indeed in places of holiness." The emissary raised his hands high. "Until then, let us pray."

Everyone bowed their heads, Asher last. A current of anger rose in him, acidic with self-disgust. This is the moment, he said to himself. The perfect time to reveal yourself. Don't commit another forgery, don't say one more false prayer—but the priest had already begun.

This time he spoke in Latin. Asher could no more mimic that language than the emissary could converse in Yiddish. He stared past the people, light in the front as the main door opened and closed again. Marie, like him, was skipping the prayer.

"Amen," the priest said.

"Amen," said the others.

Asher, torn between triumph and deceit, said nothing.

The emissary sent Denis for his overcoat, donning it at the entry. "Make no mistake about what I have said today. You people have changed the art of stained glass. You have transformed it. I am blessed to be the first to witness."

The door opened with a blast of sunshine, the priest charging out into the afternoon. The instant the entry was dark, everyone erupted in cheers.

"Well done," the nameless man said to no one in particular. "Well done."

"There you go," Denis replied, shaking Simon's hand in both of his, for once tolerating noise inside the cathedral.

"Where is the c . . . ?" Marc shouted, silencing them all. "The c . . . Where is this crucifix he said something about? I can't find it."

Scurrying over to the wheelchair's handles, Henri backed Marc up the aisle to where the priest had stood. Squatting, his arm on Marc's shoulder, he pointed.

"Yes, I see the c . . . cross on the altar. I'm no idiot."

Henri rolled his hand over, pointing beyond.

"I don't follow you," Marc said. "I don't . . . Oh, there. On the prow of the ark."

Henri leaned over him and nodded.

"Ingenious. But I'm not satisfied yet. I have m . . . more questions."

As the men drew nearer, Brigitte stepped aside. Asher thought she seemed anxious, her hands worrying a pair of gloves.

"How the hearts shine yellow and then fade," Marc said. "How the t . . . t . . . tops of the waves are dark blue, but lighten as you move deeper in the water—which, need I remind you, is the opposite of reality."

"Asher calculated," Etienne explained, "and we did not have enough chemicals to give the animals halos. He had the idea of a strong yellow within the creatures, which faded gradually. An internal halo."

"The priest said it was the immortal soul," Simon interjected.

"He was carried away with himself," Marc said. "What about the ocean?"

"The same principle," Etienne answered. "Put a strong blue on the water's surface, but let it fade in the adjoining glass. You can see the dark blue diamonds he added randomly below, to reinforce the suggestion of water. Otherwise, the idea was to let the congregations imagine the rest."

"That's more flaky than my grandmother's pie," Marc growled. "Last q. Q . . . last question. The dove's red halo. I don't like it. Halos are yellow. But that hue. Deepest red I've seen. I know f . . . firsthand that we were out of gold. Explain."

Henri waved Asher forward several times, till at last he stepped up. "The glass was left over, sir," he said. "From Henri's red sun in the first side window."

"Nonsense." Marc shook his head. "I saw that w . . . window. I would remember a red this bold."

"We used layers."

"What are you talking about?"

"The halo is two panes thick."

"Two p . . . two panes thick?" Marc glanced around himself. "Is that allowed?"

Asher shrugged. "Allowed by who?"

Marc raised his disabled hand, waved it in the air, let it drop into his lap. He heaved a monumental sigh. "The emissary was infatuated with himself. But he was right about one thing. You have t . . . t . . . transformed windows forever."

"May I say a word about the religious aspect?" Simon stepped out of his pew.

"In brief," the nameless man answered.

"Please," Brigitte said. "The short version."

"Simply this." Simon tugged down on his rain-soaked vest. "Most stained glass is concerned with Christ. His life, deeds, disciples. A few favor a saint, or a pope, or the king who paid for them to be made. But the New Testament is the primary inspiration."

Simon gestured at the central window. "Here we have Noah's ark. Also Abraham and Isaac. Both from the Old Testament, from the Hebrew prophets, long before Christ was born. Do you understand? Asher's technique is so rare, we notice that first. But we must not overlook this other innovation: reaching back further in scripture, to invoke the more ancient spiritual tradition—"

"I've got it!" The nameless man stepped forward, eyes blazing. "Finally, finally, finally, I figured it out."

"Excuse me," Simon said. "I was about to—"

"Why did it take me so long, when the evidence was so obvious?" He swaggered forward, laughing loudly and freely.

"I beg your—"

"Come here." The nameless man waved at Asher. "Come out, come out."

"I was trying to say—"

"Silence," the nameless man roared at Simon. "This is much more important. Isn't it, Asher?"

"I don't know," he answered, a knot of dread in his belly. He had never heard the nameless man laugh before.

"Time for the day's second unveiling." The nameless man held out both arms. "Come, stand before your friends."

Brigitte leaned down to Marc. "This doesn't feel good."

"Come, we are all praising your genius. What is there to be shy about?"

Asher was halfway to the aisle, when the nameless man put an arm around his shoulders and dragged him to the center. "Our friend here, our talented trusted friend, has a secret. I've suspected it forever, but Simon just proved it for me."

All at once Asher understood why that lead-cutter in his pocket kept intruding on him all day: for this moment, this danger, this temptation. That arm around his shoulders felt like nothing but hostility, and he could end it in two seconds. But to do that, he would have to forget the starving man who had stood in exactly this spot, two years before, watching a crow fly through an opening his window now occupied. He would have to dismiss all the distance he had traveled, in body and in soul.

Meanwhile, Marc was banging a fist on his chair arm. "What are you t . . ." He frowned. "What in hell are you talking about?"

All Asher had to do was slide the cutter from his pocket and spin to his right, and the killer he had been would become the killer he always would be. Kill this man, and simultaneously kill every friendship he had made, every window he might make.

"How I wish I had a sheet to pull down." The nameless man hugged Asher tighter. "This man here? This impostor? He's a Jew."

"What?" Simon said. "What are you talking about?"

"He's Jewish, I tell you."

"So what?" Etienne said.

"So *what?*" The nameless man's eyes went wild like those of a frightened horse. "He has infiltrated us. He has won our trust with a lie. Deceived his way into our good graces. And now?" He laughed again, an acidic sound. "Now we have a permanent installation in a holy cathedral built by a person who does not even practice our faith."

He shoved Asher away. "Isn't that right? Isn't that the truth?"

Asher looked at him, at the hideous triumph written on the nameless man's face. He could reveal the man's own deception, and the children who died on his watch. Or he could pull that lead-cutter from his pocket, and put him out of everyone's misery.

Instead, Asher was surprised to feel the heat of retaliation dissipate.

Why should the truth provoke an act of violence? Why should honesty inspire revenge? He could choose to reject fear. He could experience relief at being known. Genuine relief.

"Answer me," the nameless man shouted. All of the others were frozen.

Asher looked at each of them in turn, his heart saying farewell to all the deception, regardless of what other departures might result. Releasing the cutter, standing tall, he gave his answer.

"*Modeh ani lefanekha melekh hai vekayam shehehezarta bi nishmati b'hemlah, rabah emunatekha.*"

"What language is that?" Etienne asked.

"What in blazes?" Denis exclaimed. "I'm as confused as an upside-down horse."

But for Asher, their astonishment brought another old prayer to mind, one he felt entitled to say, reciting their blessing before every meal for all those months: "*Barukh ata Adonai Eloheinu, melekh ha'olam, hamotzi lehem min ha'aretz.*"

"See?" the nameless man crowed. "He speaks Hebrew. I caught him, the liar."

Marc combed his fingers through his beard. "I knew that already," he replied. "And it d . . . does not matter."

"It does matter, sir," Simon said. "Not because of his religion, but because he has lied to us continuously for all this time."

"Exactly." The nameless man pointed at Simon. "Exactly what I—"

He was interrupted by Henri giving a long cry, "Naaahh," as he dashed past Marc's wheelchair, down the aisle, and out the cathedral door.

"What is happening?" Denis asked. "Can someone explain?"

"I'm not surprised by your anti-Semitism"—Simon gestured at the nameless man—"but I would not have expected to see it in Henri."

"That's n . . . not what it was," Marc said.

"Not to contradict you, sir," Etienne said, "but we saw it with our own eyes."

"Hear me, then," Marc answered. "I know why he d . . . did that, and it is not for the reason you think. I will explain it to you later."

Asher had fallen back against one of the pillars, hand over his eyes. Expulsion he could withstand, he had prepared himself for it, but he had never expected the pain of his friend running away.

Denis cleared his throat. "Would *someone* please explain this to me?"

"T . . . tomorrow at dinner," Marc continued. "You'll see. Do not be concerned."

"What can you tell us tomorrow that you cannot say today?" the nameless man persisted. "You knew Asher is Jewish. You know why Henri ran out. You're holding all the secrets, but we're the ones who have been betrayed."

"You have some nerve," Brigitte said, shaking a fist at him. "Challenging the trustworthiness of the man who has made this château's survival possible."

"We have all made it possible," the nameless man replied, though his tone was quieter. "It has required all of us."

"That inc. Inc . . . that includes the two men who have left us here," Marc said.

"Two?" Simon asked.

They looked forward again, and realized that Asher also had made his exit. The canvas sheet he'd been holding now lay on the floor like something abandoned.

HE HAD NEVER TRULY WALKED in the city before. Even in his time of wandering, the path was always through a place—daylight creeping across the squares, someone singing from an upstairs window, the scent of dinner cooking, lovers canoodling in the shadows, a peal of laughter from down the lane. Were the people as divided as the old woman had said on the afternoon of the fiddler? Everyone as angry as Bondurant, offended to the verge of violence over the name of a donkey? Was this still a nation of gunshots in the night, fires in the distance? Were those men beside the well still punching each other?

Or were these only symptoms, an outward manifestation of his troubled heart?

If so, it felt considerably less troubled that evening. In fact, now that he was real, was true, he felt like he'd shed a great burden. His window had succeeded and would endure. He had not committed any acts of violence that day. After the weight of deception, he felt light and relieved. He was a member of the city, not a passerby who arrived starving and left hungrier. All that time he had walked with his head down, and was now beginning to lift his gaze.

Like a fish, he thought. A creature who somehow has leapt clear of the water, and there—there is the world.

IN THE END HE RETURNED to the château because he had nowhere else to go. Asher made sure to arrive long past dinner. By habit he checked the garden wall, and yes, the jar was there—empty this time. He might never know what that was all about.

People were still in the dining room, their conversation droning out the window. He skirted the courtyard, entering in back at the wood delivery doors. They were ajar, a dim light inside, and Asher hesitated. If Henri was in there, what should he do? Leave? Hurry past? How do you reconcile with a man who does not speak?

While he considered, out came Simon, shaking a broom.

"God in heaven," he said, dropping the broom with a jump. "You scared me to death."

"I'm so sorry," Asher said. "I'm sorry about everything."

"I'll survive." Simon smiled, collecting himself. "Besides, here's your influence. Before the new work begins, I thought I would organize things. And scrub the studio, for once." He picked up the broom. "I'm glad to see you."

"You're not angry with me?"

Simon assumed the stance he often adopted for one of his lectures. "Some people believe in evolution," he said. "We come from one family, ascended from the apes. Personally, I follow the Bible. It too teaches that we are descended from one family, one mother and father in Eden. Either way, Asher, we're all kin."

"But I hid something important from you. All this time."

"Each of us has done worse. Besides"—he held the broom to one side and shook it, dust flying—"we are all children of God."

"Do you sincerely believe that?"

"It's my faith. And didn't we fight a horror of a war, based on that principle?"

"Maybe," Asher said. "Maybe that was part of it."

"There's a thing I've wanted to ask you." Simon fanned the air in front of his face, trying to clear the broom dust. "Did your brother keep his promise from the day at the waterfalls?"

"Which promise was that?"

"The one to show up, to save your life."

Asher scuffed his boot. "One time a Nazi soldier was plunging his sword into hay bales where he thought members of the Resistance were hiding. He came so close to me, he cut my shirt. I sure wished that day that my brother would appear. Like everyone, though, he had his own war to fight."

"You were in the Resistance?"

Here was an opportunity to discard one more deceit. "I was."

"And here I called you all animals." Simon lowered his head. "When I never knew for certain who had attacked me."

Asher reached into his pocket, and handed Simon the lead-cutter he'd been carrying all day. "In a way, it was true. But in wartime, every person is an animal."

SNEAKING THROUGH THE HOUSE, ASHER tiptoed up the stairs. He did not hazard a lamp. Entering his room, he could tell no one had been there. How could there be no consequences? Of course there would be consequences.

He poked his head out the window. A moonless sky, spangled with stars. He wished he'd learned the constellations, and whatever wisdom the heavenly scale of time might teach him. He breathed in—delicious, verdant, spiced by all living things in reach of his senses. He breathed out.

An uncertain wind blew across the lowlands, stirring the trees below. With his concealment ended and the windows finished, there was room in his thoughts for other things. Aube first, always first. Hair blown back from her handsome, strong-jawed face. And Rachel, who had the same determined expression, but her father's softer eyes. He ached with longing for them, to relive the least, most pedestrian moment with them. Let them rise on the wind of his memory, rise above the pain of their deaths, elevate far beyond his sorrow. He knew this now: grief was a form of love.

They rise, he imagined, until their memory finds a place among the stars, their faces forming constellations all their own—not Orion or Cassiopeia or any antique notion of how to make the night less frightening, but a certain and memorable shape nonetheless. This line of lights in the north was Aube's jaw, that glimmer in the east was Rachel's eyes—arrangements as fixed in his mind as pieces of cooled glass, so that out of all the creatures on earth, there would be one being who recognized that combination of stars and knew it as them. His wife and daughter were never coming back. Never. Never. Yet their constellations would remain there, vast and distant, visible on every cloudless night for as long as he lived, whenever he should think to lift his eyes.

It was a long way from his garret window to the grass below. All that distance his tears fell, landing without sound.

IN THE MORNING, DISPATCHED BY Marc to bring Asher first thing, Etienne encountered a room of creative chaos: drawings on the sheets, on papers, on the walls and draperies and one torn shirt. He found Asher asleep against the wall, just below the window, a charcoal pencil in his hand.

CHAPTER 36

I knew the d . . . the first day you arrived here."

"How is that possible?"

"The name your parents gave you." Marc pulled one wheel on his chair, angling from his desk toward Asher. "Perhaps you're unaware that I have s . . . studied in a seminary. Asher led one of the twelve tribes of Israel."

"Yes, he did." He did not try to abbreviate the conversation. With the truth out, here was the expulsion he'd avoided for so long. In a way, he was ready.

"Also, you have no creativity in last names." Marc smiled. "Mister Asher *Verte*."

"Why didn't you expose me at the beginning?"

Marc sighed. "Ev . . . ev . . . every man here has something to hide. You may not know that you talk in your sleep. Something you did nineteen times still haunts you."

"That is terrifying."

Marc shook his head. "It t . . . it tells me that you have a conscience. Therefore, my role has been to protect you. Though I do wish you had not attended Mass. You should have said you were ill. A small lie is preferable to sacrilege."

"The priest could tell I was faking anyway."

"So could the almost-priest." He waved Asher behind his wheelchair. "D . . . down the hall and back, would you, please?"

"Yes sir." Asher pushed, but the wheelchair had a mind of its own—wheels wobbling in all directions—until he took sterner control. Then it was easy.

Meanwhile, Marc was reminiscing. "When we reclaimed the château, and began accepting people to live here, Brigitte and I decided to safeguard their secrets. It made sense at the time. The war was t . . . too recent. The pain too fresh. Yesterday we learned otherwise."

"What did we learn, sir?"

"C . . . concealment no longer makes sense here. For anyone."

Asher slowed at the end of the hall. "I feel cleaner with the truth out."

Marc stroked his beard. "T . . . t . . . tonight at dinner I will share everyone's history. Thereafter, we will live as our actual selves."

Was this a ray of light? Of possibility? Asher wheeled the chair back toward Marc's office. "I regret that my dishonesty was hurtful to others."

"I prefer to think of you opening a d . . . a door. You and the nameless man together, ironically. One that should already have been open. We have been striving in common purpose for too long. Can you imagine anything these men might confess at this point that would alter your view of them?"

"I already know them by their deeds. I'm not sure what else I need to know."

Marc raised his disabled hand, bringing them to a halt. "What about Henri?"

"I'm saddened by his reaction yesterday," Asher said. "He is my teacher, colleague, and trusted friend. It's a real disappointment."

"So, there is room for understanding? And perhaps forgiveness?"

"I suppose there is. I'm not the one who fled the room."

"Excellent." Marc's grin was like a slice of melon. "J . . . just as I'd hoped."

"Why is that?"

"Allow me to show you two things." He pointed. "Open that window and crane your head to the left."

Asher did as he was told, seeing nothing, bending farther, until it struck him like a slap: a swastika, carved in the stone. Someone had left his mark. He returned to the room speechless.

"When the enemy aban . . . abandoned their headquarters here," Marc was saying, "squatters were a legitimate threat, people whose homes had been destroyed. Had they arrived here first, eviction would have been impossible. But we had a larger plan, as you see, rescuing a place that has been in Brigitte's family for four centuries. Henri came and found us, the day the house was unoccupied. He helped me reconnect the electricity. He f . . . f . . . he found Marie to deliver fresh food. He modified the kilns to operate on wood until natural gas returns."

"So we are all in his debt," Asher said.

"Up to our chins. Which is the second thing to show you." Marc leaned his head to one side and yelled, "Henri." He waved his hand again, directing Asher to roll him to his desk. "*Henri,*" he called again. As the small man trotted in, Asher felt his entire body go on alert. There was a letter opener on the corner of the desk, and he moved near it.

"Henri," Marc said. "Tell your brother in glass the truth."

Short as he was, Henri stood at attention, chest out. "My name is Heinrich."

FOR A LONG TIME, ASHER could not stop laughing, though it was not mirth but surprise. "You can speak?" he choked out eventually. "And you're German?"

"*Jah.*" His voice was low, as gruff as chains pulled over a gunwale.

"I ought to kill you," Asher gasped, sobering. "After what your country did."

Heinrich nodded. "Moral argument for you kill of me can be reasonable made."

Asher made his way to an armchair. "Your silence all this time—it was an act?"

"To conceal my accent."

Marc laid his good hand on the desk. "As I said, we have guarded many secrets."

"We are protect ourselves," Heinrich said. "All of us."

Asher felt the keen blade of betrayal. Was it larger than his? Smaller? He did not know, only that rage boiled up in him. "How many Jews have you killed? How many Frenchmen?"

"I am mechanic." He pantomimed with his hands. "Fix engines in motor pool."

"But those vehicles go to places where the driver and passengers kill Jews and other French people."

Heinrich coughed into his fist. "It is likely."

"Damn, Henri, but—"

"You continue to call me by this name?"

"It's how I know you."

Heinrich shrugged. "And I know you as Christian."

Asher fell back into the chair. "So, it's what, a tie?"

"No," Heinrich growled. "You? Maybe Marc send away, maybe nothing. I forgive deceit, accept you as Jew. Me? You wish to kill."

Asher held the sides of his head with both hands. "What do we do now?"

"I'd like you both to spend time in silent thought," Marc answered. "Separately. It doesn't have to be prayer, though that may help. But you need to digest this news, and decide what it means for your partnership."

"What partnership?" Asher countered. "The one based on mutual horseshit?"

"The one that designed and built a window so unique, it saved this atelier and everyone in it." The vein on Marc's forehead stood out. "That partnership."

"This is why I run from cathedral." Heinrich stood squarely, and

Asher thought speaking made him more confident. There was nothing childlike about him anymore. "I am learn you are as bad as me."

"Except that your country was the killer, and my people were the killed."

"My country is kill, but not me. And I do not go home. Ever."

"This tone of argument is why I want you to think separately," Marc said. "Both of you have been dishonest. Therefore, dispute within yourselves first. Now I need to rest." He waved his good hand toward the door. "If you would excuse me."

"What?" Asher shook his head as if to clear it. "What happens next?"

"When you are both ready," he answered, "we will sit together to make a plan."

"What type plan?" Heinrich said.

"A way that you two can continue to make windows."

"Not a chance," Asher said. "Too false."

"This place." Marc wagged his head. "This glass château. It has been home to artistic temperaments for more than four centuries. Why should today be any different?"

"The war changed everything," Asher replied, rising from his chair. "Now the world is too fragile."

THE GOATS HOPPED DOWN FROM their pedestals, a broken tabletop and the roof of an old shed, trotting up to snatch grass from Asher's hands.

"Hello, my friends," he said, holding freshly pulled greens over the fence. Any plant out of reach was the one they wanted most. "Why do I like you so much? Because you never lie to me?"

The ram butted his ewe, shouldering forward for a flower. "I always thought they would expel me. I never imagined I would want to leave. But what else can I do?"

One of the kids zipped over, stiff-legged and feisty. He bumped his father's rear, but instead of responding, the ram jutted his head forward, wanting more.

"That's all." Asher held his hands out empty. "Something incredible has just begun for me. I'd hate for my life in glass to be over."

Leaving the pen, he considered the handsome building there, on the height of land. "If the next thing that happened is that the château fell down on me, I would not be surprised." He picked one more wild-flower, holding it so the kid could get some after all. "It would not be the first home of mine to collapse."

The little goat snatched the offering and trotted away, his odd mouth chewing. Asher hiked his uncertainty back up the hill.

In the courtyard he could see a rainbow moving here and there on the stones—Etienne in his spot, playing with the prism. Asher was not in the mood, and reversed toward the atelier's rear door. Checking as always, he saw that the jar had been refilled. Could he leave without ever knowing its secret? His curiosity grew keener with that possibility, so for once he took up the jar. Looking right and left to confirm he was alone, Asher unscrewed the top and took a strong sniff. But he recoiled at the powerful scent: vinegar. He raised the jar. Caraway seeds, float-ing among the white leaves. He pinched some out, for a taste. Totally unfamiliar. He brought the jar into the kitchen.

"There he is," Brigitte said, flour on her hands, dough on the counter. "I haven't had a chance to congratulate you on your triumph."

"My triumph? When was that?"

She continued kneading. "The window, silly man. It's brilliant and gorgeous. The bishop's own emissary said you transformed the world of stained glass."

"That feels like a long time ago."

"Yesterday afternoon, my friend. And it's not yet lunchtime today."

He picked at a bit of sauce, hardened on the cutting board. "Still."

Brigitte paused, a wrist on her hip. "You've been talking to Marc."

"I have."

"I think it's wonderful." She pushed on the dough. "There will be a period of adjustment, but we won't be uncomfortable for long. We'll have more compassion when we know what each of us has been through. Then we'll have work and meals, our old routine, to help us mend."

"Brigitte," he said, holding up the jar, "what is this?"

"Oh, Asher." Her hands went still. "I suppose it's another secret."

Asher shook the jar, liquid sloshing. "I don't want to know, but I need to know."

"I tried several times to warn you."

"Hints don't count. You knew what I was getting into."

Brigitte wiped her hands on the apron. "I make no apologies for respecting each person's pain. I have honored other people's secrets as I honored yours."

Asher struggled to respond, to calm himself. "I knew all along who was filling the jar. Now I have a guess about the rest."

"Can you please listen to me about this, for once?"

He nodded, eyes down.

"Marie has lived her whole life here. Never been farther than she could walk in a day. I have known her sorrow, her suffering, her need for comfort. You were not the only source within reach."

His jaw was tight. "That is an excellent understatement."

"She is much better now. You deserve some credit. And what she's done with those gardens and her delivery business is miraculous."

He tapped the jar's lid. "Tell me straight, please. What is this stuff?"

"Asher." Brigitte sighed, but her expression could not have been kinder. "It's sauerkraut."

CHAPTER 37

He wore an old waistcoat to hide the knife. He'd snatched it when Brigitte was busy. He brought the jar too. Two jobs to do, two tools to do them with.

"No more concealments," he told the elm trees that arched over the lane. "No more secrets," he told the poplars in the lowlands. "No more lies," he told the bridge as he marched hard-heeled across. The sky was cloudless, breezes as light as a wren.

If he had simply lived at the château for two years, eating and sleeping safely, it would have been enough. If all he accomplished was to win the trust of men he respected—Etienne, Marc—it would have been enough. If he made one window and saw it installed in a cathedral, it was beyond enough. If he had made a friend and enjoyed a lover—oh, he could not finish the prayer. Deception made none of it enough.

He would not be using the knife, Asher told himself repeatedly. It was for defense only. First he would confront Marie, then Heinrich. He was an open man now. "One last concealment to reveal," he said, kicking a stone away.

The man on fire had been especially horrifying that night. He'd held a lead-cutter in each hand. Behind him lay Aube and Rachel, Eli and Levi, the soldier who put his boots in the way, the nineteen, a whole crowd of people Asher had known in his time of wandering, and all of their throats were cut. The nameless man was to be next, and after him Heinrich, and Marc, Etienne, Brigitte, Marie, a long line into the future. In the strange logic of dreams, Asher looked down and the lead-cutter was in his hand, his own hand, and he was the killer of those people in the past, and those people to come.

He awoke with a shout. The château was silent, darkness all around. What if all this time the man on fire was not some abstract horror, but himself?

He reached the bridge, and beside it, the dirt path to the river, which he could not resist. Standing at the bank's edge, he accepted that, no, it would not be easy, breaking with her. No, a new woman had not erased his grief. She was her own humanity, with her own experiences and flaws and gifts.

Squatting, Asher cupped water in his hands. At one time, he had thought his hands would never be free from the stain of leather. And then the stain of blood. Yet here they were, clean. How had that happened? How had that even been possible? He splashed water onto his face, and he hiked back to the bridge and down the road.

Still, he arrived at her house unprepared for what he saw. The chair with the permanent umbrella, the one she'd always kept him from sitting in, had an occupant. With Clementine curled in his lap. It stopped Asher cold.

"Now, there is big surprise," Heinrich said, rubbing Clementine's ears. "I am thinking separate prayer time is end."

The cat. The man had been here long enough, and often enough, to win its affection. Asher nearly staggered with the implications. "I brought you something," he said instead, tossing the jar.

Heinrich jerked up his hands to catch it, which sent the cat darting into the grass. He looked at the jar without opening it. "Important I am tell you something." He tilted his head toward the cottage. "All this time I am not knowing about you and her."

"I didn't know about you either," Asher said, "but I was starting to suspect. When you were late for the unveiling, I couldn't think of any other reason."

"Similar for me on morning we arrive at cathedral and you are already there."

"And the night I was working on the window, and you arrived with wet hair."

"Ha. That night is first time not speaking is advantage to me. I have no explain."

"So," Asher said. "At least we were not knowingly deceiving one another about her."

Heinrich sighed. "We are agree. Also, no more ask of specific times, please. I am not wish to know who and when."

Asher sidled over to the corral fence. Pétain eyed him from the other side. "It is very strange to hear you speak."

With a wistful expression, Heinrich put the jar on the ground. "I am like better when we are work together and I am not speak."

Asher stood a moment, considering the small man in the chair. Pétain came forward, snuffling at his sleeve. "What do we do now?"

Heinrich sighed heavily. "I am leave."

"You can't. This place depends on you. Marc can't live without you."

"You already say you want kill me. Others will want kill too, when they find out. I am leave is only safe way."

"What about the new commissions? There's plenty of work."

"You, Etienne are expert at make. Nameless is good at install. Simon helps. Everyone fine." He shrugged. "Marc fine too."

"We both know that's not true. And what about what you and I did together?"

"It is my first happy since war."

The house door opened. Marie appeared in a sky-blue dress and a maroon beret. She could not have stopped more abruptly had she run into a tree.

"Hello, Marie," Asher said.

"Hello also," Heinrich added.

In that short a time, she had collected herself. "You have both come here without an invitation. You broke the one and only rule." She started toward the donkey's pen. "So it is over. For both of you—over."

"Nice try," Heinrich said. "But you are explain for us first."

"We deserve that," Asher said. "Given the degree of betrayal here."

"Betrayal?" Marie laughed. "I never lied to either of you, not one word. You were the one concealing your religion, Asher. And you"—she waved at Heinrich—"were hiding your country. Meanwhile, you both presumed I was your possession. But I am my own property, no one else's."

"Well argued," Asher said, "and your color is up quite beautifully." He bent, pulling grasses to feed Pétain. "But it's not that simple."

"Not simple," Heinrich agreed. "We are deceive by you."

"Both so confident," she scoffed. "So ready with your half-declarations of love, you never imagined there might be another. Or questioned if you were enough for me."

Heinrich lowered his head. "Is cruel thing to say."

"As cruel as both of you deciding to keep me a secret? If you had been open about me up at the château, you would have known about each other from the start. And I would not have sometimes felt like I was your whore."

Asher spoke slowly, mildly. "If your conduct is so unimpeachable, Marie, and this is a case of selfish men carried away by infatuation, please tell me how you knew about the nameless man's past."

Heinrich spun toward him. "What you are talk about?"

"The only person he would tell his terrible secret," Asher continued, "is someone he thought was incapable of passing it along. But actually, that person *could* speak, and he confided in you, because he trusted you. And he was wrong to do so."

Heinrich slapped his hands together at Marie. "You swear you tell no person. You promise me."

"Asher's the only one," she answered.

"Are you also tell him about motor pool? Is that how he find?"

"I . . . I—"

"She showed it to me," Asher said. "Yes. Was that where you were stationed?"

"I am. Three years after war it is there, no one knows. One day you find, like magic, and we take all glass. Horrible day for me, to go back there. Horrible."

"Telling him saved you, Henri." Marie folded her hands in calm. "Saved the château."

"Probably," Asher agreed. "I just thought it worth noting that your behavior has not been as morally upright as you're pretending it was."

"There was a time at the unveiling," she said. "Yesterday, though it feels longer ago. I saw you two from the back of the cathedral, I saw those glorious windows you'd made together, and I thought, okay, the work is done, now it's time to tell you both."

"But you didn't," Asher replied.

"We are tell each other first," Heinrich added.

Her face softened. "You beautiful confused men." Marie took off her hat. "Do you know why I always closed my eyes?"

"She did that with you too?" Asher asked.

"Passion, *mein schatz*," Heinrich said. "I am imagine you surrender to passion."

Marie shook her head. "I was thinking of my husband. I was trying to feel something. After all I've survived, I deserve to feel something."

"You're still in the war," Asher said.

"Me?" Marie frowned. "Suppose you take out your weapons. Show the truth, which is that you both are also still in the war. We all are."

The men looked at one another. Asher reached into his waistcoat, brought out the kitchen knife, and dropped it to the ground. Pétain bent his long neck over the fence to sniff at it. From a strap by his boot Heinrich drew the big knife, placing it by his chair.

"Listen, please," she said. "This is what I have learned. And I learned it from you, from the two of you."

"What you are learn, *liebe?*"

Marie opened the gate, entering Pétain's corral. The donkey raised his head.

"I used to make my rounds with a hatchet under my seat. Not anymore. A few months ago, I would have been content—or even excited—to watch you men fight over me. Like I'm some princess of old, and you're jousting for my hand. Not anymore."

She rubbed Pétain's muscular neck. "Whatever we do with the time left in our lives, it cannot be about fighting. We saw Bondurant's rage, we saw neighbors who couldn't enjoy a fiddler together. Conflict and anger are the opposite of what our country needs, and what we need to repair ourselves. Whether I am a good person or not is beside the point. The disputing must stop. It must. We need all of our strength for rebuilding."

"The world is not safe yet," Asher said. "We were smart to keep our secrets."

Marie tapped her chest. "We are the ones who must make it safe. You each had a duty during the war. Think of it that way now. A peacetime duty."

"What would you have us do?"

"It's easy for me. All I know how to do is grow vegetables and flowers. And to sell them to all kinds of people with all kinds of politics, which a little bit brings them closer to one another. So that's my duty. You both are capable of much more. So my advice . . ."

They waited while Marie paused, considering, until a sly smile came to her face. "Come to think of it, I *do* have advice. Why don't you make something of yourselves? The world always has enough foes. Together, you could be something better."

"Easy saying, *schönheit*, hard doing."

"Try saving a farm when your husband's dead," she snapped. "Try digging his grave all alone. Plenty of things are hard doing."

Marie momentarily stepped into sunlight reflected off a window of her house. She raised a hand to shield her eyes. "I heard what that stuffy priest said. You two transformed an art. That's what you are capable of. Before you kill one another, remember what you have built together. A successful atelier. Amazing windows. And maybe remember too all that you have done for me, to help me begin to heal. And then, imagine what else you could build together. What else you could heal."

"Like what?" Asher said.

"I don't know." Marie pulled the beret snug onto her head. "But you know what? You have a role model. Try to be the equal of that children's choir."

Heinrich squinted at her. "Who?"

"You know what I mean. All three of us were there, when they made something beautiful together, and it gave us a moment of peace. Try to be as good as they are."

Marie was gentle as she led Pétain to the wagon. Securing the braces, she paused. "Henri, wherever you go, whatever you do, I will tend your gardens at the château for the rest of my life."

"*Mein liebe*," he said, hand to his chest.

"Asher." She reached into the collar of her dress and pulled out the pendant, a royal blue crescent of glass. "I will wear this often, and treasure it always."

His heart a windstorm of emotions, he was barely able to speak. "Thank you."

"I have to make a delivery to the doctor." She climbed up onto the seat, and took the reins. "Do as you like. Just don't take too long deciding. There's work to be done, and it won't wait."

As she reached the road, Asher called out, "Is the doctor your lover too?"

"Yes," Heinrich said. "He is?"

She did not hesitate one second. "You will never know."

They watched the wagon roll away. Clementine nosed out of the grass, keeping her distance. Crickets violined the air, an orchestra waltzing the day toward evening.

"Do you know," Heinrich said, "how badly I am want to tell you I am

German? How many times I feel terrible friend, because I am conceal my country?"

Asher kicked at the ground. "I have kept plenty of secrets myself."

"That first day you are join us at assembly. Two minutes of Marc teaching, and you move leaf to superior place. *Two minutes* and you are better. I am want so badly to explain that you are have gift. A natural of gift."

Asher stammered, unable to reply. "I saw your knife at the cathedral."

"My father is carry in Great War. Hand-forged in Oslo." Heinrich smiled. "Brigitte is kill you, when she sees best favorite vegetable knife missing."

"It was all I had an opportunity to grab."

"Very dull. That would hurt going in."

They shared a laugh, then the crickets sang again.

"What we are do now? Be better than choir. Hah."

"There was a time," Asher began, "when I thought that she was the answer."

"Marie?" Heinrich shook his head. "Lovely, but no."

"The war crushed me, though. She brought me back into the world."

"You lose wife and daughter. She lose husband and son. Is same broken."

"Wow." Asher picked a long stem of grass. "Somehow I hadn't thought of that."

What had Marie given them? Sex, yes. But only of the sort that she wanted. Not love, either—or at least not a kind that would be enduring. Yet she had dismissed his killings as an ugly necessity of war. She had dispensed with Heinrich's military service in the same way. Perhaps they had been able to transform the art of glass because, in her damaged way, she had transformed them—by forgiving their deeds in the war.

Heinrich rose from his chair, happening to straighten precisely into the light reflected off Marie's front window. For a second, Asher thought, he looked like . . .

He staggered backward as if struck. Heinrich looked like a man on fire.

In fact, he always had. At work in front of the furnaces, backlit and glowing. Bent to garden in the afternoon sun. Saving Marc from falling into the fireplace. Standing at the unveiling in the exact place to receive golden light. Heinrich was the true man on fire—not for Asher to flee, but to embrace.

"You are all right?"

"I am excellent," Asher answered. "I have found two answers."

"What answers you are have?"

Clarity had arrived, and the sail of his heart filled with wind. "You. And glass."

Heinrich was strapping the knife back into place on his leg. "I am listen."

Asher crossed the dooryard to put a hand on Heinrich's shoulder. "Come with me to the river. There's a fish I want to tell you about."

CHAPTER 38

A sher and Heinrich stood at attention, waiting while Marc gazed
out the window. He'd called for them first thing that day, greeted
them, then faced away. Over the back of his wheelchair they could see
a long view down the valley, where morning mist hovered over the river.

"Before the war, I had a brother." Marc moved his neck in a circle, as
though he wore a too-tight necktie. "He was an actor, brilliantly gifted.
P . . . p . . . primarily he was traveling."

"Yes sir," Asher said.

"He brought home g . . . great stories. Audiences, tricks onstage, the
character of certain cities. Not one to hide his vanity, he often said that
what he loved most, above all else, was taking a bow. Applause, p . . .
people cheering, he would bend low as if to say, no, he was unworthy,
while adulation poured over him."

"Must be great pleasure," Heinrich said.

Marc piloted his chair around. "You know, gentlemen, that your
idea is genius, yes? T . . . totally inspired."

"I am worry about leave you."

"Etienne will manage the atelier and make glass. Our nameless man
will repair and install the salvaged windows. Simon will learn to operate the crucible and annealer. We will hire laborers to carry wood and
shovel sand."

"It sounds like a new chapter," Asher said.

"More than you know." Marc fiddled with the brake on his chair. "I've made a decision."

"What it is?" Heinrich said.

"Did either of you notice anything the bishop's emissary left out the other day? Anything missing?"

The two men looked at one another. "Not really," Asher said.

"The medallion. In all his commentary, he never mentioned the one component designed and assembled by the director of the atelier."

"It is masterpiece," Heinrich said at once. "He does not mention because it shows tradition."

"Thank you, but I will not be p . . . patronized," Marc answered evenly. "We three know the reason. It is perhaps my best medallion, the finest I have made. But installed above what is arguably the most innovative and expressive window in all of France, it looks crude. My time has come to step down."

"To use your favorite word," Asher said, "nonsense. In every way, you are the foundation of this atelier."

"I am an artifact," Marc insisted. "Your window is the future."

"I know who gets up in the middle of the night to feed the kilns. We would all be starving if not for you."

"Hear me," he shouted. The vein on his forehead bulged. "Listen to me."

They were silent again, while Marc rolled himself back and forth using his good hand. When he had gone still again, he drew himself upright in the seat.

"We have n . . . as your window says, we have all navigated through a flood, haven't we? We have weathered the st . . . the storm of war. Now the waters recede. The dove arrives with his olive branch—in the form of a pompous priest who has assured us of years' more work. It is r . . . it is right to accept with humility and honesty that the time has come for me to give w . . . w . . . give way to the skill and spirit of the next generation."

Heinrich shook his head. "Impossible."

Asher felt hollow. "I don't know what to say."

"It's done." Marc folded his hands in his lap. "I've decided. Now tell me your p . . . preparations."

Heinrich, haltingly, detailed the equipment they had loaded on the wagon the night before: blowpipes and cauldron bowls, iron frames and cutting tools, tongs and ingots of lead. All of it potential weaponry, Asher thought—or none of it.

"I approve of your thoroughness," Marc said. "I d . . . did some preparation of my own. On my desk you'll see an envelope with what cash we can spare. Also letters of recommendation you can show to any who question your craft or competence."

"That is incredibly generous," Asher said, while Heinrich retrieved the envelope.

"It's less than we'll receive for your work, so consider it p . . . partial repayment. But." He held a finger up. "There is one last thing."

He shifted his wheelchair, raising both arms, and began to clap. It was not hearty, with one of his hands disabled, but he kept clapping nonetheless.

Asher glanced at Heinrich to see what they should do, but he looked puzzled too. Then he smiled, a light coming on. He faced the master of the atelier, and he bowed.

"Bravo," Marc shouted, applauding still, "bravo."

Heinrich put an arm around Asher, and while the old man continued clapping, they took bow after bow.

SIMON WAS WAITING AT THE bottom of the stairs like a groom for his bride. "God is so proud of you right now. So proud of what you're doing."

Asher answered on the way down, "Let's hope he's good to us on the journey."

"God is always good."

"Well," Asher said, "except for the war."

"Didn't the right side prevail, though? In the end?"

"Not to argue with you, my friend, but at what cost?"

Simon took a step backward. "I want to apologize for all of my preaching, without considering that anyone here professed a different religion. My presumption in those days humbles me today."

"But Simon." Asher took him by both arms. "You gave me the side window idea. When you told me to think about great acts of faith."

He brought a hand to his mouth. "I did do that, didn't I?"

Asher hugged him, and there was no scent of wine. Meanwhile, Heinrich gave Simon a deep and formal bow.

They found Etienne lounging on the courtyard wall, fiddling with rainbows again. "The seasons are changing," he said. "Don't you want to wait till spring?"

"Now is time," Heinrich replied. "To wait is to waste."

Color glinted in Asher's eyes. "Why are you always playing with that prism?"

"I'm not." Etienne moved his long slender fingers. "I'm playing with light."

"And what has become of our nameless man?"

"He's down at the cathedral, smoking up a storm with his new friend. And scrubbing those gorgeous old windows. Happiest I've ever seen him."

"Please tell him . . ." Asher paused.

Etienne laughed. "Take your time with that one."

"Oh, why not? Say that I wish him well."

"Bully for you." Etienne angled his wrist to flash red and orange into Asher's eyes. "I imagine they'll have light where you are headed."

"I expect so."

He directed the prism elsewhere. "I hope you capture all of it."

That was how Asher last saw Etienne, aiming the colors as he chose. Heinrich gave another bow, before leading to the kitchen.

"I've packed you some meals." Brigitte placed two baskets by the door. "It can be a long way between inns."

"It's only four days to the border," Asher said. "We should be fine."

"I remember what you looked like when you arrived here. Skinny as a wet cat." She stood, wiped her hands on her apron, and put a hand on each of Asher's shoulders. "Now look at you. Solid, strong, healthy."

"I have you to thank."

"Among others, yes, you do." She sat back on her stool. "You're really going?"

"It's not easy," Asher conceded. "What do you think about Marc's decision?"

"He's probably right," she answered. "And he's my hero for deciding now, while he's still strong and able, instead of waiting till things are . . ." She drifted off for a moment. "It's always painful to see someone you love be diminished."

"I'm glad Etienne and Simon will be here for continuity."

"And man with no name," Heinrich added.

"Yes." Brigitte smiled at them. "It's a silly thing to think about, I know, but I suppose I'll have to stop flirting so much. I don't want Marc having any doubts."

Asher smiled back. "All the world will mourn."

"Oh, but look." Reaching up to the knot at her neck, Brigitte untied the apron, revealing the smock he had sewn for her. "Worn today for you. So maybe I'm ready to be more chaste."

"It's holding up well," he said.

"Too well," she said with a wink. "You preserved my modesty, but diminished my admirers."

"Not a bit." Asher elbowed Heinrich. "Did you ever stop looking?"

Grinning, he shook his head emphatically no.

Brigitte gave an easy laugh. "Oh, my beautiful orphans," she cried, pulling both men into a fierce hug, swaying them side to side.

"Now go do great things," she said, pushing the men away. "Go."

"I'll miss you most of all," Asher said, lingering.

She waved a dishrag. "Be gone with you. I have dinner to make."

OUTSIDE, HEINRICH SHOWED ASHER THE contents of Marc's envelope. There was a bundle of francs, as he'd said. But when he unfolded the letters, the handwriting was illegible. Three copies, and they could not decipher one word.

"Do you still think we should go?" Asher asked.

Heinrich folded up the letters. "Others are help now. We are work to do."

They stepped around the corner and stopped cold. The wagon was transformed. The evening before, it was loaded with gear. Now it was festooned with flowers. Marie must have come in the night, or in the earliest brushstrokes of dawn. The plain planks and sturdy frame were all decorated, blooms twined down each side, over the running boards, in an arc over the driving seat.

"Someone visit us," Heinrich croaked. "Beautiful parting gift."

Asher snapped his fingers. "I'll be right back."

"We are need to be go," he called, but Asher was already running.

There in its cubby, lightly coated with dust, sat Etienne's flower of glass. Asher wiped it, wrapped it in a chamois cloth, and hurried to the kitchen.

Brigitte was studying a recipe. "You can't live without me after all?"

He pressed the bundle into her hands. "Please give this to Marie, with my love."

She grinned. "With your love?"

"Not like I expected," he said. "But in times like these, about as good as possible."

"I'd make a bet that she feels the same."

His throat choked, Asher kissed the top of her head and ran. Heinrich had loaded the food baskets and was strapping himself in the wagon's harnesses. Asher started to do the same, but had to untangle and start over. His mind was elsewhere—imagining that flower in a tiny vase on her table, a tangible fact about them both, and what they meant to each other. Maybe, from time to time, she might look at that glass flower and think of him.

Another image came to Asher then—an idea for a painting: a woman, joyous, swinging from the trapeze that is her life. A donkey behind her, soaring over the roof of a stone cottage. A skeptical cat nosing in from one corner. And a fish, of course a fish, holding toward the woman a bouquet of colors so brilliant, she reaches for them even as she swings from the bar. All motion and dream, primitive and sublime. He would paint the moon of glass against her chest too, just below the collarbone, how warm her skin, a memory to cherish forever.

It would have been kinder and simpler if love had saved them. But that was unlikely, given the magnitude of what they had each lost. Instead, he faced a harder road, and so did she, because that was what war required.

Running his gaze up and down the wagon's flowery rail, Asher knew that he had not seen Marie for the last time. She would appear in his thoughts, and in his art, for as long as he lived. He knotted the harness leathers on his shoulders, attempting to pull them snug. "These are looser than I expected."

"We are more small than hungriest pony," Heinrich said, double-wrapping one of the lines around his chest. "You are ready?"

Asher nodded, and they leaned forward, straining. The wagon groaned, the wheels budged, and they were on their way.

"Keep a hand tight on that brake," Asher instructed. "So we don't get run over on the downhill."

In the lane they steered left at the fork, beginning the descent.

"I have question for you," Heinrich said.

"I have a hundred for you."

"Me first. In center window. What yellow panes are about, in low right corner? They are nothing about ark. The priest is call them fangs."

"He was pretty close." Asher plodded along. "They are teeth. Of a pipe-smoking man. Next window, I'll sneak in a steering wheel. After that, a breakfast plate. Then I'll have sixteen secrets left."

"Sometimes you are make no sense."

"I'm honoring the past. And putting it in its place."

They had only reached the first switchback when a handbell

clanged from above. Heinrich pulled the brake so they could see what it was about.

Brigitte stood atop the wall, putting down the bell, lifting both arms. As the men waved in reply, with quick fingers she unbuttoned the smock. Beneath she wore nothing, not so much as a shift, her breasts pendulous now that they were free. She raised her arms again, waving both hands, and her bosom swayed side to side.

"What in hell?"

Her skin reddening in a flush, Brigitte buttoned up and dropped from sight.

"You did witness that, right?" Asher asked. "That really happened?"

"I do," Heinrich said, "but am not understand. What it is?"

"The last time of something," Asher said. "The end of an era."

"What that is?"

"I'll have to think a minute about how to explain it."

They began pulling the wagon again, both lost in thought. Eventually Heinrich chuckled. "Crimson, maybe?"

"Ha. Not that dark, I think. Definitely not scarlet. Nor pink, exactly."

"Rose, perhaps?"

Asher reached to clap him on the shoulder. "Rose."

NOT AN HOUR INTO THE lowlands, they came to an unexpected crossroads. "The maps I read did not have a crossing here," Asher said.

"We are ask girl?"

"What girl?" Asher said, but as he spoke he saw her. She was small, perhaps ten years old—about the age Rachel would have been by then. Beside her sat a mixed-breed dog, his tongue lolling while he panted. Though the war had been over for years, still Asher considered every pet a miracle. All in a dash the dog was greeting him, leaping and bounding. Asher tried petting but the animal spun in place and jumped again, trying to lick his chin. "Your dog is friendly."

"It's not my dog," the girl answered. "My parents won't let me keep him."

"Did you give him a name?"

"Not yet."

He smiled. "It's an important decision. Do you happen to know which of these roads leads east?"

She dug her heel in the dirt. "I don't know any of the roads."

"We must choose," Heinrich said. "Too soon for stop."

"Which way do you like?" Asher asked.

Heinrich leaned to his left, steering the wagon. But within a few steps the dog barked at them. It had trotted up the road's right fork.

"Pardon me," Asher said. "But we should follow the dog."

"Because?"

"Dogs never lead me wrong."

"My guess, dog guess, who can say?" Heinrich reversed the cumbersome wagon to the right. As it backtracked, however, who should be revealed behind it but Euclid and Pascal, smiling and huge.

"Running away without goodbye?" Pascal asked.

"Without farewell?" Euclid added.

"Without a parting glass?"

"Gentlemen," Asher greeted them. "How wonderful to see you, to say our *au revoirs* in person."

"How was leaving the château?" Euclid asked.

"Difficult," Heinrich replied. "Painful."

"Ha!" Pascal cried, pointing his great sausage finger. "The little man speaks."

Henrich took a small bow. "Asher is cure me."

"Leaving was indeed painful," Asher said, but then he chuckled. "Though there were consolations."

"Yes." Heinrich laughed along. "Brigitte is show us her breasts."

"No," cried Pascal, his eyes wild. "Tell me you are joking."

"We are joking," Asher answered. "But it is also true."

"Aarrgh." The giant bit on the knuckle of his thumb. "Were they splendid?"

"Of course they were splendid," Asher said.

"You torture me."

"Oh, but Pascal," Asher added, feeling that he had been unwittingly cruel. "She also gave us baskets of food for you."

"For me?"

Heinrich nodded. "For you."

"So." Pascal bobbed his enormous head. "As you said, some consolations."

Euclid wrapped great arms around his brother. "Ever is love the cause of our anguish and joy."

"Change the subject or I will weep," Pascal said. "Where are you going?"

Exchanging a glance with Asher, Heinrich spoke. "You are tell them."

"All right." Asher smiled. "We are headed to Germany."

"Such a long way," Euclid exclaimed.

"Why Germany?" Pascal asked.

"We're going to repair their stained glass windows."

"Excellent idea," Euclid exclaimed, clapping his huge hands together.

"That's not all," Asher said. Each time he had uttered it, saying it out loud, he found that his throat had choked up. Whose idea had it been, anyway? His or Heinrich's, he could not say. He turned to his friend. "You tell them the best part."

"Synagogues," Heinrich said. "We are repair synagogue windows only."

"What?" Euclid cried. "But you are German."

Asher laughed. "That's the whole point."

"We are must rebuild Germany synagogues first."

"Yaaah!" Pascal seized Heinrich, hoisting him in the air, roaring like a lion.

"Put me down," Asher told Euclid, who had lifted him like a bale of hay, and whose howl would have put hunting dogs to shame.

They did lower the men to earth, but Euclid moved to stand squarely in the wagon's path. "We are coming with you."

Pascal choked. "We are?"

"We are," Euclid said. "To save your poor, desperate loving heart."

"I see," Pascal answered wistfully. "To save my heart."

"Besides." Euclid bumped against his brother. "These two? Pull a wagon all that way? They are much too small."

"Yes," Pascal answered. Then he bumped his brother back. "Yes, they are. Very small, And weak."

"Also pathetic."

Pascal wagged his big box of a head. "They will get eaten by wolves."

"Bears," Euclid said, nodding. "Elephants."

"My goodness, eaten by elephants." Asher felt like he was glowing with the presence of such goodwill. "Would you honor us with the pleasure of your company?"

"Shove over," Pascal answered. In seconds the giant men were strapped into the braces, the leather tight on their beefy frames. In seconds the wagon was rolling.

Heinrich followed alongside, all but a skip in his step. Asher trailed, though, tempered by melancholy, though also eager for glass, for rebuilding, for light from the heavens to pour through the windows and onto the people's beautiful faces. The sky had cirrus clouds like horses' tails.

When he spied the dog ambling along, a volunteer to their caravan, Asher thought to thank the girl. He turned to say goodbye, but somehow she was gone, not visible up either of the roads behind.

"Farewell," he said anyway, waving. Farewell to the château, farewell to the river, farewell to the glimmering air.

Not half a minute later, Heinrich was calling from the other side of the wagon. "Asher, is you are tell one of your story?"

"Yes, yes," Pascal cried out. "I love your stories."

"A long one," Euclid added. "For our long walk."

"I know many short stories," he told them. "But only one long one."

"Then you'd better get started," Pascal said. "We're almost there."

"One moment." Asher considered, weighing how to begin.

"Anytime now," Euclid prompted, pulling against his straps.

"All right. Here goes." Asher cleared his throat. "After the end of a slaughter that nearly devoured a continent, the last thing anyone expected to hear was laughter . . ."

Euclid bent toward the dog, who looked for all the world as if he were smiling.

"You know what, little friend?" he confided to his canine companion. "As long as the man keeps telling stories, I say we do not kill him."

ACKNOWLEDGMENTS

This novel was written under the influence.

No, not the liquid type that has helped and hurt writers over the centuries. I mean the long shadow of one of the greatest artists of the twentieth century, Marc Chagall.

I first encountered his work in a meaningful way in 2017, in a retrospective at the Musée des Beaux-Arts in Montreal. In addition to his paintings, drawings, and theatrical designs, Chagall revolutionized the art of stained glass windows. That exhibition, which contained 340 works, sparked an interest that led me to read his autobiography. My sister Casey added fuel to the fire by sending me a book with excellent prints of his windows. Chagall's genius inspired this novel, and some of the windows Asher and Henri create resemble windows that he produced. The fantasies Asher sees—flying cows, a fish with a bouquet—likewise come from Chagall works.

In fact, he is a thread throughout the plot. Consider, for example, the fiddler on the roof. Long before it was a celebrated Broadway musical, much less a scene in this novel, the fiddler was a 1920 painting by Chagall on the wall of a theater in Moscow.

Springing from an artist's work and having a setting in the 1940s, this book allowed me to indulge in the pleasure of research. I want to express deep thanks to the artists who were kind enough to put up with my ignorance, questions, and interruptions. The glassblowers at AO Glass in Burlington, Vermont, were especially generous, from company founder Rich Arentzen to the artist Rob Beckham (who helped me make a small glass flower that wound up appearing in the novel). Jordan Gullikson, also at AO, gave me a book that expanded my understanding of what is possible in glass windows.

For design and assembly, I started with Terry Zigmund of Burlington. Next, the Louisville, Kentucky, novelist James Markert connected me with his father, Robert Markert—one of the great religious window makers in America. He was hugely helpful. But my most patient teacher was the stained glass window artist Lawrence Ribbecke, also of Burlington. Larry spent many hours explaining, loaning me books, demonstrating, and trying (as he put it) to keep me from screwing up. I probably did so anyway.

The imperatives of fiction require all sorts of abbreviation of technical elements, so I apologize to Larry and the other glass artists for my oversimplification of their highly skilled work. I bow before your talents.

This book benefited enormously from the Denis Diderot Grant I received for a residency at the Château d'Orquevaux artists' colony in France. My sincere thanks to executive director Ziggy Attias, artistic director Buelah van Rensburg, and my wonderful and hilarious fellow residents. The effect of this place was more than an opportunity to immerse myself in writing the first draft. It also changed the book's setting (originally an abandoned abbey up near Belgium). The fictional château of this novel bears more than a slight resemblance to Orquevaux's real-world influence. And if you need a name for a cathedral docent, who better than the French philosopher who helped to invent the encyclopedia?

I read deeply of the history of postwar France, and of the country's efforts to rebuild amid a politically polarized atmosphere. Rather than providing an exhaustive list, let me say that *Paris after the Liberation, 1944–1949* by Antony Beevor and Artemis Cooper is the best of the bunch.

I'm indebted to Tavia Kowalchuk—super savvy marketing director at HarperCollins Publishers, but also my good friend—for many reasons. In particular I want to thank her for an email urging me to go back to the Reims cathedral on a rainy Sunday ("Stephen, you can't have just still photos, you must have video too"). By chance, the children's choir was practicing that evening. It was an unexpected goosebumps experience, and gave me a way to keep Asher from killing Bondurant.

My dear Jenna Blum, gifted writer and cofounder of the *Mighty Blaze* social media platform for books and writers, was a great support during the early going—much as she generously helped with my novel *Universe of Two*. My great friend Dave Wolk was the source of Simon's idea that evolution and religion both say that we come from a single family. Dave lives that belief every day. My immensely generous friend Chris Bohjalian deserves my thanks for every book, because he has taught me so much about writing, publishing, and how to find readers in a busy world. But the first, last, and best reader for this particular story was my trusted friend Dawn Tripp, a brilliant novelist who spent countless hours helping me think more clearly. This would be a lesser book without her patience and genius.

I appreciate the volunteers at Unity Church in Pocantico Hills, New York, for guided tours of a chapel that contains commissioned Chagall windows in a highly accessible setting. I loved the excellent collection at the Musée Chagall in Nice, France, and at the Fondation Maeght in Saint-Paul-de-Vence, France. Thanks also to Ruth Oxenburg, who opened the doors for me to see Chagall's masterpiece *The Window of Peace and Human Happiness* at the United Nations' Dag Hammarskjöld Plaza in New York City. Bravo to Anne Soiberg-Friedkin at the UN, for an informative explanation of that window and its history. Having immersed myself in Chagall's work of his fifties and sixties, I was much moved to see a window completed decades later. The images are full of optimism and joy. Additional thanks to Stephane Dujarric for showing me more of the UN's collection of art from around the world, which is nothing shy of incredible.

As ever, this book would not exist without the faith, support, and expertise of a team of publishing professionals. Ellen Levine remains the gold standard for literary agents, and I trust her with everything. This is my fifth book that has benefited from the editing of my friend Jennifer Brehl, whose suggestions are always insightful and helpful, who believed in this idea from the very beginning, and who remains a joy to work with. This time that included an afternoon conversation late in the pandemic, while walking barefoot up a stream in rural Vermont. I am very lucky.

Jen also introduced me to the skilled people at the William Morrow imprint. Nate Lanman's self-effacing personality cannot hide the meaningful editorial contribution he makes—especially for this book. I'm a huge fan of Sharyn Rosenblum for her nonstop creativity and publicity excellence. Mumtaz Mustafa has designed smart, memorable covers for my prior novels, but on this one she outdid herself. With the interior pages designed by Nancy Singer, they've combined to make a book any writer would be proud of.

Lastly I'd like to thank my friend Bob Stannard, the harmonica bluesman now retired, for giving me a button from his great-grandfather's vest. The button is a symbol of affection in my novel *The Curiosity*, and Bob's gift was a perfectly timed reminder of how breathtakingly generous readers can be. My heartfelt gratitude to every one of you.

DISCOVER MORE BY
STEPHEN P. KIERNAN

"Stephen Kiernan has pulled off the nearly impossible, reminding us by wrapping a war story in a love story that although we hold the power for our own extinction, we also have the power to redeem, heal, and save. The most tender, terrifying, relevant book you'll read this year." — Jenna Blum, *New York Times* bestselling author of *Those Who Save Us* and *The Lost Family*

"*The Baker's Secret* will have you weeping, and then cheering. A tale beautifully, wisely, and masterfully told." —Paula McLain, author of *The Paris Wife* and *Circling the Sun*

"This many-faceted, thought-provoking story prompts soul-searching about life, war, and death." — *Booklist*

"Remarkably touching, insightful and timely.... Bridges several powerful stories of life and death that explore the cost of courage and the true meaning of heroism.... Illuminating, uplifting and ultimately redemptive." — RT Book Reviews (4.5 stars)

A gripping, poignant, and thoroughly original thriller, Stephen P. Kiernan's provocative debut novel raises disturbing questions about the very nature of life and humanity— man as a scientific subject, as a tabloid novelty, as a living being: a curiosity.

"Summer is dominated with thrilling books, but if you prefer yours more measured, more touching and decidedly more thought-provoking, this one may satisfy your curiosity." — *Star Tribune* (Minneapolis)